The Lost Classics Series

THE 9.50 UP EXPRESS

And Other Stories By
FREEMAN WILLS CROFTS

Copyright © 2020
by Crippen & Landru Publishers, Inc.
Published by arrangement with the estate
of Freeman Wills Crofts
Introduction and Bibliography © 2020
Tony Medawar

Cover artwork by Joshua Luboski

Lost Classics logo, adapted from a drawing by Ike Morgan, ca. 1895

FIRST EDITION
Printed in the United States of America on acid-free, recycled paper

For information contact:
Crippen & Landru Publishers
PO Box 532057
Cincinnati, OH 45253

Jeffrey A. Marks,
Publisher
Douglas G. Greene,
Senior Editor

Web: www.crippenLandru.com
E-mail: Info@crippenlandru.com

ISBN (softcover): 978-1-932009-34-7
ISBN (clothbound): 978-1-936363-49-0
First Edition: December 2020
10 9 8 7 6 5 4 3 2 1

The Lost Classics Series

THE 9.50 UP EXPRESS

And Other Stories By
FREEMAN WILLS CROFTS

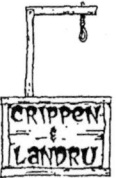

CRIPPEN & LANDRU PUBLISHERS
Cincinnati, Ohio
2021

FREEMAN WILLS CROFTS (1879-1957)

CONTENTS

The Master of Alibis   3

PART I: The Casebook of Inspector French
Meet Inspector French   15
The Vertical Line   23
The Hunt Ball Murder   35
The Match   45
Fingerprints   69
The Faulty Stroke   73
Teamwork Felonious   77
Dark Waters   81
The Target   85
The 9.50 Up Express   89
During The Night   117

PART II: The Casebook of Robin Brand
Meet Robin Brand   187
Perilous Journey   191
Danger in Shroude Valley   207

PART III: Other Stories
James Alcorn's Oversight   217
Murder by Deputy   223

Appendix A: Why I Write Detective Stories   227
Appendix B: Who Killed Cock Robin?   231
Appendix C: Bibliography   235

The Master of Alibis

"The soundest builder of them all when he doesn't get too fancy."
Raymond Chandler, *The Simple Art of Murder (1950)*

Though he himself would have shunned the title, Freeman Wills Crofts can reasonably be regarded as Ireland's greatest writer of classic crime. In a career extending over four decades, he delivered a solid series of carefully plotted novels, with a particular penchant for railway mysteries and plots built around other forms of transportation. Described by Agatha Christie as "The Master of Alibis." and by Dorothy L. Sayers as "Our cunningest fitter of jigsaws.", Crofts created Joseph French, one of the relatively few great police detectives of the Golden Age of crime and detective fiction, and for many readers the Inspector French novels epitomise fairplay and routinely deliver a smoothly engineered plot in which the only certainty is that, eventually, the truth will out.

Crofts' forebears were from Suffolk[1] in England, but he was named, like his father and his grandfather before him, after his great grandfather, who owned land in Cork in the south of the island of Ireland, where Crofts' own father was born. Crofts' mother, Cecilia Frances Wise, was born in County Down in the north east. Freeman Senior and Cecilia were married on 21 February 1878[2] at Aldershot in England, where he had been training for a career as a surgeon in the medical department of the British Army. In the autumn of the same year, while living with her father, James Wise, Cecilia found that she was pregnant, however, her happiness was short-lived, for at around the same time she learned that her young husband, who had only recently been posted to the British colony of Honduras, had died of fever on the 17th of November. A little over six months later, their son, Freeman Wills Crofts, was born on 1 June 1879 at 26 Waterloo Road in Dublin. Ireland was then part of the United Kingdom but with the Anglo-Irish Treaty of 1921 it gained independence and became the Irish Free State with Dublin as its capital. From his father, Crofts inherited the equivalent of roughly $100,000 in today's money, together with some land in Clogheen and Longstone in Cork. There were questions about the

---

[1] Some sources suggest he was descended from the Croft family of Sussex but this is incorrect.
[2] Some sources give the date, incorrectly, as 1877.

ownership of the land and in the ensuing legal wrangle, the infant had to be represented by James Wise.

In April 1883, Cecilia married again, this time to the Venerable Jonathan Harding, the canon of Dromore. It is likely that the two had met at St Paul's Church in Gilford, County Down, where Harding was also the rector. On the marriage, Cecilia went to live at the vicarage with her young son who was made the legal ward of his stepfather, whom the child always called uncle. Harding was an eminent anglican, becoming an archdeacon in 1892, and he and Cecilia ensured that, like his family for generations, Freeman Wills Crofts was raised in the Church of Ireland.

In 1891, after the Hardings moved to Belfast, Crofts took up a place at the city's prestigious Methodist College, where he won at least one school prize. He left the "Methody" in 1894 after he and a cousin, James Berkeley Wise, were selected for the initial intake of the newly established Campbell College in Belfast, where, among other things, Crofts served as official scorer for the school cricket team.

A year later, the cousins were joined at Campbell by yet another cousin, Hamilton Knutson Deane Roe. Cousin Hamilton would go on to become an actor, under the name Hamilton Deane, and his most famous role was that of Professor Van Helsing in his acclaimed adaptation of Bram Stoker's *Dracula*, which was the basis for the celebrated 1931 film. In July 1896, Crofts left Campbell College, but he retained an affection for it for the rest of his life, even serving in 1935 as president of the London Branch of the Old Campbellians' Society.

At the age of 17, Crofts took up an apprenticeship as a pupil in civil engineering on the Belfast & Northern Counties Railway, the BNCR, where his uncle, Berkeley Deane Wise, was chief engineer. Wise mentored his nephew and his career flourished. In 1899, Crofts was promoted to junior assistant engineer and was involved with the building of the Londonderry and Strabane extension of the Donegal railway line. In the following year, Crofts' stepfather Archdeacon Harding died, and Crofts was promoted first to assistant engineer and then to district engineer, after which appointment he moved with his mother to Coleraine in County Derry.

Crofts' passion for his work and his energy was boundless. In 1907, he invented a new kind of buffer coupling for railway engines and, even outside work, engineering was never far from his mind. In 1908, he designed a full-sized roller skating rink, made from rock maple and spruce, which opened in 1909. Crofts was also deeply religious, and in 1902, he was made a sidesman at Holy Trinity Church in Portrush, becoming churchwarden in 1907. He was a skillful musician, and from June 1909 to 1920 played the organ at St John's Parish church in the nearby village of Killowen, as well as at St Patrick's, Coleraine. He also designed that church's organ chamber and established its men's choir, becoming its first conductor. Crofts also took on various roles in the wider community around in and Coleraine, including chairman of the Coleraine Musical Society and, reflecting his internationalist outlook, secretary of the Portrush Esperanto Club, whose ambition to make Esperanto a global language he would still be championing over thirty years later.

Crofts also served for a while as honorary secretary of the Portrush branch of the Women's National Health Association and as master of several choirs, including the choir of the local branch of the Young Women's Christian Association, which, under his leadership, performed at the annual Coleraine Music Festival for many years, and in 1921 won the Mary Wakefield Medallion for the best women's choir. In 1909, Crofts even sang in a variety show at the Northern Counties Hotel in Coleraine, helping to raise funds for the local cricket and croquet teams. He also had many other interests, which he would pursue throughout his life, included gardening, carpentry, motoring and traveling.

In 1912, at the age of thirty-three, Crofts married Mary Bellas Canning, whom he had met at Killowen parish church some 10 years earlier; Paul R Moy, who has revealed many forgotten facts about writers of the Golden Age, has established that their first home was 11 Lodge Road, Killowen. Mary was the daughter of the manager of the Coleraine branch of the Provincial Bank and, while she and Freeman never had children, they would remain together for forty-five years.

Within two years, Europe was at war. Still in his thirties, Crofts was not called up because he was in a reserved occupation, but whether this frustrated or delighted him is unclear. As a civilian, he followed the ruination of Western Europe closely, and in 1915, he invented and patented a war game whose details, sadly, appear to have been lost.

In the second half of the decade, probably in 1916[3], Crofts fell ill as a result of contracting influenza in the pandemic. Confined to bed for a lengthy spell of convalescence, and possibly inspired by the incredible

---

[3] Crofts sometimes said that he had begun to write *The Cask* in 1919 and sometimes in 1916; the earlier of the two dates seems more likely.

by the success of E.C. Bentley's semi-satirical *Trent's Last Case* (1913) and the burgeoning growth in popularity of crime and detective stories, this almost feverishly active man decided to try writing a mystery.

He asked his wife for a pencil and a few sheets of notepaper and began to write down what to him "seemed the most absurd and improbable things I could think of." That first morning's work was followed by a second, and then a chapter was complete. Crofts read what he had written to Mary who "expressed delight (unhappily, mingled with amazement.)" Nonetheless encouraged, he continued to write what would eventually be his first novel until he returned to work. When he came across the manuscript sometime later, he found himself surprised quality of what he had written. He began to revise it, with the help of a neighbour, Dr. Adam Mathers, who acted as a sounding board. Crofts would go on to dedicate the book to Mathers and said later that "the book must have been written at least five times before the final draft was reached". But reached it was, and in 1919, with no little trepidation, Crofts submitted the final draft of the novel to an agent, Alexander Pollock Watt, regarded today as the first true literary agent and in 1919 very much in the forefront of his profession.

Watt was very impressed and submitted the novel, then entitled *A Mystery of Two Cities,* to the publisher William Collins, where it was read by the novelist John Davys Beresford. Beresford was full of encouragement, judiciously prompting Crofts to change the final section of the novel in which a trial took place. Crofts accepted Beresford's advice, commenting in later years that "I don't know a great deal about murder trials now but I have learnt enough to appreciate that no trial like that I described has ever taken place, either in this or any other country." Collins were delighted with the revised draft and, in July 1920, Crofts' first novel was published under a new title, *The Cask*, one not coined by its author.

As Crofts revealed many years later to the bibliophile Edward T Guymon, he "was the most astounded person in the universe" by the book's publication and he delighted in the praise for its "bewilderingly intricate" and "skilfully contrived" plot—whose solution, incidentally, was revealed in a contemporary review by one leading Irish newspaper. He decided to write another and the following July saw the publication of the "ably-engineered" *The Ponson Case*. The manuscript for the next book was completed by the following April, and the novel, *The Pit-Prop Syndicate*, was published that November, not long after

Freeman and Mary had moved to Whiteabbey, a small coastal village near Belfast near Jordanstown, where they lived at 22 The Oaks and Crofts played the organ at St Patrick's Church.

At around this time, Crofts also decided to try his hand at short stories. The first, "The Mystery of the Sleeping Car Express" was published in *The Premier Magazine* in 1922; Crofts later revealed that he had tested the practicability of his plot with a rope and a railway coach and the active cooperation of the District Superintendent.

In October 1922, Crofts was appointed to the position of chief assistant engineer at around the time the BNCR was being absorbed into the London, Midland and Scottish Railway, a name that says much about the sensitivities of the British authorities at the time to the growing calls for Irish independence. Crofts transferred to the railway's headquarters at York Road station in Belfast where one of his earliest assignments was to design a new railway bridge over the river Bann in Coleraine harbour; this would replace a wooden bridge whose flaws Crofts had first criticised nearly fifteen years earlier. He was also involved in the design of the Greenisland viaduct near Bleach Green on the Belfast to Larne railway line.

Notwithstanding his demanding job, Crofts managed to find time to continue writing. His fourth novel, *The Groote Park Murder* (1923), is set in South Africa and Scotland, and prompted one newspaper to hail its author as "a distinguished member of that little group of public benefactors, the writers of really good detective stories." Crofts became increasingly confident that he could consider a career as a writer and a writer of detective stories and, either of his own volition or—perhaps more likely—in response to pressure from his publisher, Crofts decided to create a series detective.

At school, Crofts had been "immensely" impressed by Conan Doyle's stories of Sherlock Holmes and his favourite writer of detective stories was R. Austin Freeman, creator of the preternaturally intelligent Dr. John Thorndyke and the best-known practitioner of the inverted detective story that would also be a feature of Crofts' work. However, Crofts decided that he would do something different, eschewing the idea of creating a "superhuman" sleuth or even a "character detective" as created by the likes of Philip Macdonald, S.S. Van Dine, and Christie. Instead, and building on the various police officers that had appeared in his first four books like Inspector Tanner, the main investigator of *The Ponson Case* he created Joseph French, "an ordinary man, carrying out his work in an ordinary way [without any] special characteristics except being thorough, painstaking, persistent and a hard worker. He makes mistakes but goes ahead in spite of them."

The first of the series was *Inspector French's Greatest Case* (1924) and, while Crofts' books were already being criticised for the scant attention to characterisation—a weakness Crofts recognised—the suave "Soapy Joe" French was an immediate success. In the second, *Inspector French and the Cheyne Mystery* (1925), the policeman appeared late in the book, resolving a puzzle that an amateur would-be investigator had failed to unravel. Over the next thirty-three years, French would appear in nearly thirty novels and over fifty short stories, as well as radio plays and a stage play.

Already acclaimed in the United Kingdom and in Ireland, Crofts began to gain popularity in other countries, including the United States where he would be hailed in 1927 as "The Crime King." Praised for his scrupulously "fair" and "logical" plotting and for creating the "plodding, painstaking," French was widely regarded as, at the time, the most realistic of fictional detectives. An unwelcome consequence of such laudation, however, was that some reviewers delighted in nit-picking, especially those working for the *Belfast News*. Thus, one review queried the accuracy of the description of the phases of the moon in *Inspector French and the Cheyne Mystery* (1926) and another the prevalence of particular types of tide in Inspector French's fourth case, *The Sea Mystery* (1928). Such comments were not always well-founded. Given his attention to detail, one can imagine how Crofts reacted to the misplaced criticism that he had erred in a later French mystery—*Fatal Venture* (1939)—by having the Royal Ulster Constabulary investigate a crime in the north of the island of Ireland rather than Eire's Garda Síochána.

Even Crofts' friends were not above tweaking his ears. The writer John Rhode—of whose work Crofts was a great admirer—once calculated that a key aspect of the plot of *The Sea Mystery*, involving a crate, was impossible. Another friend teased Crofts about a different novel in which the author had underestimated the weight of a large quantity of bank notes and the volume that it would occupy.

Regardless of minor issues, few of which were detected by his readers, Crofts was immensely popular. However, not all of his books were successful. Despite an interesting and complex problem involving serial murder, the drugs trade and the counterfeiting of silver coinage, French's fifth case, *The Box Office Murders* (1929), was poorly received, with one reviewer speaking for many when he dismissed it as "over-weighted and over-complicated". Crofts shrugged off such criticism and, recognising that he could no longer deal with the twin pressures of work as an engineer and work as a writer, he decided at the age of fifty to become a full-time author. His mother, Cecilia Harding, had died in 1929, and Freeman and Mary decided to move to Britain.

However, before they could put this plan into effect, Crofts received a most unusual assignment. In May 1930, through an appointment that may have raised some eyebrows at the time, the "popular novelist" was appointed by the Minister of Finance as an inspector to chair a two-day public inquiry to consider community and commercial objections to a drainage scheme for the river Bann near his home in Coleraine. Sensing a degree of innocent misunderstanding as well as some not so innocent obfuscation, Crofts used the bulk of the first day to examine the proposals in great detail, as a result of which many objections were simply withdrawn. After completing the hearings, he wrote up his report and supported the majority of the remaining objections, arguing that they should be addressed by compensation or modification of the scheme. His conclusions were accepted and the works began, taking 12 years to complete and costing approximately $60,000,000 in today's money.

After the publication of the report on the drainage scheme, Freeman and Mary completed their relocation, settling in the tiny village of Blackheath near Guildford in the south east of England. They bought a newly built house, Wildern, which has since come to be known as Crofts; still standing, Crofts is a charming house and, quite coincidentally, is presently the home of an Ulsterwoman who, like Crofts, attended Methodist College and at one time lived in Coleraine.

Among other community roles, Crofts played the organ at St Martins' Church in Blackheath. He also became friendly with Detective Superintendent Tom Roberts of the Surrey Police, who advised Crofts on arson and other matters for several novels set in the area, including *The Hog's Back Mystery* (1933), *Crime at Guildford* (1935), and *The Affair at Little Wokeham* (1943), the titular village being based on Blackheath.

Crofts' writing routine was simple; he worked in a spacious summer house in the garden, typing on an Underwood typewriter from nine in the morning till one and again from half past five to seven in the evening.

"I begin a new book by working out the plot in fairly complete detail, noting (a) the method of the murder, (b) what steps the criminal takes to avoid suspicion and (c) how the detectives eventually detect him—usually the most difficult of the three. Also I prepare a chronology of the main incidents, details and histories of the necessary characters, and a chronology giving the order of the happenings. All this really amounts to a detailed synopsis, and it is pretty complete before I begin to write a word."

Crofts' tenth novel was *Sir John Magill's Last Journey* (1930) whose central character, a wealthy Ulsterman, was named for the seventeenth century proprietor of Gilford, the Irish village where the author had been raised. The novel was widely regarded as a return to form, and it was the first of three books by Crofts with a Northern Ireland setting, the others being *Man Overboard!* (1936) and *Fatal Venture* (1939).

The 1930s is the decade generally regarded as the core of the Golden Age of crime and detective fiction and, at its outset, Crofts was honoured and delighted to be asked to become one of the 26 founder members of the Detection Club, a society created by Anthony Berkeley to bring together crime writers and champion the genre in the press and elsewhere. Together with Agatha Christie, Dorothy L. Sayers, and John Rhode as well as Henry Wade, Canon Victor Whitechurch, and Ronald Knox, crofts produced the round-robin mystery *The Floating Admiral* (1931), by some way the best of its kind.

By the end of the decade, in addition to taking part in two other round-robin mysteries, Crofts had published 14 full-length cases featuring Joseph French and adapted one of them for the stage. Towards the end of the decade, as Europe was escalating towards war for a second time, Crofts enlisted in the Oxford Group, a Christian organisation founded by an American pastor Frank Buchman. In 1938, as troops were being mobilised across Europe, Buchman launched a campaign for "moral re-armament," to bring about "the regeneration of society by "complete honesty, purity and love." This chimed with the personal views of Crofts who, reflecting his upbringing and possibly distaste of the nationalist sentiments that led to the partition of Ireland, Crofts was an internationalist and a strong proponent of the League of Nations. He had for some time considered that a greater sense of morality, in its purest sense, could be a salve against war as much as a cure for crime and, as a result, was greatly taken by Buchman's campaign, which he publicly supported. As well as using the principles of moral rearmament as the basis of a novel, *An-*

tidote to Venom (1938), a book described "a detective story with a clear moral purpose" by the novelist Martin Edwards, author of *The Story of Classic Crime in 100 Books* (2017). And, in the following decade, Crofts would also make a direct contribution to promoting Christian teaching through the publication of his contentious "modern biography" of Christ, *The Four Gospels in One Story* (1949).

After the outbreak of the Second World War, Crofts became even busier. Although he only published eight novels in the next decade, as well as *The Four Gospels in One Story* and a juvenile detective novel *Young Robin Brand, Detective* (1949), he worked for the British Broadcasting Corporation, contributing several series of Chief Inspector French's Cases, in which French (and the listener) were challenged to spot the flaw in a murderer's scheme and also several similarly brief spot-the-oversight plays for *Here's Wishing You Well Again* (1944-1946), a morale-boosting radio programmes for convalescing troops. Crofts also revised the stage play he had written seven years earlier and when the new version, now titled *Chief Inspector French* (1944), was produced again at a theatre in Kent, Crofts must have been delighted to learn that his play was to be produced by his cousin Hamilton with whom he had attended Campbell College nearly fifty years earlier; Hamilton also appeared in the play.

By 1948, as Freeman and Mary had begun to find their garden at Crofts too large to manage, they decided to swap with another village couple and move to a smaller home, Rose Cottage, closer to the heart of Blackheath. Crofts' health was failing and, after the completion of *Dark Journey* (1951), he put his energy into writing short stories. The main market for these at this time was the *London Evening Standard*, which operated a strict word limit, considerably lower than the 4,000 words that typically marked the length of Crofts' stories; after completing a story Freeman would cut it to meet the Standard's requirements, only to discover, when the story was published, that it had been cut again.

In October 1953, Freeman—now in his seventies—and his wife Mary moved from Blackheath to Worthing on the south coast of England, initially living on the seafront at Grenfell, 131 Brighton Road. In 1954, he began work on what would be his final book but within a matter of months he was diagnosed with cancer. In September 1956, the couple moved to 26 Warwick Gardens[4], a new home more centrally

---

[4] Some sources, incorrectly, give the address as 25 Warwick Gardens.

located, but that Christmas his doctor ordered Freeman to move into Charnwood Nursing Home where he died on 11 April 1957, only a matter of weeks after the publication of the poignantly titled *Anything to Declare?* (1957). Four days later, Freeman Wills Crofts was cremated. In his will he left the equivalent of half a million pounds, while his literary estate was bequeathed to the Society of Authors.

While his short fiction and plays are generally excellent, Crofts is best-known as a novelist. As becomes an engineer, he was above all thorough and his books are characterised by carefully constructed plots. They are memorable not for duplicitous clueing and ingenious murder methods nor for any great ingenuity in the concealment of the murderer—though some do come as a genuine surprise—but for the deliberate method and skill that French puts into the unravelling of apparently watertight alibis and the systematic deconstruction of an apparently impenetrable mystery. While a reader can be forgiven for speculating occasionally about how easy it would be to prove the case against the murderer in some of the books of Crofts' more famous luminaries—Berkeley, Carr, Christie, and Sayers—there can surely be no doubt that those who are arrested by Inspector French will face an awesomely robust case for the prosecution.

However, notwithstanding the popularity of his books, the work of Freeman Wills Crofts has never appealed to film makers, with only one film—a German adaptation for television of the non-series short story "The Level Crossing"—appearing in 1969. Yet at the time of this book's publication—which marks the centenary of *The Cask* and comes more than sixty years after Crofts' death, an Inspector French television series is in the works. This is the brainchild of the award-winning writer Brendan Foley, who was inspired by a lengthy study of Crofts' life and work included in *Masters of the "Humdrum" Mystery* by Curtis Evans, the authority on the literature and personalities of the Golden Age.

That it should have taken many years for French to appear on television is somehow very much in tune with Crofts' approach to crime and detective stories. Certainly, that "these things take time" would be wholly unsurprising to Joseph French whom the leading light of the Golden Age, Agatha Christie, once described as "a kindly, painstaking man [who] accomplishes his results by sheer hard work," a description that as aptly fits his creator, Freeman Wills Crofts.

I should like to acknowledge the various people who have helped with this book, in particular Carmina Harlow, Billie Hockley, Don Dale-Jones, Derek Martin, Andre Michielsen, and Lisa Dowdeswell of the Society of Authors.

Tony Medawar
Colchester, England

Part I:

The Casebook of Inspector French

Meet Inspector French

I have been asked to tell you something about Chief-Inspector French of the Criminal Investigation Department of New Scotland Yard. I shall do my best, but I thought it would give you a better idea of him if I were to bring the man himself to the microphone. So with a good deal of trouble I have persuaded him to come, and he'll speak to you himself. But I have put him in the next room for the moment, lest his ears should burn from my introduction.

As he's not here, then, I may say that he's really quite a good fellow at heart. He's decent and he's straight and he's as kindly as his job will allow. He believes that if you treat people decently— you'll be able to get more out of them; and he acts on his belief. Politeness is an obsession with him, and he has well earned his nickname of "Soapy Joe." He's far from perfect, but I have known him now for many years, and I don't wish for a better friend.

But I have to admit that he's not very brilliant: in fact, many people call him dull. And here I'll let you into secret history. Anyone about to perpetrate a detective novel must first decide whether his detective is to be brilliant and a "character," or a mere ordinary humdrum personality. When French came into being there seemed two good reasons for making him the second of these. One was that it represented a new departure; there were already plenty of "character" detectives, the lineal descendants, most of them, of the great Sherlock. The other reason was much more important. Striking characteristics, consistently depicted, are very hard to do.

I tried therefore to make French a perfectly ordinary man, without peculiarities or mannerisms. Of course he had to have some qualities, but they were to be the ordinary qualities of ordinary fairly successful men. He was to have thoroughness and perseverance as well as a reasonable amount of intelligence: just the qualities which make for moderate success in any walk of life.

From this it follows that he does not leap to his conclusions by brilliant intuition. He begins a case by going and looking for information in those places in which he thinks information is most likely to be found. When he gets the information he swots over it until he grinds out some sort of theory to account for the facts. Very often this turns out to be wrong, but if so, he simply tries again till he thinks of something better.

I made French an inspector of the Yard rather than a private detective because I hoped in this way to gain realism. But at once a horrible difficulty loomed up: I knew nothing about Scotland Yard or the C.I.D. What was to be done? The answer was simple. I built on the great rock which sustains so many of my profession: if I knew nothing of my subject, well few of my readers would know any more.

As a matter of fact, I have found this rock not quite so steadfast as I had hoped. It has been pointed out to me that French has at times done things which would make a real inspector of the Yard shudder. He has consistently travelled first-class railways, particularly in sleeping-cars. He has borrowed bicycles from local police-officers without paying for their hire. He has undertaken country inquiries without his attendant sergeant. And there are many other evil things has he done. Fortunately, now that he has become a chief-inspector, he is seeing the error of at least some of his ways and being more careful to live up to his great traditions.

French is a home bird, and nothing pleases him more than getting into his slippers before the fire and bury himself in some novel of sea adventure. He is married, but unlike Dr. Watson he is the husband of only one wife. On occasion his Emily helps him with his cases. But this is only when he is more utterly stuck than usual. Otherwise he doesn't think it decent—or perhaps worthwhile—to worry her with shop. I have been wondering whether he has children. It's like a dream to me that in one book children were mentioned, and that in another their existence was denied. But as I can't find either reference, I can only note the point as one to be avoided.

French's job at the Yard is distinctly comfortable, particularly since he was made a chief inspector. His promotion was decided on for a somewhat unusual reason. It was not because of his work or of what his superiors thought of him, but because so many people mentioned in letters that his promotion was long overdue. The customer, of course, is always right.

Not only, indeed, is French's job at the Yard comfortable, but he enjoys very considerable advantages over his colleagues. Two in particular are so striking as to give him an almost unique position.

The first is that he must necessarily succeed in his cases. He may become utterly discouraged and pessimistic—indeed, he does so at regular intervals. This, however, is merely a concession to the reader, who must often be feeling equally bored and wearied. But if French is discouraged it is his own fault. He knows very well—or he would know if he applied his own methods of reasoning—that he wouldn't have been put into a book if he were going to fail. Success does not come at once—the value of sus- pense in a book cannot be overlooked—but that it will come, and that not later than about page three hundred, he is well aware.

His second great advantage over his colleagues really arises out of the first. It is that definitely he will find all the clues that he wants. He is bound to find them, because they have been laid down specially for that purpose, and he is led up to them in such a way that he could not avoid seeing them even if he wished to. These clues which he will find, moreover, are exactly those which lead to the solution of his problem, though naturally he does not see this at first. A decent interval always occurs between the pick- ing up of the clue and the realisation of its significance. This is necessary, as otherwise the book would run out too short.

This plan of finding just the clues necessary to lead the investigator to the correct conclusion seems to me such an extraordinarily good way of conducting an inquiry that I offer the idea, quite freely, to the heads of Scotland Yard.

I said that French had two advantages over his colleagues at the Yard, but really he has three. He cannot be killed. He cannot even be seriously injured. The reason, of course, is that he will be wanted for the next book. So if anyone fills the room with petrol vapour and attempts to light it, as was done at Newhaven, French will, if he thinks hard, know that either the person will not light the petrol, or that if he does it won't burn. If the criminal he is attempting to arrest withdraws the pin from a Mills bomb he is carrying, he will know, again if he thinks, that either he will be able to hold the lever down, or that the bomb will prove a dud. Of course, under such distressing circumstances he never does think, as otherwise he couldn't register the amount of terror which is the reader's right and proper due.

I'm afraid I've talked too much about French, but it's really because I think a lot of him. However, with your permission I'll call him now. I give a shout that would wake the dead, and he appears. "Yes, what is it?" he asks. "Speak to these good folk, will you?" I say. He deprecatingly: "Well, I'm very glad to be able to talk to all these kind friends, and to say it's a proud day in life when - "I stop him. Goodness knows where he would otherwise get to. I ask him to tell how he solves his cases.

This is more in his line. He gives a little laugh, and starts off in his normal voice. "Huh, yes, I can do that." The answer is that I don't—not always.

But I'll tell you ladies and gentlemen how I make things look pretty well: I just don't mention the failures. Sir Mortimer and the boys at the Yard may know about them—as a matter of fact, they do; but you don't. That's my thoughtfulness for you, of course: I don't want to worry you with anything that's not just absolutely so." "But," I tell him, "you know you usually do succeed. They would like to hear your methods." "Well," he explains, "I have two principal ways. Either I get a good clue or I have a stroke of luck. And you may take it from me that the luck's the best way. It saves endless trouble and difficulty." The stream of his inspiration seems to come to an end, and I start him off again. "You've been in one or two tight corners," I suggest. "You might tell them, about your worst five minutes."

He warns to it. "At the Yard we do get occasional nasty turns, but of course they're all in the day's work. Since you've asked me, I think my worst was in the case I just heard you speak of— Did you know the door wasn't shut? I mean the case in which two financiers were murdered on an abandoned yacht off Newhaven, and a lot of diamonds were missing. You may remember it. Well, a man called Nolan was my suspect, though I couldn't prove his guilt. But I thought there was just a chance that I might be able to make him commit himself. So I laid a trap for him. I pitched him a yarn that made him think he'd left a clue on his launch, in the hope that he'd try to destroy the launch and we could take him in the act.

"The launch was lying in Newhaven Harbour, and the next night Sergeant Carter and I took cover on the wharf and settled down to watch. It was a wet night, and we got our fill of it. But it was worth it. About three in the morning we saw Nolan creeping down and slipping aboard. We followed him as close as we dared. He disappeared into the little engine-room. I crept after him to the door and peeped in. He was working with a torch, and you can imagine my feelings when I watched him take the missing diamonds from a hiding-place and put them in his pocket. This, of course, was all the proof I could have wanted. But then things grew nasty. He flooded the place with petrol and put a canister on the floor with a clock attached. So I thought it was about time to make a move.

"As a matter of fact, it was past the time. Before I could do anything he had flashed his torch on me, and I found myself looking into the wrong end of a pistol. He spoke quite quietly. He said he had feared a trick, but that he had gone through with the thing on chance. He said that as long as I lived he was in danger of being hanged. Therefore he was going to kill me. If he could get away afterwards himself, he would; if not, we would die together. "You'll understand that I could do nothing, for if I'd made a move he'd have fired, and if he'd fired, the whole place would have gone up in a sheet of flame. It was nasty, and no mistake."

French pauses, and I prompt him again.

"Tell them how you escaped."

"Ah, that was where my bit of luck came in. Carter was behind me, and Nolan didn't see him. So Carter nipped on deck, lowered himself over the side, and shot Nolan through the porthole. He got him in the hand, but the flame from the gun didn't get in, so there was no fire. But Nolan was desperate, and in spite of his wound he went for me all out. I tripped over a pipe and fell with my side against the motor, I broke some ribs, but managed to hold off Nolan till Carter got back and pulled him off."

"And after that you think you can be killed! French, my dear fellow, you're a humbug!"

He grins, and indicates pointedly that he is now due at the Yard. So I have to let him go.

The Vertical Line

The sweat was running down Arnold Wilde's forehead as from his sitting-room window he watched Chief Inspector French and Sergeant Carter leave his house. It had been a bad half hour, that which was just over, the worst he had ever known in his life. For French was close to the truth, hideously, damnably close, and it had taken all Wilde's brains and skill to preserve his secret intact.

But he had preserved it! That was the great outstanding fact: the only fact which really mattered. French could guess and suspect as much as he liked, but he could *prove* nothing. He, Wilde, had been too clever for him. He had been too clever for any detective who could be put on the job. His scheme was without a flaw and he had carried it out with absolute precision.

For Wilde was a criminal. He had just committed a murder— and he was getting away with it.

Arnold Wilde was a technical assistant in the firm of Scott & Son, analytical chemists, of Barchester in Wiltshire. In skill, knowledge, and ingenuity, he was quite first class, and would quickly have risen in his profession had it not been for a certain impatience or recklessness which made him quick to meet an emergency, but intolerant of humdrum or routine work.

It was this very quality of impatience, coupled with a healthy but uncontrolled love of adventure, which led him into the mad break from which all his later troubles had come.

He had fallen in love and he had not money enough to carry on the courtship as he desired. He could not take Alys Deane to theatres and on weekend excursions, nor give her the continuous presents she so obviously considered her due. He was desperately in love, and he was desperately afraid of losing her. Then the chance of helping himself to the firm's money had come, and with his fatal desire for short cuts and immediate results, he had taken advantage of it.

Though Wilde had never allowed himself to be bound by moral scruples, it was the first time he had gone in for theft on a large scale, and five minutes had not passed before he bitterly regretted his action. But it was ten too late. The opportunity of replacement had passed. Restitution would have involved confession, and whatever confession would have meant, it would have included the loss of Alys Deane. Instead he set himself to cover up what he had done, managing to divert suspicion from himself by inventing a mythical individual, traces of whose forced entry to the principal's room he carefully provided.

His scheme had succeeded to the extent of taking in his principals and the local inspector of police who was sent to investigate the theft. After a few days of sharp anxiety, Wilde began to breathe more freely. But he had exulted too soon.

On the third evening, he was called mysteriously aside by one of the laboratory assistants, a man named Hubbard. Hubbard was indirect in everything he did and it was some time before Wilde realised the significance of what he was hearing. But when he did so, the knowledge was like a blow between the eyes.

Hubbard knew the truth. He had seen Wilde arrange the evidence of the mythical thief.

At first, Wilde pictured immediate ruin: dismissal, the police court, prison. But he soon learned that this was not Hubbard's idea. Hubbard was on to a good thing and he was going to make the most of it. In short, his knowledge was a marketable asset, at the disposal of Wilde—for a consideration.

Wilde had paid—he could not help himself. Then, like others before him, he had discovered that his payment was only temporarily effective. A further payment was required. And still another...

After a year, Wilde found himself being slowly bled to death. Most of the money he had stolen had by this time found its way into Hubbard's pockets. Alys had not, it was true, formally broken with him. But he had not improved his position with her, and he was under no misapprehension as to how the present state of affairs would end.

And now Hubbard had made a further demand for a slice of Wilde's pay. It was a demand which, if admitted, would definitely bring the Alys Deane affair to an end. Wilde swore bitter oaths to himself that nothing would induce him to submit to it.

But what could he do?

He knew what he could do. All those months of thrawldom had not passed in vain. They had bred a Plan. Yes, he knew what he could do.

Very carefully he worked out the details. His former scheme of the Mythical Thief had been a brilliant success. He would try it again. He would create a Mythical Murderer!

He temporised with Hubbard. He could not pay during the present month: he had spent too much of his salary. He would begin with his next month's cheque.

Hubbard was taken in. He agreed; and Wilde began the carrying out of the Plan.

First he disguised himself: not ignorantly with a wig and false moustache, but skilfully with glasses, different clothes, a cap instead of his usual hat, and small pieces of rubber in his cheeks. In London he bought an airgun. It was a toy in the sense: scarcely a serious weapon. But Wilde was going to fire into Hubbard's head from only a couple of inches away and he knew it would kill. At shops in different areas he bought also a pair of rubber gloves, a small crowbar, and a second-hand pair of hobnailed shoes, two sizes too big for him, "to help a chap I know to get a job."

The laboratory in which the two men and three other workers were employed was to be the scene of the crime. It was a large ground floor room overlooking the garden of the suburban house used by the firm. The garden was hidden by trees from the observation of neighbours, and Wilde was sure that if the house itself were empty, he could approach and leave the window unseen.

The room was furnished with the usual apparatus for four working chemists. Of these Wilde was one, and Hubbard was assistant to the four. Hamilton, the senior, who overlooked the others' work, had in addition a large roll topped desk. This desk was placed with its back against the wall, and beside it on the right was the sink, bench, and stink cupboard Hamilton used. The stink cupboard was in the corner of the room, and close by in the wall at right angles was a window. The top of the desk bore a heterogeneous collection of personal treasures, which Hamilton guarded as the apple of his eye. Besides the telephone there was a curiously marked piece of feldspar which he had picked up on the slopes of the Matterhorn, a rain gauge which he had said for months he was going to set up in the garden, a large barograph whose records he carefully studied week by week, a bottle of Dead Sea water whose purpose no one had ever been able to discover, and another bottle containing the vertebrae of a snake which he had killed in the Pyrenees.

Work normally stopped at half past five, but it any of the men were in the middle of a test at quitting time, they usually waited to complete it. Hubbard seldom got away till after the others, as it was his business to clean up and put away the apparatus they had used.

With the plea ready of extra work in case he should be observed, Wilde on several nights returned late to the laboratory to test out the Plan.

He went over its every detail till he was absolutely satisfied it would not fail him. Then he began to watch for an evening to put it into operation.

The conditions were simple. All that was necessary was that he and Hubbard should be alone in the building. He made it his business to learn his companions' plans, so as to be sure that when they had once left for home, they would not return.

A suitable evening soon came and Wilde seized the opportunity. He delayed over his work till the others had gone, pretending that a series of tests had run out longer than he had anticipated. Surreptitiously he watched Hubbard moving about the laboratory, collecting test tubes and other dirty apparatus and carrying them to the sink beside Hamilton's desk, where he would presently wash them.

Except for occasional distressing qualms, Wilde had up to this been cool enough about his terrible undertaking. But now that the moment was upon him he realised what it was he was doing and grew almost sick with fear and horror. However he had provided against this also. From his pocket he took a bottle of brandy and fortified himself with a good nip. It pulled him together and he became once more his own man.

With the feeling that the action constituted a burning of his boats, a making irrevocable of his dreadful intention, he heaved an audible sigh and exclaimed: "There, thank the Lord that's done!" going on presently: "I've got a few test tubes for you, Hubbard. I'll bring 'em across."

Hubbard, his head bent over the sink, grunted. Wilde seized his airgun, which he had hidden in his locker, and walked boldly across the room. Hubbard did not look up. Wilde presented the muzzle of the gun to the back of the man's neck. It was almost touching, and as the head was bent down, the bullet would certainly penetrate to the brain.

Suddenly suspicion seemed to arise in the assistant's mind. He dropped his test tubes and began to swing round. But before he could do so Wilde fired. The report was negligible. Hubbard hung for a moment motionless. Then with a soft choking cry he fell sideways on to Hamilton's desk and from there slid slowly down to the floor. A convulsive tremor passed over his body and lay still.

In spite of the brandy Wilde grew cold and faint. Then once again he pulled himself together. Now was the time for care and coolness!

If he made a mistake now, he was lost.

Quickly he began to work. And first as to the position of the body. A glance told him it was satisfactory. Anyone could see that the man had been working at the sink when he was hit, and as the question of powder blackening did not arise, anyone might suppose that he had been shot through the window. So far, so good.

The next thing was to supply the traces of the assailant. Putting on his rubber gloves and taking the crowbar and shoes, Wilde let himself into the garden. It was almost, but not quite dark: just light enough to see what he was doing, just dark enough to be practically safe from observation. Keeping on the hard walks he went to a small gate leading in from the land behind the houses. He let himself out with the communal office key, locked the gate behind him, and with the bar forced the lock from the outside. Then he put on the nailed shoes and again went through the motions of forcing the gate, for though the ground at the place was hard, he thought the nails might show. He walked out along the comparatively soft lane till he reached hard road, then returned, taking care not to tread on any of his outward bound footsteps.

Continuing on to the window, which, being normally open at the top, was unlatched, he pushed up the lower sash while standing on the rather untidy flower bed alongside the house. Then he entered, stepped beside the body, and knelt down as if to search it. He straightened himself up again, climbed out of the window, and leaving the lower sash fully up, walked back to the gate. This time he was careful to tread on at least one of his previous prints. At the gate, he changed his shoes once again, and carrying the nailed pair, he returned over hard walks to the laboratory.

Here was the trail of the Mythical Murderer, to provide which was the second part of his Plan. But there was still a third. There must be proof that the Mythical Murderer was not himself.

Retaining his rubber gloves, he quickly reconstructed the apparatus with which he had so carefully experimented. Taking from his pocket a piece of find thread with the ends knotted together to form a loop, and which at one point he had frayed half-through, he put it over the telephone hook. Then he got a large beaker or glass jar and placed it in the sink adjoining. He fixed it so that it leant inwards at an angle of forty-five degrees, its base standing across the angle between the side and bottom of the sink. It was just balanced, but to make sure it remained in position he slipped the loop of thread round it close to its top. He had made the loop just large enough to fit tightly. The beaker was thus, as it were, supported by the loop of thread from the telephone hook.

Wilde then removed the telephone receiver. This he could do without calling up the exchange, as the thread loop kept the hook down. Stretching the flex to its fullest extent, he seized Hubbard's right hand and closed it on the receiver. The hand would not of course remain gripped, so Wilde let it fall to its former position. The receiver he left swinging on its flex.

Wilde now had a good look round the room to see that he had forgotten nothing. Then having fastened previously prepared weights to the nailed shoes and the gloves, he put these in his pockets, hid the airgun and bar under his jacket and down his trouser leg, and covered all with an overcoat.

There remained but one further detail. Just before leaving, Wilde turned on slightly the water-tap at Hamilton's sink. He had placed the beaker with its top beneath the tap. In from twenty minutes to half an hour, the glass would fill sufficiently to overturn. The thread would break, the telephone hook would rise, and a call would be made at the exchange. This would fix the hour of the tragedy. At that hour he, Wilde, would be dining with a number of friends at a small club he frequented.

Wilde was well pleased with his scheme. It contained nothing that could possibly give him away. The upturned beaker and the dripping tap would suggest only that Hubbard was actually at work when he was shot—which would be the truth. The thread was of the kind continuously in use in the laboratory and its presence would therefore be normal and unsuspicious. Moreover, it could not draw attention to the telephone, as the position of the frayed portion would insure that it would break over, and come clear away from, the hook.

Close to the house ran the deep river on which the town was built. It was crossed by a footbridge but little frequented after dark. Wilde ran out on to the bridge and threw the air-gun, bar, shoes, and gloves into the black water, as far down stream as he could. They disappeared with hollow splashes. Ten minutes later, he was in his club, and with an innocent but carefully thought out remark had called the attention of his companions to the time.

The next day or two had been a ghastly ordeal, but as time passed Wilde grew reassured. He was safe. No one could know what he had done.

But at this last interview with French and Carter his confidence had been rudely shattered. French's questions had been terribly disquieting. It seemed certain that he suspected the truth. He had at all events discovered the trick of the alibi. Wilde struggled to hide the panic he felt creeping over him. Again and again, he told himself that French could guess and suspect as much as he liked, but he could *prove* nothing. And as long as French could *prove* nothing, he, Wilde, was safe.

All the same, as he watched French and Carter going away down the street, he sweated with real fear.

A little later Chief Inspector French and Sergeant Carter were back for the nth time in the laboratory. French was looking worried.

"That blighter's going to get away with it," he growled. "He's as guilty as sin, but his counsel would work that telephone stunt with the jury and get him off."

Carter mumbled an unwilling agreement.

"We must get him, no matter what it costs us," French went on. "Just let's go over the blessed case again. Perhaps one of us may see something we've overlooked. I'll put it to you and it may help us both."

French began pacing slowly backwards and forwards as he talked.

"What struck us first was the receiver lying off the telephone. Owing to the disappearance of the gun, the case was an obvious murder, and the idea suggested was clearly that the deceased saw his danger and was about to call for help, but that before he could do so, he was shot."

Carter nodded, a wary eye on his chief.

"But," went on French, "can you or anyone else imagine the murderer leaving the receiver off? As long as it remains off it is a signal to the exchange that something is wrong. It's at least on the cards that they may ring up some close by to have a look. If—as actually happened in this case—one of the partners rang up Hubbard to give him some altered instructions for the next day, he would be gold something was wrong. He was told in this case and the tragedy was discovered. Now the murderer would not want that discovery to be made till the last possible moment.

"On the other hand, if the receiver is replaced on the hook, it only means that it was lifted in error. Surely if Hubbard had really tried to phone, the murderer's first act would have been to replace the receiver?"

Carter nodded more appreciatively.

"This is of course a purely speculative point which proves nothing whatever, but it does suggest that this telephone signal *may* have been a plant, probably intended to fix an erroneous hour for the crime."

"That's right, sir." Carter agreed heavily.

"We test the receiver for finger prints and what do we find? Again something suggestive, though inconclusive. We find that if the deceased picked up the receiver, he gripped it in a particularly awkward way: diagonally across his hand, too far from the wrist opposite the thumb, too near it opposite the little finger. He might in his hurry have so grasped it, but it's unlikely. Again there's the suggestion of a plant."

French turned towards the sink. "Here in the sink we find an assortment of objects. A dripping tap; a large beaker lying on its side beneath it; under the beaker a broken loop of thread, partially frayed at the break. Nothing suspicious there—at first."

"That's where the value of routine work comes in, sir," Carter said with slightly exaggerated innocence.

French glanced at him keenly. "Yes, I have pointed that out, haven't I?" he returned drily. "And I was right this time—if never before." He glared and Carter's manner grew less assured. "Routine work told us that none of the men in that room had used either a beaker or a piece of thread of that length that day."

"Pretty neat, sir," Carter remarked ingratiatingly. "Incidentally, though we didn't suspect Wilde so far, that's where he made a bad mistake. He should have been able to prove that he had used both. However he didn't twig that till too late."

"The beaker, the thread, the telephone," Carter murmured. "Something fishy about all three."

"Quite: it's easy to repeat a well-known argument. Was there a connection? Not easy to see one. Then at long last the position of the thread under the beaker and the length of its broken ends does suggest something. We find if the beaker was partially raised, the loop would just go over the telephone hook. We get another thread and reconstruct. Then we turn on the tap and watch what happens. We see the beaker slowly filling till it turns over and snaps the thread and releases the hook. That takes about twenty minutes. The beaker and thread fall where they were found. So there is no longer any doubt."

"But w can't prove it, sir."

"Ah, Carter, how wise you are! We can't. However, to continue. Routine work again tells us the time at which each member of the staff left the place, and we learn that Wilde was the last to go. We ask him what time he left and he tells us six o'clock. We have no reason to doubt it. But the telephone rings at 6.20, and we note that that was just twenty minutes later. At that hour, 6.20, all the members of the staff, including Wilde, have watertight alibis. We wonder if one of them arranged the time plant. If so, it could only have been Wilde, as he was the last to leave."

"It's a good case, sir, if you ask me."

"I don't ask you," French returned, "because I know you're wrong. We then look for motive. Who could have desired this man's death? And here at last our excellent routine work gets something more encouraging.

"The deceased was undoubtedly living beyond his income. From some unknown source he was getting cash. Where was it coming from?

"More routine work. Was anyone else concerned living below his income? Great trouble to find this out. A week's work for half a dozen of us. But worth it when we get the answer. Wilde had a decent salary, but lived as if he was chronically hard up. And he had saved nothing."

"We can't prove the money passed from Wilde to the deceased."

"No. Neither can we prove blackmail, though our present line of enquiries may tell us that. Then there was the question of the footprints."

"The best bit of work I ever heard of."

"I admit it wasn't too bad," French said with more complaisance. "The length of the pace was small for the size of the shoes. That set us thinking. And we found that the length of the pace, and more important still, the angle at which the toes were turned out, were precisely those of Wilde's normal walk. Practically conclusive to you or me, but still not good enough for court."

French had continued to pace the room, but now he pulled up at the desk. "The position of the body showed that it hit the desk in falling. Let's move the desk a bit. Something might have rolled underneath it."

They pushed the desk sideways. It clung to the oilcloth, then slid with a sudden jerk. Both men searched the floor. There was nothing.

"I didn't expect anything," French admitted, "because though I hadn't moved it, I had already looked below it. Let's have it back again."

But instead of pushing it back, French stood rooted to the ground, staring straight before him with excitement growing in his eyes. Then like a madman he began striking the desk, with his shoulder, with his fist, while still he gazed. "Carter," he gasped, "have we got that blighter after all? Show me the photographs."

Carter took from a despatch case prints of the photographs which had been taken first thing on the arrival of the police, some hour after the crime. French hurriedly turned them over and selected a large detailed view of the front of the desk, showing everything in and upon it with great clearness. He whipped out a lens. A glance through it was evidently sufficient. He smote his high a mighty blow.

"We've got him, Carter! We've got him! Proof, absolute and complete and as neat as we could wish! Come one: we'll go and see him again."

Wilde had sweated after his ordeal as he had watched French and Carter leave his rooms. He grew positively sick with terror when he saw them coming back. If all were well, why should they come back? Hurriedly, he crossed to a cupboard and took out his bottle of brandy.

"Just another question or two, Mr. Wilde," French said gravely when they were seated. "But first I'm bound to warn you again that whatever you say will be taken down and may be used in evidence. Also that you need not answer my questions unless you like. But you said you wished to make a statement and did so. Are you willing to add to that statement?"

Momentarily Wilde hesitated. "I've nothing to hide," he said with an assumption of ease. "I'll answer your further questions if I can."

French immediately began. But he surprised Wilde. He repeated questions which he had already asked, inoffensive questions, irrelevant questions even. Wilde began to breathe more freely. There was nothing to be alarmed about. It was simply a case of official stupidity.

"You stated that you were alone in the laboratory with the deceased from about half past five, when the others left, to about six, when you left yourself. Do you stick to that statement?"

"Certainly."

"Where were you working?"

"At my bench, as I said." Relief was growing in Wilde's mind and was reflected in the tone of his replies.

"From your bench you could see Mr. Hamilton's desk?" "Yes, it was straight in front of me."

"Now during that half hour did anything heavy strike the desk?"

Wilde's relief suddenly evaporated. With terrible clarity he saw in his mind's eye the body growing limp, crashing against the desk, and from it to the floor. Why had French asked this question? Could it be—that he knew? And what should he, Wilde, answer? If yes, what could he say had fallen? If no, would be give himself away?

With a dreadful feeling of misgiving, he realised that he was delaying his reply. Delay would be fatal. He plunged. Nothing had struck the desk.

"I want to be absolutely certain about that, Mr. Wilde," French went on with relentless insistence. "Your definite statement is that while you were in the room between half past five and six, the desk was not struck a heavy blow? Is that correct? Think carefully before you speak?"

Wilde, terror stricken lest a trap should lurk in the question, now wished he had said he had himself fallen against the desk. But it was too late. He dare not reverse his statement.

"I have already said," he declared, striving desperately for composure, "and I now repeat, that nothing struck the desk while I was in the room."

French nodded, paused, and then gathered himself with something suggestive of an animal crouching to spring. "I told you that we had discovered the plan by which telephone call might have been given some twenty minutes after the murderer had left the room: the beaker and thread and so on?"

"Yes, but that has nothing to do with me," Wilde murmured through dry lips.

"Let me finish," French persisted. "The medical evidence indicates that the deceased struck the desk in his fall. The only question then is, when did he fall?"

Panic was closing down on Wilde. He could not see where this was leading, but there was something utterly terrifying in French's manner. He nodded without speaking. He could not speak.

"Let me tell you what happened just now," French went on. "We, Sergeant Carter and I, had occasion to move the desk. It stuck to the oilcloth, then came free suddenly. The effect on the desk was a sudden shock, much the same as if a body fell on it."

Wilde could only stare helplessly.

"Do you know what happened as a result of that shock? Well, I'll tell you. The pen of the barograph vibrated. It recorded a tiny vertical line across its ordinary trace. You see?" French paused, then took the photograph from his case and with a lens handed it across. "Now here," he went on, "is a photo taken about seven on the evening of the crime.

Let us look at the trace of the barograph. What do we find? We find the pen pointing to seven o'clock with the trace leading back from it, every hour being shown on the scale. Across that trace is a vertical line—one vertical line. Since there is only one, it must represent the fall of the body. Now do you see the hour? That line was drawn at just a quarter before six."

There came a slight sound in the ensuing silence. Wilde had fainted.

The Hunt Ball Murder

Howard Skeffington had reached the end of his tether. He sat, hunched forward and staring unseeingly into the fire, as he faced the terrible conclusion to which inexorably he was being impelled: that his only escape from ruin lay in the death of his former friend, Justin Holt.

He, Howard Skeffington, must murder Holt! If he didn't, this pleasant life he was living, this fortune which seemed almost within his grasp, would be irretrievably lost. He would have to leave the country and everything he valued, and looked somewhere abroad for a job. And what job could he get?

To a certain extent, Skeffington was an adventurer. Possessed of a good appearance, charming manners, and an admirable seat on a horse, he had made friends at Cambridge with some of the young men from this Seldon Sorby country, this centre of the hunting life of England. At their homes he had spent vacations, riding their horses with skill, if not distinction. Alone in the world, and not drawn to any career which involved hard work, he had conceived the idea of settling down at Seldon Sorby, and, if possible, marrying money.

The first part of this scheme he had carried out successfully. He had taken rooms in the district and been accepted as a member of the Hunt. He had joined an associated and very select club, and his social prospects seemed flourishing.

But he was up against one difficulty—money. His capital, he had estimated, would last him for four years, and on these four years, he had staked his all. If before the end of that period he was unable to bring off the second part of his programme, he would be finished: down and out.

His chances in this respect, however, he considered rosy. Elaine Goff-Powell, Sir Richard Goff-Powell's only daughter, would have enough for any husband. Moreover, he was sure she admired him, and he made himself very agreeable to her father. Elaine was neither a beauty nor a wit; in fact, in moments of depression, he realised she was, as he put it, damned plain and damned dull, too. But this gave him all the more hope. It wiped out the most dangerous of his potential competitors. As yet, he had not risked a proposal, but he felt the time would soon be ripe and he had little fear of the result.

Unhappily, while the affair was moving, it was not moving quickly enough. Unless an engagement could be achieved soon, his resources would not stand the strain. Another five or six hundred would undoubtedly enable him to pull it off. As it was, the thing would be touch and go.

He had done what he could to borrow, but with indifferent success. Professional moneylenders would not touch him. Friends who might, with luck, be good for a tenner, certainly would not stretch to anything more: and it would take a good many tenners to be of use to Skeffington.

In this difficulty, he had embarked on a course which normally he would have avoided like the plague. He had taken to cheating at cards. He realised very fully the risk he ran, but he did not see that any other way was open to him.

For some weeks he had managed successfully, and he had determined to put his fortunes to the test at the Christmas Hunt Ball, which was to take place in a few days. With reasonable luck he would be accepted, and then this dreadfully wearing period of his life would be over.

But now, five days before the ball, disaster had overtaken him.

His cheating had been discovered.

And yet not wholly discovered. What had happened was this. During a game at the club, one of the men, this Justin Holt,

suddenly ceased playing. His face took on an expression of agony, and after swaying about for a moment, his head pitched forward on the table, the cards dropping from his nerveless fingers. The others jumped to their feet, but before they could do anything Holt raised himself. He was covered with confusion, and apologised profusely. He had, he explained, got a severe pain and giddiness. It had come so suddenly that, for the moment, it had bowled him over, but already it was better. Infinitely he regretted breaking up the party, but with the others' consent he would go home and lie down. When they wanted to help, he hesitated, then asked Skeffington, who lived in his direction, if he would mind seeing him to his quarters.

The affair puzzled Skeffington, who had never before seen such a seizure. But for him the mystery was soon cleared up. When they were alone, Holt suddenly found himself able to walk normally and the expression of pain vanished from his face.

He remained, however, looking extremely worried.

"I did that little bit of play-acting for a reason, Skeffington," he said. "The truth is, I saw what you were doing. I've been suspicious for some time, and so, I may tell you, have been a number of the others. But tonight I watched you, and I saw the whole thing. Skeffington, you're finished at Seldon Sorby!"

To Skeffington it sounded like a sentence of death, but he quickly pulled himself together. Staring at Holt as coolly as he could, he said: "Perhaps you'll kindly explain what you're talking about?"

Holt shook his head irritably. "Don't be a complete fool," he begged. "I tell you I saw it. There's no use in your pretending. I know."

"You can't know anything," Skeffington returned doggedly. "If you had seen anything at that table, you'd have said so at the time. You didn't."

"I didn't," Holt explained, "for an obvious reason. I have some thought for the Hunt, if you haven't. I didn't want to make a scandal. If we had been by ourselves I would have spoken. But with outsiders present, naturally I didn't."

"Very thoughtful," Skeffington sneered. "It hasn't occurred to you that your consideration has rendered your story useless? Even if you had seen anything, which I deny, you can't prove it."

"I can tell what I saw."

"That's not proof. I shall deny it, and then where will you be? You will have made a libelous statement which you can't prove. I think, my dear Holt, you, and not I, will be the one to retire."

Again Holt shook his head. "That sounds all right, Skeffington, but you know as well as I do that I would be believed. You know, or you ought to, that several of the men suspect you as it is. If I describe what I saw you do, they will believe me."

"You just try it on," Skeffington said, as contemptuously as he could. "It doesn't matter what anybody believes or doesn't believe privately. You can prove nothing, and you'll be the one who will suffer."

"That may be," Holt admitted, "but I'll tell you what I shall do. I'll give you three days to think it over. If by then you have sent in your resignation from the Hunt, I will never refer to the matter again. If you have not resigned, I shall tell the committee. You do as you like."

Though Skeffington had attempted a mild bluff, he knew that Holt had the whiphand. It was true what the man had said: he would be believed rather than Skeffington. Holt's transparent honesty was universally recognised, whereas Skeffington was aware that his own reputation was by no means too secure. His phenomenal luck had been remarked on jokingly—or was it jokingly?—by several members, and the somewhat spectacular wins which had produced these remarks would be remembered—if Holt told what he had seen.

Skeffington rapidly considered the matter. He must somehow get Holt to keep silence. There must be no scandal, for scandal would mean complete ruin. The least breath, and all chance of marrying Elaine Goff-Powell would be at an end. Indeed, if he didn't pull off an engagement at the ball next Tuesday this last hope would be gone. He could not propose again for some weeks, and his money would not stretch to that.

But what could he do to restrain Holt? Nothing! Holt was one of those men who believe in doing what they consider is their duty. No, he could not hope to influence Holt. Then first occurred to Skeffington the terrible idea that there was a way in which he could silence his enemy. One way: and only one.

Skeffington felt that he was at the most dreadful crisis of his life. To give up his present position and, practically penniless, to begin looking for a job—for which he had no training—would mean destitution, misery and death. And he could look forward to nothing else—if Holt were to live. But could he face the alternative: if Holt were to die? . . . Drops of sweat formed on his forehead.

He realised, of course, that his future did not depend solely on Holt. If Elaine turned him down he would equally be ruined. Therefore, if Elaine turned him down, there was no need to consider Holt any more. He was down and out in any case.

But if Elaine accepted him? Then Holt's actions would become vital. In this case . . .

All Skeffington's instincts were now prompting him to gain time. At all costs he must close Holt's mouth till after the ball. Then he, Skeffington, would either disappear and go under, or he would somehow deal with Holt. He turned to the man and spoke quietly and with more hesitation.

"Don't be in a hurry, Holt; I must think this over. Without admitting anything, I see you can do me a lot of harm. You have given me an ultimatum: resign or take the consequences. I want you to compromise."

"Compromise?" Holt was shocked. "How can I compromise on a thing of that sort? Why, it's fundamental! You're not a fool, Skeffington; you must see that."

Skeffington shrugged. "I suppose you're right," he admitted presently. "Well, I'll tell you. I'll agree to your conditions provided you give me six days, instead of three, to make my arrangements. And what's more, during these six days, I promise not to enter the cardroom. At the end of the six days, if I haven't resigned, you can go to the committee. Hang it all, Holt, that's not too much to ask. I must fix up some reason for the resignation. I'll have an uncle die in America and leave me money, or something of that kind. Then I'll go abroad and that will be the end of me so far as you're concerned."

Holt hesitated.

"Look here," went on Skeffington, "I'll not ask six days. Give me till the ball. We'll meet there and I'll let you have every satisfaction."

"But, damn it, Skeffington, you mustn't come to the ball."

This was what Skeffington had feared. He shrugged, then turned away. "Oh, well," he said coldly, "if you're going to be unreasonable, I withdraw my offer. You tell the committee now, and when I am approached. I shall deny everything and ask for your proof. And if you don't give it, I shall press for your expulsion, and if you don't leave I shall start proceedings against you for defamation of character. A worse scandal that than my going to the ball!" He paused, then continued in a pleasanter tone. "But I don't want to do that. If you will wait till the ball it'll give me a chance to explain my departure. That's all I ask." He suddenly changed his tone. "I'm not attempting any extenuation, Holt, but try to imagine the ruin this means for me. It's not like you to kick a man when he's down."

There had been some further argument, and Skeffington had triumphed. Holt had agreed to say nothing, provided that at, or before, the ball Skeffington resigned.

Left alone, Skeffington hardened his heart and began to work out the solution of his terrible problem. First, if Elaine refused him. By borrowing from his friends and selling some of his stuff he could raise, he thought, a couple of hundred pounds. He had better do this at once and buy tickets to the Argentine, where he thought his knowledge of horses might stand him in good stead. No doubt before leaving he could borrow a little more. Enough to get past the immigration laws, at all events. It would be hell after what he was accustomed to; but it would be at least a chance for life.

But if Elaine accepted him?

Then he was set up for life, with all the money he could want; his future absolutely assured—if only Holt were dealt with.

Skeffington took care to speak to various members of the committee and others to whom Holt might have told his story, and in every case he was satisfied from their manner that they had heard nothing. Holt, therefore, was the only danger. If he were silenced, Skeffington would be safe.

For three days, Skeffington thought over the problem, and then at last he saw the man might be eliminated, and with absolute secrecy. Admittedly, there would be a little risk at one point, but, that point once passed, no further hitch could arise. Carefully, Skeffington made his preparations. He avoided the club on the excuse of private business, and kept rigorously out of Holt's way. At last the fateful night arrived, a dark and bitter evening, with the ground like iron and a frosty fog in the air. The Christmas Hunt Ball was *the* Social event of the year, when the local four hundred thronged the Seldon Sorby Town Hall, and everyone who was anyone felt he must be present. The somewhat drab building was transformed out of all recognition with bunting and greenery, and the hunt colours made the gathering what the local paper invariably called a spectacle of sparkling brilliance. The first two essentials of Skeffington's plan were to drive some people to the ball and to park his car in a secluded place near the back entrance of the hall. The former he managed by inviting a young married couple called Hatherley and a bachelor friend named Scarlett to accompany him; the second, by a careful timing of his arrival, coupled with his knowledge of how the park filled. The market at the back of the hall was used as a park, and there he succeeded in placing the car in the corner he desired. He knew that before long it would be completely surrounded and that no one was likely to remain near it.

In the car, hooked up under the dash, was a heavy spanner, round which he had wrapped a soft cloth. It was so fixed that he could lift it out by simply opening the door and putting in his hand.

He had taken just enough whisky to steady his nerves, and in spite of the terrible deed which was in front of him, he felt confident and in his best form.

To his delight, Elaine had greeted him with more than her usual warmth. For half the evening he had danced exclusively with her, and now he led her to a deserted corner and, with trepidation, put the vital question. A thrill of overwhelming satisfaction shot through him when he heard the answer. As soon as Skeffington could, he returned to the young woman.

How he endured to the end of the proceedings, Skeffington scarcely knew. But at long last Elaine departed with her family, and he went in search of his friends.

"I'll bring the car to the steps," he told the Hatherleys, then adding to Scarlett: "You might come and help me, if you don't mind. It's a job to get out of such a jam."

Reaching the car, Skeffington opened the near forward door for Scarlett, then went round to the driver's side and got in himself. He thus had a witness of all his proceedings, while Scarlett had not seen the body.

As Skeffington pulled in to the steps, a commissionaire opened the rear door for Mrs. Hatherley. He lifted away the rug, then swore hoarsely, while Mrs. Hatherley gave a shrill scream.

What happened then seemed a confused muddle to Skeffington. He got out and tried to edge round to the door through the dense crowd which had instantly formed.

"What is it?" he heard himself shouting. "What's wrong?"

He heard murmurs all about him. "A man!" "Seems to be dead!" "There, in the back of the car "—then an authoritative voice, which he recognised as that of the chief constable of the county: "Keep back everyone, please, and let Dr. Hackett pass. Doctor, will you please have a look here?"

Everyone but Skeffington and Scarlett moved back. Someone provided a torch. For a moment time seemed to stand still, then the doctor said slowly: "It's Holt, and I'm afraid he's dead. A blow on the head. Must have been instantaneous."

Time began to move once more; in fact, it now raced so quickly that Skeffington could hardly keep up with it.

As if by magic, police appeared. The guests were politely herded back into the ball-room. Skeffington was asked by a sharp-looking young inspector if he could give any explanation of the affair, and when he replied that he could not, he was told, not so politely, to wait where he was for a further interrogation.

The whole place buzzed as if a swarm of colossal bees had invaded it. Then, gradually, people began to leave, their names and addresses taken, and a few questions put and answered. At long last the police returned to Skeffington.

He had taken a little more whisky, enough to subdue his fear and steady his hands, but not enough to make him stupid.

"Will you tell me what you know of this affair, Mr. Skeffington?" asked the local superintendent, who had now arrived and taken charge of the proceedings.

Skeffington replied without hesitation. He had driven Mr. and Mrs. Hatherley and Mr. Scarlett to the ball. He had parked in the corner of the market. All had then got out and gone into the hall. When Mrs. Hatherley was ready to go home, he and Scarlett had gone for the car. He had driven it to the steps, and when the rear door had been opened the body had been found. The affair was just as great a mystery to him as to the super.

It was a simple story, and Skeffington told it well. Superintendent Redfern asked many questions, but he could not in any way shake the tale, and at last he thanked Skeffington and said that would be all.

Rather shakily, Skeffington drove home.

During the next couple of days events moved quickly at police headquarters at Seldon Sorby. The place had been shaken to the core. Such a murder, taking place at the most fashionable event in the town's year, and involving the death of a relative of Lord Bonniton, the Master of the most famous hunt in the country, seemed almost a national disaster. The Chief Constable was frantic, and without delay had wired to Scotland Yard for help. A couple of hours later Chief Inspector French and Sergeant Carter had arrived to assist in the inquiry. French had heard all that had been done, had studied the various statements made, and had examined the Town Hall and market.

As he had not thereupon laid his hand on the guilty party, the Chief Constable had asked querulous and suggestive questions.

"Silly fool!" French grumbled to Carter as that night they went to their hotel. "Does he think we're thought-readers? If he was in all that hurry, why didn't he do the job himself?"

Later that evening French sat smoking over the lounge fire and imbibing cup after cup of strong coffee, as he puzzled his brains in the attempt to find some line of investigation which would give him his solution. He had put in train all the obvious inquiries: about Holt's career and recent activities; who had seen him at the ball; who had been in the market while the cars were parked; and suchlike; but he wanted to find some short cut, some royal road, almost, to the criminal.

Sir Mortimer Ellison, the Assistant Commissioner at the Yard, had given him a hint before he started. "It's a society place," he had said, "and the big bugs are society people. You'll find them touchy down there, because this case will get them on the raw. Hence, the quicker you pull it off, the better for all concerned." And now he had been down for the most of two days and he was no further on than when he arrived.

For three hours he considered the matter, and then a point struck him, a very simple point. It might not lead to anything; but, on the other hand, it might. The following day, he would try a reconstruction.

Accordingly, next morning he demanded a man of the approximate build of the deceased and a car like Skeffington's. These he took to a secluded corner of the police yard and set to work.

The dummy was a young constable named Arthurs. He grinned when French explained that he wanted to smash in his head.

"Right, sir," he agreed. "I hope you'll remember the wife and kiddies when I'm gone."

"No one, I'm afraid, will know how it was done," French assured him. "Now, Arthurs, just where you're standing I hit you a bat on the head and stove in your skull. See? "

"Yes, sir."

"Well, go ahead, man, You don't want me to do it in reality, I suppose? "

"I'm afraid, sir, if my skull—"

French jerked round. "Good heavens, man! Use your brains! Collapse!—"

With a sudden look of comprehension, Arthurs sank quietly on to the ground beside the car—while French adjured him to relax all muscles completely.

"Now, Carter, lift him into the position the dead man occupied." Carter opened the rear door, and, lifting the grinning Arthurs beneath the arms, tried to get him into the car. But, like Skeffington, he found he couldn't do it from where he was standing. He also had to go round to the other side and draw him in. "Can't you pull in the legs? "French prompted.

Carter tried. "No, sir," he returned: "I'll have to go back and lift them in."

French watched him, a smile of satisfaction playing on his lips. "I rather thought that might happen," he declared. "Come along to the mortuary." He looked into the car. "Thank you, Arthurs, we've done with you. I'll admit you'd make a good corpse."

On reaching the room where Holt's clothes lay, French took out his powdering apparatus and dusted the deceased's patent-leather shoes. Several fingerprints showed up. French blew away the surplus, then photographed the prints.

"Now the deceased's fingers," he went on.

Soon the ten impressions were taken and photographed in their turn. A proper comparison would require enlargements and detailed observation, but a certain amount could be learnt from mere casual inspection. French quickly satisfied himself. Most of the prints belonged to the deceased himself, but certain others were not his. From their position, they might well have been caused by lifting the feet into a car.

Two hours later, the club started a new waiter in the bar. Gradually a row of used glasses accumulated, each neatly labelled with the name of the drinker. At intervals French tested and compared the fingerprints. Suddenly the affair clicked. Skeffington had lifted Holt's shoes.

The correct line of investigation was now indicated. Judicious inquiries brought to light Skeffington's financial position and

mysterious luck at cards; Holt's strange illness, and the fact that Holt had asked Skeffington to accompany him to his rooms. The fact of the latter's engagement also became known. Here, French saw, was all the motive he needed.

"He thought putting the corpse in his own car would absolve him from suspicion, but the prints on the shoes are proof positive that he did it," he concluded his statement to the Chief Constable. "We're ready for an arrest, I think."

"Tonight," nodded the Chief Constable.

The Match

I

Claud Sefton sat huddled forward over the fire in his study, his face pale and drawn, and an expression of horror and loathing stamped on his features. And not without reason, Claud Sefton had just reached a terrible decision. He had determined to kill his acquaintance, Roger Locke.

His position was desperate. If Locke lived, it meant for him utter and complete ruin. It meant the loss of his money and position, it meant beggary for his wife, it meant prison for himself. Claud Sefton couldn't face it. Anything, he thought, rather than that.

And yet he shrank with almost equal dread from the only alternative. To murder Roger Locke! Locke with whom he had played golf and bridge, with whom he had shot, at whose house he had dined. Locke, who had always been pleasant and who had never done him any harm. Sefton's whole being revolted from the idea. And bad as was the idea of abstract murder, the actual carrying out of the deed would be a thousand times worse. Sefton grew physically sick as he thought of it. Heavens! Could he bring himself to do it?

But if not, there was ruin for himself and his wife. Prison ...

So for some days Sefton had hesitated, oscillating from one standpoint to another, torn between conflicting fears and desires. But now he had reached a decision. His lower and more cowardly side had won. He would buy his own safety with Locke's life.

Claud Sefton was a solicitor in the not inconsiderable town of Bridgebury, some five-and-twenty miles south of London. He had a good practice, and though at his age, just past fifty, he could no longer hope for success of a spectacular kind, he had no reason to be dissatisfied with his lot. He had a circle of pleasant acquaintances, a small but comfortable villa in the suburbs, a wife with whom, after twenty years of married life, he still remained on good terms, and an income which ran to a car, theatres when either felt inclined, and an annual holiday abroad.

Sefton indeed could have been very comfortable in a mod est way, had it not been for one disastrous factor which ruled in his life. Discontented with his moderate income and hope ful of increasing it, he had some years earlier taken to speculation on the Stock Exchange. His experience as a solicitor should have warned him that no outsider can make money in any such way, but there was something of the gambler in his blood, and each fresh deal seemed so promising that he could not resist its appeal. Needless to say, he lost. But the fascination of the thing grew on him, and in spite of his better judgment he went on and on.

Gradually, his capital became reduced, but always he believed the next speculation would rehabilitate him. Instead it usually left him worse off. Soon he was actually in debt. Now, it might have been thought, was the time to stop. But he could not bring himself to give up hope. He felt he must go on till he pulled off some profitable coup. But no profitable coup presented itself, and at last he became faced with a very terrible temptation jeweler—He had been solicitor to a certain Walter Denman, a wealthy landed proprietor of the old school. Denman had died some years earlier, leaving his money to his widow and appointing his brother John and Sefton as trustees. Hermione Denman was no business woman, and John was lazy and careless and left the whole of the work to his co-trustee. Sefton therefore found himself in practical control of a small fortune.

For months he fought the temptation. Then at last, after a particularly disastrous reverse, he fell. If he were to borrow a little of Mrs. Denman's money, he would be able to make what would enable him to pay it back, besides getting him out of his previous difficulties. Once again he lost. In a sort of gambler's dream, he borrowed and lost, again and again. At last he came to himself to find that a considerable portion of his client's money was gone.

This sobered Sefton. Once and for all he determined he would forswear gambling. He would go straight in future. He would cut down his expenses to the minimum and save every possible penny. He kept his word and began to pay off what he owed. Given time, he was certain that he should be all square.

Then suddenly a terrible blow fell. Mrs. Denman became engaged to marry Roger Locke.

Locke was a financier and a wealthy man. He lived a couple of miles from Sefton on the fringe of one of the still unbuilt-on heath districts of Surrey. As has been said, he was a pleasant enough man, but he was shrewd and had the reputation of getting every available penny out of his deals.

It was at once obvious to Sefton that his period of grace had come to an end. It would be only a short time till Locke would look into his wife's money matters, and Locke it would be impossible to deceive.

Then the matter was brought to a head by a letter from Mrs. Denman, saying that no doubt Sefton had heard of her approaching marriage, and that she wished he would kindly explain her affairs to Locke, who thought that certain reinvestments might be desirable. Sefton had replied agreeing to carry out her wishes, but by raising technical difficulties he had managed to delay the disclosure for the time being.

But only for the time being. Another week represented the extreme limit to which he could postpone the crash—if Locke lived.

But if Locke were to die, the situation would be altered. Mrs. Denman and her brother-in-law had neither the will nor the ability to investigate complicated financial affairs, or, if they tried, they could easily be hoodwinked. He, Sefton, would gain the time he required—due time to make good what he had taken. It was the difference between safety and ruin.

So Sefton had argued, and so he had come to his terrible conclusion.

But now having reached it, besides a creeping horror, he found his mind filled with misgivings. The thing was not so simple as he had supposed. The alternative was not merely to commit murder and be safe: to refrain and be lost. There was a third contingency to be faced. Suppose he committed the murder and still were lost? Suppose he committed the murder and were found out?

The sweat broke out on Sefton's forehead as he considered this possibility and all it involved. For a moment his resolution faltered. Better social and financial ruin: better a term of imprisonment—than that! He thought of the many who had tried the way he was proposing—Crippen, Mahon, Rouse and a host of others—and a wave of deadly fear swept over him. In the grip of a momentary panic he grew sick. He got up and staggered across the room. With shaking hands, he poured out a stiff tot of whisky and tossed it off.

It pulled him together, steadying his nerves. The affair presently ceased to be personal and terrifying and became an abstraction which he could examine coolly. He settled down to think it out as he would think out any other problem which came to him in the course of his business.

How did one commit a murder so as not to be found out? It was a question to which Sefton had never before given a serious thought. But now as for the first time he did so, he began to grasp its terrible difficulty.

It was probably true, he thought, that a police investigation of a suspected murder would in a majority of cases mean the conviction of the criminal. He, Sefton, must avoid this risk. No such investigation must take place. His idea was that no murder must be suspected. The affair must be arranged to look like suicide. But could he manage this?

What, he reminded himself, was the first step in facing any problem? Why, to get the conditions clear in one's mind. Very well. He would go over the conditions, and no doubt while doing so some workable scheme would suggest itself. Whatever he did would presumably mean a visit to Locke's. This would probably have to be paid in the evening, as on most days the financier went to Town. What were the chances of paying such a visit secretly?

Three main items had to be considered: the actual journey, the leaving of his own house, and the arrival at Locke's.

With reference to the journey, there was first the situation of their respective homes, his in the suburbs of Bridgebury, Locke's some two miles farther into the country. The houses were con- nected by a secondary road, passing mostly through woods, and upon which traffic was light. Moreover there were few buildings along it, the chief exception being the Crown Inn, some half-mile before reaching Locke's and just before the road crossed the deep and sluggish Surrey Ouse. At present the moon was new, and a chance meeting would not mean recognition. So far as the actual journey was concerned, a secret visit to Locke should be possible. But what about his own home? There his wife and Bella, the cook-general, had to be considered. Though Sefton knew that if he retired either to his study or workshop—he made a hobby of carpentry—he could count on remaining undisturbed, yet he felt he could not safely leave the house for any considerable time without the knowledge of one or both of these women. A reason for his absence must therefore be supplied.

As to the situation at Locke's, he was naturally not so clear, and yet he knew it pretty well. Not only had he dined there more than once in a purely social way, but he had been on business both during the daytime and in the evening. Locke was captain and Sefton a member of the committee of the local golf club, and he had dropped in occasionally to discuss policy. Also he had once bought a second-hand shotgun from Locke, which had involved a couple of calls. Perhaps he had been in the house a dozen times altogether.

"The Cedars," Locke's house, was a small but exceedingly well-furnished bungalow standing high on the side of a valley from which it looked out over a charming vista of wooded Surrey downs. The other three sides were surrounded by woods, which cut off all view from the road. The approach to the house could therefore be made unobserved.

Entrance could be obtained just as privately. Locke's library, in which he invariably sat when alone, had a french window. A knock on this would bring Locke himself to open it. If the murder were then committed, exit could be made in the same way.

And it was very unlikely that such an entrance or exit should attract attention in the house itself. Locke lived entirely alone except for the married couple who acted as cook and butler. They had rooms at the rear of the building, and at the hour Sefton contemplated calling there would be nothing to bring them away from their own apartments. After a lot of thought, Sefton came deliberately to the conclusion that he could pay an entirely secret visit to "The Cedars."

But what exactly should he do when he got there?

For the whole of the evening he pondered the problem. Then suddenly, an idea flashed into his mind. He considered it with growing excitement. Rudimentary and with the details still hazy, he yet believed it would work. Yes, at last he saw how Locke could be killed, and without the slightest chance of suspicion arising. Better still, even if murder were suspected, even if murder were proved, it could not by any possible chance be connected with him, Sefton. His plan was safe and it was certain. Some courage would be required, a rather dreadful ten minutes would have to be gone through, and— Locke would be dead.

And he, Sefton, would be safe!

II

Sefton saw that if he were to carry out his plans to encompass the death of Locke before the question of Mrs. Denman's securities came up, he could lose no time.

On the night on which he made his terrible decision, he went to bed at his usual hour, but he did not sleep. Hour after hour he lay tossing from side to side, too excited and upset to remain still. His brain, abnormally active, seized on the outline of his plan and began working out its details, devising expedients, overcoming difficulties, revising here, eliminating there. It was a wearisome night, but in the morning his scheme was cut and dried, complete in every detail, ready to be put into operation.

He had first to carry out some simple experiments, and that day he began by going to Town and buying an assortment of balls of string, as well as cotton, silk and linen thread, wool, and some saltpetre.

In the evening, he made a saturated solution of the saltpetre, and in it steeped samples of his other purchases. When these had taken up all the chemical they would carry, he dried them and cut off exactly six inches of each. These pieces he laid side by side on a board, numbering them to correspond with their source of supply. Then one by one he lit them and carefully noted, first, the time they took to smoulder through their entire length and second, the kind of ash they left.

After various experiments he selected the cord which gave the best results. It smouldered slowly, left comparatively little ash, and of the ten pieces he eventually tried, not one went out.

Next he got his gun, a 12-bore double-hammer shot-gun, and tried certain experiments with it. These succeeded better than he could have hoped, and well-satisfied, he turned to his next item.

Taking a piece of flat iron bar about the size of a heavy ruler, he ground some three inches of one side to a sharp edge. This made a weapon like a crude single-edged sword, of which only a small piece at the top had been sharpened. Well pleased with this also, he locked it away with his prepared string.

He had now to get hold of a bicycle. He would have preferred to borrow it—without informing the owner. But as this did not seem possible, he had decided that he must buy. His plan for doing so was ready. It had been founded on the fortunate feet that on the following Thursday his wife was going to the Isle of Wight, where she would stay overnight. This would supply him with the excuse he wanted for spending a solitary evening at the theatre.

The next day, Wednesday, Sefton pleaded business in Town and went up in the middle of the day. This was not exactly an invention: he had business, though whether it could not as well have been settled by letter was perhaps a moot point. However, he went up and did the business. But he did more. He had taken with him in a dispatch-case an old and stained waterproof. Now, in a street lavatory, he put this on over his well-cut cloth overcoat, at the same time turning down irregularly the brim of his smart Homburg hat. At a theatrical supplies shop he bought a pair of dark-rimmed spectacles, and as he put them on he pulled his small moustache out of its neat curl and dragged it down untidily over his mouth. He chanced to catch sight of himself in a mirror, and was surprised and delighted with the excellence of his disguise.

Taking a Morden train at Leicester Square Station, he got out at Stockwell and walked down the Stockwell Road till he came to a bicycle shop, the address of which he had already found in the directory. There he bought a bicycle of a cheap make, saying it was to enable a young man for whom he had got a job, to reach his work. He paid for it and asked the shopkeeper to have it sent to Waterloo and left in the cloakroom, the messenger putting the ticket into an envelope addressed to Mr. J. S. Hardy, passenger to Weybridge, which, he would leave at the enquiry office to be called for. This the shopkeeper agreed to do. Sefton then returned to Victoria, buying a pair of rubber gloves on the way. He reverted to his normal appearance in another lavatory, and caught a train which brought him to Bridgebury in time to reach home at his usual hour.

It was next day that his wife was leaving for the Isle of Wight, and that afternoon after she had gone he rang up his home and told the maid that he was going up to Town to a theatre that evening and would not be home till late. He took the 5.30 train to town and an hour later entered his accustomed restaurant near Charing Cross. There he made it his business to chat with the manager, incidentally impressing on him the fact that it was Wednesday. He left about half-past seven, having mentioned that he was going to the Adelphi Theatre, He did go to the theatre and impressed his identity on an attendant by questioning him as to the hour at which the show would be over. Then surreptitiously he slipped out of the building, and having put on his disguise, hurried to Waterloo. At the enquiry office, he asked if there was a letter for Mr. J. S. Hardy, passenger to Weybridge, and on its being handed over, he obtained the cloakroom ticket and took out the bicycle. He booked to Lenfield, some twenty miles from the town, on another branch than Bridgebury. There he arrived about 8.30. With his waterproof turned up round his ears and his hat pulled low, and walking with a slight limp and bent forward as he wheeled the bicycle, he was satisfied that even should some acquaintance see him, he would escape recognition. Once outside the station, he was safe. Apart from the darkness, merely to be riding a bicycle would be a sufficient disguise.

Bridgebury was only ten miles from Lenfield, and Sefton covered the distance under the hour. He approached his own house with care, and made sure that no observer was in sight when he wheeled the bicycle into the drive. Five minutes later, the machine was hidden under some old cement bags in his workshop, the shop was locked, and Sefton was once more out on the road.

Now came the most dangerous part of his programme. He had to walk nearly three miles to Carrington, a village from which he would get a bus which did not pass through Bridgebury. He stepped out briskly, though holding himself ready to drop into his limping slouch should he meet anyone. His luck, however, held. He caught the bus unseen and by eleven o'clock, he reached Hammersmith Broadway. There he took the District Railway and in due course arrived at Victoria. A change in the station lavatory recreated the normal Mr. Claud Sefton, and he caught his usual 11.30 theatre train. His luck held further in that he found a couple of acquaintances to travel down with, and to these he was careful to praise the Adelphi show,

So far, so good. All the preparations for his terrible deed were now complete. With what patience he could muster, he waited for the first suitable evening.

This depended on the weather. It must be fine and pleasant for walking, and not wholly dark. In other words, as there was no moon, it must be starlight.

Friday was wet, but Saturday proved an ideal evening. Sefton, however, hesitated to act, as Locke usually had weekend visitors. Monday was always equally suitable, and Sefton decided he dare no longer postpone action.

At dinner he told his wife that he was going over to see Locke on business, and in strict confidence he mentioned what that business was. A certain Major Knowles had been giving trouble at the golf club, drinking too much and becoming abusive to servants and visitors alike. Sefton was going to consult privately with Locke as to whether he should not be asked to resign. That Knowles had been drinking was true: that there was any idea of asking him to resign was false.

Next Sefton rang up Locke. As he had expected, the butler answered. Sefton said that he had some business with Mr. Locke, and if Mr. Locke was alone and could see him, he would go over immediately. It was a fine night and he, Sefton, wanted some exercise, so he would walk over. It was now just ten minutes to nine, so he would arrive about half-past. Would this suit Mr. Locke?

Presently Locke himself answered. "It's those securities of Mrs. Denman's," Sefton explained. "I'll hand them over to you and you can look through them at your convenience. Then we can have another meeting and decide what changes if any, are to be made." "Delighted to see you, whatever the cause," Locke answered pleasantly.

The friendliness in his voice gave Sefton a feeling of sinking horror. Could he go through with it? Then he told himself, he must. Was he going to face prison? Was he going to see his wife down and out and penniless, for she had no money of her own on which she could live. He went back to the dining-room and helped himself lavishly to whisky. It steadied his nerves. Coolly he carried on.

When he had put on his coat, he looked into the sitting-room. "I shall not be long," he told his wife, then glancing at the clock, he went on in an undertone, as if counting up. "Ten to nine, get there about half-past nine, say twenty minutes discussing poor old Knowles, and back here by half-past ten." In a leisurely way he left the room and presently Mrs. Sefton heard the slam of the hall door.

But the moment the door was shut, Sefton's leisureliness dropped from him. He hurried to his workshop and took out the bicycle, stowing his iron weapon, the string, and the rubber gloves in his pockets. Mounting, he rode quickly away.

He had counted on the road to Locke's being deserted on this cold October evening, and his calculation was justified. He met no one, and without incident reached "The Cedars."

He glanced suspiciously round in the darkness, then extinguished his lamp and wheeled the bicycle into a lane which passed up at the side of the house. Standing it behind a bush, he crossed the wire boundary fence into the grounds of "The Cedars." His footsteps made no sound on the grass and presently he reached the library french window.

To his satisfaction it was lighted up, and through a chink in the curtain he saw Locke reading by the fire. He knocked lightly. Locke smiled when he saw who it was.

"I thought you were going to walk?" he observed as he opened the window.

"So I intended," Sefton returned as easily as he could, "but Stanford overtook me in his car and insisted on giving me a lift."

"You didn't bring the securities?" Locke went on, glancing at his visitor's empty hands.

"Yes, rather," Sefton answered. "Under my coat." He began to feel inside the large loose waterproof.

A sick qualm swept over Sefton as he realized that at last the awful moment was upon him. But once again the thought of the alternative stiffened him. And the bad time would be over quickly. One supreme effort and he would be safe. He braced himself setting his teeth.

"Good," said Locke, though there was clearly something of surprise in his voice. "Just let's pull these curtains again and then we can sit down and have a drink."

As Locke spoke, Sefton's hand closed on the iron bar. Stealthily, he drew it out of his pocket and slipped it behind him. In as natural a way as he could he moved close behind Locke, and when the curtains were pulled and Locke began to turn round, he swung up the bar and brought it down with a sickening crash on the man's temple.

With a faint choking cry Locke collapsed on the floor on his back. Blood spurted from the ghastly wound, then soon ceased flowing. Locke was dead.

III

For a moment Sefton stood petrified, staring down at the motionless body at his feet. Locke was dead! The secret of Mrs. Penman's securities was now safe. A few minutes' effort and he, Sefton, should be at peace, relieved from the ghastly anxiety which had been turning his life into a hell.

But as he stood with the sweat running down his forehead, it came to him that never again in this world would he know peace. Always that gaping wound would haunt him, always that choking cry would ring in his ears. Already, not a minute after the crime, he would have given everything he had if only he could recall it.

He strove desperately to break the dreadful paralysis which was settling down on him. If he didn't act, and immediately, he was lost. He had little enough time at the best for all he had to do. A short delay, and it would be no longer possible. Longingly he looked at the decanter of whisky on the side table. But he daren't finger it.

That reminded him. In his perturbation he had forgotten his rubber gloves! Now he drew them on.

The action calmed him, and he began in a sort of dreadful dream to carry out the plan he had devised.

Taking some paper from the waste basket, he carefully wiped the blood off the bar, burning the paper in the fire. To his immense relief, no blood had got on to his hands or clothes. He had struck from the side with the object of avoiding this, but he had not been sure that his precaution would succeed.

He replaced the bar in his pocket, and going to the gun-rack in the corner, he took down a 12-bore double-hammer shot-gun which he knew was there. It was an old gun of inferior quality to some of Locke's hammerless models, but it had been Locke's first gun and he had kept it among the others. From the box nearby, Sefton took a couple of cartridges to suit. Then, kneeling down, he pressed Locke's fingers over certain parts of both gun and cartridges.

Now came the critical operation. Handling the gun only where there were no prints—so that the marks of the rubber gloves should not show—he raised both hammers to full cock and tied them back by the thumbpiece to the stock with his saltpetred string. One of the two ends of the string he cut off at the knot, the other he measured carefully to burn for ten minutes. Then he pulled both triggers, leaving the hammers held up by the string, slipped in the cartridges, and dosed the gun. When the smouldering of the string reached the knot the loop round the stock would part, the triggers would fall, and both barrels would go off.

Next to get the gun into position. In this Sefton's determination nearly failed him. He had to lift that ghastly head and prop it up against the leg of a chair. However, with set teeth he did it. Then he laid the gun across the body with the muzzle resting on the forehead just below the wound. A heavy chair, moved slightly forward, made a resistance for the butt. When the shots were fired all trace of the original injury would be blown away, leaving a still greater wound. But this would be a gunshot wound, not a cut. One or two small details remained to complete the scheme.

Sefton tied a piece of ordinary string to the triggers, passed it round a rung of the chair at the butt, and brought the end back to the body's hand. The arms he folded over the gun. Then he turned to the french window, and by sticking a pencil through the loop of the key, he locked the door on the inside, while leaving Locke's fingerprints on the key.

This completed his preparations. After a keen look round to see that he had forgotten nothing, he took a book of matches from his pocket, lit the string, and threw the match into the grate. Then he silently opened the door to the hall and stood listening.

This was the most nerve-racking moment of the whole affair. If the butler saw him he was a lost man. If Sefton had heard a sound he would have closed the door again and made his escape through the window. But as he had expected, in the hall all was still. He crept on tiptoes to the hall door, opened it softly, and softly drew it after him. The well-oiled Chubb lock closed noiselessly as he had counted on, and he was out of the house.

Now, he told himself, the worst part of the affair was over. He had only to complete the much easier portion still remaining, and he would have no more cause for alarm.

He hurried round to the bicycle and wheeled it back to the road, once again taking care that he was not seen. The road, however, was deserted, and he mounted and rode quickly back towards his own home.

In five minutes he came to the bridge spanning the Surrey Ouse. Here again he wanted secrecy. He looked up and down the road. No lights were in sight, no sounds of vehicles or footsteps were audible. Quickly he stepped to the parapet, lifted the bicycle, and threw it into the water. The rubber gloves, tied to the iron bar, followed. All trace of his journey was now gone. At last he was safe. But he wished to be safer. Hurrying to the Crown Inn, he walked into the bar and asked for a double whisky. "I was having a walk and got some kind of weak feeling," he told the barman.

"It never happened to me before."

The barman murmured sympathetically.

"Your clock's fast, surely?—" Sefton went on." I didn't think it was so late as twenty past nine."

The barman consulted his watch. "No," he answered, "I think it's about right." Sefton took his drink to an unoccupied table and slowly sipped it. He allowed himself ten minutes, till half-past nine. Then with a 'Good night,' he left the inn.

The fresh glass of whisky had still further steadied him, and as he walked quickly on towards "The Cedars,: he felt himself cool and competent to carry out the small portion of his plan still remaining.

He reached the house about twenty minutes to ten to find a car at the door, which was open, and a policeman in the hall. He walked up boldly.

"Hullo," he said. "Anything wrong?"

The policeman looked at him searchingly. "I'm afraid so, sir," he answered. "Who might you be, if you please?"

Sefton stared haughtily. "I should have thought you might know," he returned coldly. "I've been in court often enough. I'm Mr. Sefton, the solicitor, of Bridgebury."

The constable saluted. "Excuse me, sir. I'm a newcomer to the district. I have seen you in court, but for the moment I didn't recognize you."

"That's all right," Sefton said easily. "But what's going on here?"

The constable hesitated, then evidently feeling he had demonstrated the majesty of the law sufficiently, he answered in a sort of confidential aside. "Shot himself, Mr. Locke has. Just now. Butler heard the shot and ran in. Found him dead with his head half-shot away."

Sefton contrived to register an expression of incredulous horror. "Shot himself?" he repeated in awed accents. "You're not saying Mr. Locke has shot himself?"

"I'm afraid he has, sir. Friend of yours, was he?"

"Good God!" Sefton had only to allow his real feelings to show to obtain the feeling he wanted. "I can't believe it! Why, I was speaking to him not an hour ago, and he sounded absolutely normal then."

"What, sir?" the constable returned more sharply. "You were here tonight before, were you?"

"I telephoned him – from my own house. I asked if he could see me if I came over. He said he could. He was expecting me."

The constable considered this. "I think in that case, sir," he pronounced presently, "the Inspector would like to see you. Perhaps you wouldn't mind stepping in?"

"I was going to do so in any case," Sefton declared, determined to hold his end up. "I want to see whoever's in charge to hear further details."

As he spoke, Wilton, the butler, appeared in the hall. His face was ghastly and he seemed to have gone all to pieces. He saw Sefton and came forward.

"You've heard, sir?" he said in shaky tones.

"The officer has just been telling me," Sefton answered, still allowing the agitation he really felt to show in his voice and manner. "My God, I can't believe it! How did it happen?"

"I heard the shot and went in and I saw—" Wilton, as it were, cowered back and put his hands over his face. Then turning as if he could no longer trust himself to speak, he disappeared towards his own quarters.

"Upset, he is," the constable considered. "If you wait a moment, sir, I'll fetch the inspector."

Inspector Dobson of the Bridgebury Borough Police was well known to Sefton. He saluted and was civil in manner. But his civility did not prevent him from carrying out his duty with efficiency. Beyond the mere fact that Locke had shot himself, he gave no information. On the other hand he obtained from Sefton a complete statement of his relations with the deceased and the reason for his visit.

Sefton found the interview less trying than he had expected. His greatest effort was not required: to hide his feelings. It was reasonable that he should be upset by such dreadful news, so he could allow his manner to be natural;. And he had no trouble with his story. He had thought it out so carefully as to be sure of the details.

After pledging the inspector to secrecy, so far as this was possible, he explained about wishing to consult privately with Locke on the behavior of Major Knowles at the Golf Club, about ringing him up to fix the time, about his own want of exercise and decision to walk over. He told how on the way he felt a little unwell—probably due to his chronic indigestion —and how he had gone into the Crown Inn, which was on his way, for some whisky. He had stayed there drinking it for five or ten minutes and then had come straight on. He couldn't say how distressed he was by what he had heard on arrival, nor could he understandwhat could have happened to Locke, as he had seemed perfectly normal when he telephoned less than an hour earlier.

Inspector Dobson was sympathetic and obviously unsuspicious. A certain comfort began to flow back into Sefton's mind as he realized that so far his awful experiment had succeeded. Dobson thanked him for his statement, indicated that the interview was over, and pointed out that Sefton's evidence would probably be required at the inquest. Tactfully Sefton wished him good night and withdrew.

On the road he heaved a sigh of unutterable relief. The worst was over. He had now only to sit tight and say nothing. His courage had freed him from his difficulties. All would now be well.

IV

Claud Sefton's optimism lasted till he had reached home, told his wife of Locke's death, and gone to bed. But as he lay awake through the long hours of the night, his mood changed. Dreadful doubts began to creep into his mind. Inspector Dobson had seemed satisfied, but that after all meant little. When the police suspected anyone they didn't show it. They waited quietly till they were sure: then suddenly they acted. If they suspected him, he would hear nothing of it—until, probably late one evening, there would be a ring, a heavy tread of feet in the hall, and then ... He shivered. Dawn was breaking when Sefton fell into a troubled sleep. He awoke unrefreshed and went down dreading the day. At breakfast he had an earnest fear of what he might expect. He found his wife's comments on the tragedy almost unbearable. It took all the effort of which he was capable to answer her in a normal way, and even then he thought that more than once she looked at him curiously. It was worse when he reached his office. The death of Locke seemed to have attracted enormous attention, and everyone he met insisted on talking of it. People called, and after avidly discussing the details, expected him to attend to intricate legal business as if nothing had happened. If he hadn't brought a flask and taken nips at frequent intervals, he didn't think he could have got through the morning.

But his worst shock came in the afternoon. He had been expecting all day a summons to attend the inquest, but none had come. It must, he supposed, have been postponed until the following day. All the same he was surprised not to have heard.

Then a caller, bubbling over with importance, revealed the hideous truth. The inquest had been opened. It had been summoned for three o'clock. Formal evidence of identification had been taken, and it had then been adjourned to enable the police to make further inquiries!

Sefton made use of a trick he had learnt at school. He sneezed violently and covered his face with his handkerchief. It gave him time, a little time, to recover from this dreadful shock. For a postponement of this kind could mean one thing and one thing only: that murder was suspected.

How Sefton got through the interview he didn't know. Fortunately his visitor was so full of himself and his news that he had temporarily lost his critical faculty. When he left, Sefton gave orders, that he was not to be disturbed. Suspicious or not suspicious, he couldn't face anyone else.

He let it be known that he wasn't feeling well, to cover any lapses of manner and to account for the smell of whisky. He walked home by a slightly circuitous route to avoid any of his usual companions.

He got through dinner somehow—his wife hadn't heard of the adjourned inquest and he didn't inform her—and then retired to his study 'to finish some work.' There once again he set himself to go over in his mind everything he had done, to see if he could find any point, no matter how slight, in which he could have given himself away.

First, as to his preparations. No one could possibly trace his purchase of the bicycle. He was not known where he had bought it, his disguise had been reasonably effective, and he had given a false name. The purchase was such an ordinary transaction that the shop assistant would give it no special attention: from his manner he obviously had not done so. He, Sefton, had brought the machine home in an absolutely secret way. No one knew of its arrival. No one was aware that he had it. Nor had anyone seen him taking it out on that awful Monday evening. Finally, he had hidden it in a place in which it was never likely to be found. And even if by some extraordinary chance it were found, it could never be connected with him.

Secondly, there was the evidence he had prepared to prove the death suicide. The more he thought over this, the more satisfied he became with it. There was first the room with the door locked on the inside and Locke's fingerprints on door and key. There were Locke's own gun and cartridges, both also bearing Locke's fingerprints. There was the natural position in which the body had fallen, the wound on the head actually caused by the shot, the string to the trigger. There was the absence of any other wound or cause of death. There was the blood, which would show that the man had been shot while alive, not after death. This had been one of Sefton's greatest difficulties, and he had surmounted it by using a weapon which would break the skin in the first instance. He tried to picture what must actually have occurred. Wilton had doubtless heard the shot and rushed in. He would find his employer in a pool of blood, shot in the temple, and with the library french window locked on the inside. Before he could make any kind of detailed examination the last scrap of the smouldering string—the loop round the gun—would have disappeared. The recoil would have broken and scattered any ash the string left. No suggestion of delayed action could possibly remain. Yes, it was certainly well arranged.

Lastly and most important of all, there was his own alibi. At the moment the gun had gone off he had been seated in the bar of the

Crown Inn, half a mile away. That, together with the facts already considered, that there was only the gunshot wound on the body, and that there could be no evidence of delayed action, would alone be amply sufficient to prove his innocence. In short, he had carried out in a perfect manner an entirely watertight scheme. He had left no loophole anywhere which might give him away. He was safe!

All the same, the next couple of days were a nightmare. Fortunately for him, a terrible aeroplane accident took place near Bridgebury, which turned popular attention from the Locke case. By Thursday evening, he was beginning to feel almost normal. But on Thursday evening came the most dreadful shock of all.

He was sitting in his study, thinking that he might now really consider the worst over, when he heard the doorbell ring and heavy steps in the hall approach his door. His blood froze. The sounds were those he had heard in his most awful dreams. Quickly he gulped a glass of whisky which he had mixed for the evening's consumption.

There entered two men, one slightly undersized with a pleasant, clean-shaven face and keen blue eyes, the other tall and obviously a policeman in plain clothes. Sefton stood up, fighting hard to preserve his calmness.

"Good evening, sir," the shorter of the two men began. "I'm Chief Detective Inspector French of Scotland Yard, and I've called to ask for some help in an enquiry I'm making into the circumstances of Mr. Locke's death."

This was unexpectedly polite, even friendly. Sefton desperately pulled himself together,

"Yes?" he said, as coolly as he could. "A dreadful business! I knew Mr. Locke and it has much upset me. Won't you sit down?"

They sat down.

"I didn't know," Sefton went on, "that Scotland Yard had been called in, I suppose this means that what we thought at first was not true: that it was suicide?"

"Well, sir, that's just it. We don't know. We can't find a motive for suicide. I wondered if perhaps you could help me there? Did you know the deceased well?"

"Not particularly well," Sefton returned, his fears beginning to moderate. This was surely not the attitude the police would take to a suspect. "I've played golf and so on with him and we've dined in each other's houses a couple of times, but we were not really intimate."

"I understand. Quite." French waited while the plainclothes man wrote in his noteook. Sefton suddenly remembered a test he had heard of. He did not smoke himself, but he kept cigarettes for visitors. Now he held out the box. "Will you smoke?"

French hesitated momentarily. Then he helped himself. "That's very kind of you," he declared. "We don't usually do it while on duty, but," he smiled, "an occasional exception proves the rule."

Sefton was breathing more freely. He had heard that police will never accept a smoke or drink from a suspect. He was all right! He was a fool to have been so upset.

But French was fumbling in pocket after pocket. "I'm afraid, sir, I'll have to trouble you for a match," he said at last. "Thank you."

As Sefton handed over his book a move of the plain-clothes man's hand knocked his fountain-pen off the table. He gave a muttered exclamation and stooped quickly.

"I'm sorry, sir," he apologized, examining the carpet. "I don't know how I came to do that. It leaks, but fortunately it hasn't done so on this occasion."

"You should mind what you're about, Carter," French said sharply, then with a change of manner he handed back the matches. "Thank you, sir. When did you last see the deceased alive?"

Fear and relief waxed and waned in Sefton's mind during that long enquiry. French was the personification of politeness and understanding, but his questions were both persistent and penetrating. The detailed history of Sefton's relations with Locke, the cause of his going to "The Cedars" on Monday evening—"Please don't repeat this, Chief Inspector: I shouldn't wish it to come to Major Knowles' ears,"—anything of Locke's affairs that he had heard him mention, any business dealings he had had with the man: it seemed to Sefton the questions would never stop.

When it was over Sefton felt battered, but on the whole satisfied. He had certainly done well. Particularly about his walk. The statement sounded convincing. He had been working pretty closely in the office for some days; he felt he was not getting enough exercise; the night was fine and inviting, and he decided to walk the two miles, returning, if he felt like it, by bus. When he had rung up and found that Locke could see him, he set off to walk. He enjoyed it for a mile or so, then he began to feel rather upset. He didn't know exactly what was wrong, but he supposed it was indigestion, from which he suffered. He thought a glass of whisky would do him good, so he called at the Crown Inn. He had not remained there long, perhaps ten minutes. The whisky made him feel all right and he walked on to Locke's, to find the police in charge. That was about twenty to ten. No, he wasn't sure exactly when he left home, but thought it must have been a few minutes before nine.

French seemed satisfied, too. He expressed himself as much obliged for the clear statement, read over the notes which had been taken and got Sefton to sign them. With more heavy trampings the two men took their leave.

That night Sefton once again lay wakeful. What, he puzzled desperately, had made them suspicious? Surely it must be something more than mere inability to find a motive for suicide? Was there nothing more tangible? Had he made a slip? For the thousandth time he went over everything he had done. No, he had made no slip. His plan was perfect: he had carried it out perfectly. By no possibility could there be evidence against him.

And yet. . , . No, he told himself, he was safe. He must be.

Again and again, he repeated the phrase.

But his fear remained. At times stark panic gripped him. What had been discovered? Had the enquiry been dropped? Or were the police working ceaselessly, remorselessly, worming out evidence? If only he knew what was happening! He would have given his life to know. But he daren't ask.

So the days began to pass: ghastly hideous days of suspense and terror.

V

A few evenings after Chief Inspector French's call upon Sefton, a conference took place at the Bridgebury police station between the local Chief Constable and his staff, on the one hand, and French and his sergeant, on the other.

"I'm pleased to tell you," French was saying, "that at last I've got a complete case. I think when I put the evidence before you, you'll see that you're sure of a conviction and that you may carry out the arrest at any time."

There were murmurs of applause. "Very gratifying," the Chief Constable declared. "I'm now," he smiled twistedly, "only sorry that we didn't do it ourselves. However, one can't have everything. Go ahead, will you, Chief inspector, and let's have the details."

"Perhaps I might first remind you of what you yourselves discovered before you decided to call in the Yard, in order that you may realize what I had to work on and follow why I did what I did. Besides, it'll make the case complete."

The Chief Constable nodded. "Nothing could be better," he approved. "Take a cigarette and go ahead. We'll all be interested."

French lit up and settled himself more comfortably in his chair. "Then I'll begin with Wilton ringing you up on Monday night to say that his employer had shot himself. You, inspector Dobson, went out to the house with a couple of men.

"From the very start you were puzzled about the affair, because you knew that the deceased was rich, healthy, and about to marry a charming woman. In other words, he seemed to have no motive to die, but a strong one to live. You therefore decided to look very carefully into the details before coming to a conclusion. That's so, isn't it?"

"That's right, sir," Dobson agreed.

"When you reached the room you examined everything critically. It certainly looked like suicide. The house was closed, the French window was locked, and the dead man's fingerprint was on the key. The gun was the deceased's, his fingerprints and only his were upon it, and there was a string tied to the trigger by which the deceased could have fired. I needn't go over all the details: you all know them as well as I."

There was a murmur of agreement.

"But there was one thing you noticed, Dobson —that on the hearth lay a yellow cardboard match. Someone had obviously intended to throw it in the fire, but it had fallen short. You searched for the book it had been torn from. But there was no book there.

"Feeling dissatisfied, you questioned Wilton. He told you two things,. First, that he had never known the deceased to use that type of match. Locke always used either his lighter or a wooden one. Second and more important, that he, Wilton, had swept up the hearth while Locke was finishing dinner, and that the yellow match was not then there.

"No this *proved* nothing. Locke might have bought the book and thrown it into the fire after using that match. But considering probabilities only, it looked to you as if someone else had been in that room that evening. Am I right so far?"

"Yes, sir: that's just what happened."

"If I may say so, it was a first-rate bit of work. Well, you discussed the affair with your superiors and it happened that you, sir," he looked at the Chief Constable, "knew Mr. Locke personally. You knew his prospects were particularly happy, and also you didn't think he was the type of man who would commit suicide. So you were suspicious too. Your own men were busy on other work and you decided to call us in. I was sent down here."

"A very accurate summary, Chief inspector."

"Then I started in. I had a more careful look at the site and I discovered three additional facts. The first was that on the side of the gun, just towards the back of the trigger-guard and about an inch or more behind the hammer pivot, was a discoloration as if the metal had been heated. This puzzled me, as I could not see how heat could be applied just at this place. However, my second find gave me the clue.

"That was a little piece of burnt string about half an inch long. It was lying on the ground near where the triggers of the gun must have been when the shot was fired, for as you know, the gun had moved a good deal as a result of the recoil. I searched more carefully and presently I found several pieces more. All were short, some as short as the eighth of an inch. Were these connected with the affair, and if so, what were they for?

"I found out from Wilton that the room had been cleaned out that day. The string had then been burnt during the evening. The burnt string: the mark on the gun; the match on the health. Was there any connection?

"Suddenly—though I admit not till after some hours' thought— the solution occurred to me. If the string had been used to tie the hammers back, and been prepared to act as a fuse, the heated spot might represent the burning of the knot, and the discharge might have been a case of delayed action.

"If so, what must have been done was clear enough. The deceased must have been killed by a blow on the temple, since no other cause of death was found. The discharge, by making a larger wound, would remove all traces of the first. This was theory. Could I prove it?

"I found I was able to do so to my own satisfaction, though probably not to that of a jury. I collected all the burnt string I could find and had it analysed. I was informed that it had been steeped in saltpetre."

"Good!" exclaimed the Chief Constable. "Very good indeed!" "So much," continued French, "for the gun. But I made a third discovery. In the lane adjoining the house I found the mark of a bicycle. It chanced that a rabbit had thrown out some loamy soil from a fresh burrow, and the bicycle wheels had passed across it, leaving a clear trace. The soil, I noted incidentally, could scarcely have been seen at night.

"I took a cast of the marks while I wondered whether this bicycle could have been used by the murderer. Further enquiries seemed to indicate that it had, because I was unable to find any authorized person who had had a bicycle in the lane. Who then could have used it? If I were right so far, it must have been someone living within cycling distance of "The Cedars."

"Then another point struck me. How did this presumed murderer get in and out? Obviously he must either have had a key of the front door, or Locke must have admitted him. How did he leave? There could have been no way but through the front door. Enquiries from Wilton showed that he had been all the evening in his own quarters with his wife, so that this would have been possible.

"But—and this struck me as important—such a person must have known the house. Not only that, he must have been well known to Locke.

"Then I saw that there was another reason for believing the murderer knew the house. If I was right at all, the affair had been carefully thought out beforehand. That is to say, before he went to the house the murderer knew that Locke had a hammer gun—for he couldn't have carried out his trick with a hammerless—and also where it and the cartridges were to be found.

"I had thus reached the stage of believing that the affair was murder and that the murderer must fulfil three requirements: he must live within cycling distance, he must be familiar with the house, and that he must have been well known to the deceased. It should not be hard, I told myself, to find such a person."

"Good!" the Chief Constable exclaimed again. "A very pretty piece of work."

"Here again I wasted a good deal of time," French went on, "in getting out a list of persons to whom the conditions would apply. And then suddenly a point struck me about Sefton, whose name of course was on the list. Sefton had referred twice to the hour of his movements on that Monday evening. He had mentioned the time of his departure from his home in his 'phone conversation with Wilton, and he had called the attention of the barman in the Crown Inn to the time at which he got his whisky. Why had he done so?

"At once the idea of some sort of alibi occurred to me, and I seeded down to think out how such a scheme could have been carried out. Obviously there was only one way. Sefton had said he had walked to "The Cedars." Suppose he had bicycled? He would then have arrived in time to carry out the murder, leave the house, ride back along the road, make his alibi at the Crown Inn, and then walk up to the door and be surprised at what had happened. "But if he had done this, one important matter would have to be dealt with. He must get rid of the bicycle. To be found with it in his possession would be dangerous. And he must get rid of it there and then, before the crime was discovered and enquiries began. " I acted on this. Was there any place where the machine could have been hidden? I had a walk about the neighbourhood of the Crown Inn and at once I saw the ideal spot."

The Chief Constable nodded. "So that's why you worried us to drag at the river bridge?" he remarked. "Well, we caught a fine fish."

"As it happened, it worked out all right," French admitted "We got the bicycle and the tyre registered with my cast."

"I had now little doubt in my mind as to what had happened but still I hadn't the proof I wanted. I thought over it and thought over it, and then I determined to try a long shot."

French laid on the desk a burnt match of the cardboard or book type. "That's what Dobson found on the hearth. Look at it, please. Do you see those creases?"

About a third of the way from the head creases in the paper showed that the match had been bent sharply upwards, though now it was partly straightened out again.

"I wondered if I could get anything through those creases," went on French. "I'd heard that Sefton didn't smoke, so if he had supplied that match, he might still have the same book on him. It was worth the trial.

"I bought a similar book and called on Sefton. To my great satisfaction he offered me a cigarette. If he hadn't, I should have asked his permission to smoke, on the grounds that I couldn't otherwise concentrate. I accepted with seemly hesitation. Naturally I hadn't a match. I could scarcely hide my delight when he took a book from his pocket and passed it over. The Sergeant promptly dropped his pen and started the hare that the ink had leaked on to the carpet. While Sefton was looking at the floor I substituted his book for mine, tore out about the number of matches that he had used, and handed him my book. And now, gentlemen, will you look at this?"

With the air of a showman introducing his star turn, French dramatically laid a book beside the single match. The others stared. Across the few remaining matches—which bore the same printed legend—ran a sharp upward bend, exactly similar to that of the single one.

The Chief Constable hesitated. "Congratulations, Chief Inspector," he said a little uncomfortably. "Awfully good and all that. But are you sure this is enough? These books do get bent pretty often, you know."

"It's not enough for Court, of course," French admitted, "but it was enough for me. I knew I was on the right track and I went ahead. The rest was easy. Through the serial number of the bicycle it was possible to trace the shop where it had been sold. The salesman, hidden in a car at the door of the Bridgebury Club, picked out Sefton as the man who had bought it. Good enough, I think, sir?"

"Good enough indeed! And the motive?"

"Confidential enquiries at Sefton's bank and elsewhere told me he was exceedingly hard up. I then asked myself if any change had recently taken place in the relations between Sefton and Locke. When I learnt that Sefton was Mrs. Denman's trustee, and that she had recently become engaged to the keen financier, Locke, I thought I had my motive. But I'm afraid, we'll have to wait for proof till we go through the man's papers after the arrest."

The search, when it came off, revealed the motive only too clearly. Sefton's conviction was a foregone conclusion, and in due course he paid the dreadful penalty that the law demands.

Fingerprints

Jim Crouch was a writer, precariously supporting himself while slowly developing the masterpiece which was to bring him fame and fortune. It had been a hard struggle from the start, but now was harder than ever.

Recently he had fallen for Elsie Lee, and the courtship took money. It was when for the sake of a little ready cash the loss of Elsie seemed inevitable, that his thoughts turned, not for the first time, to Nicholas Jacobs, his somewhat miserly uncle.

Jacobs lived alone in a tiny cottage in the suburbs. A charlady came in morning and evening to make breakfast and supper and look after the house, and he went out each day for dinner.

He was not rich, though well enough off in a small way. His nephew, Crouch, was his only near relative and, as he had more than once told him, would be his heir. He was old, depressed, and in poor health, and recently had gone rather rapidly downhill.

Crouch could not help dwelling on these facts, as well as on some others which seemed relevant. He also lived alone. He had a small ground floor flat in a quiet neighbourhood. It had the advantage to anyone at odds with the law, that after dark a secret approach was possible via the window.

Crouch had often stayed with his uncle and knew every detail about the old man's habits and the house itself. This enabled him to devise a plan which he felt would be adequate while entirely safe. No weapon or apparatus would be required save a pair of rubber gloves, a bottle of aspirins, a small pestle and mortar and a short glass rod, and these he unobtrusively acquired. All other essentials were already in the house.

Having screwed his courage to the sticking point, Crouch, on the predetermined evening, left his flat between eight and nine. He had fitted his reading lamp and switch on a flex, and this he pushed out through the open window.

Turning off the light lest he should be seen from the road, he dropped out between the drawn curtains. Then from outside he switched the light on again. Should he be asked how he spent the evening he would say he had been working in his flat. He could not therefore risk a report that the room was in darkness.

Normally he wore a hat and walked briskly, but now, with a cap low over his eyes and a muffler high above his neck, he slouched. The evening was dark and, as far as possible, he avoided the street lamps. It was about a mile to his uncle's house. He reached it without incident and, he felt sure, unobserved. Jacobs opened the door.

"Why, it's Jim," he exclaimed. "And what might you be wanting at this hour of the evening? Well, come along in anyhow."

Crouch left his coat in the hall and followed the old man to the sitting-room. They sat down and chatted desultorily for a few moments, then Jacobs went on: "Well, I don't suppose you came here to talk about the weather and my health. What's the trouble?"

This was an opening, and Crouch seized it. "You're right, uncle," he answered, "and I'm afraid you won't be very pleased when I tell you. But the fact is I'm absolutely stuck for a few pounds."

His uncle refused. Crouch pleaded, but when he saw it was hopeless, he gave up. The die was cast.

"Oh well," he said, rising. "I'll manage somehow. Don't trouble to get up, uncle. I'll let myself out."

This was an essential part of his scheme. If Jacobs accompanied him to the door, the affair would be off for that evening. But the old man didn't move. He said good-night, and Crouch left the room, closing the door behind him.

In the hall, Crouch put on his rubber gloves and hid his coat and cap under the table. Then he stepped noisily to the door, opened it, and remaining himself inside, banged it shut.

He listened. All was still in the sitting-room. Now for it. Stealthily he crept upstairs. In a moment, he was in his uncle's room.

There on the table by the bed were his two essentials. The flask of hot milk which the charlady left out each night and which the old man drank after getting into bed, and his bottle of sleeping pills. On a recent visit, pleading inky fingers from a leaking pen, Crouch had gone to the bathroom for a wash, and had then found that the bottle was nearly full.

Now he took the pills and the flask to the bathroom. He emptied the pills into a mortar and replaced them with an equal number of aspirin tablets. These looked so similar that even if Jacobs were to take one, he would not notice any difference.

Having ground up the pills, Crouch emptied the powder into the flask, stirring it with a glass rod. He had read that rubber gloves left prints, which, though they would not identify the wearer, would show that some unauthorised person had been present.

He therefore carefully wiped both flask and bottle before replacing them by Jacob's bed. Having looked round to make sure that he had left no other traces, he tiptoed into a spare room and waited.

Time passed slowly, but his uncle went to bed early and soon he heard him come upstairs. Crouch cold see across the passage the light under his door. There were movements in the room and at last he heard the bed creak. Then there was silence, but the light remained on.

Two hours, Crouch had decided, must pass before he attempted any research. Again the time seemed long, but at last it passed. He crept across the passage and softly opened Jacob's door. A glance showed that the milk had been poured out and drunk. His eyes passed on to the bed. His uncle was lying on his back, very still. He went closer. Yes, there was no doubt of it. He was dead.

Though Crouch's heart was beating as if to suffocate him, he forced himself to act coolly. Only one thing remained to be done. Picking up the pill bottle, he emptied the aspirin tablets back into their original bottle and replaced this in his pocket.

Lest he should have smudged Jacobs's prints he once more wiped the pill bottle and lid clean, and pressed the dead man's fingers on both. Then he placed them on the table where Jacobs would have put them down after emptying the contents into his milk.

Looking round as before to make sure he had forgotten nothing, he went downstairs. He could see into the sitting-room through the open door, and on a sudden impulse went in to satisfy himself that here also he had left no traces.

Feeling with a kind of sick relief that the worst was over, he put on his coat and cap and let himself out. On the way home he took off his rubber gloves and threw them, together with the bottle of aspirins, pestle, mortar and glass rod, into the canal. A few minutes later he was back in his flat, with the flex disconnected from the lamp.

He was well satisfied with what he had done. Whoever found Jacobs would necessarily conclude that he had committed suicide. His bottle of sleeping pills was open and empty, and an analysis of the dregs of the milk would show where the pills had gone. The pill bottle, flask and glass bore the old man's prints and no others. He himself, having worn gloves, could have made no prints, in fact, he had left no traces of any kind. There was, indeed, no evidence to suggest that any stranger had been in the house. Therefore nothing but suicide was possible, and this could be accounted for by Jacobs' depression and poor health.

Finally, the articles he had himself used were too small to be recoverable from the canal, and even if they were fished up, no connection with himself could be proved. He was, in fact, absolutely and completely safe.

It happened that superintendent French of Scotland Yard was at the local police headquarters when Inspector Ransome, who investigated the death, was reporting. The inspector had been called early that morning to the house by the charlady, Mrs. Crossley.

She had, she explained, taken up Jacobs's morning tea and had found him dead. In reply to questions, she had stated that on the previous evening he had seemed perfectly normal. After supper he had gone to his sitting room where they had discussed certain household matters. He had been neither excited nor more than ordinarily depressed. She had heated his milk and left it in his bedroom as usual, and had gone home. Ransome had examined the room, and detailed what he had found.

As he finished, his superintendent was called away. French turned to him. "You've done a lot for me, Ransome, and I'd like to help you in return. Be careful you don't make a mistake. You've been speaking of suicide, but what you've described is murder."

Ransome stared.

"Think if over," French went on. "I'll give you a hint. The fingerprints on the flask."

"There were no prints on the flask, sir; I mean, except Jacobs'."

"Exactly. Why weren't there?"

Ransome smote his thigh. "I missed that, sir. Mrs. Crossley'd handled it and her dabs should have been there. Since they're not, they've been rubbed off."

"That's it," said French. "Now get back and go over that house with a comb. If you're lucky you may find some other traces."

Ransome did. On the handles of the sitting-room door were prints belonging neither to the dead man, nor to Mrs. Crossley, though both had fingered them on the previous evening. No one had called while Mrs. Crossley had been there; therefore the visit had been paid after she left. When it was learned that Crouch was Jacobs's heir and that he was in low water, his prints were secretly obtained ...

His strenuous denial that he had left his room, and his collapse when confronted with proof to the contrary, sealed his fate.

The Faulty Stroke

At last I see my way. At last I can get even with Upson. Eleanor is a good wife. She has always been true to me, till that snake got into the house and began to steal her away.

I don't blame Eleanor. Upson has a lot of things that I haven't. He's better looking, tall, slim, and elegantly built, and with the face of the usual Greek god. I'm hefty myself, but not such a good shape, and my face as it is, got burned in the RAF.

Upson has a manner that would wheedle blood out of a stone, but I can never shine in company.

Above all, Upson makes tons of money, whereas I've only just enough to carry on. As I say, I don't blame Eleanor, but when I saw the way things were going I swore that if Upson didn't lay off, I wouldn't rest till he was dead.

Now his time has come. At last I see how it will happen. He'll walk out into the night and never be heard of again. And nothing who ever connect me with the affair. I'll be as safe as if such a man as Claud Upson had never lived.

It's true that I've got special facilities for a job of the kind and I'm going to use them. Why not? Since I was demobbed from the RAF I've been working on an invention. It's connected with blind flying, and the Air people are interested. They've let me have a small two-seater Midge and all the permits necessary to go up when I want to. I can take off from and land on my own field. I haven't a hangar, but I've good arrangements for mooring and locking up, and the aeroplane's as safe at night as if it was under cover.

Upson and I met in hospital while we were recovering from war wounds, and when later he came to live at a posh residential hotel not far from my tiny house in Sussex, I was fool enough to ask him in for a drink. He's a portrait painter and has a studio in Town, where most days he goes up to work. Pretty good, he's supposed to be, but personally I think a child of six could do better.

There's a bit of road between the station, and his hotel which runs through a wood. It's short but lonely and behind the trees lies my field. This is where the affair will take place and all I want for it is a spanner. There's one just the size in my kit.

Upson's an exercise maniac and always walks to and from the station. About 7.00 he usually passes though the wood.

Well, on the evening I'd chosen I went to the place and waited, the spanner under my coat. It was October and dark under the trees, with a fine rain driven searchingly by a cold wind. Upson was late, but at last I heard his step. When he came up I spoke to him and he stopped. I manoeuvred into position and raised the spanner.

As I did so he swung around. Instead of taking the blow on his hat, which would have saved the skin he got it below the temple. He fell without a sound, but blood begun to ooze from the wound. This was unfortunate, but there was so little I didn't think it mattered.

Now I had to get the body quickly away in case someone came by. With a lot of difficulty I raised it on to my shoulders, and having made sure with my torch that no traces had been left, I staggered off through the wood. Once off the road I was safe. No one walked among the trees after dark.

It cost me a bigger effort that I'd foreseen, but at last I got the body to the aeroplane and lifted it in. With a small chain I attached some old firebars to the ankle. I covered it with a rug, locked up the aeroplane, and went home. It was a time at which I frequently arrived and my appearance caused no comment.

I cannot pretend I slept that night. If some extraordinary accident happened and suspicion were aroused, the police might search the place. I kept on assuring myself that no such accident could happen. All the same I was glad when a growing light indicated that the night was over.

At breakfast, I felt sure that Eleanor nothing amiss with my manner. "The usual flight this morning," I called as I went out. "Back to lunch."

I went to the plane trying not to hurry or show eagerness. Everything so far was all right. But when I lifted the rug I wasn't so pleased. There had been quite a bit of bleeding, indeed there was quite a little pool on the aeroplane floor. Though Upson had been unconscious, clearly he hadn't died immediately.

I pulled off my coat. Yes, there on the back were stains. They were slight, but enough to finish me had they been seen.

I stood thinking. The coat was easy to deal with and I quickly fastened to it another set of firebars. But to account for the blood wasn't so simple, for I couldn't wash out the stain.

Suddenly I saw my way. I got a chisel and trimmed some parings off a wooden strut supporting my invention. Then, gritting my teeth, I ran the chisel into my hand. From the first-aid outfit I quickly bandaged the cut. It didn't take long yet all the time I was in a panic. If anyone had come past I'd have been for it. I can tell you I was glad when I was in the air.

I turned south and passed out over the sea near the Birling Gap. Twenty miles took me well out of sight of land. I'd rigged a sort of automatic pilot for my experiments and now I brought this into operation.

I went back and opened the aeroplane door, and after a look round to make sure no ship was in sight, pushed out first the body and then the coat. The aeroplane staggered and pitched but in couple of seconds I was back at the stick and had her steady again.

I got back shortly after noon, my usual time. As I circled to land I saw two black specks on the grass. They gradually grew into an inspector and sergeant of police. I tried to get out before they could reach the aeroplane, but they were there waiting.

"Good day, sir," said the inspector. "I've come to ask for a little information." Then he saw the blood. "Oh, you've had an accident?"

"Yes," I answered. "This morning. Cut my hand. But it's nothing to signify."

"I see, sir. How did it happen?"

"I hit the strut when I was lifting in my box of tricks and split a piece off the edge. I was smoothing down the roughness when the chisel slipped."

He seemed satisfied and went on: "You knew Mr. Claud Upson, I suppose?"

I explained how we'd met in hospital. He asked which hospital. I told him. Next he asked did I know Upson was missing.

I put on, I think the right amount of surprise. Then followed increasingly unpleasant questions: When had I seen Upson last? Where was I at 7.30 on the previous evening? And such like.

It almost seemed as if they knew something. But when they said they'd like their doctor to see my hand I was delighted. The cut was genuine, so the doctor's statement could only support my own.

The interview was satisfactory. Reassured I went in to lunch as if nothing had happened. All was well. I'd saved Eleanor and I was myself absolutely safe.

Two evenings later, the police returned. Then my complacency was shattered and I stiffened into frozen horror as the officer pronounced the incredible words: "I'm sorry, Mr. Crossman, but I hold a warrant for your arrest on a charge."

"It was hard luck on so ingenious and painstaking murderer," said Inspector French when he was discussing the case, "that his admirable scheme should have failed through so trifling an error. His mistake was to strike Upson where it bled: a faulty stroke.

"The luck was against Crossman in another way. That evening Upson had invited a nighbor to his hotel for a game of chess. So by 8.30 it was known that something unusual had occurred. Upson was punctilious about keeping appointments and advising the hotel of changes of plan therefore when next morning came without news, the manager informed the police.

"On this one of the local constables came across with something interesting. It seemed he was walking out with the Crossmans' daily help, and she had told him that she'd once overheard Upson and Mrs. C. Talking. She said they were what she described as too thick to be wholesome. So there was what might be a motive. "Well, the local inspector learned that Crossman was out on a flight and met the plane. On the floor he saw blood. Crossman explained that he'd cut himself, but the inspector doubted the story, for he thought a chisel cut would have produced scattered drops rather than a pool.

"He was puzzled for a bit and then he saw his way. He drove Crossman to the doctor to check the existence of the cut—which he hadn't doubted—and while they were away the constable took a sample of blood. Its group was quickly established.

"The next step was chancy, though if it hadn't come off he still could have got his information. He sent a man to the hospital where Upson and Crossman had been treated. Luckily their records hadn't been destroyed. Their blood belonged to different groups, and that on the aeroplane was of Upson's group, not Crossman's.

"As I said it was hard luck on Crossman because for an improvisation it wasn't a bad effort."

Teamwork Felonious

John Rennison was an engineer, and desperately hard up. So was his friend, Thorpe, a chemist. They had been gambling and losing.

There was plenty of money coming to Rennison, if only he could get it. He was due to inherit from his cousin, Mark Hazlewood, who was rich. Not only rich, but old, and living alone, save for the man and wife who looked after him.

Bui Rennison could not see any safe method of hastening the old man's end since the inheritance would point unerringly in his direction.

Then he began to examine the possibility of a joint murder with Thorpe on a 50-50 basis: a joint murder giving each of them an alibi, and each to be too much involved to give the other away. He sounded Thorpe, who was willing to co-operate. They developed their plan, which was built round the fact that Thorpe was a member of the local dramatic society.

Rennison started by handing Thorpe a duplicate key of his car and by obtaining false number plates, arranged for quick changing.

At the same time Thorpe bought a policeman's uniform from a theatrical costume maker in London. They decided on an evening when the local dramatic society was having a rehearsal.

After dark on that evening Rennison took the parcel of policeman's clothes and put it in the back of his car. Then he changed the number plates and ran the car to a quiet street near Thorpe's flat where he parked it.

He walked back to the residential hotel where he lived, dropped into the bar and unostentatiously established the time. He was asked to join in a game, but said he had unfortunately brought some work home.

This was true; he had set the work out in his room. But on reaching his room he did not even look at it. Putting on a dark coat and beret, he left the hotel by a side-door and Thorpe picked him up nearby with the car.

Thorpe had been working to time, too. Half an hour before his rehearsal was due to begin he had left home, explaining that he was going to walk. But he did not do so.

He hurried to Rennison's car and drove to a call-box. There he rang up Hazlewood.

"This is Superintendent Richards speaking from the police station," he said in a deep voice. "I regret to say that a man whom we think may be Mr. Rennison has met with a fatal accident. I should be grateful if you would help to identify him. I am sending a car to pick you up."

Thorpe went back to the car, drew on the policeman's uniform over his clothes, and drove Hazlewood's house. He rang the bell and the housekeeper opened the door.

"Oh, you're the policeman," she said. "The superintendent has just rung up. Mr. Hazlewood will be down in a moment."

Hazlewood came out. "What is all this?" he said.

"I don't know, sir. I was simply told to drive you to the scene of the accident." Hazlewood got into the car beside him and they started off towards Rennison's hotel.

They paused to pick up Rennison who jumped into the back seat and promptly seized Hazlewood by the throat. It was at least quick. In a short time the old man was dead.

Thorpe drove to a deserted road near to the rehearsal hall. He stopped the car.

Quickly the two men changed places. In the back Thorpe threw off the policeman's uniform. Leaving the car, he entered the rehearsal at about the time he should have arrived had he walked from his flat.

The Rennison drove out into the country. Switching off his lights, he turned from the road into a narrow lane.

The place had been chosen beforehand. He had no time to lose. Tying the dead man's wrists together, he slipped his head between the arms. Rennison got the body on his back, passed through a gate into a field, and reached a small fenced enclosure that he had selected in advance.

It contained a round hole, one of the many dene-holes in the district. He tipped the body in, hurried back to the car, got the policeman's uniform, and dumped it also.

Driving the car again without lights till he reached the road, he returned to his garage, changed the number plates, and slipped unseen to his room. On his way he threw the number-plates into the canal.

Now for his alibi, he went down to the bar for a drink, and once again called unostentatious attention to the time.

All had gone well. Both he and Thorpe felt safe.

Rennison was definitely in the bar when the policeman called for Hazlewood, and the only time that Thorpe was out of sight of other people was while he was walking from his flat to the rehearsal; in any case too short a time to drive the body to the dene-hole, for its early discovery had been intended.

"We started with three clues," said Superintendent French. "First, the murderer had a car. Second, he had a police uniform. Third, routine inquiries had produced the usual list of possible suspects. Of the names on this list we believed that only Rennison need be seriously considered. This view was confirmed when further investigation revealed his powerful motive. But Rennison was unquestionably at his hotel when the bogus policeman called for Hazlewood.

"We had Rennison shadowed, and made a list of his contacts. Thorpe was one of them.

"Inquiries into the various backgrounds showed that Thorpe had gambled with Rennison, and was equally hard up.

"A joint murder was the obvious suggestion. We worked out how it could have been done.

"But we felt that no murderer would risk using his own car for such a purpose without first changing the number-plates. So we had Rennison's car examined. When we found that its number-plate fastenings had recently been slackened we felt we were on the right track.

"We now estimated the time during which the car would have been available for the disposal of the body.

"This gave us the area in which the latter must have been hidden. Searching this, we found the dene-hole, and so obtained both body and uniform.

"Inquiry gave us the theatrical supplies firm from which the uniform had been bought—and the salesman was able to identify Thorpe as the purchaser.

"Evidence against Rennison came more easily still. Gazing upon the well-starched collar of the victim, we made a test. On each side of the collar were prints of Rennison's third and fourth fingers."

Dark Waters

For years, Weller, the solicitor, had handled Marbeck's affairs, and when he received the old man's letter saying that he wanted to realise some securities, it struck him like a sentence of death.

For the securities were gone. In order to recoup some unlucky operations on the Stock Exchange, he had sold the lot. Marbeck was no business man, and as his dividends continued to be paid with unfailing regularity he had suspected nothing.

For Weller, discovery would mean the end of everything. He would not escape prison. His business in the nearby town, his charming house on the Thames, his position and his friends—all would be gone. He could look forward to nothing but poverty and misery.

But there was an alternative. He scarcely dared to put it into words, but if Marbeck were dead he could undoubtedly produce papers which would convince the executors that he had sold at the old man's request and paid him the money.

He saw very clearly how the deed could be done, and with complete safety. The Thames! What was the river for, if not to meet the problems of those who lived on its banks? A little care, an unpleasant five minutes, and then—

Weller's house was on the north bank. He was not married, but his sister kept house for him, helped by a woman who came morning and evening to clean and cook. He would have to choose a time when his sister was away from home, as he must have the house to himself in the late evening.

On Wednesday nights for years past, he and three friends had met at each other's houses for a rubber of bridge. There was a dentist, an architect and Marbeck, who was a returned professor of music. The first two lived near Weller on the north bank, but—and this was where the river came in—Marbeck's house was on the south bank almost immediately opposite. There was no bridge close by, and all four had light skills which in suitable weather they used as ferries, preferring to scull directly across rather than to get out cars and drive some miles round.

This was Thursday, and on the coming Wednesday the meeting was to be at Weller's. Till then he could easily put Marbeck off with assurances that the sale of the stock was in hand. Wednesday indeed would suit from every point of view, for his sister was going to some friends in Torquay for that entire week.

Two small preliminaries required attention. At a London chemist's Weller bought some of those "sale" sleeping tablets obtainable without a medical prescription. The shop was large and full of customers and he was satisfied that the purchase had attracted no attention.

On Wednesday evening he dissolved two tablets in a little whisky, then destroying the remainder. It was the custom for the four men to have drinks when breaking up at the end of the game, and as usual Weller set out the decanter, siphon and four glasses. Into one of the glasses he poured the prepared whisky. While standing at the side table he could see the liquid, but it would be invisible to his seated guests.

The other preliminary Weller dealt with shortly before his friends were due. Going to his boathouse, he made sure that his boat was ready for instant use, with rowlocks and oars in place and water gate open.

In due course the men arrived and settled down to their game. Weller threw himself desperately into the play, partly as the best way of passing the time, partly lest he should make some error which might later give rise to comment.

The evening, the longest he had every spent, came to an end at last. He and his partner had lost, but without, he felt sure, any suggestion of carelessness on his part. They settled up their few shillings' debt and then he turned to the glasses. Marbeck was the senior and Weller poured the whisky for him first.

After interminable delays the whisky was drunk, second helpings being offered and, as usual refused. Further delay followed as the guests made their way to the hall and put on their coats in the most leisurely manner. But finally they left and strolled off together down the drive. Weller stood watching them, then slowly closed the door.

Now he could drop the pretence of composure. In the hall cloakroom he put on a cap and dark waterproof. Hurrying to a side door, he let himself out and made his way noiselessly towards the Thames.

It was not completely dark. More by sound than sight he located Marbeck. The old man was on his. Weller's, boat slip, a tiny pier adjoining, but outside his boathouse. Marbeck had moored his skiff, as usual, at the slip. Weller heard him getting in and unchaining his sculls. His movements were slow and fumbling, the result, no doubt, of the dope. But at last he cast off and floated out, a shadow of deeper jet on the dark waters.

Weller now worked frantically. In less than a minute his boat was following the other. He tried to steady the thumping of his heart, reminding himself that everything was going perfectly. He overtook Marbeck in mid-stream, just as he had intended. "Marbeck!" he called softly.

"Yes, yes? Who is it?"

"Weller. A small matter I forgot. Ease up a moment."

The other held water and the boars drew together. Weller unshipped his sculls, laying them parallel to the gunwale at either side. Then, as the skiffs touched, he gripped the gunwale of Marbeck's, pushed it downwards, and then raised it with all his strength. The skiff rolled violently and then righted itself. Marbeck was overboard.

The victim's single cry would not invalidate Weller's plan: in fact it would help it. But further cries might give him away. He swung his skiff round to where Marbeck was struggling, and leaning over the gunwale, seized the figure and pushed it under.

His waterproof caught somewhere, impeding him, and he jerked it roughly free. He was counting on the dope making the old man stupid. It appeared to have done so, for his feeble struggling soon ceased.

One more point and Weller had finished. A glance showed him that Marbeck's boat was as he wanted it: one oar caught in the rowlock, the other overboard. What had occurred would be obvious to everyone. Some slight indisposition or carelessness, and Marbeck had lost an oar. He had made a sudden effort to recapture it before it floated away. The light skiff was unsteady in the water and its sudden roll had taken the old man unawares.

Weller now moved at top speed, though still silently. He rowed to his boathouse, replaced the boat, and hurried to the house. There he had a wash and brush up. He thought another whisky permissible while he waited for the next development.

Half an hour later it came, just as he had intended it should.

Mrs. Marbeck rang up to ask if her husband had left.

"Yes, Mrs. Marbeck," Weller hastened to reply. "He left at his usual time, nearly an hour ago."

"Well, he hasn't arrived here and I'm rather anxious."

"I'll come across at one," Weller declared and rang off.

This call was really part of his scheme. The wet oars, the drippings in his boat, the damp sleeves of his waterproof: all such awkward items would be explained by the speed with which he had hastened across.

Everything continued to go exactly to plan. He made his report to Mrs. Marbeck, they rang up several houses at which the old man might have called. Then at Weller's suggestion they telephoned the police.

Inspector French was at the house within minutes. He listened to statements and said he would start an immediate inquiry. Then came a period of waiting.

Mrs. Marbeck urged Weller to go home, but his sickening anxiety prevented him. Fortunately his presence was not suspicious since politeness also required him to stay. At length, two hours later, the inspector returned. To Mrs. Marbeck he broke his news with genuine kindness. Her husband's body had been found lower down the river. He had evidently fallen overboard while making the crossing. Then he turned to Weller.

"I'd like , sir, to go over to your house to get some further details about Mr. Marbeck's start. If you'll take me over in your boat, I'll send the car round."

"Right," Weller answered. He put on his waterproof and said he was ready.

But the inspector was looking at him very strangely. Weller's heart missed a beat. All had been going perfectly; what could now be wrong? "I said I was ready," he repeatedly shortly.

Inspector French bent forward. "Excuse me, sir, I see you've lost a button from your coat."

Weller glanced down. This was what he had left. No doubt it had jammed under the oar. "My own fault, inspector," he said with truth. "It was loose and I omitted to have it resewn."

French took something from his pocket. "It's not lost, sir. I think this is it. Yes: colour, shape, size and even thread are the same. And do you know where I found it? Gripped Mr. Marbeck's fingers: I could hardly get it out."

The Target

Make a mistake once and you're finished: it dogs you all your life. At least that is what has happened to me.

When I was younger I helped myself to someone else's money and went to prison. It was not for long: only six months, but it meant the end all the same. For the result now is that I have just three weeks more to live.

I was absolutely sure I was safe that evening two months ago when I called to see Jasper Lavender.

My father served with him during the war and Lavender felt in his debt. So when my father told him of my trouble, and begged a start for me in his firm, he didn't refuse.

I joined under a new name and was beginning to make good when a horrible thing happened. I fell for Vera Lavender, Jasper's daughter and heir.

Worse still, Vera fell for me. She wanted an engagement, but of course I had to put her off. Was it likely that Lavender would allow his daughter to marry a jailbird?

I was so sure of my safely on that fatal evening that no misgivings distressed me. Lavender, I knew, would be alone in the house.

As I expected, he opened the door. "Bless me, Brinton, what do you want?"

"A rather delicate matter sir. I thought I should have a word with you about it. It won't take long."

Again as I expected, he led me to his study. I knew it well, for Vera and I usually sat there when her father was not home.

He now stood with his back to the fire, and without asking me to sit down, said: "Well, what is?"

I had my answer pat. "I want, sir to marry Vera, and I want to be sure you've no objection."

Now Lavender had a nervous disorder which made him subject to fits of uncontrollable fury, during which he scarcely knew what he was doing.

He reacted just as I had expected.

"G-g-get out," he stuttered, stepping towards me." And you can g-g-get out of the works, too! N-n-never let me see or hear of you again!"

It was perfect. Just what I had hoped for. I clenched my fist and let him have it on the chin.

He went down like a stone. His chin was bruised, so were my knuckles.

Now I had to be careful, for mistake might give me away. I moved the body a little back so that the head just reached to the raised corner of the hearth. Then I lifted the torso and with the poker struck the head where it might have fallen on the stone.

I laid the body back in the correct position and cleaned the poker with a spare handkerchief which I then burned.

I raised the right hand and gave the lower part of the wrist a blow with my fist. So much for Lavender.

With the blade of knife I pulled out a certain drawer of his desk, thus avoiding smudging possible fingerprints.

Vera had once opened this drawer and I had seen in it the automatic pistol I now wanted.

I picked up the pistol and loaded it without leaving prints on any object. Then I returned to the position from which I had knocked Lavender down, and pointing the pistol upwards, fired. The bullet entered the chimney breast near the ceiling.

Quickly I cleaned my prints off the pistol and pressed on Lavender's.

I placed the pistol on the floor where he would naturally have dropped it.

Haste was now essential. I ran to the telephone, dialled the exchange and asked for police.

Sergeant Railham soon arrived with a doctor. When it was established that Lavender was dead I told my story. I had called to see Mr. Lavender on a delicate mission. In fact, I wanted his permission to marry Miss Lavender.

But, at the suggestion he had gone off the deep end. I was, he said, a pauper. I had explained that it was not so simple as that, since Miss Lavender wished to marry me. At that he had choked and said that if she did, it would be the wedding of two paupers.

That had riled me and I was sorry now for what I had answered: that if his self-conceit was more important to him than his daughter's happiness, she'd loathe him as much as I did.

I thought then that he'd have burst from fury. His face got dark red and seemed to swell. Suddenly his last shreds of self-control had given away. He had swung round to his desk and pulled a pistol from a drawer, aimed it at my face, and fired.

I had struck wildly at his wrist, fortunately knocking it up. Then in self-defence I had hit him on the chin. He had gone over like a pine-pin and struck his head on the corner of the hearth.

The tale went down well. The sergeant asked me some questions, then thanked me and said not to leave the town, as I would be wanted at the inquest.

I can tell you I was sweating when at last I got away from the house. It had been a ghastly time. But it had been worth it. Now I was free to marry Vera and she would be rich.

Superintendent French happened to be at the local police-station on other business when Sergeant Railham returned from his investigation.

He said he had thought that Brinton's statement was somewhat improbable, but he had been forced to accept it because of the supporting evidence. The dead man's fingerprints, and his alone, were on desk, drawer, and pistol. There were bruises on his chin and beneath his right wrist, and Brinton's knuckles were cut.

The bullet had been fired from the pistol beside Lavender's hand, and its entry high up on the chimney breast showed that the pistol had been knocked up as Brinton had said.

This was further confirmed by the position of the ejected shell.

The dead man had a nervous complaint which had rendered him liable to fits of ungovernable rage, and when Brinton insulted him he might well have acted as the young man had stated.

"You interest me extremely, sergeant." Superintendent French told Railham when he had finished. "But don't you see that if your statement's correct, Lavender was murdered by Brinton?"

Railham gazed at French incredulously. Superintendent French suggested going round and making a reconstruction.

"Now," French said when they reached the study, "I'll be Lavender and you Brinton. Let's get into position. I stand here with my back to the fire so that when you hit my chin I fall backwards with my head on the hearth. That right?"

"Okay, sir."

"Then think," French advised.

Railham saw it. "Bless me, sir, the bullet went the wrong way! If Lavender had fired, it would have gone away from the chimney breast, not towards it."

"That's it," French agreed. "Brinton had been standing facing the fire during the whole interview, and in his excitement he forgot to turn round when he began to play Lavender. It'll put paid to his defence."

It did.

The 9.50 Up Express

CHARACTERS
in order of appearance

ACKROYD
ALICE
LOXTON
CHIEF SUPERINTENDENT GRAY, Scotland Yard
SUPERINDENDENT DYSON, Scotland Yard
CHIEF INSPECTOR FRENCH, Scotland Yard
INSPECTOR MANT

ACKROYD: (*Speaks always in an undecided, rather emotional way*) Good evening, Alice. Is Mr. Loxton at home?
ALICE: Yes, Mr. Ackroyd. He's in the library. May I take your coat?
ACKROYD: Thanks. It's a cold evening.
ALICE: Yes, sir. Very cold.
ALICE: Mr. Ackroyd, sir.
LOXTON: (*Speaks in a bluff, hearty and direct way. Preferably a bass*) Hullo, Ackroyd! Delighted to see you! Come in.
ACKROYD: I hope you're not busy, Loxton?
LOXTON: Doing nothing. Where will you sit? Over here?
(*Sound: The door closes*)
ACKROYD: (*In a low voice after a pause*) Thanks.
LOXTON: (*In a tone of surprise*) Hullo, what's the matter with you? Not feeling well?
ACKROYD: I've got some bad news.
LOXTON: (*Quietly*) What is it?
ACKROYD: (*In a low intense voice*) I've seen Frazer.
LOXTON: (*After a silence*) Frazer? You mean—
ACKROYD: Yes. Melbourne.
LOXTON: Tell me.
ACKROYD: He's seen you too. He knows we're living here.
LOXTON: (*Quietly*) He does, does he?

ACKROYD: (*On edge*) What's the good of talking like that? Don't you know what it means?

LOXTON: Blackmail?

ACKROYD: He's got us, Loxton; got us in the hollow of his hand!

LOXTON: Don't be dramatic, man. Go ahead with your story.

ACKROYD: He saw you in Town and trailed you here to this house. Then he saw us together and railed me to mine. He knows we're both well off and he knows I'm married.

LOXTON: And what does he want?

ACKROYD: What do you think he wants? Money!

LOXTON: (*In a low growling voice*) For heaven's sake, get to the point. What does he propose?

ACKROYD: He proposes to send duplicate anonymous letters to Sir George, to the secretary of the golf club and two or three others who matter here. Do you want any more?

LOXTON: Yes, damn it. Let's have no hints nor guesses.

ACKROYD: Those letters will say that their respected neighbours, Loxton and Ackroyd, are thieves and old lags; in short that they're Edgar and Smithore, formerly staff of a public library officials, who got seven years in Melbourne jail for stealing part of the building fund for the new premises.

LOXTON: The end of us here.

ACKROYD: Absolutely. It would be ruin for you and worse for me. My wife! I can't bear to think of it.

LOXTON: Bound to have come. We both know that, even if we didn't say it.

ACKROYD: Damn it all, Loxton, you take it calmly. Don't you *see* the man can ruin us?

LOXTON: Where is he living? Did you find out?

ACKROYD: Yes, he has a secondhand bookshop in Brighton.

LOXTON: His library training coming in handy? *He* didn't need to change his name.

ACKROYD: Well, he didn't go for the library money.

LOXTON: And now he's going to reap the reward of virtue? Does he know what we did after we left Australia?

ACKROYD: He knows the library never got the money back.

LOXTON: So that we're worth plucking? How much does he want?

ACKROYD: Two hundred and fifty a year each. He says he'll be straight with us, and as long as we pay we'll never hear from him again.

LOXTON: They all say that. Did you tell him that if we chose to leave this place, his power would be gone?

ACKROYD: That and a lot more like it. He just laughed.

LOXTON: He was right there. I don't know what you feel about it, but I'm not going to move for fifty skunks like Frazer.

ACKROYD: Then you mean to pay?

LOXTON: Pay be damned! What do you take me for?

ACKROYD: But hand it all, Loxton, there's no use in talking like that. We can't help ourselves.

LOXTON: (*Slowly and with meaning*) Oh, we can't, can't we? Can't we help ourselves, Ackroyd? Can't we?

ACKROYD: (*Uneasily*) I don't know what you're getting at. You know as well as I do that if he sent his letters—

LOXTON: Don't be a fool. You know as well as I do that no one can afford to pay blackmail. Once you start, you're done for. He terms just keep on mounting.

ACKROYD: But what can we do?

LOXTON: (*Grimly*) There's an alternative.

ACKROYD: (*Uneasily*) There's no alternative that I can see—except—murder. You're not suggesting that, I presume?

LOXTON: There's no other way/

ACKROYD: Good, Loxton. I can't believe it's you speaking! Murder! No, no.

LOXTON: Then you prefer to give up your home and have your wife leave you with most of your money? (*There is a silence*) Now look here, Ackroyd, the reason I'm cool about this is that it doesn't come as a surprise. I've foreseen that it might happen and I've worked out a method to meet it; an absolutely perfect method. Some modifications are necessary since he lives at Brighton and has a bookshop. But that's easy.

ACKROYD: I can't believe you're serious.

LOXTON: Serious as death.

ACKROYD: This is ghastly! We couldn't—commit a murder. We'd be caught.

LOXTON: We shall not be caught. An accident would happen to him, that's all.

LOXTON: Suspicion.
LOXTON: Impossible. I tell you it's an absolutely safe plan.
ACKROYD: A lot of people have said that before now. Crippen and Mahon and Rouse and a lot more.
LOXTON: They made silly mistakes. I've guarded against such mistakes.
ACKROYD: I couldn't do it.
LOXTON: Right-oh. I'll clear out and you can fix it up with Frazer.
ACKROYD: One reason neither of us could do it is that Frazer might have written out a statement and left it somewhere.
LOXTON: Not on your life! He may say he has done so, but no blackmailer will supply written evidence of his own crime. In any case, that's a risk we've got to take. Come along, Ackroyd. I've never known you to shirk what was necessary.
ACKROYD: (*After a pause and in a changed voice*) All right. All right. What's the plan?
LOXTON: Oh, thinking better of it, are you? You're willing to join in?
ACKROYD: I suppose so. I hate it, but I suppose I must.
LOXTON: That's more like you. We've been in tight corners before now, and we've always pulled through.
ACKROYD: I see you're right. There *is* no other way.
LOXTON: Then look here. Come closer, man; I don't want to shout the think out. (*His voice drops*) Suppose we were to ask Frazer to come here .....
(*Sound: The voices fade out to indicate the passage of time ... The voices come back up again*)
LOXTON: Well, there it is, Ackroyd. Safe as a house! Satisfied now?
ACKROYD: I hate it; I dread it. But I admit it's a clear scheme.
LOXTON: Hate it myself. But it's our only hope. We'll have a bad five minutes and then we'll be safe. Safe for the rest of our lives. It's worth it.
ACKROYD: (*Dejectedly*) I hope so.
LOXTON: Of course it's so. Now let's run over the whole plan again to make absolutely sure we've got it right.
ACKROYD: Yes, we can't risk a mistake. Now you start it by buying the

first edition.

LOXTON: Yes. I go to some distant city —perhaps— Edinburgh, a sort of literary flavour—and buy a valuable first edition; something that will cost anything up to fifty pounds. I bring it home and hand it to you.

ACKROYD: Then I see Frazer. I tell him that we agree to pay up, but we want to put up an alternative proposal which we think would pay him better.

LOXTON: Would pay us *both* better.

ACKROYD: Yes, yes, yes, would pay us both better. I suggest that we meet to talk it over and that it would be wiser to do this openly.

LOXTON: Right. Point out that if a secret meeting were discovered, it might start rumours.

ACKROYD: Quite. I suggest Thursday evening at this house, "and here," I say, handing him the book, "is the excuse."

LOXTON: Right.

ACKROYD: "Show that," I tell Frazer, "to your assistant and tell him that you think you can sell it to a Mr. Loxton of Pethurst-St-Mary, and that you're going to see him about it on Thursday night."

LOXTON: That's it.

ACKROYD: I tell Frazer to bring it along with him and that we'll hand him forty pounds in exchange, which of course will be part of what we're going to pay him. When he goes back he's to show the forty pounds to his assistant, and that'll keep *him* from being suspicious.

LOXTON: Then about trains?

ACKROYD: I tell Frazer—what he knows of course—that your house is near the station, but that the bus goes to the village a mile away. Therefore he should come by train. A suitable train arrives at Pethurst-St-Mary at 9.50, and there's one back at 9.55 which he could catch.

LOXTON: And the path?

ACKROYD: I tell him to take the path across the field, as it's so much shorter than round by the road.

LOXTON: Seems everything. Then you'll come over yourself that evening before he arrives?

ACKROYD: I'll come over to talk about the proposed changes in the Golf Club rules.

LOXTON: Good. Then as well as getting the first edition, I have some small things to do here. To have coats and gumboots ready and the whisky and so on.

ACKROYD: I think that's all.

LOXTON: Think so. Then I'll go to Edinburgh tomorrow and buy the book, and you'll see Frazer and keep him sweet till everything's ready?

ACKROYD: Yes. I'll do it, Loxton, but I don't mind tolling you the thought of it makes me sick.

LOXTON: (*Grimly*) If you funk it, we'll both hang. Pull yourself together, Ackroyd; it'll soon be over. Well, here's to good luck on Thursday night.

(*Sound: Voices fade out; As before, a bell rings and there are light footsteps and the sound of the opening door*)

ACKROYD: Good evening, Alice. I think Mr. Loxton's expecting me.

ALICE: Yes, Mr. Ackroyd. He's in the library.

ACKROYD: (*Entering*) An unpleasant evening.

ALICE: Yes, sir. I'll put your coat here.

ACKROYD: Thanks. It's rather wet, I'm afraid.

ALICE: Mr. Ackroyd, sir.

LOXTON: 'Evening Ackroyd. Glad you were able to come. Take a pew. By the way, Alice, I'm expecting a Mr. Frazer shortly. If he comes, show him straight in.

LOXTON: (*In a low tone*) Well? Everything ready?

ACKROYD: Yes, he's all set to come. He says he'll be reasonable and all that. If we have another proposition, he'll be glad to consider it.

LOXTON: Looks as if he was afraid. All to the good.

ACKROYD: God! I wish it was over!

LOXTON: (*Sharply*) None of that. We're committed to it and we've got to see it through. I won't give it away nor will Frazer. Will you?

ACKROYD: (*Offended*) I don't know what you mean.

LOXTON: I mean you're the only danger we have to face. So bear that in mind.

ACKROYD: I'm all right. You needn't be frightened. I could do with a drink all the same.

LOXTON: You can't have one. We'll have to drink with Frazer and we don't want to take too much. Let's see those papers about the Golf rules. Remember we're here to discuss them and we must know what we've said.

ACKROYD: There they are. (*There are sounds of papers falling on the table*) There's nothing more to be said about them. We've already been over our supposed conversation.

LOXTON: Very well. Then here are the coats and the gumboots. Your own coat will stay in the hall. Still raining?

ACKROYD: No, it's over.

ACKROYD: Then about the interview. There must be a little bitterness; that would be natural. But Frazer mustn't ever doubt that we're going to pay up.

ACKROYD: (*Wearily*) I know. I know. You needn't go over it all again.

LOXTON: All right if you remember it. Then just one other thing; don't forget to be normal before Alice.

(*Sound: There is a distant ring*)

ACKROYD: (*Excitedly*) There he is!

LOXTON: Now keep calm and leave everything to me.

ALICE: Mr. Frazer to see you, sir.

LOXTON: (*Genially*) Come in, Mr. Frazer. Sorry for bringing you out at this hour. This is Mr. Ackroyd, a friend of mine. How are you?

(*Sound: The door closes.*)

FRAZER: (*Nervously and in a whining tone with a Scotch accent*) I've already met Mr. Ackroyd.

LOXTON: (*In a more brusque tone*) Sit down, Frazer, and let's talk this over. This is not a social gathering, but I feel like a drink. Expect we all do. Just hand me another glass from the table, will you, Ackroyd, of course. Say when, Frazer.

FRAZER: Thanks. I can do fine with that.

LOXTON: Well, Frazer! Didn't expect to see you here.

FRAZER: Nor didna want to neither, I'm thinking.

LOXTON: Well, we didn't, and that's a fact.

ACKROYD: We wanted to forget Australia.

FRAZER: But you're no going to; he, he, he.

LOXTON: Oh, drop all that. Your return train leaves pretty soon.

FRAZER: You're wanting rid of me already?

LOXTON: Don't be a fool. What I mean is, we haven't too much time. Let's get to business and keep the reminiscences for another day.

FRAZER: Suits me. It was to do business I came.
LOXTON: Then give me the first edition; the Keats. Here's the forty pounds. Better count it.
FRAZER: (*After a pause*) Eight fives. Correct. Dirt cheap for an uncut Lamia.
LOXTON: Now that's why you came here tonight and don't forget it.
FRAZER: Aye. Mr. Ackroyd told me.
LOXTON: Good. And when you go back tell your assistant all about it. That's to keep the blackmail a secret.
FRAZER: I know right well what it's for.
ACKROYD: Did you tell your assistant you were coming here tonight?
FRAZER: Snelgrove? Aye, I told him. Wasna that agreed? Well, I'm keeping my word.
ACKROYD: All right. I was just asking.
FRAZER: You didna need to.
LOXTON: Of course he was right to ask. Now about this other money. Before we pay we'll want some guarantee that you'll hold your tongue.
FRAZER: (*Grumbling*) You'll no get any guarantee. How could you? Except that if I talked I'd be killing the goose with the golden eggs. Not meaning anything personal, you know, he, he, he.
ACKROYD: Yes, Frazer put up that point; that our secret was only valuable to him as long as it was a secret.
FRAZER: You gentlemen pay reg'lar and you won't ever hear of the thing again.
LOXTON: Very well, leave it at that. Keep your mouth shut and our money goes on. "Spill the story and it stops. But you know that and we didn't bring you all the way from Brighton to tell it you.
FRAZER: I didna think it, Mr. Loxton.
LOXTON: What we wanted you for was to put up an alternative proposition; one that would cost us less and bring you in more.
FRAZER: You're no fool, Mr. Loxton, if you can do that; he, he, he.
LOXTON: Well, that's what we want to talk about. Do you know Anderson and Truscott?
FRAZER: Of Charing Cross Road?
LOXTON: Yes.
FRAZER: Aye. They're one of the biggest firms in the world in my line of business.

LOXTON: Quite. Know them personally?

FRAZER: I've spoken to Anderson. I never saw Truscott.

LOXTON: I happen to know Anderson pretty well. Not him not long ago and he mentioned that Truscott was retiring.

FRAZER: Retiring, is he? I didna know that.

LOXTON: Retiring in a couple of months. Now Anderson's looking for a partner. Do you see what I'm getting at?

FRAZER: I'm no making any guesses, Mr. Loxton. What are you getting at?

LOXTON: If you had the cash and would like the job—you might get it.

FRAZER: Me? About as likely as the Home Secretary's.

LOXTON: Well, I happen to have a pull with Anderson; did him a good turn once and he hasn't forgotten it. I'm not urging you, but if you'd like it I'd see Anderson and find out his terms.

FRAZER: I wouldna have a chance with a man like Anderson.

LOXTON: I agree. If you went to him without money and influence, you'd have none. But with both—it might make a difference.

FRAZER: I'm thinking I'd better off with my five hundred
and stay where I am.

LOXTON: Go up and see him. See here, I'll write him tomorrow—or tonight for the matter of that— and you slip up to Town and see him.

FRAZER: I'd maybe be as well—

ACKROYD: If you don't like it, there's no harm done; we can go back to your own plan.

LOXTON: Yes, don't be fool enough to turn down a god offer before you've looked into it. But you've finished your drink and so have I. Have another?

FRAZER: Thanks. I don't mind if I do.

ACKROYD: What sort of man is this Anderson?

LOXTON: Quite a good chap, keep and efficient and all that.

FRAZER: Straight, is he?

LOXTON: Far as I know. Go and find out for yourself. If you like him and he likes you, we'll fix the money part. If you don't take to him there's no harm done. We can the reconsider your own plan.

ACKROYD: Remember that with your plan you stay as you are. As partner to Anderson, there's practically no limit to your profits.

LOXTON: That's right. Depend on yourself. Now this is Thursday. I'll write and make an appointment for you on Saturday morning and you slip up to Town and see Anderson.

FRAZER: (*Doubtfully*) I might do that. (*With conviction*) But this is no shuffle out for you. If I dinna like Anderson we'll go back to the two-fifty from each.

ACKROYD: I've already said so.

LOXTON: We've both said so. Then that's settled. Now I'll do better than write. I'll go up and see Anderson in the morning. You ring me up tomorrow evening—from a street box—and I'll tell you if he'll consider it.

ACKROYD: That's an idea. A personal interview is always better than a letter.

FRAZER: Well, I suppose there's no harm in asking the question.

LOXTON: Then the only point remaining is to fix up our next meeting.

ACKROYD: What about Monday night?

FRAZER: Suits me.

LOXTON: Right. But we can't have it here or at Mr. Ackroyd's or at your place. Where do you suggest?

ACKROYD: What about one of those shelters along the Brighton sea front? At this time of your they're deserted. Say the one opposite Bourneville Avenue?

LOXTON: That'll do. Then we meet at the shelter at nine next Monday night? And you'll ring up from a call box tomorrow night about this time?

FRAZER: I'm likely to forget.

LOXTON: Very good. (*Speaking earnestly*) Now a last word. There's just one thing you've got to understand, and that is that if we're in your hands, you're in ours.

FRAZER: I dinna see that, Mr. Loxton: really I dinna.

LOXTON: Well, the sooner you see it, the better. You take this money from us and you keep your bargain, and all goes well. Break it and we simply shut down payment.

FRAZER: You wouldna be so unwise as to do that. Mr. Loxton: not that I'm going to break my word.

FRAZER: That's what we'd do. You'd then presumably tell your story. I agree that would ruin us here— we'd have to leave. But we *would* leave: we'd start fresh in another country. No real difficulty in making a new home. But what would happen to you?

FRAZER: I'd follow and start fresh too.

LOXTON: Oh no, you wouldn't. That's just there you're making the mistake. You'd stay behind in prison. You couldn't hurt us without giving away the blackmail, and you'd get a longer stretch for that than we get in Australia. So just keep that in view as an aid to temptation.

FRAZER: You're a hard man, Mr. Loxton: he, he, he.

LOXTON: Right then: I see you understand. Now you've just time for another drink before you go.

FRAZER: (*Doubtfully*) I'm thinking I've had enough.

LOXTON: Nonsense, man. I'm offering another to Mr. Ackroyd and I'm having another myself. You must join us.

FRAZER: Well, maybe—

LOXTON: Your glass, Ackroyd. (*Here sounds of pouring out*) Well, here's to an amicable settlement. (*A pause while they drink*)

FRAZER: Well, thank you, gentlemen. I'm no thanking you for the cash, which is my due, but for the drinks.

LOXTON: That's all right, Frazer. Sometimes it's your turn to get on top, and sometimes it's ours. Don't want to hurry you, but it's time you were off, if you're to catch your train.

FRAZER: Aye, it's all that.

LOXTON: Just touch the bell, will you Ackroyd?

(*Sound: A sound of steps, a distant bell and more steps*)

LOXTON: Now, Frazer, you're here as a bookseller to dispose of a first edition Keats. Remember that when Alice comes in.

ACKROYD: You came by the path across the field from the station, I suppose? It cuts off a long round.

FRAZER: I came by it and I'll go by it because it's short, but it's a bit muddy after the rain.

LOXTON: Look out: here's Alice. Well, Mr. Frazer, if you can get me the companion to that edition, I'd be glad to have it, particularly with that same front and tooling.

FRAZER: I'll look out for it, sir. I think I can get it. Then good night, sir. (*Sound: Movement*)

LOXTON: Good night. Sorry for giving so much trouble.

FRAZER: No trouble at all, sir.
ACKROYD: Good night Mr. Frazer.
FRAZER: Good night sir.
(*Sound: Steps and the door closes. The footsteps retreat and probably the closing of the front door is heard*)
LOXTON: (*In a low urgent tone*) There he goes, Ackroyd. Now coats and boots quickly. (*There are shuffling*) Ready? (*A pause*)
ACKROYD: (*Almost in a whisper*) Ready.
LOXTON: This damned French window creaks and I was afraid to oil it. (*A noise of a creaking window being opened*) There you are. Out with you. (*A noise of the window being closed.*)
ACKROYD: You think of everything, Loxton.
LOXTON: I daren't leave it open in case it would slam. Now I know this place better than you. Catch hold of my arm.
(*Sound: Soft steps*)
ACKROYD: It's terribly dark.
LOXTON: (*Urgently*) I tell you, hold on to my arm. You don't want to go crashing into anything.
(*Sound: During the remainder of the scene their voices are low and urgent and their movements stealthy. Their steps continue. There are pauses, so now, while only the steps are hard*)
LOXTON: He'll not walk fast. We'll overtake him in plenty of time.
ACKROYD: We'll hear his steps. We can hang back till the right moment.
LOXTON: Yes. Now don't forget, Ackroyd. When we get behind the shelter I'll say: "Now there's another point," and you'll shine you torch on his face. Just for a moment, you know. Got your torch ready.
ACKROYD: Of course I have.
LOXTON: "Now there's another point." That clear?
ACKROYD: Yes, yes. For heaven's sake don't harp on it.
(*Sound: A pause while steps only are heard*)
LOXTON: Here's the gate. Steady: don't crash into it. Are you outside?
ACKROYD: Yes: I can see now dimly. It's not so dark as I thought.
LOXTON: I can see the road. Now we mustn't miss the path. Frazer will have found it with his torch. But we can't use a torch.

(*Sound: A short pause with steps only*)

ACKROYD: There's the path. I can see the gap in the hedge.

LOXTON: Right. I see it. Walk as quietly as you can. (*The sound of the steps is reduced*) it's gone well so far. He suspects nothing.

ACKROYD: That's what it so horrible.

LOXTON: Forget it. Do what I tell you and we're perfectly safe.

(*Sound: Short pause with steps only*)

ACKROYD: Suppose my torch is seen?

LOXTON: Won't be. I tell you there's no one about the station but the signalman, and the platform shelter will hide us from his box.

ACKROYD: I suppose that's right.

LOXTON: Then he express pauses up on our side as nine-fifty, and it's not till nine-fifty-five. Five minutes later, that the stopping train comes in on the other side: the train Frazer was going for.

ACKROYD: *Was*!

LOXTON: I hear his footsteps. We're just going to overtake him at the right place. (*Faint additional steps are heard*) Now a bad five minutes and we'll be done.

(*Sound: A pause in which the other steps grew louder*)

LOXTON: (*Calling, but not loudly*) That you, Frazer?

FRAZER: Eh? Who's that?

LOXTON: Loxton. Sorry to barge in again, but we've made a mistake. We had to follow you to tell you.

FRAZER: What's wrong?

LOXTON: You can't ring up tomorrow evening.

FRAZER: Why not?

LOXTON: I've got a dinner in Town. Forgot all about it till I looked up my book. We'll have to put the thing off for one day.

FRAZER: You're meaning till Monday?

LOXTON: Yes. You go to Town Monday instead of Saturday. You ring me up Monday evening. We meet in Brighton on Tuesday evening. That all right?

FRAZER: Oh aye, that'll do.

LOXTON: Right. *Now there's another point.*

(*Sound: A momentary silence, the click of a torch, the rustle of clothes, a blow, an explosion of breath suggesting effort, and a fall to the ground*)

LOXTON: Put off your light, you fool! Here, put it on again, lowered. Let's see him.

ACKROYD: (*Almost whispering*) Loxton! You've killed him!

(*Sound: All speech to the end of the scene is low or whispered and gasping*)

LOXTON: I. He's just knocked out. Got him square on the chin. That'll do. Put off that torch.

ACKROYD: He looks... like death.

LOXTON: Come on now, we haven't got all night. I'll take his shoulders and you take his knees. (*A pause with shuffling movements*) Got him? Now go ahead.

ACKROYD: Wait. I haven't got him yet. (*More shuffling*) That's right now.

LOXTON: You go first and look sharp about it. (*Stumbling footsteps are heard*)

(*Sound: The footsteps continue*)

LOXTON: Faster, Ackroyd. There's the green signal for the express.

(*Sound: The footsteps get quicker and more irregular and the breathing more gasping, to indicate the carrying of a weight*)

ACKROYD: Here are the platform steps. Slowly a moment.

LOXTON: Get on, man. We haven't time to wait.

(*Sound: Stumbling up steps*)

LOXTON: Now to the right. Hurry: it's not far to the end of the platform.

ACKROYD: (*With horror in his voice*) Loxton: this is awful! Couldn't we simply lay it on the line and get away?

LOXTON: Suppose he came to? Besides, haven't I told you that the injuries might give the show away?

(*Sound: A distant whistle*)

LOXTON: (*Urgently*) There she is! For heaven's sake look sharp.

(*Sound: The steps redouble their speed, then stops*)

LOXTON: Now, Ackroyd, one more effort and we're through. When I say "Let's go!" heave him off the platform.

ACKROYD: (*With a groan*) I know.

LOXTON: And for heaven's sake don't go over yourself!

(*Sound: The distant sound of an approaching train heard, travelling at a high speed. *The sound increases quickly, and Loxton's shouted "Let go!", just before it reaches maximum, should only just be heard. The train roars past and the sound diminishes and fades out. There is a short pause*)

ACKROYD: (*In a trembling voice*) My God! That was awful!

LOXTON: (*Intensely*) Come away. It's over. Come quickly.

ACKROYD: It—Was it all right? I couldn't look.

LOXTON: All right? Absolutely! The engine hit him. I saw by the buffer lamp. Come along.

(*Sound: The steps begin again*)

ACKROYD: (*Tremulously*) It! I didn't know it was going to be like this.

LOXTON: Shut up. Will you. Do you want to hang? Let's get off this damned platform, then we'll have to run.

ACKROYD: Did he—feel anything?

LOXTON: Of course not. Unconscious. Come on, run!

(*Sound: The steps break into a slow dragging run and fade out momentarily to indicate the passage of a short time*)

(*Sound: The steps, walking, fade in again, one set on gravel, the other softer, on grass*)

LOXTON: (*In an urgent whisper*) Got on to the grass, can't you? Do you want to wake the entire neighbourhood?

(*Sound: The gravel steps cease, and both sets become soft, as if on grass. There is a general sound of movement*)

LOXTON: Here's the French window. Keep still while I open it.

(*The window creaks as before. There are sounds of entering*)

LOXTON: There. Take off your coat and boots and sit down and get your breath.

(*Sound: The window creaks again. A sound of gumboots being dropped softly. Soft steps in room*)

LOXTON: Give me those boots. I'll hide them here in the meantime and wash them later. The coats too. I'll drop them behind here.

(*Sound: Movement to correspond*)

ACKROYD: (*Faintly*) A drink! Give me a drink.

LOXTON: Help yourself. No, don't: you'd spill it. Sit down there at the fire and I'll get it for you— (*He speaks with normal loudness*) And talk normally.

ACKROYD: A drink!

LOXTON: Time enough. It's coming. There, put that down. And for pity's sake pull yourself together. Now we have to suggest on alibi. I'm going to ring for Alice.

ACKROYD: (*On edge*) Y'll never get over this. Not as long as I live.

LOXTON: (*Fiercely*) Stop it!

ACKROYD: (*Slightly hysterical*) But don't you realise it? We're murderers! *Murderers!*

LOXTON: For God's sake! If you go on like that, as sure as fate we'll hang!

ACKROYD: Blood on our hands! Blood! We'll never get it off! (*Gives a sob*)— I'm sorry. It's all right. I'll be quiet.

LOXTON: (*Relieved*) That's better. Calm yourself while I'm emptying the siphon. (*The window creaks*) Damn this window! (*There is the sound of emptying a siphon and the door creaks again and is shut and bolted*) Now I'm going to ring for Alice. (*Steps across road and the distant bell is heard*)

ACKROYD: Don't ask me to speak to her.

LOXTON: You won't have to. Just sit where you are. I'll sit here at the desk and be writing. Now—it'll only be for a moment.

LOXTON: (In his normal voice) Oh–er–Alice, I'm afraid our soda's out. Can you find another siphon?

ALICE: Certainly, sir.

LOXTON: (*In a joking tone*) Rather underestimated our visitor's capacity, I'm afraid. (*Then to Ackroyd*) Then, as I was saying, Ackroyd, we'll vote for the motion. If that's carried, it'll be all right.

ACKROYD: (*Weakly*) How can you do it, Loxton? How can you? With that old man—

LOXTON: (*Drily*) Well, someone's got to do it.

ACKROYD: And to joke about him—and he's lying—Can you bear to think of him at this moment?

LOXTON: No. Don't think of him. Think that Alice will be back in a minute or two with the syphon.

ACKROYD: I don't follow all this syphon business. How will that help our alibi?

LOXTON: it won't, but it'll strengthen the suggestion that we've been here all the time. Too well worked out on alibi would be suspicious.

ACKROYD: I see that.

LOXTON: And you also see that all we've done will look quite natural. First, Alice shows Frazer out and swears that we stayed all the time in here. Second, your coat and hat were in the hall. Third, almost before we've had time to o to the station and back we ring, and she finds us sitting here talking about golf.

ACKROYD: But we might have done—just what we did.

LOXTON: Of course we might. But why should we? Don't you see that that's our strength? We could have had no motive. Everything tonight has been perfectly normal.

ACKROYD: Normal!

LOXTON: Yes: don't you see? The whole episode of Frazer coming here to sell the Keats is absolutely normal. His assistant has seen the book and known he was coming. The book is here now. The forty pounds is in Frazer's pocket. Nothing suspicious there, if only we act normally.

ACKROYD: It's not that.

LOXTON: Then what is it?

ACKROYD: It's—what happened at the station.

LOXTON: But that's absolutely normal too. It's dark in the blackout and Frazer has taken too much drink. Remember that's why we'll be upset about— because we gave him too much drink and so unwittingly were the cause of his accident.

ACKROYD: I know that's our line.

LOXTON: Then Frazer arrives at the wrong platform and wants to cross. Fuddled with drink he misses— or funks—the footbridge: thinks he will cross on the luggage level crossing at the end of the ramp. He knows nothing about the express and gets run over.

ACKROYD: It sounds all right.

LOXTON: Of course it's all right. Now the police may come at any time. Depends on when they find him. The appointment may be in his notebook. And we've to tell them the exact truth. Everything except that we left this room. The story's perfectly good.

ACKROYD: I know: I'm not an utter fool. (*Suddenly anxious*) But, Loxton, have you thought? There may be a bruise on his chin—where you hit him!

LOXTON: A bruise! For God's sake, Ackroyd! Have you ever seen a man who's been run over by a train?

ACKROYD: No.

LOXTON: Well, I have.

ACKROYD: All the same— If only we could be sure! Loxton, are *you* sure—they can't find out?

LOXTON: Don't be a bloody fool. How could anyone find out? Now light a cigarette. Here's Alice coming with the soda.

(*Sound: Movement fade out*)

GRAY: Well, French, You asked for this conference at a propitious moment. Here am I, just back from America, and the first thing I learn is that you've been having murders and what not in my own village.

FRENCH: Mr. Dyson said you were arriving this morning, sir, and that suited me very well. I'm ready to report on this Frazer case.

GRAY: Good: I want to hear all about it. There you are, super. Here's French ready to tell us all about the Frazer case.

FRENCH: Good morning, Mr. Dyson.

DYSON: Good morning, Mr. French. I hope I didn't keep you waiting, sir?

GRAY: Not a bit: just arrived myself.

DYSON: I've said nothing to the Chief about the case, Mr. French, so you may begin at the beginning.

GRAY: French looks pleased, super: I deduce a completed case.

DYSON: I hope you're right, sir.

GRAY: But you have your doubts? Well, we'll see. Now, French, as I was saying, you asked for this conference, and here we are.

FRENCH: Yes, sir. I wanted the interview because I believe I have *completed* the case.

GRAY: What did I tell you, super? Delighted to hear it, French. Go straight ahead.

FRENCH: As you're not familiar with the details, sir, I'd better begin by summarising what took place before I took over. Before that, Inspector Mant had done a lot of useful work. And may I say that I'm sorry about his accident and that he can't be here today.

GRAY: Yes, I'm sorry about him too. Good fellow, Mant.

FRENCH: Well, reporting for Inspector Mant, the first intimation received was a phone early on Friday morning from the railway station at Pethurst-St-Mary, saying that a body had been found on the line. Inspector Mant got in touch with a doctor and went down with a couple of men.

DYSON: He got Dr. Wright, the police doctor.

FRENCH: So, I understand, sir, Mant found the remains were those of an elderly man, and they were on the up line at a luggage 1 level crossing at the end of the platform. The body had evidently been there some time.

GRAY: Not seen in the dark, I suppose?

FRENCH: No, sir: that was it. Mant then did what might be expected. When the doctor had examined the body, he moved it off the line and then went through the pockets. Papers showed the deceased was Andrew Frazer, a secondhand bookseller of Shore Street, Brighton.

GRAY: I've seen the shop. Quite a small place.

FRENCH: So Mant found out later. There was nothing remarkable in the pockets except a roll of eight five-pound Bank of England notes. Mant sent the body to the mortuary and then had a look round, but without finding anything of interest.

DYSON: He assumed it was an accident.

FRENCH: It was natural, sir. The body had been found by a signalman named Bell, and Mant then interrogated him.

(*Sound: The voices fade out to indicate a change of scene*)

MANT: Tell me, Bell, had you seen the deceased before?

BELL: Yes, Mr. Mant. 'E came off the 9.50 from Brighton. I took his ticket, the outward 'arf of a third return from Brighton.

MANT: Did you see in which director he left the station?

BELL: Off the up platform, sir.

MANT: To the up or west side of the line: I see. Now have you any idea what train he was killed by?

BELL: Yes, sir: the 9.50 up express last night. There was a call this morning all along the line asking 'ad there been an accident, the driver 'aving found blood on the engine.

MANT: Pretty conclusive. Can you suggest what the deceased might have been doing on the line at that time?

BELL: Coming to get the 9.55 back to Brighton, I suppose.

MANT: You mean there's a train to Brighton just five minutes after the express passes?

BELL: Yes, sir.

MANT: But isn't there a footbridge?

BELL: Yes, there is, and 'e should 'ave used it. But you know what people are. They won't climb steps when they can walk on the level. But you'd think in the blackout—

(*Sound: The voices fade out*)

FRENCH: So Bell's statement made it seem likely that the deceased was coming for that 9.55 train, and in crossing the line, as he would have to do, he was knocked down by the express.

GRAY: Fairly obvious, I agree.

FRENCH: Mant then went to the address in Brighton. There, as you said, sir, he found the shop was a small one with one assistant, Snelgrove. Snelgrove said the deceased had gone to Pothurst-St-Mary with a first edition Keats to try and sell it to a resident there, a Mr. Loxton

GRAY: The explanation of the eight fivors?

FRENCH: Yes, sir. The sale had evidently gone through. Mant brought Snelgrove back with him, and he identified the deceased as his employer—as far as was possible, for the face was badly smashed up.

DYSON: A fair dither he was in too, was Snelgrove. I saw him at the mortuary, and if I'd been in a suspicious frame of mind, I'd have put a man on him.

FRENCH: I was doubtful about Snelgrove myself, Mr. Dyson, but I was wrong. He was only nervous and frightened about is job.

DYSON: No doubt.

FRENCH: When Mant got back he saw the doctor. He reported that death had occurred from the injuries, which might have been caused by the train, that the deceased probably occurred between eight p.m. and midnight on the previous evening, and that there was a fair amount of alcohol in the stomach.

GRAY: Again all supporting the accident theory?

FRENCH: Entirely. Mant then went to see Loxton who lives about five minutes walk from the station by taking a short cut across a field.

(*Sound: The voices fade out*)

LOXTON: Yes, inspector, it has given me a great shock. I was just going over to report to you. I suppose you know that it was to see me that the unfortunate man came to Pethurst-St-Mary?

MANT: I understood so, Mr. Loxton. Perhaps you would tell me about it?

LOXTON: There's not much to tell, I'm afraid. I'm interested in first editions, and he had supplied me on various occasions. You knew, of course, that that's his business? Some days ago he rang me up to say that he had an uncut first edition Keats which he thought I'd like, and might he bring it for my inspection? I said certainly and we fixed up last night.

MANT: I understand, sir.

LOXTON: Well, he brought the book—there it is—and I liked it and bought it.

MANT: Can you tell me what hour he left?

LOXTON: He was going for the 9.55 train and he left about ten minutes earlier. I hurried him out indeed, because in the blackout I thought he should have plenty of time.

MANT: Had he taken drink, sir?

LOXTON: (*Hesitatingly*) Yes, I'm afraid he had, and that's why the accident has so much upset me. I'm afraid I gave him a lot of whisky. Mr. Ackroyd happened to be here when Frazer came, and he had some, and I couldn't do anything else but offer it to Frazer.

MANT: How many glasses did he have?

LOXTON: Four or five, I think; all small of course. Frazer was not in the slightest degree drunk when he left here, but I confess there was a slight— well—he was growing a bit facetious, if you know what it mean.

MANT: No other signs?

LOXTON: None, and I need scarcely say that night Mr. Ackroyd nor I suspected he was, or we'd have seen him to the station.

MANT: Oh well, sir, I don't see that you can blame yourself. A man should know what he can carry...

(*Sound: The voices fade out*)

GRAY: Seems straightforward.

FRENCH: So Mant thought. He then saw the maid at Mr. Loxton's. She had let Frazer out on the previous evening, and she said that in her opinion he was not drunk, though smelling strongly of whisky.

GRAY: Confirmation?

FRENCH: Complete, sir. Mant next called Mr. Ackroyd, who lives not far away, and he also confirmed Loxton's statement, though without adding anything fresh. So far Mant had gone before I came on the scene.

GRAY: Mant then put up a theory.

DYSON: Yes, sir, he told me about it. He supposed Frazer had taken more drink than he was accustomed to because his prospective customer offered it to him. As you know, you can antagonise a man by refusing a drink. Then going out into the cold, sir, would increase the effect, so that by the time he reached the station he would be fuddled. There he thought he'd avoid the footbridge steps by using the crossing. He knew nothing about the express. When he heard it he probably thought it was his train and hurried on and so got knocked down. That at least was Mint's idea.

GRAY: Very reasonable too.

FRENCH: Then, sir, perhaps I may repeat how I came into the affair. Down here on the Foxfield case, I was held up waiting for some information from the Yard. At a loose end I walked up with Mant to the mortuary. I happened to notice the deceased's overcoat. The back and shoulders were stained with mud, a whitish chalky mud. At first I supposed he'd been knocked on the back by the engine.

GRAY: And wasn't he?

FRENCH: No, sir. It didn't occur to me till later, but there's no mud of that kind on the railway. Broken stone ballast might have oil or dust or rust on it, but not chalky mud.

GRAY: That's right.

FRENCH: Then I noticed something else. The injuries showed that the deceased had been knocked on his face, and sure enough on the breast of the coat were just the stains of rust and dirt that one would expect from the ballast. It was therefore obvious that he had fallen on his back before the accident.

DYSON: If you thought he was drunk, what's remarkable in that?

FRENCH: Perhaps nothing, Mr. Dyson. And yet I thought, except when going down steps or a slope, a drunk would be unlikely to fall on his back. More likely, surely, to trip and fall forward?

DYSON: You may be right.

FRENCH: As I said, I was at a loose end, so I strolled over to the station and had a look round. The path across the field leading to Loxton's house was muddy after the rain: just that some sort of whitish mud.

(*Sound: The voices fade out*)

(*Sound: The distant bell, followed by the opening of the door, all as before*)

FRENCH: Good afternoon. My friend, Inspector Mant, who was here today about Mr. Frazer's accident, asked me to call and ask you one question he forgot to put. You are Miss Alice Smith, aren't you?

ALICE: Yes, sir. Will you come in?

FRENCH: No thanks, one word is all I want. Did you take Mr. Frazer's coat when he called last night?

ALICE: Yes, I hung up his coat and hat.

FRENCH: Did you happen to notice if there were any stains of mud on the back?

ALICE: No, sir; there weren't any. I should have seen them if there were. There's quite a good light in the hall…

(*Sound: The voices fade out*)

FRENCH: The deceased had fallen on his back then crossing the field on his way to the station. I kept on wondering why.

GRAY: An interesting question certainly.

FRENCH: I strolled back along the path and had a look round for marks. I found some prints that I thought rather suggestive. You remember the layout of the station, sir? The main buildings on the down platform and a shelter on the up?

GRAY: I know it, of course.

FRENCH: the path runs behind the shelter and at that point it is screened from the platform. It was there that I saw the prints—the only screened part.

GRAY: I should have thought you'd see prints anywhere along that path.

FRENCH: That's true, sir, the whole centre was a mass of them. But these were at the sides. There were two pairs of heel marks, blurred and useless for identification, but they showed that two men had stood at opposite sides, facing the centre.

DYSON: A couple of friends stopping for a chat?

FRENCH: There was more than that in it. Those marks weren't opposite each other. One pair was about three feet further along the path than the other.

GRAY: I don't know that I follow.

FRENCH: Suppose the two men had stooped to pick up a third who was lying on his back on the ground, they would have left prints in just those places.

GRAY: Yes.

FRENCH: Then I had a word with Dr. Wright, but he couldn't help me. Without a post mortem he couldn't tell if the deceased had been drugged and the face (was mutilated by the train?) had been too much injured to show previous injuries. Then I told you, super, what I suspected, and you asked me to carry on a little further.

DYSON: I thought it the best thing to do, sir.

GRAY: I, think you were absolutely correct, super.

DYSON: Thank you, sir.

FRENCH: I started then with the possibility that the deceased had been murdered, and the next question was: who was the man? From the information I had, Snelgrove was the obvious first suspect. He had both knowledge and opportunity. By the way, Mr. Dyson, some of this will be new to you too.

DYSON: Yes, we haven't discussed it since.

FRENCH: I know of no motive for Snelgrove, but of course he might have had one. In any case I went down to Brighton and saw him. I don't think I need go into the interview, except to say that I satisfied myself that he was innocent.

GRAY: I think for completeness sake you might just indicate the nature of your conclusions.

FRENCH: Well, there was the question of Frazer's fall. I couldn't tell whether other or chloroform had been used, but if he'd been knocked out, someone knuckles might bear traces.

DYSON: What about a spanner on the top of his head?

FRENCH: I thought that unlikely, first, because it might have caused bleeding and second, because the wound might have been found.

GRAY: How did you test for the knuckles?

FRENCH: I had brought down an old charm I had used before in similar cases. I held it out on the palm of my hand and said it had been found near the body, and asked Snelgrove had he seen Frazer with it? He couldn't tell without picking it up, and he couldn't pick it up without exposing his knuckles. They were not bruised.

GRAY: Good!

DYSON: No fear of his having used the other hand?

FRENCH: I considered that. He used his right, and I saw that he was righthanded. All the same he might have padded his hand or used a spanner and I wasn't satisfied. I therefore asked him where he was on the Thursday night. He had an alibi, and I checked it up and found it watertight.

GRAY: Snelgrove eliminated.

FRENCH: Negative progress, sir: always useful. Then I made the usual routine enquiries: went through the deceased's papers and so on, but I could learn nothing helpful. Apparently he was an Australian and had been in the book business in Melbourne.

GRAY: Search for another suspect then?

FRENCH: Yes, sir, and not so easy to find one. I felt it was probably someone in Brighton, but I had no line on anyone there. Then the idea of Loxton occurred to me, simply because he had the opportunity. But this seemed farfetched.

DYSON: No motive?

FRENCH: That was the snag. There were also the facts that neither he nor Ackroyd had gone out with Frazer, and that a few minutes after Frazer left Alice had taken a siphon of soda to the library, and both men were then sitting quietly discussing golfing matters.

GRAY: Not an absolute alibi, you know.

FRENCH: By no means. However I could think of no one but Loxton, so on chance I called and produced my charm. He reacted better than Snelgrove.

DYSON: He used the wrong hand?

FRENCH: Yes. He picked it up with his left hand, but I saw from his movements that he was righthanded. Try as I would, I couldn't get a glimpse of his knuckles.

GRAY: Looking more hopeful?

FRENCH: Well, he made me a bit more suspicious. Then I saw Ackroyd and put up the same tale about the charm. He made no attempt to hide his knuckles.

GRAY: A difficult situation.

FRENCH: Very, sir. I don't mind confessing that I didn't know what to do next. But I saw that if I were to make progress, I must get some further evidence.

GRAY: Easier said than done.

FRENCH: I was lucky. I got absolutely conclusive evidence, and without addressing another word to Loxton.

GRAY: I admit I don't see how. Do you, super?

DYSON: I know what the Chief Inspector did, sir.

GRAY: (*Laughing*) Very discreet, super. Well, French what was the evidence?

FRENCH: I reasoned this way. If Loxton had murdered Frazer, it was not done on the spur of the moment. It had been carefully thought off. Therefore was not all this business of the Keats first edition a plant of Loxton's to get the deceased into his power?

GRAY: Possibly.

FRENCH: I wondered how it could have been done. Then I thought Loxton could first have let the deceased know he wanted the book....

GRAY: Yes?

FRENCH: And then have himself bought the book...

GRAY: Yes.

FRENCH: And then under another name have sent it to the deceased.

DYSON: You mean so that the deceased would have approached him about it?

FRENCH: Exactly. If so, Loxton could have said: "Bring it down for my inspection on Thursday evening."

GRAY: It's certainly possible.

FRENCH: It was a pure guess of course, but on chance I put out a general call to trace such a purchase. Fortunately the book is rare, or I mightn't have succeeded.

GRAY: You found it?

FRENCH: Yes, sir. Goldie and Mackintosh of Edinburgh had sold one like it a week earlier. What was more, their salesman identified Loxton as the man who bought it.

GRAY: That was better.

FRENCH: It satisfied me that I was on the right track. But still, I hadn't enough proof for court. Luckily I thought of something else.

GRAY: It's a good tale, isn't it, super? What was the next brain wave?

FRENCH: Something very simple, sir. Thursday night was damp and cold. Therefore if Loxton had gone out, he would have worn an overcoat.

GRAY: Yes?

FRENCH: Could he have carried a man whose back was covered with mud without getting the mud on his own coat, particularly about the knees?

GRAY: Yes—

FRENCH: Mant and I thought we would test this. We called at Loxton's when we knew he was out, and said we'd wait for him. We were shown into the library. When the maid went away we had a search round and we found two coats stained with the same whitish mud of the path. They'd been brushed, but not just well enough.

DYSON: They all make a mistake somewhere.

FRENCH: Another point. Ackroyd was with Loxton all that evening. Therefore he was surely in it too. The second mud-stained overcoat confirmed this.

GRAY: Excellent!

FRENCH: I took the opportunity to have a look through Loxton's papers, but I found nothing helpful. But I had got so far that I felt I couldn't be beaten. There were two facts which suggested a line of enquiry. First, the reference to Australia in Frazer's desk and second, the fact, I got that from the Sussex Post Office, that Loxton and Ackroyd had come to the district at the same time, it was generally believed, from abroad.

GRAY: Ah.

FRENCH: You can guess my next move, sir. I called on Loxton and Ackroyd and gave each a nicely surfaced card, saying I'd found it in Frazer's desk, and asking had they had any dealings with the man whose name it bore.

DYSON: (*Chuckling.*) A hoary trick.

FRENCH: The old ones are the best, as you know, Mr. Dyson. I developed the cards and got excellent fingerprints. Then I wired these to the Australian police. When I got their reply I saw that I had the whole thing.

GRAY: What did they say?

FRENCH: It was the Public Library business: you may remember it's Loxton and Ackroyd, under other names, were accountant and clerk in one of the largest public libraries in Australia. Frazer was a messenger. Loxton and Ackroyd stole £15,000, which had been collected for rebuilding. Frazer was suspected, but acquitted.

GRAY: Blackmail?

FRENCH: Not a doubt of it, sir. Frazer evidently found out where these birds were living and put on the screw.

GRAY: And they counter attacked? Between ourselves, French, their plan was so good that they deserved to succeed.

FRENCH: They made one oversight and that gave them away.

GRAY: You mean?

FRENCH: The weather. The plan would have been good enough in dry weather, but they forgot that the rain would cover that path with mud.

GRAY: By Jove! An easy mistake to make too. The plans of mice and men! Well, French, I must offer you my congratulations. A fine job of work! Now will you and the super get together and make arrangements to bring them in tonight.

DYSON: I'd like to add my congratulations to the Chief's. Well then, Mr. French, about bring them in. I think if we went out about nine....

(*Sound: The voices fade out.*)

During The Night

CHARACTERS
in order of appearance
ANNE DAY
SYBIL GRINSMEAD
EDITH CHEAME
RICHARD GRINSMEAD
MAXWELL CRAWLEY
MRS. GRINSMEAD, Senior
IRENE HOLT
CHIEF INSPECTOR FRENCH, Scotland Yard
SERGEANT CARTER, Scotland Yard
THE STRANGER

SCENE
(*The action takes place in the lounge of the Grinsmeads' house, near Ashbridge, Kent.*

ACT I
Scene 1 Tuesday evening.
Scene 2 Wednesday morning

ACT II
Scene 1 Later on Wednesday morning
Scene 2 Thursday morning.

ACT III
Evening five days later.

TIME
The present. A week in November.

ACT 1
SCENE 1

(*The time is about nine on a Tuesday evening. It is dark. The lamps are lighted and the curtains closed. The room is comfortably furnished, as befits the home of a prosperous country solicitor. There are two doors, to the right and left of the back wall which has a long window with french doors in the centre. The door on the left is the main door into the room and leads to the rest of the house, including the front door of the house. The door on the right leads to Mrs Grinsmead's bedroom. There are two armchairs centre stage. There is a small chair on the back wall and a fireplace down stage right, with the fire lit. There is a picture over the fireplace and a telephone on a desk on the left-hand wall of the lounge.*

As *the curtain rises Anne enters with a coffee tray. Anne is if anything plain, but she gives an impression of kindliness, honesty, and sterling worth. She is dressed in semi-evening dress. She puts the tray down on small tea table, walks to the right-hand door and knocks.*)

ANNE: Coffee's ready, Mrs. Grinsmead, when you are.

SYBIL: (*Off*) Just coming. (*Anne goes to the tea table. Sybil enters. She is about thirty-five, tallish, and rather thin, but has evidently been handsome in a cold sort of way. Her face is pale and haggard, and she conveys the impression of being unhappy and in poor health. She also is dressed in semi-evening dress.*) I thought I'd bring in the coffee myself. Gladys is clearing up the dinner things.

SYBIL: (*Smiling in a weary sort of way*). You're a lenient housekeeper, Miss Day. You spoil Gladys.

ANNE: Oh, I don't think so. (*Sympathetically.*) Tell me, how do you feel now? Headache better?

SYBIL: (*Trying to be bright.*) Oh, it's not so bad, thank you. (*Sits on the settee.*)

ANNE: The coffee may help it; it's nice and strong. (*Sits in an armchair and pours two cups of coffee.*)

SYBIL: Yes, I dare say it will. It's been better lately, I think.

ANNE: It's that special brand you like. I chased round till I got some.

SYBIL: How good of you! Oh, Miss Day, I'm glad you came here! You're the only one in this house who really cares anything for me.

ANNE: (*Holding up a warning finger.*) Now you must'nt say things like that. Everyone cares for you.
SYBIL: We needn't argue about it. But you can't think what a relief it is to have someone I can really talk to.
ANNE: I'm glad you feel like that.
SYBIL: (*Emotionally.*) Thank God, I've found a friend at last! It means a lot to me, after having been for a year without one.
ANNE: Now, here's your coffee. (*Passes the cup.*)
SYBIL: Thank you. (*Sipping the coffee*) Yes, that's nice. Where is everyone?
ANNE: Mrs. Cheame's with the children. She'll be down in a minute. Mrs. Grinsmead and Mrs. Holt went up to see a dress they were discussing at dinner.
SYBIL: I heard them.
ANNE: They said they didn't want coffee. The men of course didn't expect to be home for dinner. Maxwell's gone up to town to get his car and Mr. Grinsmead is detained at the office.
SYBIL: Then we'll only have my esteemed Australian sister-in-law. You get on pretty well with her?
ANNE: (*Surprised*). Oh yes, of course I do. Why do you ask?
SYBIL: I just wondered. *I* disliked her from the moment she entered the house and I'm sure she hates me.
ANNE: Oh, Mrs. Grinsmead, how can you say such a thing? I'm certain Mrs. Cheame doesn't hate you.
SYBIL: I know she does.
ANNE: I admit her manner is sometimes a little difficult.
SYBIL: Difficult? It's just dreadful at times.
ANNE: But can you wonder? It's only what the poor thing has been through.
SYBIL: That on the top of carping and bad temper.
ANNE: Oh no. After all she suffered, I wonder her reason didn't give way.
SYBIL: I allow for that. But even so.
ANNE: I think she's terribly to be pitied.
SYBIL: You've made friends with her at all events. By the way, you may call her Edith to me, since you do it to her face.
ANNE: She asked me to. Maxwell also.
SYBIL: He *ought* to call her Aunt Edith.
ANNE: (*Smiling.*) He forgets the "Aunt" every time.
SYBIL: I admit she's carrying out her part of our bargain. She's certainly looking after the children and in return we're certainly giving her a

home. And though it's a purely temporary arrangement she hasn't said anything about moving on.

ANNE: I don't think she knows what she wants to do.

SYBIL: Well, if she can't make up her mind she ought to go back to Australia.

ANNE: (*With a warning gesture.*) Here she is.

(*Mrs. Edith Cheame enters. She is a tall, well-built woman of about thirty, but not specially good looking. She looks capable and determined, but her face is hard.*)

ANNE: (*Jumping up.*) You're just in time, Edith. Let me pour you out a cup.

EDITH: Don't get up, Anne. I'll sit here. (*Sits in the other armchair*)

SYBIL: (*To Edith.*) Children in bed?

EDITH: In bed and asleep. I was afraid that Johnnie was developing a cold. But it's nothing. His chest is quite clear again.

SYBIL: I always forget. You're half a doctor.

(*Anne passes a cup of coffee to Edith.*)

EDITH: Oh no. My father was a doctor near Melbourne, as you know, and I thought of being one too. I took part of the course, but when my father died I had to support myself. I became receptionist to one of the Melbourne surgeons.

SYBIL: And you were there when you became engaged?

EDITH: Yes. Your brother consulted my specialist and in that way we met.

SYBIL: He was a most uncommunicative man, but he did tell us that.

(*A car is heard approaching and stopping.*)

ANNE: Here's Mr. Grinsmead. (*Looks at Sybil.*) Is the coffee helping your headache?

SYBIL: Well, it's still a little troublesome.

ANNE: What about some aspirin? It generally does you good.

SYBIL: Yes, thanks, I think I'll take some.

ANNE: (*Jumping up.*) I'll get it.

EDITH: I don't know *where* you'll get it. I was looking for it this morning and couldn't find it.

ANNE: It was in the medicine cupboard.

EDITH: It isn't there now.

ANNE: (*Moving to the main door.*) I'll have a look round at all events. (*Exits the main door.*)

EDITH: It's funny, because there was half a bottle there yesterday. Someone must have taken it out and forgotten to put it back.

SYBIL: Perhaps Gladys.

EDITH: Very likely.

(*Grinsmead enters. He is about 43, a big powerful man with a strong jaw and a determined manner. He gives the impression of ruthlessness and strong will. He is dressed in a dark lounge suit.*)

GRINSMEAD: Ah, coffee still here? That's good. I'd like a cup. (*Moving towards the armchair.*)

EDITH: As I'm beside the tray, shall I pour it out? (*Does so.*)

GRINSMEAD: Thanks, Edith. Sorry I couldn't get here earlier, specially as Mrs. Holt was arriving this afternoon. She did come, I suppose? (*He stands in front of the fire and looks at Sybil.*)

SYBIL: (*Coldly and looking away.*) Yes, she's upstairs now with your mother.

(*Edith carries Grinsmead's coffee to him, with cream jug and sugar basin. Grinsmead helps himself.*)

GRINSMEAD: Thanks.

(*Anne enters*)ANNE: I'm awfully sorry, Mrs. Grinsmead, but I can't find it anywhere.

GRINSMEAD: What is it? Anything lost?

(*Edith replaces the cream and sugar on the table, and sits.*)

ANNE: The aspirin. Mrs. Grinsmead has a nasty headache and she thought it might do her good, but we can't find the bottle.

GRINSMEAD: (*Putting his hand in his pocket and pulling out a small bottle.*) I'm afraid I'm the culprit. I'm so sorry, Sybil. I had a touch of toothache this morning. I took the bottle and clean forgot to return it. (*He hands the bottle to Anne, who opens it. When Grinsmead produces the bottle it seems to upset Sybil dreadfully. She sits staring at it with an expression of fear and horror, but makes an obvious effort to control herself.*)

SYBIL (*Breathlessly.*) Thanks so much, but on second thought … I won't have any. Aspiring sometimes upsets me, you know.

ANNE: Oh, won't you? You know it has often helped you.

SYBIL: (*Desperately.*) No, I won't take it! I won't! (*Pauses, then adds unsteadily.*) I don't feel it would do me any good.

GRINSMEAD: (*As Anne hesitates.*) Don't press her if she doesn't want it.

ANNE: Of course not. (*She puts the bottle on the table.*)

SYBIL: (*Rising.*) I think I'll go and lie down. (*Anne makes a move to go with her, but Sybil shakes her head.*) No, no, Miss Day, please don't move. Sit down and finish your coffee. (*Hysterically.*) I don't want anyone. I just want to lie down quietly.

GRINSMEAD: (*Speaking very quietly.*) All right, Miss Day; let her do as she likes.

(*Sybil goes to her room. Anne sits again in the armchair, looking puzzled and anxious. Edith looks angry and Grinsmead sad. There is a short silence.*)

ANNE: What was it, Mr. Grinsmead? Did I do anything g to upset her?

GRINSMEAD: No, no one did anything to upset her. (*He remains silent for a moment, then sighs and with an obvious effort goes on.*) I don't know that I care to discuss her, and yet I'd like your opinion.

EDITH: Our opinion?

GRISNMEAD: I mean as to how you both think she is. (*He pauses, then goes on as if the subject was painful to him.*) You know there's never anything to be gained by burying one's head in the sand. I'm afraid we must admit it's her mind.

ANNE: (*Shocked.*) Oh, don't say that! I can't believe it.

GRINSMEAD: She's been growing worse now for the last year. Before that she was as bright as a button and an absolute sport. Now she's … well, you can see what she is; unhappy and resentful and aloof.

ANNE: (*Sorrowfully.*) I know she's unhappy.

EDITH: That's true. All the same I don't think it's as bad as you imagine.

GRINSMEAD: I'm afraid you can see the trouble in all sorts of ways.

EDITH: How do you mean? Such as?

GRINSMEAD: Well, first of all, she undoubtedly has a persecution complex.

EDITH: But that's not serious.

GRINSMEAD: It's symptomatic of something serious behind. I'm not saying its very developed. Thank God she has no suicidal tendencies.

ANNE: Oh, no! No indeed!

GRINSMEAD: Then there are other things. Look for instance at her insistence on sleeping in that room. (*He motions towards the door through which Sybil exited.*)

ANNE: I've often wondered about that, but didn't like to ask.

GRINSMEAD: She used to sleep upstairs, you know. Then one day without rhyme or reason she announced that she could never sleep upstairs again; that if a room couldn't be prepared for her on the ground floor, she'd leave the house.

ANNE: And you arranged it?

GRINSMEAD: Yes. She was so worked up about it we had to bring down her bed that very day.

EDITH: There must have been some reason for it.

GRINSMEAD: We could never find any. Then there was that electric bolt she had put on the door, that she works from her bed.

ANNE: I wondered about that too.

GRINSMEAD: That was the same thing. There had been no question of bolting her door, and then one morning she insisted on having a bolt on then and there.

ANNE: And can nothing be done?

GRINSMEAD: She's been to doctors and specialists, but none of them seem to have done her any good. Then I thought that perhaps she had too much on her shoulders, and six months ago you, Miss Day, took over the burden of the housekeeping. Then two months ago, Edith, when you kindly suggested that you might look after the children, I was glad to accept your offer.

EDITH: You've made me an adequate return. Indeed I feel I should be moving on.

GRISNMEAD: I sincerely hope you won't, for the present at all events.

ANNE: I don't think Mrs. Grinsmead is getting worse. Not in the last six months in any case.

GRINSMEAD: That's really what I wanted to ask you. Do you agree with that, Edith?

EDITH: I do. I'm positive she's no worse since I've come.

GRINSMEAD: Well, that's something.

(*A child's cry is heard faintly off. Edith listens.*)

EDITH: (*Jumping up.*) Goodness, what are those children up to? I left them asleep. Excuse me, please. (*She hurries out.*)

ANNE: She's awfully good to the children.

GRINSMEAD: She seems to be.

ANNE: Oh yes, and she helps in all sorts of ways in the house. She does messages in Ashbridge when she takes the children out. She deals with the letters; sort them in the morning and posts them in the evening. She gives Gladys a hand -

GRINSMEAD: Yes, yes, I'm sure she does and we're all grateful. (*He pauses, then sits on the settee and goes on with some embarrassment.*) I've been wanting to have a word with you, Miss Day, quite between ourselves, and I dare say this is as good an opportunity as any.

ANNE: Yes, Mr. Grinsmead?

GRINSMEAD: I imagined —I don't know if I'm right?— that you and my wife had grown more — er —intimate lately? Is that so?

ANNE: Yes, it is. She's been very friendly recently.

GRINSMEAD: Well, now, if you're in her confidence I wonder if you'd do me a favour?

ANNE: Why of course! Anything I can do!

GRINSMEAD: It's not very easy to speak of. I don't know if you've noticed it, but our marriage has grown rather — well, things are — er — unfortunate.

ANNE: (*Softly.*) I was afraid so.

GRINSMEAD: Up to a year ago we got on famously, but now — (*Shrugs.*) It's miserable for her, and it's not very happy for me either.

ANNE: I'm so sorry.

GRINSMEAD: I've often wondered whether she'd like a divorce. It would be a disaster for me. I rather think it would hurt my practice, because in a town this size people are as narrow-minded as ever they were, and I need all I can make to live as we do. But I'd risk that if it would help things otherwise.

ANNE: Oh, but wouldn't that be the last resort?

GRINSMEAD: I'm afraid we've got to the last resort. Now what I want to ask you is this: Do you think you could sound her out about it? Some time when you get an opportunity? You see, she never gives me a chance to approach her about anything.

ANNE: (*Reluctantly.*) Well, if you really wish it, I will.

GRINSMEAD: I don't want you to urge her either for or against you know; only to try and get her reactions to the idea.

ANNE: I understand. I'll try.

GRINSMEAD: I'll be ever so grateful if you will.

(*Edith enters.*)

EDITH: Peace has now been proclaimed upstairs, at least an armistice has been signed — if that's anything to go by. (*She looks from one to the other.*) I'm not interrupting, I hope?

GRINSMEAD: Of course not. Matter of fact I was just going. (*Gets up.*) What you've both told me about Sybil is a great comfort to me. (*He pauses at the door.*) Do you know if Mrs. Holt will soon be down?

ANNE: I should think so. She and Mrs Grinsmead only went upstairs to look at a dress.

GRINSMEAD: (*With a dry smile.*) Only? An evening gone. (*He goes out.*)

(*Edith crosses to the fireplace, takes a cigarette from the box on the mantelpiece and lights it, all with jerky movements as if on edge.*)

EDITH: (*Trying to speak normally.*) It's all very well, this illness and persecution complex and all the rest of it, but he knows the truth as well as you or I. (*She throws herself down on the settee.*)

ANNE: What do you mean?

EDITH: I mean that's what's wrong with my respected sister-in-law is just selfishness and bad temper.

ANNE: Oh no, Edith! It's all part of her illness.

EDITH: Well, I've had enough. She hates me and I'll have to go. And I don't want to. I'm comfortable here and I've nowhere else in sight..

ANNE: Mr. Grinsmead doesn't want you to go.

EDITH: It's not him I have to deal with. There, sorry, forget my grousing. I'm a bit on edge tonight.

ANNE: We all are, I think. At least there seems to be a strain in the atmosphere.

EDITH: Maxwell's the only completely healthy person in this house.

ANNE: A bit sweeping, surely. (*After a pause.*) By the way, that sleeping draught notion of yours has turned up trumps.

EDITH: Is she going to take the draughts?

ANNE: Yes, but there was trouble enough to get her to.

EDITH: I'll be there was.

ANNE: It was really rather queer. She got into such a state when I suggested it. As excited as if I wanted her to take poison. It quite upset me.

EDITH: What was it all in aid of?

ANNE: That's just it. I don't know. She asked whose idea it was.

EDITH: You said mine?

ANNE: Yes. Then she asked if I'd mentioned it to Mr. G. I told he he had said I was to consult the doctor. Then she wanted to know what Dr. Roome had said. She made a whole song about it.

EDITH: And what *did* Dr. Roome say?

ANNE: He didn't much like the idea, but at last he said he would prescribe the draughts if someone else kept them locked up.

EDITH: (*Looks impressed.*) I see. Then who's to give them to her?

ANNE: I am.

EDITH: Well, I'm glad I suggested something right! It's about the first time.

ANNE: Funny the fuss she made, though. She gave me the impression of being frightened.

EDITH: Frightened? Good Lord! Of what?

ANNE: I don't know. An overdose perhaps.

EDITH: What rot! Why should she take an overdose? (*There is the sound of an approaching car.*) Hullo! Listen! Sounds like Maxwell.

ANNE: Been up to town for his new car. He's talked of nothing else for days.
EDITH: You're telling me! I thought it was second-hand?
ANNE: New to him, I mean. He bought it from a friend.
EDITH: (*With sarcasm.*) I know: profits on the deal, one car; losses, one friend.
ANNE: I'm all for optimism myself, Edith, but don't overdo it.
EDITH: he was getting something done to it?
ANNE: Yes, having it re-cellulosed. I gather the Daimler's day is done.
EDITH: Huh! Maxwell's swans have a goose-like sub-stratum.
(*Maxwell Crawley enters. He is a pleasant-looking youth of about 24, healthy and commonplace. He wears sporty clothes.*)
MAXWELL: (*Cheerily.*) Hullo, everybody! I say, I've got the bus. Done up just like new.
ANNE: Grand! Is she as good as you hoped?
MAXWELL: Hundred per cent. Got 63 out of her on the way down.
EDITH: How many people killed?
MAXWELL: Oh no, only a few. She just leaps ahead when you shoot her the gas.
EDITH: (*Getting up.*) The "Kangaroo" or "Bounding Bus." I can see her loping along with you two in the little pocket. (*She moves to the door.*)
ANNE: Be an angel and take the tray if you're going out.
EDITH: I must run upstairs. I'm afraid I left the light on. I pity you while he's getting it off his chest.
ANNE: Oh, for heaven's sake go and see to your light.
(*Edith exits with tray.*)
MAXWELL: I say, Anne, she was right about my wanting to take you for a run. What about it?
ANNE: In the middle of the night? When I go out I like to see the country. (*She gets up and has a look round the room, putting the tea table back and generally tidying up.*)
MAXWELL: Well, hang it, the headlamps throw plenty of light.
ANNE: Quite. But I'm not interested in tarmac.
MAXWELL: What about tomorrow then? Do come, Anne! Tomorrow afternoon.
ANNE: I *might*.
MAXWELL: Right! I'll be ready after lunch. Let's go to Friar's Crags.
ANNE: Why Friar's Crags?
MAXWELL: Because I love the place. It was there I met you first.

ANNE: (*Shivering.*) Oh, I don't like Friar's Crags.
MAXWELL: Why not? What's wrong with the place?
ANNE: It was there I met you first! (*She sits at the end of the settee. Maxwell sits beside her.*)
MAXWELL: Just for that you're going to give me a kiss!
ANNE: (*Fending him off.*) Just for that I'm going to do nothing of the sort.
MAXWELL: (*Putting an arm round her.*) Anne, don't be an absolute pig. (*Edith enters left.*)
EDITH: You two had better cut out the love-stuff. Mrs. Grinsmead's just coming in and then you'll have to watch your step. (*She sits in the armchair.*)
MAXWELL: Oh, Grin? She's all right. She's an old sport.
EDITH: I didn't say she wasn't. I said she was coming in.
MAXWELL: (*Getting up.*) That's OK by me. Anyway I must go and put the car away. (*He exits left.*)
EDITH: The boy's right sbout the old lady. She really is a good sport.
ANNE: (*Doubtfully.*) Yes, I suppose so. But I do think she's unkind about Sybil. She's terribly bitter about her.
EDITH: What do you expect? She sees Sybil doing her damnedest to ruin her's son's life. No wonder she hates the sight of her.
(*Mrs. Grinsmead enters left. She is a widow of seventy, with a pale face and white hair. She looks old and frail, but alert, and suggests the determination noticeable in her son.*)
ANNE: (*Jumping up.*) Come over to the fire, Mrs. Grinsmead, won't you? It's turned quite cold. (*She gives Mrs. Grinsmead her place on the settee and sits on a chair.*)
MRS. G.: (*Sitting on the settee.*) It *is* cold. I wonder my son doesn't put in gas or electric fires? They *are* so convenient.
EDITH: One was installed in Sybil's room lately. She wanted a fire all night without having to get up to stoke it.
MRS. G.: Pity it was only done in her room.
EDITH: Well, you see, hers was so easy to fix. The only gas in the house was to the kitchen cooker, and as the kitchen's just behind's Sybil's room, it only meant running a pipe through the wall.
MRS. G.: Of course to do the whole house would have been a big job.
EDITH: Oh, I don't know. I heard Richard say he had ordered electrics for the other rooms.
MRS. G.: Has my son come in yet?
EDITH: Yes, a few minutes ago.

MRS. G.: I can't make out what's the matter with Sybil. She's evidently upset again this evening. (*She pauses.*) I'm very much distressed about her — about the situation here.
ANNE: She really isn't well, you know, Mrs. Grinsmead.
MRS. G.: (*Frigidly.*) I don't mind her attitude to myself, but when I see the way she behaves to my son, my blood boils. I know I shouldn't talk like this about my daughter-in-law, but I'm afraid of something happening. What *has* upset her so much tonight?
ANNE: (*After a pause and doubtfully.*) I don't think she likes Mrs. Holt very much.
MRS. G.: H'mm. *Whom* does she like?
ANNE: She never did like Mrs. Holt: I can't think why not.
MRS. G.: Mrs. Holt seems a very nice woman to me. Who is she exactly?
EDITH: The widow of a naval man. Till a couple of months ago she lived quite near here, but now she's moved up to town.
ANNE: She's come for a week.
MRS. G.: She was showing me a dress she made herself: charming, I thought, but too youthful for me.
(*Irene Holt enters left. She is a smartly dressed woman of about 40, extremely good-looking. She is wearing make up, and gives the impression of being very much a woman of the world. Her face is rather hard and her manner conventionally polite, but not cordial.*)
MRS. G.: (*To Irene.*) I wonder how it was we didn't meet when I was here last year? I understand you were living in the neighbourhood then?
IRENE: Yes, until a couple of months ago. Then my lease was up and I had to move. As a matter of fact, that's what has brought me down now.
MRS. G.: Yes?
IRENE: The landlord has brought an action against me for not doing repairs which he should have done himself. The case is coming up to-morrow.
MRS. G.: What a horrid bore!
IRENE: Mr. and Mrs. Grinsmead were so kind. They've asked to stay here till it's over.
(*The door left opens and Maxwell puts in his head.*)
MAXWELL: Hey, Edith, those kids are monkeying with the bath and the water's beginning to come down the stairs. (*He winks surreptitiously at Anne.*)
EDITH: (*Jumping up.*) Drat the little beggars. I'll 'water' them. (*She hurries out. Maxwell grins at Anne, disappears, and the door shuts. The others*

laugh.)

ANNE: I think he's only pulling her leg. He's always trying to get a rise out of her.

MRS. G.: I dare say she gets her own back.

ANNE: (*Smiling.*) With interest as a rule.

IRENE: She wasn't here in my time.

MRS. G.: Oh, don't you know? She's Sybil's sister-in-law, her brother's widow. An Australian …

IRENE: Oh indeed. Is she going to live over here?

MRS. G.: I don't think she has made up her mind. Poor thing, she has had a rough time. Edwin Cheame, Sybil's brother, was a sheep farmer, a comparatively young man. He was doing well and everything seemed promising when his horse put its foot into a hole and fell. It rolled on Edwin. He was taken up dead.

IRENE: How tragic!

MRS. G.: Edith sold up, I understand very advantageously, and came to see what England was like. She had a terrible experience on the way. Tell her, Miss Day. You know the details better than I.

ANNE: Oh yes, it was perfectly ghastly. She was on board the *City of Brisbane*. You remember? It was sunk in collision with the loss of nearly four hundred lives.

IRENE: Oh poor thing! Was she on that?

ANNE : She was in the third boat: the one that wasn't picked up for ten days. Mr. Grinsmead kept the newspaper account of it, if you'd like to read it.

IRENE: I should indeed.

ANNE: (*Getting up and taking a scrapbook from a drawer. She sits again in the armchair.*) The whole thing was just unspeakable. This cutting appeared ten days after the collision, you understand. I'll read it.

IRENE: Please do.

ANNE: (*Reading.*) "Another boat from the ill-fated *City of Brisbane* has been picked up. It will be remembered that she was rammed in a fog by the 12,000 ton Argentine freighter *Santos* about 800 miles south-east of Cape Guardafui and sank in less than an hour. The *Santos* picked up two boatloads of survivors, and though herself badly damaged, was able to make port. Seven other boats were unaccounted for, and it was feared that in the great gale of four days later all had perished. Now a third has been picked up by the British liner *Dungeness*, due in London on 17th. The rescue of the crew in the heavy weather appears to have been an epic of the sea equal to anything in the past,"

IRENE: The poor souls; First the collision and then the storm! What a time they must have had!

ANNE: (*Reading.*) "Fourth Officer Grayson was in charge of the boat, and of the forty-two people who left the ship in it, only thirty-one remained alive."

IRENE: Thirty-one out of forty-two!

MRS. G: Edith was certainly one of the lucky ones.

ANNE : Oh but fancy, in the boat through that gale and eleven of the people dying! She never could be the same again.

MRS. G.: You notice the strain in her manner sometimes. Shows temper too.

IRENE: Can you wonder? Then she took charge of the children here?

ANNE: Yes. She was at a loose end: had never been in England before and knew no one. Mr. and Mrs. Grinsmead asked her to stay while she was looking round, and she offered to help with the children in return.

IRENE: An admirable arrangement for both parties, I should think.

ANNE: Yes, but of course it's only temporary.

(*Grinsmead enters*)

GRINSMEAD: How d'you do, Mrs. Holt? Nice to see you again. So sorry I wasn't home for dinner. The old excuse, you know: detained at the office. (*He crosses to Anne and shakes hands. Turning to Mrs Grinsmead, senior*) Hullo, Mother! Haven't seen you since yesterday.

MRS. G.: (*Smiling.*) No, indeed.

IRENE: We were just speaking of the case. I feel like a stormy petrel bringing discord into the peaceful atmosphere of Ashbridge.

GRINSMEAD: Oh, you didn't *bring* the discord, Mrs. Holt. I mustn't talk shop, but it really is a disgraceful case for any landlord to bring.

MRS. G.: (*To Irene.*) Shall you have to attend court tomorrow?

IRENE: Oh yes, I'm afraid so.

(*Edith enters the main door. She grins at Anne with a gesture as much as to say, "I'll murder him!", but does not interrupt conversation.*)

MRS. G:. I do sympathise.

GRINSMEAD: Oh, you won't find it too bad. By the way, what about coming along to the study and going over one or two of the points? It won't take long and we shall have got the thing straight in our minds.

IRENE: (*Standing up.*) Yes, I should like to. It's very good of you.

GRINSMEAD: Not at all. We can't let old Fraser have everything his

own way. (*Grinsmead and Irene go out. Edith sits in the chair.*)
MRS. G.: It is really hard luck having to spend a day in a musty old court being badgered by — what do they call them? — 'hostile counsel'.
EDITH: I believe English lawyers can be dreadful.
ANNE: Mr. Grinsmead won't let them annoy her.
MRS. G.: (*Drily.*) You have great faith in my son.
(*Maxwell enters.*)
MAXWELL: Hullo, Gran! I've got the car! (*Sits on pouffe.*)
ANNE: (*Speaking together.*) She's dark green and she's a pippin! Sorry and all that, but we've heard it before.
ANNE: Well, if you'll excuse me, I must go and lock up. (*She goes out left.*)
EDITH: (*To Maxwell.*) You'll be able to drive Mrs. Holt to the count tomorrow.
MAXWELL: (*Disparagingly.*) Oh? Has *she* come?
EDITH: Yes. Aren't you pleased?
MAXWELL: (*Shrugs.*) She's not my type.
EDITH: (*Getting up.*) My! Listen to the man of the world! Excuse me, Mrs. Grinsmead, I must run away too. I've some things to attend to. (*She goes out left.*)
MRS. G.: And what exactly is your type, Maxwell?
MAXWELL: What about old Anne?
MRS. G.: (*Glancing at him keenly.*) You admire Miss Day then?
MAXWELL: I should say I do! Don't you?
MRS. G.: Yes, very much.
MAXWELL: (*With sudden interest.*) You do, Gran? You do really? (*Gets up and walks about.*)
MRS.G.: I do really.
MAXWELL: (*Very confidential and enthusiastic.*) Oh, Gran, there's nobody like her! I'll tell you something no one else knows. I want to marry her!
MRS. G.: Are you sure no one else knows it?
MAXWELL: Well, she knows herself; I've told her.
MRS.G.: And what does she say?
MAXWELL: Can't get her pinned down. But she'll say yes: I know she will — in time.
MRS.G.: (*Puts her head on one side as if trying to recall.*) I seem to remember: (*Glances at him quizzically.*) There was once a young lady of Ashbridge. (*She rhythms it like a limerick.*) But of course I shouldn't know —
MAXWELL: Come now, Gran, that's not fair. There never was; not really,

you know. This is different. (*Sits on the settee beside Mrs. Grinsmead.*)

MRS. G.: I wonder.

MAXWELL: It's quite different. You see, Gran, the whole thing —I've been wanting a chance to tell you. It —really — depends on you.

(*During this conversation Mrs. Grinsmead is knitting. Maxwell picks up her ball of wool and absently unwinds it. Mrs. Grinsmead twice takes it from him.*)

MRS. G.: On me, does it? Funny now, I should have thought it depended on her. (*She smiles.*)

MAXWELL: On you, really. You see, my salary's not quite what — it ought to be. It'll be all right of course in time. And you know that under grandfather's will there's money coming to me. But just now— I haven't really got enough — not to marry on. You know what I mean?

MRS. G.: (*As if a light dawns on her.*) Why, I believe I can guess.

MAXWELL: Yes. That's it, you see. And she hasn't —well, I don't think she has much at all. So that my salary's important.

MRS. G.: Very important, I should think.

MAXWELL: Well, there you are. I wondered, Gran I wondered if you could possibly see your way to — well, make us a sort of loan, something I could pay off later. How about a mortgage or something on what's coming to me?

MRS. G.: But you tell me Miss Day isn't — er — *pinned*, I think you said. Wouldn't it be better to settle that part of it before embarking on financial arrangements?

MAXWELL: Good Lord, I'm trying hard enough. I mention it every day, but so far there's nothing doing. But she will: I'm sure of it. You see, what I want is to be able to say to her, "We can be married at once. We won't have to wait." It might make all the difference.

MRS. G.: Let's see; how old are you now?

MAXWELL: Twenty-four.

MRS. G.: (*Reminiscently.*) I can see you in your cot squalling for a teddy bear; just like yesterday. You were a hideous baby.

MAXWELL: I say, Gran!

MRS. G.: And a revolting child.

MAXWELL: But now a cultured and charming young man.

MRS. G.: Said he, modestly. Oh well, this is rather a shock to me, but if you must commit matrimony I'd rather it was Miss Day than anyone else. She's a very fine young woman.

MAXWELL: Fine! She's absolutely it!
MRS. G.: Well, go and ask her again. If she consents, I don't say I mightn't consider the money.
MAXWELL: Gran! How splendid you are!
MRS. G.: I only said, might, remember. Oh dear, talking of money reminds me of a letter I must write.
MAXWELL: Never mind it now. You've missed the mail.
MRS. G.: (*Getting up.*) No, I mustn't be so lazy. The postman will take it in the morning.
(*Mrs. Grinsmead goes to the main door and Maxwell rushes to open it for her. She smiles at him and goes out. Maxwell takes a cigarette, then in pantomime goes through all the motions of proposing to a girl. As he is finishing by kneeling on one knee at the settee Anne enters. He jumps up and dusts his knee.*)
MAXWELL: Good Lord, Anne, what a time you've been;
ANNE: (*Stopping short and looking at him.*) Well, I like that! Since when have I been at your beck and call?
MAXWELL: Oh, don't be an owl! I mean that when you're not here everything sort of stops. Look, Anne, I may have mentioned it before, but it's got overlooked. Will you marry me?
ANNE: Incidentally, on your way to golf?
MAXWELL: No, do be serious. I have my eye on a little cottage.
ANNE: Why a *little* cottage? I prefer large houses. (*Sits in an armchair*)
MAXWELL: (*Walking up and down.*) If I get the cottage will you marry me? What about it, Anne?
ANNE: I must live in the heart of the country at least ten miles from anywhere.
MAXWELL: That's easy! The further from town, the cheaper the cottage.
ANNE: But I must also have electric light, gas, water, main drainage, and be two minutes from church and bus.
MAXWELL: Oh, we won't bother with buses. What about a Rolls?
ANNE: H'mm. Must be pink with scarlet upholstery.

MAXWELL: Anne, do be serious for a moment, there's a darling! I've got a bit of news. I was just telling the old lady that I was going to be married and what do you think she -
ANNE: *What* have you told her? Whom are you going to marry? I am interested.

MAXWELL: Of course you're interested. Concerned, really. Vitally concerned in fact.
ANNE: What *do* you mean? What have you been saying to your grandmother?
MAXWELL: Asking her blessing, my dear! And she was all for it. More than that, what do you think she's going to do? Make me an advance so that we can be married at once. What d'you think of that?
ANNE: (*Jumping up and rounding on him.*) What did you say to her? Tell me at once !
MAXWELL: Why, just that. I asked her for an advance to get married on and she's considering it.
ANNE: Do you mean to say you mentioned my name?
MAXWELL: I mentioned your name. How else would she know who I was talking about? She asked if you'd promised to — er — come into the scheme. I said, well, not exactly, but I had great hopes. She said there was nothing she'd like so much.
ANNE: (*Steps towards him. He steps back.*) Well! of all the nerve! How dare you say such a thing? (*Edith enters left, unseen.*) When did I ever give you the slightest excuse? You really are the limit. I never heard of such a thing !
EDITH: (*Moving to them.*) That's the stuff! Slap him down, Anne! See what a hell the rest of your life's going to be, young man. Didn't think she had it in her, did you?
ANNE: (*Stamping her foot.*) That's enough from you, Edith! You're impossible too.
EDITH: Come now, my dear. Come off it. Why should you *mind* what he says? What did you say any way, oaf?
MAXWELL: (*Very injured.*) Nothing; only that I hoped to get married and -
ANNE: Now that's enough! I've told you !
EDITH: You'd better lay off the subject, young man. Can't you see when the sky's stormy? Look here, Anne, I have a yearning to go out and see whether Trixy's pups have materialized. Will you come?
ANNE: Rather. But I think it's too soon. They weren't expected till tomorrow.
EDITH: It won't take a moment. (*To Maxwell .*) And you'd better go while the going's good.
MAXWELL: (*Still very injured.*) But I only said -
EDITH: You *are* a mutt! Come along, Anne.

(*Anne and Edith go out through the French windows after each has bestowed a dirty look on Maxwell.*)
MAXWELL: (*As they go.*) Yes, but hang it all, Anne — (*He kicks the pouffe.*) Oh Lord, this must be Friday the thirteenth. (*He follows them out through the French window.*)
(*The main door opens and Grinsmead looks in. He looks round room, then back to the hall.*)
GRINSMEAD: No one's here. They've all gone. (*He holds the door open and Irene enters.*) Oh, by the way, there's the picture; the one I was telling you about. (*Indicating the picture over the fireplace.*)
IRENE : Oh of course, I want to see it. (*She moves over and looks at picture.*)
GRINSMEAD: It's supposed to be valuable, though I never could see much in it.
TRENE: I like it.
GRINSMEAD: It must be good, I think. Sybil's R.A.[1] friend thinks no end of it and he ought to know. (*Stands gazing at it as if he was in a trance.*) A little further back. You're too close, according to him.
(*Irene, still looking at picture, backs into the pouffe and Grinsmead springs forward and catches her in his arms. The contact with her seems too much for him. He holds her for a moment, then crushes her in his arms and kisses her passionately. Her handbag falls unnoticed by the tea table.*)
IRENE: (*In a low desperate voice.*) Richard! Are you mad? Not here! Someone may come in !
GRINSMEAD: I don't care who comes in. You're mine now, Irene, and I'll never let you go.
IRENE: (Pushing him away.) Oh please, *please* don't! Suppose your wife were to come in.
GRINSMEAD: Wouldn't it be better if she did? We'd end this nightmare once and for all! Look at me, Irene.
(*Grinsmead takes her face between his hands and kisses her passionately. Irene resists at first, then clings to him.*)
IRENE: Oh, Richard, I can't bear it! We can't go on like this !
GRINSMEAD: My darling!
IRENE: It's too dreadful, this life! Just meeting in public as strangers. I tell you I can't stand it !
GRINSMEAD: Now listen, dear. Things will soon be different.
IRENE: Just a stolen moment now and then. Oh, Richard, if you love me you'll do something.

---

[1] Royal Academy of Arts, an independent, privately funded institution in London, England.

GRINSMEAD: You *know* I love you more than my life!
IRENE: I know you love me, dear. But we can't go on like this. Now let me go. Someone will come in.
GRINSMEAD: Well, give me another kiss.
(*He takes her in his arms once more and they kiss passionately. As they do so the door left. opens and Anne enters. Grinsmead and Irene do not see her. Anne stands transfixed.*) I'll find a way, darling.
 IRENE: You must! You must or I'll kill myself!
GRINSMEAD: Oh, please don't talk like that! I tell you I'll find a way.
(*Anne horrified, withdraws silently.*)
IRENE: Now let me go.
(*Grinsmead releases Irene and they look at each other sadly.*)
GRINSMEAD: The case can't take all day tomorrow. We'll have a little time together.
IRENE: A little time! That's all it ever is. Just enough to tantalize!
(*Grinsmead and Irene move towards the door. Irene's hair is slightly rumpled. She runs her hand over it.*)
IRENE: Oh, my hair! What on earth do I look like? I mustn't meet anyone.
GRINSMEAD: You look perfect, darling; you always do. (*He opens the door left*)
IRENE: No: I mustn't be seen. (*She listens, then speaks softly.*) Someone's coming!
GRINSMEAD: (*Pulls aside the curtain and opens the French windows.*) We'll go out this way and in by the side door. Then you can slip up to your room. (*Grinsmead and Irene go out.*
(*The curtain swings back into place and the closing of the window is heard. The handbag remains under the tea table. Anne, approaching noisily, enters left, takes a quick look round the room, looks relieved, walks to the other door and knocks. As she does so the door opens and Sybil enters.*)
SYBIL: So sorry to ring for you, Miss Day, but I think after all I'll take the aspirin. Do you know where it was left?
ANNE: (*Picking up the bottle of tablets from the tea table and unscrewing the top.*) Here we are. Two?
SYBIL: Yes, please. I didn't want it just now, but my headache's no better.
ANNE: I'm sure it'll fix you up. Water?
SYBIL: (*Taking two tablets.*) Please.
(*Anne moves towards the door left, but Sybil stops her.*)
SYBIL: By the way, how long does it take for letters to come from Aus-

tralia?
ANNE: (*Pausing at the door.*) Oh, I don't know. Quite a time. Is it airmail?
SYBIL: Yes.
ANNE: I should think about a fortnight, there and back. But I don't really know.
SYBIL: I thought so, but it must take longer.
ANNE: Why do you ask?
SYBIL : I wrote some time ago to those photographers in Melbourne who took the portrait of my brother that Edith brought home, asking if they had any more family pictures. I told them to send any they had by airmail. They haven't come.
ANNE: I think there was a reply. I saw a letter from Melbourne in the box.
SYBIL: I haven't seen it.
ANNE: It's been mislaid somewhere. I'll look for it. I suppose Edith told you what pictures there were?
SYBIL: (*Bitterly.*) I didn't consult Edith and I don't want you to either. I don't discuss anything with her if I can avoid it.
ANNE: Oh, Mrs. Grinsmead, I do think you're too hard on her. It's as I said, her manner is difficult, but it's what she's been through.
(*Grinsmead enters; he searches for and finds Irene's bag. Sybil sits motionless.*)
GRINSMEAD: Mrs. Holt dropped her bag. (*Sybil looks like thunder. He notices it and goes on speaking.*) We've been going over the ground in connection with the case tomorrow. (*Pauses.*) I think — she'll win. (*He goes out.*)
SYBIL: Win! Of course she'll win! (*With a vehement gesture she throws the aspirins into the fire.*) Oh, I can't stand it! I can't! In my own house!
ANNE: (*Her face falling.*) What is it, Mrs. Grinsmead? What can't you stand? (*Anne approaches Sybil.*)
SYBIL : That woman! Actually staying here — in this house! (*Wildly.*) I shouldn't say anything about my own husband, but I must! I must! For a year I've kept it bottled up, till I felt I was going mad! I *am* going mad, I think!
ANNE: Dear Mrs. Grinsmead, you're no more mad than I am.
SYBIL: Haven't you seen what's going on? Do you mean to say you don't know? Oh, I thought everyone must know!
ANNE: Know what? I —
SYBIL: Don't you know that all he wants is that woman: that all *she* wants is him? Don't you know that they want me — dead! (*Her voice rises*

almost to a scream.)
ANNE: (*Shocked.*) Mrs. Grinsmead, don't say such a thing.
SYBIL: They're waiting their opportunity, biding their time! There'll be an accident, or it may look like suicide. But the result will be the same. I'll be dead.
ANNE: No, no: please don't talk like that! You're wrong! They don't wish you any harm.
SYBIL: Haven't you seen them together? Where are your eyes? Do you mean to tell me you never suspected?
ANNE: (*Hesitatingly.*) I did think they were fond of one another, yes. But the other —! Oh no, it's too dreadful! They couldn't possibly think of such a thing!
SYBIL: (*Despairingly.*) I know it!
ANNE: No! You must put such a thought out of your mind. It's not true!
SYBIL: It *is* true! Oh Anne — I must call you Anne and won't you call me Sybil? — You're the only friend I have. What am I to do? (*She makes a despairing gesture and comes to Anne as if for support. Anne guides her to the settee and sits down beside her.*)
ANNE: Sybil dear, I just hate to think what you must have gone through with such thoughts in your mind. But that's all over now. (*Pause.*) You don't mind my speaking frankly?
SYBIL: (*Wearily.*) Say anything you like, only help me, Anne.
ANNE: I'm absolutely certain you're wrong in these terrible suspicions. But if you're really convinced about it, why not go away for a time?
SYBIL: Away?
ANNE: Why not leave here, if only temporarily, if it would ease your mind?
SYBIL: I've nowhere to go. My people are dead and I've no money.
ANNE: I'm sure Mr. Grinsmead would take care of that.
SYBIL: To get rid of me? No, that would be no good to him.
ANNE: What about a divorce?
SYBIL: No proof, no evidence. They're too clever for that. He wouldn't have a divorce because it would ruin his practice.
ANNE: (*With a triumphant air.*) Well now, Sybil, I can tell you you're wrong. Absolutely and completely wrong. Mr. Grinsmead *would* consider a divorce.
SYBIL: (*Sitting up and staring wildly.*) What do you mean? What *do* you mean, Anne.
ANNE: He wanted to speak to you himself, but he thought it better to

send a message through me.
SYBIL: Yes? Yes? Go on!
ANNE: He admitted that your marriage had turned out unhappily, and he asked me if I would sound you as to whether you'd consider a divorce.
SYBIL: (*Greatly excited.*) Anne! (*Clutching her arm.*) Was it his own suggestion?
ANNE: Why yes: of course.
SYBIL: Anne! Don't you see what he means? Don't you see?
ANNE: See what? What do *you* mean, Sybil?
SYBIL: (*Almost screaming.*) That it's the end!
ANNE: The end?
SYBIL: Yes! He's going to act! He wants your evidence on his side! Oh, Anne, don't you see?
ANNE: Sybil, how *can* you think such a thing?
SYBIL: I tell you he wants to have you on *his* side if anything should happen to me! He wants you to say he was trying for a divorce! Think of it and you'll see how strong your evidence would be! Oh, Anne, what am I to do? (*She bursts into tears. Anne puts her arms round her.*)
ANNE: Now look here, Sybil, we'll fight this thing together. We'll find a way out.
SYBIL: (*Sobbing.*) It's too late.
ANNE: It's not too late. Sybil, do get this thing off your mind for good and all. Just *exactly what* have you feared?
SYBIL: (*After a pause.*) Murder!
ANNE: Has anything definite occurred to frighten you?
SYBIL: (*Hesitating.*) Nothing has actually happened. But I've been afraid.
ANNE: Of what?
SYBIL: (*Speaking with hesitation and after a pause.*) Well, if you must know, of fire.
ANNE: Of fire?
SYBIL: Yes; it was something I read. (*There is horror in her voice.*) A man had wanted to murder his wife. He gave her a sleeping draught and then set the house on fire.
ANNE: Oh, how awful! (*A light dawns on her.*) Was that why you suddenly decided to sleep downstairs?
SYBIL: Yes, that was it. I thought I could escape by the window. And that's why your idea of my taking sleeping draughts upset me so much. I thought it was *his* suggestion and that I knew what he was going to do. (*She shudders.*)

ANNE: You poor dear! How perfectly awful! But you know now you were wrong in this? You know exactly whose idea it was?

SYBIL: (*Dully.*) Yes, you told me. I *was* wrong that time. But I'll not be wrong the next.

ANNE: Now have you told me everything? You'll find it such a relief to get it off your mind. Were you afraid of anything else?

SYBIL: Yes: that he would come into the room at night and ... (*She shudders.*) I've lain awake hour after hour expecting every moment to see the door slowly open ... I've almost screamed. Then I thought of the bolt. I've felt safer since.

ANNE: Well, things are going to be different from now on. You must put all these thoughts behind you. Now that I know what the trouble is, I'm sure I can help you. Come now, it's time for bed, isn't it? D'you feel like going?

SYBIL: I suppose so. (*She looks at Anne, puts an arm round Anne and impulsively kisses her.*) Oh, Anne, thank God for you! I've found a friend! Why didn't I find you sooner?

ANNE: Of course I'm your friend. (*Becoming very practical.*) Now I hope your gas fire's burning? It's a cold night.

SYBIL: Yes, Gladys lit it. But she left it full on. That was too much: I turned it down to half. (*She is gradually becoming calmer.*)

ANNE: That's all right. Now another thing. I suggest a sleeping draught. It'll quiet you down. What do you think?

SYBIL: Very well: I didn't take the aspirin after all. And then I'll bolt my door.

ANNE: That's right. Bolt the door and you're absolutely safe.

SYBIL: I hope so.

ANNE: And I'm there night and morning. I won't go away till I hear the click of your bolt, and I'm at the door with your tea before you open it in the morning.

SYBIL: You *are* sweet to me, Anne.

ANNE: Now off you go to your room! I'll get your sleeping draught.

(*Anne goes out. Sybil moves slowly to the door to her room., listens, registers nervousness and looks into the room before entering. Finally she enters the other room and closes the door behind her. Edith enters the room, looks around, and is going out again when Anne comes in behind her.*)

EDITH: Oh, I was just looking for you. I didn't have much dinner and I thought of making myself a cup of tea. Care for some?

ANNE: I never say "No," to tea. I'll join you in the kitchen when I've given

Sybil this sleeping draught.
EDITH: You're not going to sit with her tonight?
ANNE: No, she's tired and wants to go to sleep.
EDITH: Right! I'll have it ready when you come.
(*Edith goes out of the main door. Anne examines the bottle to check the dose she should give Sybil. Satisfied that it is OK, she goes to the door to Sybil's room and knocks gently.*)
ANNE. It's Anne, dear. May I come in?
SYBIL. (*Off.*) Come in.
(*Anne enters, leaving the door open.*)
ANNE. (*Off.*) Here you are, Sybil. Everything all right?
SYBIL. (*Off.*) Yes, thank you.
ANNE. (*Off.*) Good night then, dear, and sleep well.
SYBIL. (*Off.*) Good night. And oh, Anne, God bless you!
(*Anne re-enters the lounge with an empty glass in her hand. She shuts the door to Sybil's room and stands by it, listening. The click of the bolt is heard. Anne tries the door. It is fast. She looks round the lounge and then at the glass in her hand. She switches off the light and goes out of the main door.*)

ACT 1
SCENE 2

(*The next morning. Daylight outside the windows lights the room dimly through the curtains. The fire is out. Anne, dressed in an overall, enters the main door with a tea tray. She puts it on the table and pulls back the curtains. The room becomes light. Anne picks up the tray and goes to the door to Sybil's room and knocks. There is no answer. She waits a moment.*)

ANNE: (*Knocking again.*) Sybil!
(*There is no answer.*)
(*She knocks again.*) Sybil!
(*There is no answer.*)
(*She knocks louder.*) Sybil!
(*Again, there is no answer. Anne sniffs the air. For a moment she stands motionless, then hurriedly putting the tray down on cabinet beside door, she flings herself at the door, trying to open it. It is fast. She cries "Sybil" with dreadful urgency. There is no answer and she screams desperately, then shouts*

"Help! Help!". Anne continues to shout and scream till the others come. After a suitable pause, Grinsmead hurries in by the main door, wearing a dressing gown; Edith, also in a dressing gown, does the same. Mrs Grinsmead Senior follows, fully dressed. Maxwell rushes in a dressing gown.)

GRINSMEAD: (*Urgently.*) What is it?
ANNE: (*Stabbing with her finger towards the door to Sybil's room.*) Gas! Smell it!
GRINSMEAD: (*Stoops and smells at the keyhole, then recoils, shouting.*) Heavens! Open the windows! Turn off the gas at the meter!
MAXWELL: (*Shouting.*) Right! (*He rushes out of the door. Edith throws open one window and Mrs. Grinsmead another.*)
GRINSMEAD: (*Pointing to the cabinet.*) Miss Day! Tools in there! Quick!
(*Anne opens the cabinet and hands some tools to Grinsmead, who snatches them from her then drives a chisel in between the door and frame and prises. After some work, the door cracks and swings open just as Maxwell rushes back into the lounger through the main door.*)
GRINSMEAD: Maxwell! Quick!
(*Grinsmead and Maxwell disappear into the bedroom. After a few seconds they re-appear, carrying Sybil. All indicate a difficulty in breathing. Sybil is wrapped in a rug and not clearly seen.*)
EDITH: (*Pointing at the settee.*) Here! Here! Lay her here!
GRINSMEAD: (*As he and Maxwell carry Sybil to the set tee.*) Ring up Dr. Roome.
(*Anne rushes to the telephone. Maxwell closes and makes fast the bedroom door. Mrs Grinsmead Senior goes to the settee, still with hands clasped.*)
ANNE: (*On the telephone.*) Hullo! Four two one. Quickly, please …four two one.
(*Grinsmead lays Sybil down on the settee. The body is never clearly seen. All but Anne stand round watching him.*)
ANNE: (*On the telephone.*) Hullo! Is that you, doctor? Oh, doctor, please come quickly! Mrs. Grinsmead… gas poisoning … I'm afraid so … Do hurry… Right! (*She replaces the receiver and crosses to the others.*) Dr. Roome's coming at once.
(*Edith and Grinsmead bend over Sybil examining her. The others stand watching. Irene enters with a surprised and frightened face.*)
IRENE: What is it? What has happened?
ANNE: Mrs. Grinsmead. Gas poisoning. We've just found her.

(*Irene gasps and murmurs unintelligibly. She looks at Sybil and stands as if turned to stone.*)
MRS. G: I'd get some blankets, I think.
MAXWELL: (*Nods.*) I'll get them. (*He hurries out.*)
MRS. G: I suggest a hot bottle.
ANNE: Right! (*She is hurrying out, but Edith looks at her and shakes her head. Anne pauses irresolutely.*)
GRINSMEAD: (*To Edith.*) What do you think? Should we try artificial respiration?
EDITH: (*Much agitated.*) Oh, Richard, how can I say it? (*Wrings her hands.*) It would do no good! Nothing would do any good now! She's — she's — dead!
(*Grinsmead stares as if transfixed. All stand overcome with horror.*)

CURTAIN

ACT 2
SCENE 1

(*About eleven o'clock that same Wednesday morning. The fire is burning. All are in day clothes. Edith is seated in an armchair. Anne enters by the main door.*)

ANNE: (*With a gesture.*) Oh, Edith, isn't it *awful*! I simply can't undestand it.
EDITH: I feel it too and I don't know why, for I thought that after what I'd seen, I'd never feel anything again.
ANNE: I'm afraid I'm selfish. Compared to what you've been through, this is — well, it's not much. But still — the poor, poor thing! (*She sits on the settee.*)
EDITH: What happened to her was what she wanted herself.
ANNE: Oh I know. But just think what she must have suffered — to want it.
EDITH: It's worse when people want desperately to live and have to sit

quiet and watch death coming nearer.

ANNE: And you've seen that! I don't know how you kept your sanity!

EDITH: I don't know myself. (*Pauses then, as if her self-control breaks, she wrings her hands.*) I think there must be some curse on me. Wherever I go there's tragedy.

ANNE: Edith, don't say that! It *is* awful for you having this on top of your other experiences, but that's just chance.

EDITH: It's more than chance. (*She becomes excited and slightly out of control.*) It was worse on the steamer — worse than anything I told you.

ANNE: Worse?

EDITH: Far worse. I saw —(*She breaks down and sobs.*) I saw— my best friend on board — killed! Before my eyes!

ANNE: Oh, Edith! How *awful*! (*Pauses.*) Tell me — if you care to.

EDITH: (*Struggling for self-control.*) It was when the collision occurred. We were walking together on deck. Some huge thing, I think it was a mast, fell on one of the boats and crushed it like an eggshell.

ANNE: Yes?

EDITH: The shock knocked us both down. I rolled clear of the boat, she fell under it.

ANNE: How horrible!

EDITH: When I picked myself up and went over, her head was pinned under the keel and her face was covered with blood. She was obviously dead.

ANNE: You poor thing! What a ghastly shock!

EDITH: I felt quite numb. When the boat station signal sounded, I formed up with the other people as if in a dream. The smashed boat was ours and we were sent to another.

ANNE: Oh, Edith, I *do* sympathise. Had you known the poor thing long?

EDITH: (*With a great effort regaining her self-control.*) Only on the voyage. We shared a cabin.

ANNE: I can't say how I feel for you. And then — this!

(*Maxwell enters by the main door.*)

MAXWELL: The police have gone.

ANNE: What did they say?

MAXWELL: Nothing that I heard. They were with Uncle.

EDITH: It wasn't so bad, their questioning, I mean. I've always heard police enquiries were dreadful.

MAXWELL: (*Sitting beside Anne on the settee.*) Oh well, this is different. It's not as if they were investigating a crime. To them this is only a routine affair.

ANNE: Routine! How can you speak like that, Maxwell?

MAXWELL: I mean, it's what it would seem to them.

EDITH: What's been happening? I've been with the children all morning except just when Inspector Kendal questioned me.

MAXWELL: Well, as you know, Inspector Kendal and a sergeant arrived from Ashbridge and went into everything. They said the inquest will be on Friday. Purely formal of course. Anne dear, you'll have to go. But it won't be bad. You'll be all right.

ANNE: Oh, what does it matter about me? It's Sybil who matters! You seem to forget her.

MAXWELL: Old thing, we don't forget her, but these things have to be done.

EDITH: Yes, that's the way to look at it. Of course it's easy for me. I won't be here. I didn't mention it, but Richard has just asked me to take the kids to the sea till everything's over. We're going to Brighton.

MAXWELL: Lucky for you.

ANNE: Brighton! Lucky! How can you both! How can you forget that poor thing -

MAXWELL: Anne, dear, control yourself. We know she was fonder of you than anyone. But then just think of all you did for her. You gave her more happiness than anyone else.

ANNE: (*Rather frantically.*) Oh, but that's just what's worrying me. I feel so — so terribly to blame. I might have prevented it — and — I didn't! (*She sobs a little.*)

MAXWELL: (*Puts his arm round her.*) You prevented it? What complete nonsense! No one could have helped her more than you.

ANNE: (*Excited and on edge and pushing away his arm.*) No, no, no! That's just it! I didn't! I knew what was worrying her and I did nothing about it!

EDITH: (*Sharply.*) What do you mean?

ANNE: She was afraid — she thought — (*She suddenly stops, embarrassed.*)

EDITH: Well?

MAXWELL: (*Getting up and standing before the fire.*) Anne, what *are* you getting at?

ANNE: (*Repressing her sobs.*) I shouldn't have said that. I — I — didn't mean …

EDITH: Go on. You've gone too far to stop. What did she think?
MAXWELL: Yes, you'd better get it off your chest.
ANNE: Oh, it's cruel! I hate to. But you know, your uncle — and Mrs. Holt … Sybil *knew*.
EDITH: H'mm. I thought there was something in that quarter.
MAXWELL: Uncle and Mrs. Holt! You don't mean …?
ANNE: I'm afraid so. They were — are, I suppose — in love.
MAXWELL: Good Lord! Are you sure?
ANNE: Oh yes, it's quite true. I found it out accidentally. But *she* knew before that.
MAXWELL: (*With a kind of shrug, he again sits down beside Anne.*) Well, suppose they were. Aunt Sybil wouldn't have … I mean, not because of that.
EDITH: How did you learn it, if it's a fair question?
ANNE: I — saw them — together.
MAXWELL: What if you did? Anyhow it wasn't your fault, you couldn't have done anything about it.
ANNE: (*Still on edge.*) Oh yes, I could. I could have told Mr. Grinsmead.
EDITH: Told him what?
ANNE: That I'd seen them together. That Sybil knew and it was worrying her — to death.
MAXWELL: Oh, I wonder. Pretty awkward thing to interfere in.
ANNE: That's just it. I funked the awkwardness and I funked losing my job. If I hadn't been such a coward they might have had it out and — she'd be alive now.
MAXWELL: Don't you believe it! Aunt Sybil was mental; there's not a doubt of it. Nothing you could have done would have made any difference. Don't you agree, Edith?
EDITH: Of course I agree. I think, Anne, you're mental too. Why Dr. Roome said it was her mind. Didn't you hear him?
ANNE: (*Wonderingly and doubtfully.*) Oh, if I could believe that! What a relief it would be!
MAXWELL: That's better. No one could possibly blame you. Blame you indeed! I like that!

(*Mrs Grinsmead enters.*)

MAXWELL: (*Jumping up.*) Come and sit here, Gran.
MRS. G: Thank you, my dear. (*She sits.*) Do any of you know what's going on?
MAXWELL: The police have just gone. They've finished

their enquiries.

MRS. G: That's at least something. They seem like a blight on the house.

EDITH: Yes; I felt that.

MRS. G: (*A little bitterly.*) I suppose I shouldn't say it, but this is going to solve a problem. I can't pretend everyone who dies is an angel. Poor Sybil's life was no blessing to herself or anyone else and she took the best way out.

ANNE: Oh, Mrs. Grinsmead, how *can* you say such a thing? She was *dreadfully* unhappy.

MRS. G: (*Resentfully.*) Whose fault was that? When I think of the way she treated my son, I can scarcely control myself. I can't pretend sorrow for what's happened.

ANNE: Oh no, no, no! She was good. She was really good and kind, but — she was unhappy.

MRS. G: Well, better let it go at that.

MAXWELL: I think Anne knew her better than any of us.

MRS. G: (*Drily.*) I think so. (*A pause.*) Mrs. Holt was wondering about her case. I suppose you haven't heard anything of it?

MAXWELL: Not a word.

(*Irene enters.*)

MRS. G: Ah, here she is. I was just asking if anyone had heard about your case.

IRENE: (*Sits in an armchair.*) So good of you, Mrs. Grinsmead. (*To the others.*) I do feel dreadful for intruding my own affairs at such a time, but you see, it's rather urgent. The case was listed for twelve this morning and it's past eleven now. I don't know whether to go into Ashbridge and I don't like to bother Mr. Grinsmead.

MRS. G: (*To Maxwell.*) Where is your uncle?

MAXWELL: He was in the study. He was talking to the police there.

MRS. G: Better find him and ask him about the case.

MAXWELL: Right! (*He moves towards the main door but meets Grinsmead as he enters.*)

GRINSMEAD: Ah, I wanted to see you all.

MAXWELL: I was just going to ask you about Mrs. Holt's case.

IRENE: I do deeply apologies for intruding it on you, Mr. Grinsmead. But it's only to know if the case has been postponed. You see, it's almost time to start.

GRINSMEAD: (*Moving into the room.*) It's I who should apologise. I should have told you. It's postponed. I'm afraid I simply phoned the office to cancel all my engagements. (*Maxwell follows Grisnmead into the room.*)

IRENE: I'm so glad you did.

MRS. G: Naturally. They couldn't expect you to go on as if nothing had happened.

IRENE: Well, in that case — it sounds very heartless, I'm afraid — but I feel I ought to leave. You're too kind to say it, but I know you'd like to be alone. I think, if I may, I'll go back to town this afternoon.

GRINSMEAD: I admit you'd be far better away from this house at present, Mrs. Holt, but I'm afraid you can't go. And you can't take the children to Brighton, Edith. We'll all have to stay here for the present. I came in to tell you — some bad news.

MRS. G: What is it?

GRINSMEAD: The police are not satisfied that — that — Sybil committed suicide. They want a further enquiry.

MAXWELL: What? Old Kendal back again? Well, he's not really a bad sort of chap.

GRINSMEAD: Unfortunately it's worse than that. They've called in Scotland Yard!

(*All stare.*)

CURTAIN

ACT 2
SCENE 2

SCENE. (*Thursday, about mid-day. The fire is burning. On the table are two leather dispatch cases, papers and a note book. On a small chair are piled two coats and two hats. French and Carter are seated at the larger table. French is, if possible, a man of slightly below middle height and rather stout, with a clean shaven face, blue eyes, and a pleasant expression. He speaks in an educated way, and is always courteous and pleasant, almost to kindliness. Carter is a bigger man, more of the police type, and contrasting in appearance to French. He is neither so well educated nor so polite. French and Carter are in lounge suits.*)

French has papers before him on the desk, but is sitting back, not looking at them. Carter has his notebook in his hand and is looking at it.)

FRENCH: Now, Carter, before we leave, let's just run over what we've got. I'll pretend to know nothing and question you. That'll tell us if we've overlooked anything.

CARTER: (*Turning over the pages of his notebook.*) Right, sir. Where'll I begin?

FRENCH: At the beginning. Let's have why the local people applied to the Yard.

CARTER: (*Finding his place, glancing at his notes, then sitting back and summarizing.*) Just the set up. The usual triangle. Man sick of his wife and in love with another woman. Mustn't have a divorce or his respectable solicitor's practice goes west. In these circs the wife suddenly pops off. A bit well timed, the super thought.

FRENCH: And the evidence?

CARTER: As to the wife, the beat constable picked up gossip through the maid about conditions in the house.

FRENCH: Gossip's probably the word.

CARTER: About the other woman they had a report filed away. It's dated the 2nd of September, just ten weeks ago. Constable Dodd wrote: "*About 4.30 A.M. when on patrol, I passed* The Limes, *occupied by Mrs. Holt. It was moonlight and I saw a man leave one of the windows and proceed in a stealthy manner towards the road. I thought he was a burglar and prepared to take him as he came past, but when he got close I saw it was Mr. Grinsmead. I followed him to his house and watched him let himself in.*"

FRENCH: Nothing in that.

CARTER: No, sir, but there's more in the doctor's statement. He thinks death didn't take place till between two and three. If so, the gas must have been turned on, say, between one and two. But the deceased had taken a sleeping draught about ten, and therefore, was presumably asleep at that time.

FRENCH: So that she couldn't have turned it on herself? You're right; there's more there. Very well, the conditions aroused suspicion. This Grinsmead is a big noise in the place and the super didn't want the dirty work. So you and I are for it.

CARTER: That's about the size of it.

FRENCH: Well, get on with it. Run over what we found here.

CARTER: (*Looks at notebook.*) In the late Sybil Grinsmead's room there's a gas fire. The tap was turned partly on, and on the tap was the deceased's thumb and finger print, one on each side. Here's the enlargement. (*He hands over a photograph, at which French glances.*)

FRENCH: Yes?

CARTER: The fire was on when the deceased went to bed. To get gas in the room the tap must therefore have been turned off and on again. Therefore, no cord arrangement under the door could have been used.

FRENCH: Because these gadgets turn the tap in one direction and then disengage. Right. What's next?

CARTER: The door. The door was bolted on the inside and that electric bolt couldn't have been tampered with without showing marks.

FRENCH: And there weren't any. Yes?

CARTER: The windows were all securely fastened inside.

FRENCH: Well, that's the room. The gas turned partly on and the deceased's prints on the tap. The door and windows bolted on the inside. That's what was found after the tragedy. And we've got nothing more, though we've gone over the place with a comb. What do we get from that?

CARTER: Could be nothing but suicide, sir.

FRENCH: First, because she turned on the gas herself, and second, because no one else could have got into the room. Seems O.K. Now the evidence of the witnesses?

CARTER: (*Turns the pages of his notebook and after glancing at it, puts it down.*) First, we have the doctor. Dr. Roome says the deceased had a persecution complex which in his opinion predisposed her to suicide.

FRENCH: In other words, a suicide subject?

CARTER: Yes. Then there was Miss Day. She said the deceased was fanciful and definitely unhappy.

(*French nods.*)

Everyone else agrees. In fact, there's little doubt that the deceased's mind was affected. Her sister-in-law, Mrs. Cheame, says she treated everyone as an enemy. Grinsmead admits that his home life was not happy. The old grannie says the same. Mrs. Holt says she was strange in her manner and very rude.

FRENCH: Very well. All the evidence points to suicide except the doctor's estimate of the time of death.

CARTER: That's what he estimates. But you know what doctors are.

FRENCH: As bad as that, you think? Well, allow a bit of error in his estimate and say the death took place earlier.
CARTER: Might be a couple of hours earlier.
FRENCH: Could be. Then with that large room and the tap only half on, it would take quite a time to get a dangerous mixture.
CARTER: So she might have turned the tap on before she went to sleep.
FRENCH: (*Beginning to collect his papers.*) O.K. it's not often we get such conclusive evidence.
CARTER: (*Collecting his papers and beginning to put them in his dispatch case.*) It's been an easy case.
(*French finishes with his papers, stands up, looking down at the table. Then he picks up the photo of Sybil's prints.*)
FRENCH: Good enlargements, these. (*He looks at it idly.*)
CARTER: Yes, they were clear dabs. (*He stands with his case open, waiting for the photo, which French is examining closely.*) I suppose we'll get the 2.30 back to Town? (*French, engrossed in the photo, does not reply. Carter looks at him in surprise. French becomes even more engrossed.*) What's the excitement, sir? What are you looking at?
FRENCH: Give me the sketch of the stove, showing the position of the tap. (*Carter takes a paper from his case. French compares it with the photo. For a moment French does not reply. Then slowly he turns to Carter and says, impressively*) Carter, I hope the story of this trip'll never get out. I'd be the world's prize idiot — except of course for you. There's evidence here we've both missed. (*Holds out the photograph.*)
CARTER: (*Surprised. Looks at the photo then back at French.*) I don't get you, sir.
FRENCH: Now this is important. Get the old turnip to work. We've had a bit of luck in that this is a new stove and the tap's stiff.
CARTER: I don't see …
FRENCH: You can't get power to turn a stiff tap by gripping it in the middle. The thumb and finger must be near the ends of the cross bar.
CARTER: (*Looking at the photo.*) That's right. That's the way they are here.
FRENCH: Exactly. (*Impressively.*) But which ends of the bar are they at?
CARTER: (*Standing with a puzzled expression.*) Which ends?
FRENCH: (*Suddenly exasperated.*) Oh, for heaven's sake, don't stand gaping like a boiled haddock! Use your eyes, man!
CARTER: (*With a gesture of amazement.*) Holy smoke! She turned it off!
FRENCH: Got it at last? The dabs are at the wrong end of the crossbar?
CARTER: She turned it off! Bless me, sir, that's not what you'd call evi-

dence for suicide!

FRENCH: (*Quietly and grimly.*) No, Carter, we've been barking up the wrong tree. The super was right. This is murder.

CARTER: (*Whistling.*) It's got me guessing, this has. What about the bolted door and the rest of the evidence?

FRENCH: (*Grimly.*) Means we've been had. This is murder and that's all there is to it.

CARTER: Holy smoke! We'll not get that 2.30 this afternoon.

FRENCH: No, nor tomorrow afternoon either. (*He jokes and digs Carter in the ribs.*) You'll have to send her a wire. (*Serious again.*) Maybe that doctor wasn't so far wrong after all. Looks as if someone was about the house in the night, turning on the gas.

CARTER: No one heard anything in the night.

FRENCH: So they said. It looks as if someone was lying. We'll have those blessed witnesses in again. (*He unpacks his papers.*)

CARTER: (*Also unpacking his papers.*) I'd have said they were a bunch of George Washingtons. But what I can't get over is the bolted door.

FRENCH: Never mind the bolted door! We'll take it in its turn. Get Miss Day in, will you? (*Carter goes out. French sits down at the desk as before. He spends some time arranging his notebook and looking again at the photograph. Presently Carter ushers in Anne. French rises.*) I'm sorry, Miss Day, to trouble you again, but one or two further questions have arisen. Won't you sit down?

(*Carter settles Anne in an armchair facing the desk. He sits.*)

ANNE: (*Wearily.*) I shall be glad to help.

FRENCH: I appreciate your attitude, madam, and I'll be as brief as I can. (*He pauses, looks at his notebook and goes on, while Carter prepares to write.*) Now I want you to go back to Tuesday night. You said the gas fire was burning when the deceased went to bed. Who lit it?

(*At each answer Carter writes.*)

ANNE: Gladys. She did it in time to have the room warm before Mrs. Grinsmead went into it.

FRENCH: Quite. Then the deceased herself did not touch the tap?

ANNE: As it happens, she did. She mentioned that Gladys had left it full on, and as that was too much, she had turned it back to half.

FRENCH: But she didn't turn it out?

ANNE: Oh no.

FRENCH: I see. Now you said you gave the deceased a sleeping draught. When exactly did you do so?

ANNE: Just before she went to bed. That was about ten.

FRENCH: And I understand after taking it she bolted her door.

ANNE: Yes. It was an electric bolt worked from her bed. I waited outside her door till I heard it click and then I tried the door. It was fast.

FRENCH: Did you always do that?

ANNE: Yes, she liked to be sure it had worked.

FRENCH: I see. Now perhaps I'd better get this from the doctor, but have you any idea how soon after taking the draught she went to sleep?

ANNE: I can only tell you what Dr. Roome said: that it would be well under half an hour.

FRENCH: So if she went to bed about ten, we may take it she was asleep by half-past.

ANNE: I'm sure she was.

FRENCH: I'm anxious to know whether anyone else visited her after you left. I suppose you can't throw any light on that?

ANNE: Oh yes, I can. No one did.

FRENCH: How can you tell that?

ANNE: For this reason. When I was taking the draught to Mrs. Grinsmead, Mrs. Cheame came in and said she was making herself some tea in the kitchen and would I join her. I did. (*Pause.*)

FRENCH: Yes?

ANNE: Well, the kitchen's just beside Mrs. Grinsmead's room and if the electric bolt had worked I'd have heard it. It makes quite a loud click.

FRENCH: I follow. And how long were you in the kitchen?

ANNE. Till nearly eleven. Gladys had gone to bed and we sat talking.

FRENCH: Can you tell me who knew that you were giving Mrs. Grinsmead a draught that night?

ANNE: (*Thinking.*) Mrs. Cheame, because she came in here at the time. I really don't know who else. There was nothing secret about it.

FRENCH: No, of course not. Now another point. You said that on that evening the deceased was slightly upset and excited?

ANNE: So she was.

FRENCH: Now here's a more difficult question: In your opinion was she sufficiently upset to have committed suicide?

ANNE: (*Readily.*) Oh no, no, I don't think so. She was upset earlier in the evening, but she had quieted down and was practically normal. Besides she took the sleeping draught.

FRENCH: But, Miss Day, have you thought that if she didn't commit suicide, only one thing could have happened to her?

ANNE: (*With a gesture of repugnance.*) Oh I know. But it couldn't have been that.

FRENCH: You mean because of the bolted door?

ANNE: (*Relieved.*) Yes.

FRENCH: But if there had been no difficulty such as the bolted door, you would have thought murder more likely than suicide?

ANNE: (*Confused and worried.*) Oh, I don't know. I suppose so. Yes, of course I would. But there *was* the bolted door.

FRENCH: Very well, you say she was upset earlier in the evening. What upset her then?

ANNE: Oh, I don't know. She used to get upset at times. Visitors in the house, I expect.

FRENCH: That was Mrs. Grinsmead, Mr. Maxwell Crawley and Mrs. Holt?

ANNE: Yes.

FRENCH: Mrs. Grinsmead was her mother-in-law and Mr. Crawley her nephew by marriage, and little more than a boy at that. You don't seriously suggest it was they who upset her?

ANNE: I didn't say so. I suggested the party as a whole.

FRENCH: Beside those two there was only Mrs. Holt. Now what about her? Was it her presence that particularly upset her?

ANNE: (*Hesitates and speaks unwillingly.*) I think it was.

FRENCH: Quite so. Now why was that?

ANNE: (*More distressed and a little wildly.*) Oh, how do I know? Sybil was not normal. Her mind was full of fancies.

FRENCH: Very well. Let us leave Mrs. Holt and consider those fancies. What did they consist of?

ANNE: I've told you all about them already. Sybil had a persecution complex. She thought everyone was against her.

FRENCH: (*Sympathetically.*) I'm sorry to ask you to repeat yourself. Believe me, there's a reason for it. Now tell me: In such cases the feeling is usually specially directed against one person. Was it so in Mrs. Grinsmead's case?

ANNE: (*Again hesitating.*) She distrusted us all, I'm afraid.

FRENCH: No doubt. But that hardly answers my question. Did she distrust one person in particular?

(*Anne does not reply.*)

FRENCH: Come now, Miss Day: she was your friend. You mustn't try to keep anything back which might throw light on her death.

ANNE: (*More distressed than ever.*) I think she distrusted Mr. Grinsmead in particular.
FRENCH: (*Casually.*) That's what I should have thought. People in her state of mind usually turn against their nearest and dearest.
(*Anne looks relieved. French watches her keenly.*)
FRENCH: (*Speaking with sudden directness.*) Now tell me, Miss Day: did Mrs. Grinsmead suppose her husband was in love with Mrs. Holt?
(*Anne shrinks back as if struck.*)
ANNE: Oh, how can you say such a thing?
FRENCH: I should say it's pretty clear from what you've told me. She distrusted her husband and was excited by the presence of Mrs. Holt. I've no doubt myself she thought they were in love. The question is: Do you know as a fact if she did?
(*Anne greatly distressed, does not reply.*)
FRENCH: Well, Miss Day?
ANNE: Oh, must I answer these horrible questions? What does it matter now? She's dead. Nothing can bring her back to life again.
FRENCH: I can't force you to do so by law, but in justice to your late employer and friend, you must.
ANNE: (*In a low voice and with evident pain.*) She thought so.
FRENCH: I was sure of it. Just what exactly did she say?
(*ANNE keeps silence.*)
FRENCH: Did she ever speak of taking her own life?
ANNE: Oh no, no; she didn't.
FRENCH: (*Pauses, then speaks gravely.*) Did she fear—someone else would take it?
(*Anne keeps silence.*)
FRENCH: I see she did. Am I not right?
ANNE: (*Softly.*) Yes.
FRENCH: To put it bluntly, she was afraid her husband would murder her?
ANNE: (*Desperately.*) Yes, but it wasn't true!
FRENCH: (*Easily and with a gesture dismissing such an idea.*) My dear young lady, I'm not suggesting it was true. This poor lady was suffering from delusions. I want to know what those delusions were.
(*Anne looks relieved.*)
FRENCH: Can you tell me what she said?
ANNE: (*Very reluctantly.*) She said her husband only wanted Mrs. Holt and she him. She said that some apparent accident would happen, but

that she would be dead. She seemed to have an obsession about it.
FRENCH: (*Rather casually.*) Quite. Now this delusion was built on the belief that Mr. Grinsmead and Mrs. Holt were in love. (*Suddenly swinging round and speaking urgently.*) Tell me, Miss Day, was she correct in that?
ANNE: (*Distressed and uneasy.*) Oh, how could I possibly know?
FRENCH: (*Relentlessly.*) You *did* know! You haven't denied it. Am I not right?
ANNE: (*Confused and distressed.*) I thought so.
FRENCH: Yes, I know you did. Why did you think so?
ANNE: Questions of this kind are intolerable!
FRENCH: (*Earnestly and kindly.*) Look here, Miss Day, I've been sent here to find out just how the deceased came by her death. You were her friend. You must do what you can to help me.
ANNE: (*Reluctantly.*) I saw them together.
FRENCH: (*Encouragingly.*) That's what I want. Where were they?
ANNE: In here. I came in unexpectedly.
FRENCH: What were they doing?
ANNE: (*After a pause and very reluctantly.*) They were in each other's arms.
FRENCH: (*Unimpressed.*) Quite so. Did they see you?
ANNE: No, I slipped away at once.
FRENCH: (*Pauses in thought, then continues.*) Were they speaking when you went in?
ANNE: (*Uneasily.*) Yes.
FRENCH: What were they saying?
ANNE: (*With a gesture of disgust.*) Oh, this is perfectly hateful! I'm not a spy. I can't tell you. I only heard a disconnected word or two in any case.
FRENCH: (*Gravely.*) You admit you heard disconnected words. I must ask you to tell me what they were.
(*ANNE does not speak.*)
FRENCH: I promise I won't use anything you say unless there's real need. If it's proved that Mrs. Grinsmead committed suicide, none of this will be mentioned.
(*Anne looks at him in dismay.*)
ANNE: But is there any doubt of that?
FRENCH: (*Easily.*) Oh well, there's doubt about everything in these cases.

(*Anne looks at him again, then puts both hands over her face.*)

ANNE: (*Horrified.*) Oh, I see why you're asking all these questions! You think it was murder! (*Shudders.*) Oh, I *knew* she never committed suicide!

FRENCH: Well, we want to be sure, you know.

ANNE: Murder! How unspeakably dreadful!

FRENCH: You see, I'm not troubling you idly. Tell me what you heard.

ANNE: (*Reluctantly.*) Mrs. Holt was almost crying. Mr. Grinsmead tried to comfort her — that was all.

FRENCH: What exactly did they say? You've told me you heard the words.

ANNE: (*Desperately.*) Oh, I don't know! He said: "I'll find a way." She answered: "You must or I'll kill myself," and he repeated, "I'll find a way."

FRENCH: Was that all?

ANNE: Yes.

FRENCH: (*Thoughtfully.*) Mr. Grinsmead said that he'd find a way. What did you understand by that?

ANNE: That he was going to try for a divorce.

FRENCH: (*Sharply.*) Eh? A divorce? What put a divorce into your mind?

ANNE: Because he had asked me to sound Mrs. Grinsmead as to whether she would consent to a divorce.

FRENCH: (*Absently.*) Oh, he did, did he? (*Thinks.*) And did you?

ANNE: I tried to.

FRENCH: Did the deceased seem agreeable?

ANNE: No.

FRENCH: No? That surprises me. What did she say?

ANNE: She didn't think it was a genuine offer.

FRENCH: Oh I see. (*Thinks.*) H'mm. H'mm. Just one more question. Did you see or hear anything unusual that night?

ANNE: Oh no: nothing whatever.

FRENCH: You slept well?

ANNE: I don't think I woke once.

FRENCH: That's all at last. No, sorry, one thing more. (*He smiles.*) I saw in Mrs. Grinsmead's address book the name of a Melbourne photographer. It looked freshly written. Do you know anything about that?

ANNE: (*Surprised.*) Curiously enough she mentioned it only last night. She wanted some photographs of her last brother, Mrs. Cheame's husband.

FRENCH: I see. How did she know they had any?

ANNE: I'm not sure that she did, but they had taken the portrait of him that Mrs. Cheame brought home and she thought it likely.

FRENCH: She hadn't then had a reply?

ANNE: No.

FRENCH: Mrs. Cheame no doubt told her?

ANNE: (*Slightly embarrassed.*) No, she hadn't consulted Mrs. Cheame. I'm afraid she didn't like her very much.

FRENCH: The poor lady's mind prevented her liking anyone. Well, that really is all. I'm sorry, Miss Day, for all these unpleasant questions and obliged for your help.

(*French and Carter rise. Anne also rises. Carter opens the door. With a little bow Anne goes out. Carter shuts the door behind her.*)

FRENCH: (*Sitting down and leaning back in his chair.*) The deceased thought her husband was going to murder her, and he told Mrs. Holt that he would find a way out. What did he mean by a way out, Carter?

CARTER: Why not a divorce, if he was making enquiries about one?

FRENCH: What about the super's argument that a divorce would ruin his practice?

CARTER: That's right.

FRENCH: Making enquiries about a divorce would be useful enough if he intended anything serious.

CARTER: (*Nodding.*) That's what the lady thought. I'll say, sir, we're not doing badly. There's motive proved on Grinsmead's part and some build up for an alibi.

FRENCH: We got more from Miss Day than I'd hoped for.

CARTER: Just the stuff we wanted. Who'll you have next?

FRENCH: Mrs. Cheame, I think.

CARTER: She's made a pretty complete statement already. (*He moves towards the main door*)

FRENCH: Yes, she's a wonder. Calm and business-like and efficient.

CARTER: (*Pausing at door.*) Why shouldn't she be?

FRENCH: Have you thought what she's experienced? First her father dies and puts paid to her medical training. Then her husband is killed in a riding accident. She comes home on the *City of Brisbane* and in the collision her best friend is killed beside her.

CARTER: She didn't mention any of that.

FRENCH: I didn't ask her: why should I? Miss Day told us and I don't doubt it. Then she's in an open boat in a storm for ten days, during which time eleven of the survivors die. How would you have stood that, Carter?

CARTER: No better, I expect.

FRENCH: Then she's not here two months till her sister-in-law is murdered.

CARTER: It's been a bad spell right enough. (*He opens the main door and looks into the hall.*) Mrs. Cheame, if you please!

(*Carter ushers Edith in. French rises as before and points to armchair.*)

FRENCH: We're sorry to trouble you again, Mrs. Cheame, but unfortunately we have to ask some more questions. Won't you sit down?

(*Edith nods gravely and sits down. French and Carter also sit down as before.*)

FRENCH: We've reason to believe that something unusual went on in this house on the night of Mrs. Grinsmead's death. I'm trying to find out what it was.

EDITH: I can't help you, I'm afraid.

FRENCH: (*Smiling.*) I hope you can. Now to make it easier we'll go through the night in detail, beginning at the time you went to bed. What time was that?

EDITH: I told you. A little before eleven.

FRENCH: You went to sleep?

EDITH: I did, quite soon.

FRENCH: And when did you wake?

EDITH: About two o'clock.

FRENCH: Oh: you didn't tell me that before.

EDITH: You didn't ask me.

FRENCH: Very well: you woke about two o'clock? How do you remember the time so well?

EDITH: I looked at my watch. You see, I went to the children's room.

FRENCH: Oh? Why was that?

EDITH: I thought I heard Johnnie shouting.

FRENCH: And was he awake?

EDITH: No, but he looked as if he'd been flinging himself about. I supposed he'd been talking in his sleep.

FRENCH: Then you went back to your room?

EDITH: Yes.

FRENCH: Did everything in the house seem normal?

EDITH: Perfectly.

FRENCH: You saw no one andheard no unusual sounds while you were up?

EDITH: (*Hesitates.*) Since you ask me, I saw Mr. Grinsmead.
FRENCH: Oh? Where was that?
EDITH: He was just going into his room as I opened my door.
FRENCH: Did he see you?
EDITH: No, I drew back till I heard his door close.
FRENCH: Very well. Did you sleep when you returned to bed?
EDITH: Yes.
FRENCH: And that was the only thing you saw or heard out of the common during the entire night?
EDITH: Yes. The only thing.
FRENCH: Then I have only to thank you for answering my questions so fully. That's all, Mrs. Cheame.
(*Carter shows Edith out and closes the main door behind her*)
FRENCH: Well, Carter, what do you think of that? See any light?
CARTER: If it wasn't for the bolted door I'd say Grinsmead had been involved in the murder, but -
FRENCH: If you mention that bolted door again, Carter, there'll be a second murder done here. Use the old turnip for once in a way. Don't you see that the gas could have been turned off and on without going into the room at all?
CARTER: Without going into the room?
FRENCH: Of course. Easy as wink. It could have been done from the meter.
CARTER: But -
FRENCH: Don't you see? Someone goes down that night to the meter. They turn the gas off from the house and wait a minute till the deceased's fire goes out. Then they've only to turn the gas on again and the job's done.
CARTER: Hang it, sir, I thought of that first thing. But surely no one would have risked that for fear of turning out other fires too?
FRENCH: Look up your notes, man! There's no gas in the house except the kitchen cooker and that one room, so there are no other fires to consider.
CARTER: (*Slaps his thigh.*) Holy smoke, sir, you're right! (*Motions with his head to the bedroom door.*) That's the only bedroom we've been into, and I just forgot the house wasn't fitted throughout.
FRENCH: Simple, isn't it?
CARTER: That's what Grinsmead was doing! Ten bob to a tanner, you've got it!

FRENCH: (*Shaking his head.*) Couldn't plunge to that extent. I'm not a blooming millionaire. Now look here, I want to have a look at that meter. But I don't want Grinsmead to know. Get him here and keep him busy with questions. See?

CARTER: Right, sir.

FRENCH: I'll send him in, and don't forget to ask him if he was out of his room on Tuesday night.

(*French goes out by the main door. Carter sits and writes in his notebook —a bit of business, Carter aping French. Presently Grinsmead comes in by the main door.*)

CARTER: (*Rising.*) Won't you sit down, sir?

(*They both sit down.*)

 I'm distressed, sir, to have to ask you to discuss this affair again, but the truth is that we're not entirely satisfied that Mrs. Grinsmead committed suicide. We're considering possible alternatives.

GRINSMEAD: (*Wary and suspicious.*) Yes?

CARTER: As of course you know, there are two points hard to square with the suicide theory. The first is that Miss Day tells us that the deceased was in a practically normal frame of mind when she went to bed.

GRINSMEAD: I know that.

CARTER: Yes, sir. The other is that she took a sleeping draught. Now, if she was normal when she went to bed and took a sleeping draught, and if no one afterwards entered her room, it's hard to believe she could have got worked up enough to take her life.

GRINSMEAD: I've thought of that. But what's your alternative?

CARTER: (*With an air of self-satisfaction.*) Simply, sir, accident. We thought that the deceased must have been a sleepwalker.

GRINSMEAD: (*Astonished.*) A sleepwalker!

CARTER: Yes. We thought that she had got up while asleep and automatically turned out the fire, and then a little later had turned it on again and got into bed.

GRINSMEAD: Bless me, that's an idea!

CARTER: From your knowledge of the deceased, what do you think of it, sir?

GRINSMEAD: (*Hesitating.*) Have you put it up to Dr. Roome?

CARTER: No, sir, not yet.

GRINSMEAD: Well — er — I'm afraid I couldn't express an opinion.

CARTER: It would explain the whole thing, sir: *if* it was possible.

GRINSMEAD: I see that. I can only say I never knew Mrs. Grinsmead to do such a thing.

CARTER: I daresay the Chief Inspector would like to talk to you about it. He'll be here in a moment. Now just one other point. We'd like to check the events of that night from your point of view. When, sir, was the last time you saw the deceased lady?

GRINSMEAD: In here shortly before ten.

CARTER: Then, sir, what did you do?

GRINSMEAD: I went to my study and then to bed.

CARTER: Quite so. (*Pauses and looks in an exasperated way at the door.*) And what then?

GRINSMEAD: (*Exasperated.*) My good man, I've told you all this before: you've got it in that book. (*Pointing.*) The next thing I heard was Miss Day's scream.

CARTER: I don't want to touch on that, only on the night. You didn't hear anyone moving about, for instance?

GRINSMEAD: No.

CARTER: You weren't up yourself by any chance? Out of your own room?

GRINSMEAD: (*Glances sharply at Carter then reluctantly.*) Well, yes, I was. I was down here about two.

CARTER: (*Lightly.*) Ah, that explains it. Someone was heard moving about. I'm afraid I must ask you what you were doing?

GRINSMEAD: No secret about that. I couldn't sleep and I felt like a drink. I came down for a whisky and soda.

CARTER: I follow, sir. And you went back without noticing anything out of the common?

GRINSMEAD: Haven't I said so?

CARTER: Sorry sir, but you know yourself misunderstandings arise very easily. Now -

(*French enters. Carter registers profound relief. FRENCH exchanges a glance with Carter who nods gently.*)

CARTER: I was just putting up your theory of the sleepwalking to Mr. Grinsmead. He can't help us about it.

(*French stares in complete mystification. Carter winks and gestures, but tries to hide it. French makes a gesture of comprehension, glances at Carter as if to say, "Well, you're the absolute limit," and recovers himself.*)

FRENCH: (*Smoothly.*) We've only put up the idea, sir. We don't say it's correct.

GRINSMEAD: I certainly think it's unlikely.

FRENCH: If we're wrong we'll have to try for something else. Well, sir, we're much obliged for your patience.
GRINSMEAD: Does that mean you're done with me now?
FRENCH: Yes, sir, and thank you very much.
(*Grinsmead nods and goes out by the main door. When the door closes, Carter turns to French who turns his right elbow towards Carter.*)
CARTER: (*Glancing at French's elbow.*) You've got some white on your arm. Let me brush it off. (*Carter brushes it off with his hand.*)
FRENCH: It's that blessed meter. It's in an awkward place up against a wall and I defy you to turn it without getting dirtied. (*Gestures as if he has had an idea. He pulls his sleeve round and stares at it, then turns to Carter.*) And (*impressively*) *that* gives me an idea.
CARTER: (*Staring and impressed.*) Holy smoke, sir, you've got something there! Maybe the end of the case!
FRENCH: Maybe indeed.
CARTER: I suppose it's a job for me — searching wardrobes?
FRENCH: You've got it in one.
CARTER: If I can find a dressing gown with a white elbow — (*Snaps his fingers with a gesture signifying accomplishment. Then with a change of tone.*) Any luck when you were out?
FRENCH: Well, the meter's possible.
CARTER: No more than that?
FRENCH: (*Shaking his head.*) Nope.
CARTER: No dabs?
FRENCH: For heaven's sake, use your turnip. Do you think any murderer would leave dabs, with detective stories round him like swarming bees?
CARTER: I suppose that's right.
FRENCH: And if he had, wouldn't they have been destroyed when young Crawley turned off the gas, and afterwards when they turned it on again to cook breakfast? Did you ask Grinsmead of he was out of his room during the night?
CARTER: Admitted it. Said he was getting a whisky and soda.
FRENCH: Probably twigged he'd been seen. You didn't ask him if he'd been sleepwalking?
CARTER: (*Injured.*) I thought that wasn't half a bad turn.
FRENCH: Oh, you did, did you? Well, you ought to know. You give a pretty good exhibition of it half your time.
CARTER: Good technique, sir. I lull people to sleep and then — (*Gestures.*) — I strike!

FRENCH: You strike me at the moment — as dotty. (*Becoming serious.*) So Grinsmead was down for whisky. (*Thinks.*) We might get something on that. Call Miss Day again.

(*French sits at table as before. Carter goes out by the main door.*)

CARTER: (*Off.*) Miss Day, if you please. Mr. French wants you again. (*He shows in Anne, follows and closes the door.*)

FRENCH: (*Rising.*) I'm really sorry to be such a nuisance, Miss Day, but I forgot one question.

ANNE: (*Sitting down as before.*) It's all right, Mr. French. I'll try to answer.

FRENCH: Thank you. It's just a little point about whisky. I take it, you as housekeeper keep it supplied?

ANNE: (*Surprised.*) Why yes, I do.

FRENCH: Can you tell me exactly what whisky was in the house on Tuesday night?

ANNE: (*Very surprised.*) Yes, I think so. It's kept here as a matter of fact. (*She goes to the cabinet and is about to take something out when French stops her.*)

FRENCH: A moment, please. (*Points.*) Is it these two?

ANNE: Yes: the bottle and the decanter.

(*French takes them out carefully, holding them in his handkerchief.*)

FRENCH: Is that all there is in the house?

ANNE: That's all.

FRENCH: Tell me about it. Did you fill the decanter?

ANNE: Yes. On Tuesday night before dinner the decanter was empty and there was just that bottle. I washed the decanter and filled it from the bottle.

FRENCH: Was the bottle full?

ANNE: Yes, it was a new bottle.

FRENCH: Did anyone have any whisky that night?

ANNE: I don't think any has been taken since. We drank wine at dinner on both evenings. When Mr. Grinsmead drinks wine he doesn't have whisky, and the rest of us seldom take it.

FRENCH: Thank you very much. Now I just want to see — excuse me a moment.

(*French, again using his handkerchief, carefully pours the whisky from the decanter back into the bottle. It fills it up.*)

FRENCH: Fills the bottle, doesn't it? Is that as the bottle was before you opened it?

ANNE: Yes; full like that.

FRENCH: So that proves no one had any since before dinner on Tuesday night? You're sure there's no more?

ANNE: Oh yes, I'm sure. It's quite clear no one has taken any.

FRENCH: Thank you, Miss Day. That's all I wanted.

(*Anne is shown out by Carter as before. Carter shuts the main door.*)

FRENCH: Down getting a drink in the night, I *don't* think.

CARTER: Holy smoke, sir, he'll find it hard to explain that!

FRENCH: We're getting on: motive, opportunity and a false alibi. All very healthy.

CARTER: You've enough for an arrest.

FRENCH: We'll go in now and have a chat about it with the super. We can get that decanter checked for Grinsmead's prints, but there won't be any.

CARTER: (*Beginning to pack his cases.*) I don't care how soon we're out of this God-forsaken place. I don't like … (*Notices French, , who is staring with an expression of amazement on his face.*) What is it, sir?

FRENCH: (*To himself and with a gesture of incomprehension.*) Fool that I am! Why didn't I see it before?

CARTER: See it? I don't …

FRENCH: (*Striking his open hand with his clenched fist.*) We've got it, Carter! We've got our case! Don't you see?

(*Carter gapes.*)

We don't want evidence about whitened elbows or whisky or anything else! We've got the whole thing!

CARTER: (<u>Helplessly.</u>) I'm hanged if I know what you're talking about.

FRENCH: Something Miss Day said. Don't you see it: staring us in the face?

(*Carter shakes his head helplessly.*)

FRENCH: Miss Day told us — and proved — just what happened to Sybil Grinsmead in the night time.

ACT 3

(*Shortly after nine five nights later. The furniture has been replaced to the positions they were in on Tuesday evening. The curtains are drawn and the lights are on. Mrs Grinsmead is seated on the end of settee with Anne beside her. Irene is in an armchair. Maxwell is on the pouffe. Edith is seated in a chair. Used coffee cups are placed near the people discovered, also a tray with coffee pot, etc.*)

MRS. G. : What Miss Day says is quite true. French does seem to have something special in his mind.

ANNE: He absolutely terrifies me! So quiet and polite and so — relentless! And question after question! The same things over and over again!

MAXWELL: They always do that.

EDITH: Relentless is the word, but he's extraordinarily polite too.

IRENE: If he's asked me once if I heard anyone moving in the night, he's asked me a dozen times.

MRS. G: And me also. It's just as Miss Day says. Question after question.

ANNE: (*With horror.*) He's not satisfied. He knows something.

IRENE: Ghastly! I felt I couldn't stand it. The house was choking me. I felt I must go away — anywhere — at once. But he wouldn't let me. He said I must stay till after the inquest.

MAXWELL: He wants us all at the adjourned inquest. After that we can do what we like.

(*Grinsmead enters.*)

MRS. G: Well, what's been happening?

IRENE: Come and reassure us, Mr. Grinsmead. Miss Day has just been frightening us all with tales of what the police are doing.

GRINSMEAD: (*Moving into the room.*) I'm afraid that once again I've got bad news. This Chief Inspector French believes, rightly or wrongly, that it — wasn't suicide.

ANNE: Oh, *awful!*

MRS. G: But that surely …

MAXWELL: He doesn't mean — *murder?*

GRINSMEAD: I'm afraid — he does. (*He stands in front of fire.*)
MAXWELL: He thinks it murder! Good Lord!
EDITH: Tragedy after tragedy! Is there no end to it?
IRENE: How inexpressibly dreadful!
ANNE: But it *couldn't* be! Who — who — I mean, *no one* would do such a thing!
GRINSMEAD: So I should have said. But he seems quite sure. And — I'm afraid it's worse than that. He appears to be satisfied that no outsider could have got into the house during the night.
(*They look at each other in horror.*)
MRS. G: But that would mean …
MAXWELL: I say, that's a bit thick! Do you mean he's accusing one of *us*?
ANNE: He couldn't mean that.
EDITH: No, no; He couldn't mean that.
GRINSMEAD: We must face it, I'm afraid. French has definitely suggested that someone in the house murdered Sybil.
ANNE: I can't believe it!
IRENE: But his suggesting it doesn't matter. It's not true. He can never prove it.
MRS. G: Of course it's not true. Wasn't the door bolted? How could anyone have got into the room? The idea's preposterous!
MAXWELL: Yes, what Gran says is right. No one could have got into the room.
GRINSMEAD: These people aren't fools. French must see that difficulty as well as we do.
ANNE: Mr. French must be on to *something*. What was he doing at the meter?
GRINSMEAD: (*Sharply.*) What's that about the meter?
ANNE: It was that morning after they'd taken the statements, you know. Gladys saw Mr. French at the meter. He plugged in a powerful lamp and worked and worked and worked.
GRINSMEAD: (*Aghast.*) The meter! My heavens!
MRS. G: What do you mean?
GRINSMEAD: I mean that that throws some light on it! He thinks someone turned off the meter and then after a little turned it on again.
MRS. G: But why? I don't see …
GRINSMEAD: Don't you? It's pretty obvious. Turn off the meter and the fire in Sybil's room goes out. Turn it on again and gas escapes into

the room.

ANNE: Then it's true!

MAXWELL: What's true?

ANNE: That we could all have done it! Don't you see? Any one of us could have gone down and turned that tap off and turned it on again.

GRINSMEAD: (*Grimly.*) I presume that's what French thinks.

EDITH: And how can we prove that we didn't? None of us can!

IRENE: I don't know where the meter is.

MAXWELL: But you can't prove you don't.

EDITH: Then any of us may be for it. (*All look self-conscious, avoiding each other's eyes.*)

GRINSMEAD: I don't think any of you need have the slightest fear. As a matter of fact, I believe French suspects me.

MRS. G: Suspects you! He couldn't!

IRENE: Oh, Mr. Grinsmead, that's surely impossible!

GRINSMEAD: I wish it were. Unfortunately I was downstairs during the night and French has found out. I couldn't sleep and I went down for a whisky and soda. (*The front door bell stops ringing.*) There's my chief clerk. He's coming to see me about some urgent business. (*He moves to the main door.*) But don't any of you worry. If we didn't do it, French can't prove we did. (*He goes out by the main door.*)

(*When Grinsmead tells about the whisky, Anne registers first interest, then surprise, and finally seems frozen with horror.*)

EDITH: Oh, I'm so distressed about this. I didn't know, of course, but I'm afraid I'm responsible for the police suspicion. It was I who told them that Richard was out of his room during the night.

MRS. G: Edith! How did you know?

EDITH: I thought I heard Johnnie shouting and went to see. Richard was just going into his room as I opened my door.

MAXWELL: Anyone else prowling about the house in the nighttime? The next thing is we'll find we all were.

MRS. G: Were you?

MAXWELL: No, Were you, Gran?

MRS. G: No, but I can't prove it.

MAXWELL: Oh, neither can I of course.

ANNE: (*Still frozen with horror.*) It's worse — it's worse than you can think! It's — I don't know how to tell you!

MAXWELL: Tell us what?

ANNE: About the whisky.

MRS. G: What about the whisky?
ANNE: (*Much upset.*) It was Mr. French. He asked me what was done about it and — I told him.
MAXWELL: Old thing, you're not what I'd call crystal clear.
MRS. G: Explain yourself, Miss Day.
ANNE: (*Tremulously.*) I said the decanter had been empty on Tuesday and I'd washed it and refilled it. He asked what I'd filled it from and I showed him the bottle. It was a large bottle, half empty. Then he asked was it a fresh bottle. I told him it was.
MAXWELL: You'd opened a fresh bottle and poured half of it into the decanter. What then?
ANNE: He poured the whisky back from the decanter into the bottle and … (*Much perturbed.*) it filled it up.
MAXWELL: Filled it up? Then …
MRS. G: (*Grimly.*) Does that mean they can prove my son didn't take it in the night?
ANNE: (*Distracted.*) I don't know! I feel dreadful about telling Mr. French, but what could I do? He asked me the direct question and I — didn't know.
MAXWELL: Of course you could do nothing else. We'd all have done the same.
IRENE: (*Embarrassed.*) Look here, I — I must tell you. I …
MAXWELL: What! More revelations?
MRS. G: Yes, Mrs. Holt?
IRENE: This is going to be ghastly; I don't know how to say it. But I can't help it. I know the truth of this and I must tell it.
MRS. G: What must you tell us?
IRENE: Oh, dear! (*Takes a breath and plunges.*) Mr. Grinsmead was not downstairs getting whisky. He was … Well, if I must say it, he was with me!
MRS. G: Oh! So that's how things were!
MAXWELL: A bit awkward certainly.
MRS. G: Has — has this been going on for any time?
IRENE: Well yes, it has. I'm deeply sorry, but I'm not ashamed. We love each other. We fought against it, but we couldn't help it.
MRS. G: Then that's what was upsetting Sybil? She knew?
IRENE: Oh no, I'm sure she didn't.
ANNE: Yes, Mrs. Grinsmead, she knew. That *is* what was worrying her and making her ill.

IRENE: Oh, Miss Day, don't say so! She couldn't have!
ANNE: She did. She told me about it.
IRENE: (*Looking terribly distressed.*) Oh, I am desperately sorry. We didn't realize it for a moment.
ANNE: She thought Mr. Grinsmead wished her dead.
IRENE: (*Horrified.*) Oh, no, no! Never! We would have liked a divorce, but she wouldn't discuss it.
ANNE: Yes, Mr. Grinsmead asked me to sound her on that.
IRENE: (*Sobbing.*) Oh, what have we done? If she committed suicide we've virtually killed her, and if not, Richard may be arrested for her murder!
ANNE: This is where I blame myself so terribly. I should have told Mr. Grinsmead she knew, and let him have it out with her.
MAXWELL: You weren't to blame.
IRENE: I must tell the whole thing to Mr. French. But will he believe me?
ANNE: He'll believe you all right. He knows about — you and Mr. Grinsmead.
IRENE: (*Incredulously.*) He knows?
ANNE: Yes, I told him.
MRS. G:. Miss Day, what are you saying? How could you know anything about it?
ANNE: I discovered it by accident. They gave themselves away. Then French — tricked me into telling.
MAXWELL: They do that. It's their job. You couldn't help yourself.
ANNE: (*Sturdily.*) I didn't want to help myself; at least, I wasn't sorry I'd done it. I was feeling bitter; thinking of Sybil, you understand.
IRENE : You were right. I am to blame.
MRS. G: Well, at least I compliment you on your courage.
IRENE: I'm afraid compliments are the last thing I deserve. I'll go now and ring up Mr. French and say I've a statement to make to him. It's the least I can do.
MRS. G: I'll go with you, my dear. You mustn't do anything rash. We'll see Richard first and talk it over with him.
IRENE: Better not tell him. He'll want to sacrifice himself.
MRS. G: We'll not let him do that.
(*Irene and Mrs Grinsmead go out by the main door. Maxwell gets up and stands before the fire.*)
MAXWELL: Good Lord! What a day!

ANNE: *Awful!*

EDITH: If you two commiserate any more I'll scream. (*Edith gets up.*) Where's that bottle of aspirin, Anne?

ANNE: I put it back in the medicine cupboard.

EDITH: I think a couple would do me no harm. (*She goes out.*)

MAXWELL: She's upset. Tries not to show it and all that. But I can see she is.

ANNE: (*Tartly.*) Do you expect her to be pleased about it? Do have some sense. (*Gets up, moves around the room, then sits on left end of settee.*)

MAXWELL: It *is* a bit of a mess, you know. This development, I mean. Apart from the original trouble altogether.

ANNE: I wonder if French *will* believe Mrs. Holt?

MAXWELL: 'Fraid that doesn't come into it.

ANNE: How do you mean?

MAXWELL: Uncle's going to Mrs. Holt's room wouldn't have prevented his cutting off the gas at the meter.

ANNE: Oh, how horrible!

MAXWELL: Well, that's how it would strike an outsider. Look here, Anne, French has got a darned plausible case. I believe he'll arrest uncle.

ANNE: You don't!

MAXWELL: Yes, I do. And I believe it'll go to trial.

ANNE: You know, that's what your aunt was afraid of. I mean, she thought he'd — murder her!

MAXWELL: I say, if French gets to know that, it'll just about put the lid on everything.

ANNE: He *does* know it. I — I told him.

MAXWELL: Good Lord, Anne! How did you know about everything? You *have* had bad luck!

ANNE: (*Sighs.*) Oh well, the mischief's done. Look here, don't let's talk of it any more.

MAXWELL: No, that's all right. (*Pause.*) I say, I'm not looking forward to the adjourned inquest, are you?

ANNE: Oh, for heaven's sake don't talk of that either! I'm fed up! I can't bear any more! Talk of something else.

MAXWELL: (*Sits on the settee beside Anne.*) Well, that's just lucky, for there *is* something else I've been wanting to speak to you about. If you have to leave here — *if* you have — you won't want a job.

ANNE: There's nothing I'll want more.

MAXWELL: No, dear, because afterwards — not now, of course but afterwards — we could be married and then ...

ANNE: Now I won't have it! With your poor aunt ...

MAXWELL: I don't mean anything *now*, you know. Only that we should have the whole thing settled, so that we'd know where we were. That's all.

ANNE: No, no, no! I won't have it discussed!

MAXWELL: (*His face clouds.*) But then of course, there'd be a snag. If uncle ... I mean, if things went wrong, the family'd be, well, sort of disgraced. I mean I could scarcely ask you then.

ANNE: (*Looks at him and begins to sob quietly.*) Maxwell dear! As if that would make any — uh
— difference.

MAXWELL: (*Suddenly excited.*) Then — then — you mean? You really will ... (*In a moment he has his arms about her.*) Oh, Anne! Anne, darling!

ANNE: (*Struggling.*) No, no! Let me go! I won't have it! Let me go at once!

MAXWELL: (*Slowly releasing her.*) Oh, if only you'd see reason once in a way!

ANNE: Maxwell dear, I feel awfully proud of what you've said, but you mustn't think of it all the same.

MAXWELL: (*Sitting back on settee.*) This is like a serial story: to be continued in our next.

(*Edith enters by the main door. She has regained her composure.*)

EDITH: Those kids are sleeping like cherubs in a nest: if you know what cherubs look like.

ANNE: Lucky little beggars.

EDITH: I envy them. (*Sighs as she stretches herself in armchair.*) Pretty interminable day, what?

(*Anne and Maxwell exchange glances.*)

ANNE: Isn't it? Absolutely endless.

EDITH: And the inquest coming on.

MAXWELL: I've just got into trouble for talking about that.

EDITH: Burying our heads in the sand won't help us. Anyway it shouldn't take long. There can't be many witnesses: Mr. G. and Anne and Dr. Roome.

MAXWELL: (*Getting up and walking about.*) Oh, for heaven's sake lay off the subject, Edith! Anne's fed up.

EDITH: And do you think I'm not fed up? Think I can't feel things like other people?

MAXWELL: Oh hell, I forgot. I promised to see to the lamp in Gran's room. Wants a new bulb. I'll not be long. (*Moves to the main door.*)

ANNE: Don't hurry away if she wants to talk.

MAXWELL: (*Exits.*) I'll not get the chance.

EDITH: She's keeping a stiff upper lip, the old lady. Over seventy and as strong as any of us.

ANNE: A good deal stronger than I am. I'm so tired. I want to sleep for a month.

EDITH: I'm tired too. It seems a month since it happened.

ANNE: Far more than a month. I want to sleep and sleep. And when I think of bursting open that door and seeing — her — being carried in, I feel I'll never sleep again.

EDITH: Well *don't* think of it.

ANNE: I don't want to, but I can't help it. I'm afraid I snapped at Maxwell, for talking about it. He *has* been splendid, hasn't he?

EDITH: I don't think splendid's the word for any of us.

ANNE: Oh, *he* has been! And what do you think he's afraid of? That his uncle may be arrested and he'll be — sort of tarnished! Fancy his feeling that! I nearly wept.

EDITH: (*Looking keenly at Anne's glowing face.*) So you've admitted it at last.

ANNE: (*Staring.*) What do you mean, admitted it?

EDITH: (*Scornfully.*) For heaven's sake, don't be such a fool! Everyone knows you're fond of him.

ANNE: (*Defiantly.*) I *am* fond of him. I'm not ashamed of it.

EDITH: Then why pretend?

ANNE: (*Eagerly.*) But he mustn't know. Promise me you'll keep it to yourself.

EDITH: You fool Anne! The boy's half crazy about you.

ANNE: But that's just it: He *is* only a boy. He's not old enough to know his own mind. Suppose we were married and the — right woman — came along.

EDITH: *All* right, all right! (*Fiercely.*) Oh, you fool! You complete unutterable fool! To have the chance of happiness like that and to throw it away! I — I ... (*She is silent for a moment then turns her head into the chair and sobs.*)

ANNE: Edith! What *is* the matter?

EDITH: (*Trying to stifle her sobs.*) Oh nothing! I'm just fed up.
ANNE: Well, I'm not surprised. I am too and I've gone through nothing compared to you. (*Pauses.*) By the way, I was forgetting, a letter's gone astray. I must have a search for it in the morning.
EDITH: What letter?
ANNE: I wasn't supposed to say anything about it, but it doesn't matter now. Sybil made a secret of it: she hadn't mentioned it to anyone else, but she told me — on the night of her death. She said she'd written to Melbourne for more photos of her brother.
EDITH: (*Uneasily.*) What was secret about that?
ANNE: I think she feared it might annoy you, sort of going behind your back.
EDITH: (*Mockingly.*) Rare consideration.
ANNE: You needn't be so bitter, Edith. But the point about the letter is that the reply came — and vanished. She never got it.
EDITH: How do you know it came?
ANNE: I saw it in the door box. I was looking for a letter for myself. Did you see it?
EDITH: Yes, I saw it. I put it on the table with the others.
ANNE: It's disappeared.
EDITH: It's fallen down somewhere. In any case it hardly matters now.
ANNE: Oh yes, it does, Edith, Anything she wanted, we must do. I feel it as a sort of trust. But perhaps Mr. G. took it.
EDITH: (*Uneasily.*) Have you asked him?
ANNE: No, I forgot to. I haven't mentioned it to anyone. But I must ask him.
EDITH: (*Tremulously.*) Oh rubbish! Let it alone! Hasn't he enough trouble without being bothered about every trifle?
ANNE: Oh no, if she was interested it's not a trifle. If it can't be found, Mr. G. may want to write for a copy.
EDITH: (*Unseen by Anne, Edith makes a desperate gesture, as if finding herself forced to a decision she loathes. She speaks breathlessly after a pause.*) I think you're a complete idiot. However, it's nothing to me what you do. (Stretches.) Oh, I'm tired! Tired enough to weep. (*She pauses and furtively feels in her pocket, brings out a little bottle, glances at it and puts it away again.*) Look here, I'm dying for a drink. We want a pick-me-up, both of us.
ANNE: Yes, I'd like something. What'll we have?
EDITH: (*Trying to speak normally.*) Whisky. I'll tell you. Let's have some

hot toddy for once in a way. Go on, Anne. It'll cheer us up and make us sleep.

ANNE: (*Getting up and moving towards the main door.*) All right. I'm not fond of whisky, but when I have to take it I like it best that way.

EDITH: It'll do you a world of good.

ANNE: I'll get the whisky and the kettle.

(*When Anne goes out Edith's face grows haggard and despairing. For some moments she stares hopelessly into the fire. Then she gives a shudder and makes a gesture as if to say, "There's nothing else for it!" She feels in her pocket, takes out the small bottle, looks at it, loosens the cork, and as Anne enters, hides it in her hand. Anne brings in a tray with two glasses, each containing whisky, a plate with slices of lemon and a sugar bowl. In her other hand is an electric kettle.*)

ANNE: I'll be quite drunk after this.

EDITH: (*Breathlessly.*) Do you good. We want to sleep tonight.

ANNE: (*Places tray on table, goes to fireplace with kettle, places it on trivet and plugs it in.*) I could only get to sleep, I believe I'd never wake.

EDITH: (*Ominously.*) Drink your toddy and you'll sleep.

(*As Anne crosses with kettle to fireplace Edith pours the contents of the small bottle into Anne's glass, rubs bottle on handkerchief, then drops it on floor by Anne's chair. To cover her movements she put slices of lemon into both glasses. Anne hears the kettle sing.*)

ANNE: Oh, the kettle's just on the boil. I didn't realise it was so hot or I needn't have plugged it in. (*She fills the glasses and replaces the kettle.*)

EDITH: (*Picking up her glass and gasping slightly.*) Nothing like really hot today! (*She points to the bottle.*) What's that?

ANNE: (*Picking up and examining the bottle.*) I don't know. I suppose the doctor or the police were using it.

EDITH: (*Obviously on edge.*) Put it on the mantelpiece and they'll get it. (*She sips her drink and never takes her eye off Anne.*) That's good!

ANNE: (*Putting the bottle on mantelpiece.*) My goodness, Edith, how can you drink it like that? It's far too hot for me. (*Sits near the tea table.*)

EDITH: (*Sipping.*) Oh, I don't know. I like things hot. (*Suddenly she listens.*) There are those children awake again. Damn the little nuisances! (*She jumps up, places her glass on the mantelpiece, and moves towards the main door.*) I won't be a moment.

ANNE: Are you sure it's the children? I heard nothing.

EDITH: I heard them. At least I thought so. I'd better go and see. (*Exits through the main door with a terrified glance at Anne.*)

(*Anne sits back, staring straight in front of her. She feels glass, registers that it is still too hot, takes her handkerchief, wraps it round the glass, raises it to her lips, puts it down quickly and re-adjusts the handkerchief. She picks it up again and is about to drink when there is a ring. She gets up, puts the glass on the table and goes out. The front door to the house is heard opening and voices then Anne re-enters, followed by French and Carter. Carter has two dressing gowns over his arm, which he places on the small chair near the desk.*)

FRENCH: I'm sorry, Miss Day, to trouble you again, particularly at this late hour, but unfortunately I forgot an item for my report.

ANNE: That's all right, Mr. French. What can I do for you?

FRENCH: I want to make a small reconstruction and I'm afraid everyone must be present. It will only take a few minutes. Is everyone available?

ANNE: Yes. Mr. Grinsmead was late and he's just finishing dinner. The rest, I think, are upstairs. But I'm sure no one has gone to bed.

FRENCH: Don't hurry Mr. Grinsmead, but perhaps when he has finished you'd kindly bring everyone down.

ANNE: Certainly. I'll tell them. (*She goes out by the main door.*)

FRENCH: (*Rubbing his hands and evidently much pleased.*) Now, Carter, five or ten minutes until these people assemble. Another five or ten while I talk to them like a father, then … hey presto! We have a full confession from the guilty party.

CARTER: (*Puzzled.*) If you can get that, sir, you'll deserve the job of A.C. How'll you do it?

FRENCH: Moral suasion: you'll see. But you shock me, Carter. How is it you haven't discovered the guilty party for yourself?

CARTER: (*Sheepishly.*) Well, I haven't, and that's a fact. I just can't see through it.

FRENCH: I admit you haven't had my chances. I got some light today when you were up in town.

CARTER: How did you get it, sir?

FRENCH: Ah, the grey matter, or so I've read. I know who's guilty and I can prove it. But when I can get a confession, I may as well have it too.

CARTER: (*Dubiously.*) I hope you'll succeed.

FRENCH: Don't let yourself be carried away with enthusiasm. (*A slight pause.*) Is Armstrong in position?

CARTER: Yes, he's outside, and Hunter's in the car with the lady.

FRENCH: Good. And you're sure of your own part?
CARTER: Yes, sir.
FRENCH: Move causally beside the window and when I give the cue, shift the blind with your elbow. Hunter'll see that and ring, I'll sign to you to open, and you'll show in the woman. Let Hunter wait in the hall to help with the arrest.
CARTER: That's all right. I understand.
FRENCH: (*Showing signs of impatience.*) I wonder when these blessed people are coming?
CARTER: They'll not hurry. Ladies among 'em.
FRENCH: You speak with feeling.
CARTER: Experience, sir.
FRENCH: Oh well, we can wait. We're accustomed to it.
CARTER: Here they are.
(*Grinsmead enters. he looks round.*)
GRINSMEAD: I understand you want to make a reconstruction? The rest not turned up yet?
FRENCH: (*Standing up.*) No, sir, but they won't be long.
GRINSMEAD. (*Moving about jerkily.*) Would it be indiscreet to ask how you're progressing?
GRINSMEAD: Irrelevant?
FRENCH: Yes, because until you learn the truth you don't know what is relevant. Suppose there are ten suspects. You must get up the life history of each. But the work on nine will have been lost.
GRINSMEAD: Surely not wholly?
FRENCH: Not wholly, of course: The information may prove innocence as well as guilt. Now in this case we've had to check the statements and the history of everyone in the house. A lot of work, and most of it will be wasted.
GRINSMEAD: I suppose you have to complete a file?
FRENCH: Exactly. Take Miss Day, for instance. None of us suspect Miss Day of any crime, but we had to check her statements: that she was the daughter of a Somerset vicar, that she had studied domestic economy at Bristol, and so on. If I hadn't done so the super would have grumbled. "Who the heck is this Miss Day?"
GRINSMEAD: (*Drily.*) It's certainly a lot of work.
CARTER: Even from Australia, sir, we've had to get information.
GRINSMEAD: You don't seem to be leaving much to chance.
FRENCH: You will understand that no slight whatever to your sister-in-

law was intended: it was simply that she is a stranger here. We had to check up on her with the Melbourne police.

GRINSMEAD: Wonderful! I had no idea you were so thorough. And what did the Melbourne police say?

FRENCH: Mrs. Cheame is well known over there. She is the daughter of Dr. Frazer of that city. And her husband, the late Mr. Edwin Cheame, was also well known and respected.

GRINSMEAD: (*Drily.*) That's fortunate.

FRENCH: Mrs. Cheame's statements have been amply corroborated. The steamship people tell us that she shared a cabin with a Mrs. Agatha Gill, who was found unconscious under a crushed boat when the ship was searched before abandonment.

GRINSMEAD: I didn't know that.

FRENCH: Oh yes, sir, Mrs. Cheame told Miss Day. She saw the accident happen and it was a great shock.

GRINSMEAD: I should think so. Poor thing!

FRENCH: She was wrong in one point, but it was a perfectly genuine mistake. She thought Mrs. Gill was dead, whereas she was only unconscious. I understand she has recovered, though she lost her memory.

GRINSMEAD: My sister-in-law will be glad to know that.

CARTER: (*Listening.*) They're really coming this time.

(*Mrs Grinsmead and Irene enter, followed by Edith. they hesitate.*)

GRINSMEAD: I suppose you want us to sit down?

FRENCH: If you please, sir.

(*Mrs Grinsmead . and Edith sit on the settee with Edith closest to the wall. Irene sits in the armchair and Grinsmead in a chair. Anne enters, followed by Maxwell.*)

FRENCH: (*To Anne and Maxwell.*) Will you kindly find a chair? (*Anne sits on the chair below the fireplace, and Maxwell on the pouffe. Standing like a lecturer, French continues.*) I'm sorry, ladies and gentlemen, to have to trouble you again in this way, but as I told Miss Day, I won't keep you long.

GRINSMEAD: It's all right. We're not in a hurry.

FRENCH: Now before we begin I must tell you the point I've reached in my investigations.

MRS. G: (*Grimly.*) We've been wondering that. We'll be glad to know.

FRENCH: (*Dropping his easy manner and becoming serious.*) Very well. As I have already stated, I have been forced to the unpleasant conclusion

that the late Mrs. Grinsmead's death was brought about by some member of the household, and If I'm right, that means by someone here.
(*All shiver and exchange uneasy glances.*)
GRINSMEAD: You said that, but you didn't prove it.
FRENCH: I'll do so now. But to take everything in order I must first tell you how I knew it was murder. The deceased's fingerprints on the gas tap in her room showed that she had turned the gas off, not on.
MAXWELL: (*With a gesture of amazement.*) Good Lord! What a give-away!
MRS. G: (*Grimly.*) They say a criminal always overlooks something, if one can only find it.
ANNE: (*Eagerly.*) But that confirms what Sybil said. She told me that Gladys had turned the gas full on, and that it was too hot, and that she had turned it down.
FRENCH: That was it, Miss Day. She moved it then and never touched it again.
GRINSMEAD: This is astonishing to me.
FRENCH: But conclusive.
GRINSMEAD: I suppose it is. Yes, we must all admit it.
FRENCH: Even if it wasn't, there's a second point which alone proves it was murder. I've already mentioned it. A little after ten the deceased took a sleeping draught and would have been asleep by eleven. But the doctor said she didn't die before about two. Therefore the gas couldn't have been turned on till long after she was asleep.
MAXWELL: In other words, she couldn't have done it herself.
GRINSMEAD: That's certainly unquestionable. So far, Mr. French, you've proved your case up to the hilt.
FRENCH: I satisfied myself that the door and window had been genuinely fastened and that no one could have entered the room during the night. The murder must therefore have been committed from the outside, and the only way that could have been done was by using the meter.
ANNE: You were seen working at it.
FRENCH: It was quite simple. First, the meter was turned off, then when the fire in the room had gone out it was turned on again, with the result that unburnt gas filled the room.
MAXWELL: That's what you thought, uncle.
GRINSMEAD: When Mr. French was seen at the meter, it was clear what was in his mind.

FRENCH: Now, ladies and gentlemen, you will see that one thing was fundamental to the crime: (*With weighty emphasis.*) that Mrs. Grinsmead must that night take a sleeping draught.
GRINSMEAD: Fundamental?
FRENCH: Yes, sir. What do you think would have happened had she been awake when the gas came on?
GRINSMEAD: She'd have smelt it, I suppose.
FRENCH: Yes, and before it could possibly have affected her. And what would she have done?
MAXWELL: Got up and turned it off, wouldn't she?
FRENCH: Much more than that, I fancy. She'd have cried out and waked the house.
GRINSMEAD: Yes, she'd have been frightened.
ANNE: And who wouldn't?
MRS. G: I should have been, I admit.
IRENE: The very idea makes me shiver.
MAXWELL: Well, suppose she *did* wake the house?
FRENCH: There'd have been an investigation. Attempted murder would have been suspected.
GRINSMEAD: Yes, that's true enough.
FRENCH: So we may take it that if Mrs. Grinsmead had been awake two things would have happened: first, that the murderer would have failed in his purpose — which, mind you, must have been vital to him or he wouldn't have attempted it — and second, that in the resulting investigation his identity would almost certainly have been discovered. You will see therefore that he simply daren't act without the sleeping draught.
GRINSMEAD: (*Looking round.*) We accept that. You needn't labour it further.
(*All nod.*)
FRENCH: (*Grimly.*) Now it's quite clear that no outsider could have had this information, and I therefore turned my attention to you. I soon saw that several of you had motives for wishing Mrs. Grinsmead out of the way. It would be painful to mention these and it's not necessary. So I'll pass on.
GRINSMEAD: (*A little unsteadily.*) We appreciate that, Inspector.
FRENCH: My problem then was: which of those in the house on that night was guilty?
MAXWELL: (*Moving uneasily.*) Ah, now you're talking.

IRENE: (*Shivering.*) Oh, this is dreadful!
GRINSMEAD: (*Grimly.*) Go on, please.
FRENCH: I had this line of approach: who knew that the deceased had taken a sleeping draught? Miss Day told me this and her statement was my first pointer.
ANNE: (*Gasping.*) I told you? I never …
(*All are giving fresh evidence of tension, avoiding each other's eyes.*)
FRENCH: (*Interrupting.*) Yes, you told me, but never mind that now. There was another matter which I have not mentioned, because it's not really essential. All the same, it gives useful confirmation. (*He looks around.*)
GRINSMEAD: Go on, Mr. French.
FRENCH: When I was looking at the meter I turned it off and on. As you know, the handle is awkwardly placed and when I had finished Carter found a patch of white on my elbow. (*All listen more attentively.*) I tried turning it again different times, and on each I got a patch of whitewash from the wall on my sleeve. This naturally gave me an idea. I examined everyone's wardrobe and I found two dressing gowns with patches of white on the elbows. (*Points to the chair.*) And there they are.
(*There is a general movement. All avoid each other's eyes.*)
IRENE: I can't bear this! It's horrible!
ANNE: Oh, nor I. Go on and get it over, Mr. French.
MAXWELL: Good Lord! Someone *has* blundered.
(*French snaps his fingers and Carter passes him one of the dressing gowns.*)
FRENCH: (*Holding it up.*) This yours, Mr. Crawley?
MAXWELL: (*Amazed and hesitating.*) Yes, that's right.
FRENCH: (*Turning up sleeve and pointing.*) The patch of white.
(*All stare at Maxwell. Carter, moving, disturbs the window blind. he draws back quickly.*)
MRS. G: (*Incredulously.*) On yours, Maxwell?
MAXWELL: On mine? No, there's some mistake. I can't believe it!
FRENCH: There's no mistake. Now, Mr. Crawley, can you account for this mark?
MAXWELL: (*Shakes his head.*) But it's impossible! No, Mr. French, I cannot.
ANNE: (*With nervous desperation.*) But I can. When we found … When the door was broken open Mr. Grinsmead shouted, "Turn off the gas!" Mr. Crawley ran down and did so.
(*The front door bell rings, off. Noone pays any attention. French signs to Carter*

to open the door. Carter leaves by the main door.)
MAXWELL: (*With obvious relief.*) That's right, Anne. Yes, I ran down in my dressing gown and turned off the meter.
FRENCH: You said so in your deposition. Then that accounts for you, Mr. Crawley.
MAXWELL: (*Looking round.*) I say, that was a nasty moment!
CARTER: (*Appearing at the main door.*) That lady from Westlake wants to speak to you, sir.
FRENCH: (*Sharply.*) Don't you see I'm busy? I can't attend to her now.
(*Carter disappears, closing the door. Grumbling, French continues.*) In my job you need to be able to do about six things and be in six places at the same time. Carter should know better. Well, where was I? About that second dressing gown. (*He moves over to pick it up.*) I tried to …
(*The door opens and Carter appears again.*)
CARTER: Sorry, sir, but I can't quiet the lady. She says what she wants'll only take a minute. She's very excited and I'm afraid she'll make a scene.
FRENCH: (*Hesitating and leaving dressing gown untouched.*) Well,—(*He looks round.*) — You'll pardon me for a moment. (*To Carter.*) Show her in.
(*Carter vanishes and returns, showing in the Stranger. Carter goes out again, leaving door closed, but not shut. The Stranger is a tall, rather good looking woman, but looks ill and is not very well dressed. She first looks inquiringly at French, then glances in a puzzled way round the room. She sees Edith and her gaze grows fixed. Her jaw drops and She stares in apparent stupefaction.*
Edith, also struck motionless, stares at her with incredulous and growing horror. The atmosphere grows tense as all move expectantly and then become rigid. There is a wild scream from Edith, who sinks back on the settee.)
FRENCH: (*Suddenly seeming to awake, motions towards the Stranger and shouts.*) Ladies and gentlemen, let me introduce you to — the real Mrs. Edith Cheame!
(*Everyone stares rigidly, as if they can't believe their ears.*)
GRINSMEAD: Merciful heavens!
MAXWELL: Edith!
ANNE: Edith! It can't be!
STRANGER: (*Putting her hand over her eyes.*) Oh, what is all this? Who are these people?
FRENCH: Your friends, madam, It's all right.

MAXWELL: But does he mean that this is Edith?
ANNE: Oh, it's too much! I can't bear it!
(*The attention of everyone is concentrated on the Stranger; Edith, looking frantic with horror and despair, slowly pulls herself up, slips round end of settee next wall, and glides towards the main door.*)
FRENCH. (*to the stranger.*) Madam, this is your brother-in-law. Your troubles are over.
(*All are looking at the Stranger; Edith, unnoticed on her way to the door, glances round at the others then seizes a flowerpot and hurls it at the desk. While all involuntarily look in that direction, Edith picks up Anne's glass and drains it. French swings round and sees her. Edith walks unsteadily to the main door. No one moves. She reaches the door, holds on to it, swaying, and turns to French.*)
EDITH: My — trick, I — think.
(*Carter is seen for a moment, then he grasps Edith and helps her out of sight.*)
CARTER: (*Shouting off.*) Hunter! Hunter! Lend a hand!
(*French, suddenly coming to life, leaps for the glass.*)
FRENCH: (*Shouting.*) What! What had she there? (*Smells the glass.*) Merciful heavens! (*He rushes out through the main door.*)
ANNE: Oh, what has she done?
MAXWELL: *Edith!* That *Edith* should …
(*Carter re-enters and goes quietly to phone. French re-enters.*)
FRENCH: Prussic acid! How did she do that? I'll swear she put nothing in, for I was watching her carefully.
GRINSMEAD: (*Much upset.*) Is she -? Will she live?
FRENCH: (*Shakes his head.*) Afraid not. Bad for me, but best for herself.
(*Carter puts down the receiver and whispers to French who nods. Carter goes out through the main door.*)
IRENE: (*In a low tone.*) Dreadful, dreadful! But, oh, what a relief!
MRS. G: My son! Oh, thank God!
GRINSMEAD: (*Incredulously.*) But what does all this mean? Are we to understand we've been harboring an imposter?
FRENCH: Yes, sir. This is your sister-in-law. The person who took her name was a Mrs. Gill. It was she who murdered Sybil Grinsmead.
GRINSMEAD: Incredible! Explain it, Chief Inspector!
FRENCH: I believed she was guilty because only Miss Day and she knew the deceased had a sleeping draught, and I could scarcely suspect Miss Day. When I found the white patch on Mrs. Gill's dressing gown I knew I need look no further.

GRINSMEAD: But *why?* *Why* did she do it?

FRENCH: That was the question I asked myself. I went to the shipping people and learned that Mrs. Cheame had shared a cabin with a Mrs. Gill, and that these two were not unlike in appearance. I learned that a lady had been found unconscious under a boat and had been picked up by the colliding steamer. This lady had lost her memory and was identified as Mrs. Gill solely by the papers in her handbag. I also learned from the Australian police that Mrs. Gill's husband had died in prison and that she was left badly off.

GRINSMEAD: (*Helplessly.*) But still I don't …

FRENCH: These facts suggested impersonation, but still I could not see my way, till unwittingly Miss Day put the missing link into my hands.

ANNE: (*Almost stupefied.*) I? I knew nothing about it.

FRENCH: You seem to have known practically everything. You told me the deceased had written to Australia for photographs. I got in touch with the photographers through the Melbourne police and found she asked for any photograph they had of Mrs. Cheame. They had sent a portrait by air mail. It arrived three days before the murder.

MAXWELL: (*Expressively.*) Ah!

FRENCH: These people print their name on the outside of their envelopes and Mrs. Gill saw it — no doubt when she took the letters from the hall door box. It's pretty clear she opened the letter. She would then have seen the game was up. The deceased obviously suspected something, and she would not have let the matter drop till she found out all.

GRINSMEAD: A ghastly story, Chief Inspector!

FRENCH: Mrs. Gill had impersonated, made false immigration declarations and stolen a lot of money. She couldn't face penal servitude and the poverty and misery that would follow it. She destroyed the letter and committed the murder. And when she found that Miss Day was also on to the truth, she tried to poison her.

MRS. G: (*Getting up.*) Look here, this is certainly ghastly enough, but while we talk Edith — the real Edith — is being forgotten. She could lie down in the morning room till we get a bed ready for her.

FRENCH: A good suggestion, madam. I think my questions brought back her memory. Then I asked her to say nothing till today.

GRINSMEAD:(*Going to the stranger.*) I'm your brother-in-law, Edith, with whom you were coming to stay. Will you rest in the other room

until we can explain all these mysteries?
(*Grinsmead takes one arm and Mrs. Grinsmead the other. They lead her out left. Irene follows. Anne begins to follow, but sinks down as if overcome in an armchair. Maxwell moves beside her.*)
ANNE:(*Overcome.*) Oh, Maxwell, I can't bear any more!
MAXWELL: Anne, dear, see what's happened! My uncle's cleared! There's no slur on the family! It's all right! (*Going down on one knee and putting his arm round her.*) Anne, darling!
(*French moves to Anne and pats her shoulder in a fatherly way. Maxwell puts his arm further round her. Anne hesitates, then suddenly clings to him. French smiles down on them as …*)

CURTAIN

Part II:
The Casebook of Robin Brand

Meet Robin Brand

Freeman Wills Crofts' juvenile detective appears in one novel and two short stories. The novel, *Young Robin Brand Detective*[1], was published in January 1947 by the University of London Press as one of a series[2] of illustrated *"junior novels by famous authors ... specially written and designed for the multitude of boys and girls who are midway between the 'children's book' stage and the whole range of adult reading."* As might be expected, however, the tone of Crofts' book, written over seventy years ago, has little in common with the dystopian sagas that are the main focus of young adult fiction today. On the contrary, Crofts' stories are gentle, Blytonesque tales of courageous children and careless criminals, complete with scouting lore, and plenty of strawberries and thick Devonshire cream for tea.

In the novel, Robin is humorously described at one point as *"the greatest amateur detective of modern times, in the direct line of descent from Sherlock Holmes himself."* It is some time after the Second World War and he is spending the long summer holiday in the Cornish town of Ryemouth with his friend Jack Carr, similarly ribbed as *"the famous authority on all matters of railway construction, operation and maintenance."* Like Crofts, Jack is *"interested in any kind of engineering"* and his father is *"the engineer in charge of the building of a large railway viaduct,"* just as Crofts had been back in County Antrim. It isn't long before the two boys become aware of nefarious goings on in the vicinity of the viaduct. They investigate and, after some near scrapes, they bring the malefactors to justice with the help of a young engineer, Cyril French, who is reminiscent of Crofts himself and, more importantly, is the nephew of Chief Inspector French of Scotland Yard. French appears in only two chapters of the book and has little to do beyond serving as a role model and reminiscing about a case he investigated over fifteen years earlier, described in *Death on the Way* (1932). Instead, the case is unravelled by the juvenile detective duo of Brand and Carr, who possibly owe their names —but nothing else — to Crofts' fellow members of the Detection Club, Christianna Brand and John Dickson Carr.

Tony Medawar

---

[1] There is no comma in the title.
[2] Others in the series were *The Emperor's Bracelet* by Manning Coles, *Caravan for Three* by Ursula Bloom and *The Knight's of St Perrans* by Clifford Witting.

Perilous Journey

"WAKE up, you lazy hog! Are you going to lie snoring there all day?" As in a dream, Robin Brand heard the voice, but when the bedclothes suddenly leaped away into space he awoke. His friend Jack Carr dropped the clothes, and though not more than two feet away, roared in a voice that would have carried to the next street, "It's fine!"

Robin sat up with a gasp of relief. It was Christmas Eve, and bad weather on Christmas Eve was not unknown. But this Christmas Eve was exceptional. Today Jack's father was taking them to try out a new type of "family" helicopter and—marvellous thought!—if it proved satisfactory he was going to buy one for their own use!

Mr. Carr was an engineer living in a London suburb and Jack and Robin were school-fellows. Robin had spent a summer holiday with the Carrs, and they had all got on so well that he had been invited back for Christmas.

Mr. Carr had first to attend to some business, but he was coming back for the boys at eleven. They were then to catch the 11.30 from Euston to the firm's private airfield near Tamworth and do some tests flights. The secret hope of each boy was that he would be allowed to take over the controls.

The morning dragged, for they were both too excited to settle down to anything. Then just as Jack was proposing a game of table tennis, Mrs. Carr appeared.

"Oh, Jack," she cried, "I've lost my bag! I think I left it last night at the Seftons." And they're not on the 'phone. Do you think you and Robin could run over for it?"

Jack was indignant. "But, mum, you can't have forgotten. We're going out with dad."

"I know, but not till eleven. It's only ten now, and you'll have heaps of time."

Jack knew it was true. They could do the errand and be back with twenty minutes in hand.

"Oh, all right," he said resignedly. "Come on, Cury."

Robin's nickname, short for Curiosity, had been given him because of his hobby. It was detection. He was always following up footprints and making deductions from clues. His school-friends admitted he was pretty good at it. They said that if he saw eggs in a nest, he would almost certainly be able to deduce the previous visit of a bird. As a matter of fact he had done better than this. He had—but that, as the books say, is another story.

They set off, discussing avidly the entrancing subject of the adoption of helicopters into families. Presently, they turned into Pacific Avenue.

A less exciting thoroughfare could scarcely be imagined. It was an ordinary quiet residential street of detached and semi-detached houses, each in its tiny area of ground, and all looking slightly down-at-heel as a result of the shortage of paint and gardeners. There was absolutely nothing about it to attract attention, yet Robin and Jack were not soon to forget it.

As they entered it Robin, who had persistently drilled himself in observation, noticed a large blue furniture van standing down the cross-street. It had evidently broken down, for the bonnet was up and the driver was working at the motor. The avenue itself was empty except for a man standing at the corner. He was clean-shaven with a long chin and was dressed in a cap and blue overalls. He did not seem to have any particular business there, and Robin supposed he was waiting for someone.

On their passage down the avenue, they were witnesses of a tiny drama. Just as they approached a detached house about half-way along, a taxi appeared and drew up at its gate. At the same time the house door opened and an anxious-looking woman came out. She pulled the door after her, shook it slightly, and hurried down to the taxi. They heard her call out "Paddington!" as she scrambled in. There was a suggestion of urgency in her manner, as if her business was vital and pressing.

The boys continued to the Seftons', found Mrs. Carr's bag, and still discussing helicopters, returned the way they had come. Pacific Avenue this time was not so wholly devoid of life. A large blue furniture van like the one Robin had seen stood at the footpath, and men were carrying tables and chairs to it from one of the houses. When they were closer, Robin noticed two things which greatly interested him. The first was that it stood opposite the house of the Paddington passenger; the second, that the long-chinned man was helping to load it.

"I say, Mock," he burst out—for unknown reasons Jack was called Mock Turtle by his friends—"I say, that van's at the same house!"

"What same house?" Jack asked disparagingly.

"Where the lady came out. You remember? She was going to Paddington."

"What of it? Any objection to her going to Paddington?" "Only that she'll be away some time if she was going by train."

"She can stay the rest of her life for me. What's bitten you, Cury?"

"Funny they'd be moving furniture from an empty house, that's all."

"How could it be empty when there's furniture in it, you owl?"

Robin sighed. Jack was in one of his crooked moods. "I mean no people in it, ass," he explained with resignation.

Jack gestured impatiently. "In the first place," he began with superiority, "you don't know there are no people in it. In the second—"

"Of course I know. Didn't you see her shake the door to make sure it was locked? She wouldn't have done that if anyone else was there."

"Rot!" Jack was scornful. "Anyhow, what business of yours is it?"

"Mock," Robin declared impressively, "I believe that furniture's being stolen!"

Jack featured kindly solicitude. "My poor fellow," he said sympathetically, "where does it hurt? Is it your head?"

"No, seriously, Mock. I mean it."

"A distressing case," Jack said sadly. "Not much hope with one so young."

"Oh, shut up!" Robin fumed. "It looks just like one of those black-market thefts that you read about."

"I don't," Jack returned helpfully.

"Well, I do. Look, you know how they're done? Suppose a gang gets to know of a house where there's good furniture or valuables."

"You mean the owner puts an ad. in the papers to tell them?"

"There are lots of ways of finding out," Robin went on patiently. "Piano tuners, meter readers, men to test that the ball valves aren't leaking, all with proper cards of authority. People with messages from friends in America, who then find they've come to the wrong house."

Jack grunted.

"From gossip with tradesmen in bars anyone can learn all they want about the people in a house. It's easy enough."

"How on earth do you know all that?" Jack seemed interested in spite of himself.

Robin ignored the question. "Suppose," he continued, "they learnt that that woman was likely to be alone in the house this morning. Well, they'd bring a van to the neighbourhood and ring her up with some story to get her out. I bet they'd found that some of her people lived down the Western Region, and 'phoned her that some accident had happened and that she was wanted. One of them would watch if she took the bait, and when the coast was clear he'd signal to the van and they'd get down to it."

"All guesswork, you cuckoo. You haven't a thing to prove it."

"Yes, I have," declared Robin, "absolute proof. When we were coming I saw the van waiting down the cross-street and the sentry at the corner where he could see both ways." He paused to heighten the tension like a B.B.C. announcer, then added impressively, "That sentry is now loading the van!"

Jack stared. "Golly," he remarked.

"More than that," went on Robin, "I noticed he was wearing rubber gloves!"

Jack was clearly impressed, and as clearly was not going to admit it.

"Isn't that the way things happen?" he grumbled. "Here we're on to a perfectly good crime and we can't wait and see it out."

Robin was horrified. "Hang it all, Mock," he objected, "we can't suspect a robbery and do nothing about it."

"Do you know the time?" retorted Jack. "If we don't get that 11.7 tube train we'll miss the 11.30."

"I don't care," Robin said stoutly. "We can't let the woman lose her furniture without trying to prevent it."

Jack seemed really annoyed. "We've been looking forward to these tests for weeks and if we're late we'll miss them. Have some sense, Cury. What's the woman and her rotten furniture to us?"

"Oh, Mock," Robin persisted, "we must do something. You know that yourself. Come back and have another look at the van. We may get a hint."

A struggle raged in Jack's mind which Robin could almost see. Then suddenly he gave way.

"I suppose you're right. Well, it won't be so bad missing the trials if we really do save a theft, but what I'm afraid of is missing them just for your nonsense."

Having by this time passed the van some little distance, they turned back and noted its registration number and the name on its sides. But they could learn nothing more. For a moment they stood talking beside it, the two men having gone into the house.

"So what?" said Jack disgustedly.

"I think we should tell the police."

"Without real proof?"

"Yes, the thing's suspicious. If we tell them what we've seen, it's up to them."

Jack made a gesture. "Then let's cut home now. We could ring them up from there and we might just catch dad."

Robin still hung back. "But, Mock, we can't! The van's nearly full. If we wait ten minutes it may be gone. Look," he pointed upwards. "There are wires going next door. Let's ask to use their 'phone."

To Robin's surprise Jack made no further difficulty. "Okay. Only let's be quick. We can sprint back and chance being in time."

As they turned in to the next gate a sudden crash came from the van, followed by a cry of pain and then a voice. "Hi, you boys!" it shouted urgently. "The piano's slipped on to my foot. Cut up to the house and get the others down to lift it off!"

Jack, always prompt in an emergency, hurried off, followed by Robin. There was no one in the hall, but voices came from a room at the back of the house.

The boys rushed in. The long-chinned man and a lanky companion were stacking saucepans on the kitchen floor. They stared at Jack as he began urgently explaining.

Suddenly, a door slammed behind the boys. They swung round. A third man stood with his back to it.

"They're on to us," the newcomer growled to his friends, then turned to the boys. "So you're going to tell the police, are you?" and his tone was mockingly polite. "And what, my brave young bantams, are you going to tell them?"

"We thought you were hurt," Jack said with an attempt at indignation.

"So you did. A harmless little stratagem. I reckoned we might have a chat, and it seemed better here than on the road."

He paused, looking at each boy in turn. Panic was slowly creeping into Robin's heart. The man's lips were smiling, but there was a cold ruthlessness in his eyes which boded only evil. Robin could see that in spite of his brave front, Jack also was frightened. "You've not been very clever, you know," went on the man. "You shouldn't have talked near the van unless you were sure it was empty. I watched you snooping round and I thought I'd lie low and hear what I could. My hunch was good. Well, you've only yourselves to thank. You'll spend the rest of the day minding your own business. Two chairs and a bit of rope, Sam."

Sam, the long-chinned man, placed the chairs in the centre of the floor and the newcomer, whose name they found was Joe, pointed to them.

"Sit down and don't make a fuss, or it'll be the worse for you."

As rather despairingly he moved towards his chair, an idea flashed into Robin's mind. If anyone were at the back of the next door house they might yet have a chance. He suddenly swung round and screamed to Jack, "Shout, Mock! Shout!" and began yelling "Help!" at the top of his voice. Jack instantly joined in with a stentorian roar. The men leaped forward with lurid oaths, clapped their hands over the boys' mouths, and before Robin could realize what was happening, he found himself tied to the chair and gagged with a cloth.

"Young devils!" Joe muttered viciously. "But I don't think they could have been heard."

"No one to hear them," Sam assured him. He moved over to Joe and began whispering. He seemed to be urging some course of action on him. Then Joe nodded. "I think you're right. We'll take 'em along."

As the men went out, the captives exchanged somber glances. Had their fate been decided? What was it to be? To judge by the men's expression, it would not be too happy. Then horror flooded Robin's mind as he remembered something he had read. Few of these black-marketeers would stop at murder. Rather than risk their liberty they would kill without scruple. Where were they taking them? And for what?

But Robin was not left long to indulge in forebodings. Soon there were sounds of something heavy coming downstairs. Then Sam returned, picked him up chair and all, and carried him to the hall. "I think it'll go in," he said, eyeing the chair.

In the hall was the upper part of a large wardrobe, and while

Joe opened the door, Sam and the lanky man lifted in Robin and his chair. The door would not close, but Joe said this would not matter if they kept a hand on it. Then Robin felt the wardrobe being lifted. It swayed perilously as it was borne from the house. Through the slightly open door he could get glimpses first of the path and then of the back of the van. It grew dark as the van roof came forward over his head. Presently, the steps retreated and he was alone.

At intervals the steps returned, and from the sounds he realised that more furniture was being packed. At last the doors were closed, leaving him in complete blackness, the motor started up and they moved off.

Alone in the darkness, unable to move, being hurried relentlessly on, his position unknown to a single friend! Despair began to take possession of Robin's mind. It might well be that he and Jack were finished. Perhaps they might never see another day. Oh, if only he had done what Jack wanted! If even they had been a little more wide awake! There was no excuse for walking into such a trap. If they had kept their wits about them, they might now have been on the way to Tamworth.

The van seemed to be going through streets and Robin imagined they were still in London. After perhaps half an hour it turned sharply to the left and stopped. A few seconds later it moved on again, dead slow. For some yards the sounds were louder, as if reflected from an arch. Then once again it stopped. The motor was switched off and all was quiet.

But not for long. Soon the van doors were opened and the men began to remove the furniture. In due course the wardrobe was slid back and lifted out. Through the chink of the door Robin caught a glimpse of an untidy yard surrounded by high decayed-looking buildings.

The wardrobe was taken into a dark unfurnished hall and there Robin was lifted out. Sam and the lanky man carried him, still attached to his chair, up eight flights of grimy uncarpeted stairs. On the top landing was an open door, and through this they bore him.

The room they entered was small and as dirty as the stairs. The walls were festooned with cobwebs and the old yellow paper was peeling off in long strips. The dust of years lay on the floor and light came from a single skylight, unscreened but with whitewash on the glass, a protection doubtless against a vanished summer's sun. The room was empty save for another chair. The sight of this gave Robin the first shred of comfort he had had since they were captured. For on it sat Jack, still gagged and tied.

The men put down Robin's chair beside the other, and while the lanky one disappeared, Sam began removing the gags and ropes. Robin was so cramped that at first he could scarcely move, and Jack seemed to be in no better case. While they were rubbing themselves the lanky man returned with a plate of bread and butter and two glasses of milk.

"Eat that and have a sleep," he said gruffly, though without looking at them. "Come on, Sam. Joe's waiting for us." They picked up the chairs and went out, locking the door behind them.

"Oh, Mock," Robin began a little tremulously, "this is my fault. I shouldn't—"

But Jack interrupted. "Rats!" he said. "My fault as much as yours. Besides, it's done. Question is, what do we do now?"

"Some milk, I suppose. I could do with a drink."

"Could you though? I'm surprised at you, Cury. Remember one time before when we got locked up and were offered milk?"

Robin stared. "Doped! I say, Mock, it just might be!"

"I thought it suspicious that fellow saying we should have a sleep."

Robin cautiously sipped the milk. "Believe you're right," he declared. "It's got a funny taste. But they couldn't have doped the bread."

"Then let's eat the bread and pour away the milk. They ought to think we've drunk it."

Jack's common sense and matter-of-fact manner was having its effect on Robin. He began to wonder how to get rid of the milk. The floor was sound and without loose boards. The skylight was far out of reach.

Then he gave an exclamation. The projecting joint between the skirting boards at the chimney breast was slightly open, and when he prised it with his knife he managed to widen the space. Further work and the short piece came away, the nails drawing out of the rotten wallplugs. A narrow space between floor and brickwork was revealed.

"Here we are, Mock," he cried. "Pour it down here."

Soon the milk had vanished and the skirting board had been pushed into place.

"When they come back," Jack went on, "I suggest we should be asleep. If they think we're doped there's just the chance they may leave the door unlocked."

Robin agreed. He had tried to speak bravely, but he did not feel brave. He did not really believe the door would be left open or that they would get away. The knowledge he and Jack had gained made them too dangerous to these men. And they were utterly in their captors' power. No one knew where they were or could find out in time to help.

Robin began to fear he might break down and disgrace himself, so started talking feverishly to Jack. Jack, perhaps for the same reason, seemed glad of it. They spoke of many things, though by tacit consent avoided the subject of helicopters. An hour dragged away: the longest that Robin had ever known. Then at last they heard steps on the stairs. "Down!" whispered Jack excitedly, "and breathe loudly."

They lowered themselves silently to the floor, and when the door opened both were clearly sunk in heavy slumber. Two men came in and stood still. Robin had a tremendous urge to open his eyes, but he controlled himself.

"Took the stuff all right," Sam's voice came presently. "They'll give no more trouble. Good stuff that: they'll sleep till we're ready for them."

There was a further pause, then the steps retreated, the door closed, and to Robin's utter despair, was locked. The steps clattered downstairs.

The boys looked at each other without speaking. They had a little time till some job or other was done. After that the men would come for them. They would find them awake, and then—

Robin just couldn't think of what might happen then.

Oh, if he had done what Jack, wise Jack, had wanted! Jack had asked what business someone else's furniture was of theirs. Jack had been right. Now they were going to pay for their mistake.

All the same Robin was amazed to find, deep down within him, a strange kind of satisfaction. A test had come to him and he had met it. He had been neither selfish nor cowardly. He had done the right thing in trying to help the lady and in fighting the black market. But why, when he had done the right thing, should he suffer for it? It didn't seem fair, and yet the satisfaction was real.

It was now beginning to get dark. There was an unshaded electric bulb hanging from a cord in the middle of the ceiling. Jack tried the switch and found the current on. It lit up the room with a bare blinding light. It wasn't much comfort, but light was better than darkness in which to face what was coming.

Slowly but inexorably the time slipped away. An hour must now have passed since the men's visit. At any time they might expect—

Suddenly an idea shot into Robin's mind. His heart began to thump. Everything might not yet be lost! Could they not even yet obtain help? Had they not a connection with the outside world after all? That naked bulb! That unscreened window!

He leaped to his feet. He was about to shout out his plan, but remembered just in time that they were supposed to be asleep.

"Mock!" he breathed. "The light! Can we signal? Look!"

He ran to the switch and turned it off. The room was now almost dark. Then he flashed it on nine times: three short flashes, three long, and three short.

Jack stared. "What is it?" he whispered.

"S O S!" Robin's voice had gone husky. "S in Morse is three shorts, O three longs. You can do it with lights or whistles or flags."

Jack instantly was wildly excited. "Oh, Cury!" he gasped, "it's a chance! How did you think of it?"

"Something I read. About Edison or someone. The wires were down and he jumped on a railway engine and morsed a message across the river with the whistle."

"It's a chance! Go on! Keep it up!"

They kept it up for what seemed like hours, till their fingers were sore and their brains reeling. At intervals they relieved each other. But nothing happened. No one came to help them. They did not speak. They no longer even looked at one another.

At last, Robin slumped down on the dusty floor. "It's no use," he groaned in utter misery. Up till now he had been the cheerful one, full of suggestions and hope. Now he seemed to have given up. Jack felt he couldn't bear it. He must do something, anything, to give his friend back his courage.

"Let's try just once more," he urged. "Suppose we each do a hundred flashes."

"All right," Robin agreed listlessly, struggling to his feet.

"No, I'll have first go. You sit still."

Jack pumped the switch up and down, counting as he did so: three, three, three, a five-second pause, three, three, three again.

"Now your turn," he said at last. Robin took over and began to switch up and down, up and down, up and—

Suddenly their crowning misfortune overtook them. The light flickered, shone up brightly for a moment and went out!

"The bulb! That's done it!" Robin groaned. He sank down again on the floor.

Jack crouched beside him. They sat there in darkness and silence. Nothing moved but Time, which dragged on slowly and inexorably.

That same Christmas Eve, a boy scout called Tony Knox was up in the attic of his home, working at a model aeroplane for his patrol competition. He was glueing on some pieces of the tail planes. At last he finished the job, opened the door, and turned out the light. As he did so a faint twinkling caught his eye. He went to the window. Yes, he was right: there were three short flashes, three long, three short again and a pause. From a skylight in the next street. A queer game to be playing! What could be the idea? Then his scouts' training asserted itself. S O S! Someone in that building was in trouble. He waited for a moment to make sure. Yes, there it was again.

Tony felt that his big moment had come. His father and mother were out, therefore he must handle the matter himself. He ran down the ten flights of stairs and out into the street. What luck! There was a policeman.

"Oh," he cried breathlessly, "someone wants help! They're S O S-ing out of a house in Duke Street!"

"Which house?" demanded the policeman surlily. He suspected all boys and their goings on.

"Come up to our attic and I'll show you," Tony begged. So insistent was he that the policeman at last consented, and toiled grumbling up the long flights of stairs. Tony threw open the door and led the way to the window. There was no winking light! They stared out into unrelieved blackness. Though Tony did not know it, Jack and Robin were just in process of changing over. He was forced to stand helplessly while the policeman's wrath descended on his head. "Bringing me up all those stairs on a wild goose chase!" growled the angry man. "I've a good mind to run you in: wasting my time like that, and—"

"Look, look! There it is!" Tony broke in eagerly.

Sure enough the little light began again blinking "S O S! S O S! S O S!" Then as the bulb gave out, it disappeared and all was once more dark.

But Constable Clutterbuck had seen enough to be convinced. Carefully he and Tony worked out the position of the window by counting the chimney pots which showed up against the night sky. Then down they went and made their way to Duke Street. As the constable saw that the window was in a building over a furniture shop beside an enclosed yard, he felt his excitement rising. For news of a theft of furniture and the disappearance of two boys had just come through from the Yard. Visions of promotion floated before his eyes. There was a telephone kiosk a little further down the street and in a few seconds he had made his call.

The message acted like a stick in an ants' nest. The station quickly hummed, for not only had the furniture been taken, but two boys who had been near the place at the time had disappeared, and an acute super told himself that morsing with an electric light was a likely enough scouts' trick. He sent an inspector to collect a squad of men, while he himself obtained a warrant to search the premises.

Superintendent Pitcairn was a general lost to the army. He surrounded the house and all those to which a passage might have been driven, then with resolution strode towards the door.

In the meantime, Robin and Jack, worn out by their anxiety, had dropped into an uneasy sleep. They were roused, cold and stiff, by the sound of heavy footsteps coming up the stairs.

"Here they are," breathed Jack. "What had we better do?" "Pretend to be still asleep," Robin whispered back. They lay with fast beating hearts, hearing their fate ascending. There were eight flights: Robin had counted them as he was carried up. The tramping had reached the top of the third flight, the fourth, when there was a ring at the doorbell. The footsteps stopped and began to go down again. Voices sounded, then an angry shout and muffled sounds which the boys could not identify. They rushed to the door and listened. A fight seemed to be going on below.

"I believe it's the police," Robin cried. "Shout, Jack, shout for all you're worth!"

They yelled as if they would burst their lungs and hammered on the door with their fists. Footsteps pounded up the stairs and a voice called out: "It's all right! We're coming!" More footsteps, crashing thuds on the door as heavy shoulders drove against it, the tearing sound of splintering wood, and the door swung open. Outside were the friendly faces and helmets of the law.

The boys had a more glorious welcome home than either could have imagined, and the Christmas Day which followed was the happiest of their lives. First, an officer called from Scotland Yard to congratulate them on having enabled the police to eliminate a gang of black marketeers which on three separate occasions had been guilty of murder.

This was good, but it was even more satisfying when the owners of the furniture came to thank the boys, and almost in tears explained that if they had lost it, they would have been financially crippled for years. A telephone message had called the lady of the house to Reading, where, it said, her son had met with a motor accident.

Lastly and perhaps best of all, it appeared that because of the interest shown in the helicopters, further trials had been arranged for a week later!

What a *marvellous* world! was the thought of both boys as they passed their plates for more plum pudding.

Danger in Shroude Valley

It was the third evening of an unexpected and very delightful holiday. To the intense satisfaction of Robin Brand and his friend Jack Carr, several of their schoolfellows had gone down with measles, and now in early June the school had been closed. As on two previous occasions, Robin had been asked to spend the time with the Carrs. Jack's father was an engineer, and was now engaged in a large railway alteration near Swinleigh, in which town he had taken a house.

The boys had been seeing a friend off at the station, and as they left, Jack glanced at the clock.

"Nine-thirty-three," he observed. "We're not due home yet. What shall we do?"

Jack's passion was for railways, and he invariably spoke as if he and his friends were trains or bales of goods or perishable merchandise. Robin wouldn't have given two hoots for all the railways in creation, had these been offered to him at the price. His hobby was detection. He was always discovering vital clues, though what these clues indicated he did not always seem to know. "Too dark to do much in the town," he pointed out. "Let's go back and get on with the jigsaw." "Okay."

It was unusual for Jack to agree so readily to a suggestion, and Robin listened with scepticism. He was soon justified. Jack stopped outside a paling.

"I say, here's a gap. Let's slip in and have a look round."

The fence encircled the works of a new bus station. Jack despised buses as being mere poor relations of genuine coaching stock, but he was interested in any kind of engineering, and here work was in hand, even if for an inferior purpose.

Unseen from the not-too-well-lit street, they squeezed through the gap. The bus platforms had been laid down with their white kerbs, but their tarmac surfaces were still unfinished. Jack decided that each platform would contain six "bays," and dilated on just how the buses would shunt to occupy them. Then they moved on to where a block of buildings was going up, the brick walls having reached a height of some eight feet.

"Offices, waiting-rooms, lavatories," Jack declared. "Let's poke through them." They moved silently over the soft clay to the first room, and were passing on to the next when they heard a man's voice. Under normal circumstances they would have backed quietly away, but the words caused them to stand rigid, scarcely daring to breathe.

"Aye," rumbled the voice, "'e said as 'ow 'e'd knock 'em out an' tie 'em up. But 'e wouldn't do 'em no 'arm. 'E weren't going' to stand for no chance of the rope, not for no money, 'e weren't." A higher-pitched voice murmured protestingly, but the words were inaudible. "'E ain't goin' to take no chances, nor me neither," came again the deep growl. "We're not standin' for no murder."

The high-pitched voice sounded once more, but Robin was no longer listening. He put his lips to Jack's ear.

"Oh, Jack, they're plotting a crime! We should listen!"

Jack glanced round, then pointed to the bricklayers' scaffold. "Give me a leg up on that and I'll look over. Steady," as Robin began to move, "wait till a bus is passing."

In spite of the late hour, buses were continually starting up from the halts in the street. Their gears shattered the silence, completely covering the slight shuffling made by the boys. Robin helped Jack on to the scaffold and was then pulled up himself. While the next bus was passing, both crawled to the top of the wall and peeped over.

Two men were standing just below, and a third was approaching from the back of the area.

"Seen the boss?" The deep voice came from a gigantic man in dungarees.

"He's coming," answered the newcomer, who was short and thickset, with fiery red hair. "Here in a minute."

A few more remarks passed and then a fourth individual walked quickly up from the rear. He was better dressed than the others and had an air of authority. He nodded briefly.

"Well, you're all here. Let's get down to it. But first, all right so far?"

The red-haired man replied: "Goliath here's got the wind up about the chance of croaking the men. And so have I. We're not standing for any risk like that."

"Tha's right," the giant agreed succinctly.

"If I've told you once, I've told you a dozen times I don't want the men hurt." The well-dressed man sounded testy. "I only want them out of action till you get the thing started: a matter of three minutes. Has that sunk in?"

There were murmurs of satisfaction.

"Now see," went on the boss, "here's the scheme and don't you forget it." He looked round aggressively. "I'll take you first, Birkett. You ride out on your bicycle, hide it in the bushes, and go to the home signal. It'll be pulled off three or four minutes before the train comes, but don't do anything till you hear the train. We don't want to give the station people time to interfere. She'll be beating hard coming up the bank and you'll hear her a couple of miles away."

"Okay, boss."

"When you hear her, cut the distant and home signal wires. Then sprint down the line to Goliath and Ginger and help them through."

"Suppose there's a down train and I can't hear ours?"

"Then cut two minutes after the signals go off."

"I got you."

The boss nodded and turned to Ginger. "You, Ginger, get the car from me tomorrow night with the extra number plates. You put it in your shed."

Ginger said he understood.

"On the night of the affair you change your plates and pick up Goliath where we agreed. You drive to near the station: I've explained where you should park, so that you can get away quick when you've finished. Both of you get on the line where the where the van will stop. Do you know the length of the train?"

"Yes," answered Ginger, "that's been measured different nights and it's always the same. And we've measured on the ground too. The place is marked."

"Good. Then when the train stops tell the guard there's an obstruction ahead and to come down to arrange the shunting. When he does so, get a cloth over his head and gag and bind him. You can manage?"

"Sure, boss. Easy as wink."

"I needn't go over the rest, we've been through it so often. You get the other fellows down, start the box, and then hook it. Now, any questions?"

"All clear to me," declared Ginger. "And to me," added Birkett.

"Clear enough," Goliath agreed, "but wotabaht the dough?" "What we settled; there's no change. I give each of you twenty-five now, and another twenty-five when the job's done. That'll be fifty pounds apiece."

"Okay."

Three lots of twenty-five notes were counted out and handed over. Then having recommended discretion to his accomplices, the boss disappeared.

When the next bus started up, Jack stabbed with his finger towards the ground, and quietly the boys lowered themselves from the scaffold.

"We'll shadow the last man," whispered Jack as they crouched at a corner from which they could see the rear exit. First Goliath lumbered away, Ginger presently followed, and then it was Birkett's turn. As soon as his figure had become a dark smudge in the gloom, the boys crept silently after him.

At the back of the new station ran the River Swinn, here canalized and with a towpath along the bank. Birkett strolled along the path, and so naturally did the boys.

Some hundred yards away a side street crossed the river, and here steps led up to the bridge from the path. Birkett climbed the steps. Instantly the boys sprinted forward, but unhappily when they reached the street he had disappeared. They dashed to the big thoroughfare at the nearest corner. There was no sign of him, and a glance at the moving crowds showed the hopelessness of a search. Jack plumped for an immediate return home. "Let's tell dad," he suggested. "He'll know what to do."

"What's the idea of cutting the signal wires?" Robin panted as they hurried along.

"Puts the signals to danger. Those fellows are going to stop a non-stop train. They know what they're doing, too."

"Why do you say that?"

"They're delaying cutting till the last minute. There are backlights or electric repeaters on the signals which tell the signalman if they go up. It's not likely he'd notice, but he might."

"You mean, the later the thing's done, the less chance of that?" "Yes, and also if he did notice, there'd be less time to do anything about it."

Mr. Carr listened gravely to the story. "The first part of it's clear enough, but what on earth does getting the other fellows down and starting the box mean? Sounds as if they were going to blow something up."

"That's it, dad: the box is a magneto!" cried Jack.

"Could it mean that something valuable is going by that train, and they hope to get it after the explosion?" Robin suggested.

'Might. In any case I think the police should know of it.

Suppose we walk round?"

Inspector Greer, to whom they reported, seemed really interested. He complimented the boys on their wise action, got from them as good descriptions of the four men as they could give, and said he would look into the matter and let them hear further. But if he had any idea of what was projected, he did not mention it. Nor did he ring up. The days went by and gradually the affair began to fade from the boys' minds.

Robin thought he had never known nicer people than the Carrs, especially Mrs. Carr's younger sister, Joan. She was, so Jack explained, engaged to a young man named Redfern, who had just taken over a nearby training stables. He had a wonderful horse, Golden Crown, which he had entered for the chief race at a famous meeting near London during the following week.

Towards dusk on the Monday evening of that week of the races, the boys were cycling home when Robin noticed a cyclist who had just turned in from a side street and was pedalling on in front of them. His heart gave a leap. Could it be? Yes, he believed it was!

"Jack!" he cried. "See that chap ahead there on the bike? I think it's Birkett!"

"Golly!" Jack declared. "You're right! Let's drop back a bit and shadow him. If it's Birkett, we've got him!"

The unconscious quarry rode on at a leisurely pace, the boys following. Then the chase turned eastwards, out of the town.

"This road runs alongside the London railway," grunted Jack suggestively.

Robin felt thrilled. "Oh, Jack! Could he be going to do whatever it is? It was to be at a station. What stations are there?"

"Shroude's the first, four miles out, then Plumpton another four."

"If there's a chance of anything, shouldn't we tell the police?" Jack seemed doubtful. "How could we? If we stop we'll lose Birkett. Besides, we're not sure. We daren't bring out the police on spec."

Robin had a profound admiration for Jack's common sense, but now he disagreed with him. They could surely tell the police what they had seen, and leave the rest to them. The more he thought of it, the more uneasy he became. A move now might prevent a crime: if they waited it might be too late.

He rode on, thinking deeply, yet not too deeply to keep his eyes open. Presently they came to a suburban crossroads at which stood a telephone kiosk.

"Look, Jack," he pointed to it. "There's our chance! I'll report what we're doing and follow on. What about it?"

Jack nodded. "I think you'd better. But don't tell them more than you know."

Robin's emergency dialing and the word "Police!" brought him an immediate reply. He quickly explained the circumstances and was cheered by the "Good lads! I'll tell the inspector," which resulted.

He put on speed after Jack. For a couple of miles out of the town the ground fell, till he crossed a river at the bottom of a wide valley. Then it began to rise again into a wilder district he and Jack had often explored, an area of hills and heather, of rocky outcrops and little mountain streams.

A mile beyond the river, he overtook Jack. Here they entered the Shroude Valley, a wild and gloomy defile just wide enough for road, rail and a tumbling stream. At the entrance was a level-crossing, where the road passed from right to left of the line. Protecting the crossing were signals, operated from a gateman's hut. A mile further up was the small roadside station of Shroude, where crossroads went up into the hills on either side.

A few score yards short of the station, Birkett dismounted and wheeled his bicycle into a lane striking off to the left. The boys also dismounted.

"That just leads up on to the moor," Jack said excitedly. "He's hiding his bike in the bushes! It looks like a true bill!"

Robin made a gesture. "We should get off the road in case he comes back and sees us."

Jack swung his bicycle round. "That's right. Let's go up to the ruined tower. From there we can see the whole valley, and if they try any tricks we can be at the station in a couple of minutes."

This seemed to make sense, and they pushed their bicycles up a lane to the top of a little cliff on which the ruin stood. It was a place they had often visited. In the daytime, as Jack had said, the view was extensive. Directly below ran railway, road, and stream, with, some quarter of a mile to the left, the station of Shroude. Nearly a mile in the opposite direction was the level-crossing, out of sight behind a bluff. Now in the growing dusk the lights of the station and signals had become the most prominent features of the landscape, but the outlines of the opposite hills were still clear and details below remained dimly visible.

'Look! There's Birkett!" Robin whispered suddenly, though they were far out of the man's earshot.

They could dimly see a black smudge on the road. It seemed to flit across it and become merged in the darker ground towards the railway.

"He's gone towards the signal, Jack! I'm glad we rang up the police!"

Jack agreed. There was silence for a moment, then he went on tensely: "Lucky we know the line here. A double line with a rising gradient of 1 in 100 all the way through the valley. That red spot to the left is what Birkett's heading for: the Shroude home signal. The crossing's away out of sight to the right. To protect the crossing there are catch-points on the up line, but of course you can't see them from here."

"You did mention those," Robin answered, "but I didn't understand exactly what they were."

In spite of their preoccupation, Jack could not resist the temptation to expound. "Where you've a long gradient like this, there's always the danger of vehicles running away. For instance, a goods might bread in two. Then the rear portion might run back down the hill, for the van brake mightn't hold it. It might go into a bus or something on the crossing and kill a lot of people. So catch-points are put into the track above the crossing to derail a runaway. The runaway would of course be smashed, but the public road or a following train would be safe."

"Good notion," Robin approved. "But how do trains pass over it safely?"

'Trains on the up grade are naturally going in the opposite direction to a runaway, so they come on the points from behind instead of in front. The points are held open by a spring, and the wheel flanges of vehicles going up the grade simply force them shut. They spring open again automatically as soon as the wheels release them. If it's necessary to run trains downhill on the up line, as for example in emergency single-line working, the points can be closed by a lever which is kept beside them. It fits into a hole in a casting at the side of the track, and when you push it over the points close."

Robin was about to comment further when Jack's hand closed like a vice on his wrist.

"There are the signals going off." He glanced at his luminous-dialled watch. "That'll be for the express: the 9.20 p.m. Swinleigh to London."

The red light near the station had suddenly gone green. Robin stiffened. If anything was going to happen, they'd soon know about it now.

A couple of minutes passed, and then Jack shouted, "Listen! She's coming!"

Far away, the beat of an engine could be heard, faint at first, but quickly growing stronger and sharper. Soon was added the dull roar of an oncoming train. The engine was working hard up the hill, and the sound increased till the whole valley seemed full of it. Then traces of steam floated up over the bluff to the right.

Suddenly, Jack gave a low cry. The green light had gone red! In a moment the headlights of the train appeared round the bluff. The engine gave a whistle, the beat ceased, and a spurt of steam roared from the safety-valve.

Robin gazed down breathlessly. He felt they ought to take some action, perhaps ring up the police again. But he seemed turned to stone, unable to do anything but watch what was happening. Jack also stood motionless, staring down with bulging eyes and open mouth.

With steadily falling speed the engine passed beneath them, followed by the long line of lighted coaches with two dark vehicles in the rear. The movement grew slower, till just before reaching the signal's red eye it ceased. There the train stood, a line of lights and jet against the grey darkness of the ground.

Now a narrow vertical rectangle of dim light appeared in the side of the first of the two dark rear vehicles. It dulled for a moment and then shone clear.

"That's the guard," Jack breathed. "He's got out."

"Then," Robin gasped, "this *is* it!" Again he felt they ought to act, and again he seemed rooted to the ground.

Suddenly the same thing took place in the rear vehicle, a shorter one than the van. A vertical rectangle of light appeared in its side. This kept getting darker and lighter for a few seconds, and then disappeared.

"Golly!" Jack muttered. "Someone's got out of that van too."

"The other man!" Robin's voice was awestruck.

"Looks like it. What on earth can be going on?"

As transfixed they started down, a narrow greyish gap appeared in the black line of the two last vehicles. Slowly it grew wider.

Jack stared as if his eyes would come out of their sockets, then he gave a scream.

"They've uncoupled the last vehicle! It's a horsebox! It'll run back down the hill and derail at the catch-points! Come on!"

He leaped for his bicycle, followed by Robin. They tore at breakneck speed down the rough lane from the tower, bumping and bouncing over the stones. Then Robin got the thrill of his life.

Just before they reached the road, a police car whizzed past, going towards Shroude. So they had acted on his warning!

He thought Jack would have stopped, but Jack instead roared— "Never mind! Come on!"

By a miracle they reached the road without disaster, and pedaled with all their strength down the hill towards the level-crossing. As he tried desperately to keep up with Jack, the probable explanation of the affair flashed into Robin's mind. A horse! The races! Something about betting! He recalled Sherlock Holmes' thrilling story of Silver Blaze, the favourite for the Wessex Cup, and how he was stolen just before the race. What if this horse was the favourite for some other important event? If the box was derailed it would be killed.

The wind whistled past their ears as they rushed along. Here was the bluff. They swung round it, cutting the corner to keep on the road. Fortunately nothing was coming in the opposite direction. There at last in front was the level-crossing. As they approached it they heard the telephone bell and saw the gatekeeper step to the instrument. He suddenly flung down the receiver and rushed out of the hut.

"Horsebox is running away," roared Jack. "Shall we close the catch-points?"

The man stared at them. "Aye!" he shouted. "Close them while I shut the gates!"

Jack tore up the line in the direction of the station, Robin panting behind him.

Some fifty yards away were the catch-points, dimly visible. Jack stooped, seized a heavy lever which was lying on the ground, and felt feverishly with his hand.

"Can't find the hole in the dark!" he cried in desperation. "A light! Quick!"

Robin turned to dash for a torch he had on his bicycle, then froze where he stood. Up the line a black, menacing shape with flaming red eyes was moving towards them through the grey dusk. Remorselessly it grew bigger. Now he heard the rolling of the wheels and the soft click of rail joints.

"The horsebox!" he yelled. "It's coming!"

Jack was sobbing aloud in his extremity. Then he gave a shout. "Got it!" He pushed the end of the lever into some socket, in which it stood nearly upright. Then he swung on its end. It did not move.

"Too heavy! Lend a hand!" he screamed.

The horsebox was close by, rolling forward inexorably. It seemed to grow monstrously. Robin hurled himself on the handle. The connections were stiff, and for a moment nothing happened. Then slowly the handle moved over. As the horsebox seemed right on top of them the points went home. Robin gave a choking gasp. Then the box had passed them and was moving on safely down the line.

When presently the boys learned that the horse they had saved was none other than Golden Crown, they could scarcely contain their delight. The engaged couple's gratitude knew no bounds.

Next evening there was a further meeting with Inspector Greer at police headquarters.

"A fine piece of work," the Inspector declared. "You boys saved a horse worth five thousand guineas and prevented an ugly bit of fraud. You rang us in the nick of time. A station in the direction you were going could only be Shroude or Plumpton, and when we saw the train stopped we knew it was

Shroude. We took the three chaps redhanded as they were running from the station. And it'll not be long till we have the principal too."

Robin's ears burned, and he was sure Jack's did also. "The whole idea's pretty clear?" Mr. Carr suggested.

"Perfectly," Greer returned. "North Star was the favourite for the principal race of the meeting and he had been heavily backed. Then news leaked out that this horse, Golden Crown, had done some extraordinary running. If he won, the North Star backers would be in the soup. What were three sums of fifty pounds to men who stood to lose thousands?"

"What exactly happened at the station?"

"They got the guard out and gagged and bound him. Then Goliath, as they called him, shouted up to the men in the horse-box—there were two. While they were speaking out of the window, Ginger and Birkett crept in by the other door and took them in the rear. They were quickly knocked out. The others uncoupled the horsebox, letting off its brake, and gave it a shove. The gradient did the rest."

"The station people must have twigged what was happening?"

"We had warned all stations to be on the lookout, but they didn't jump to it till they went down and found the men tied up. Then they phoned the gatekeeper to close the gates and catch-points, for the section was clear of following trains and the horse-box would stop safely in the hollow at the bottom of the grade. But the man had only time to close the gates. And that,"—the Inspector paused and turned to the boys—"is where you came in. As we police have learnt, it's teamwork that does it. Observation from Robin and initiative from Jack started the affair, and prompt help from both to the gateman completed it."

Robin winked at Jack, but secretly his heart glowed.

Part III:

Other Stories

James Alcorn's Oversight

James Alcorn, transfixed with horror, stood in the tiny sitting room looking down on the motionless body of his on-time friend, Leonard Crisp. Crisp had been fellow-clerk in the same office, and now he was dead.

The disaster had occurred in that simple, time-honoured way which had trapped so many short-tempered men. Alcorn, goaded beyond endurance by Crisp's gibes, had struck him on the chin. Crisp's head had fallen on the stone curb of the fireplace.

Alcorn had not meant to kill him. Though Crisp was blackmailing him in respect of his dealings with a certain cheque, he thought he had found an irregularity in Crisp's own work which would turn the tables on him. Their meeting that evening was to have been a duel of wits, not of physical strength.

But the ghastly tragedy had happened, and now Alcorn was reminding himself that he had no time to spend in bewailing it. He was in real danger. If he were to save himself he must act, and at once.

He had called at Crisp's bungalow in the housing estate, ostensibly to get his advice on a difficult investigation he was working on out of the office. Mrs. Crisp had opened the door, so he could not deny his visit.

Fortunately she had then gone out, saying to her husband that she would be back in time to get their usual cup of tea during the Nine O'clock News. There was therefore no witness. But could be deny what had happened?

His first impulse, indeed, had been to ring up the police and tell him the exact truth, in the hope of getting off with a light sentence for manslaughter. A faint hope, he now saw! There was no chance of his being believed. The charge would undoubtedly be murder, and the verdict guilty.

The sweat stood in great drops on his forehead as he wrestled with the problem. Its very urgency prevented him from thinking clearly. He sat down in Crisp's armchair and concentrated.

Then, as if sent by some evil power, a train roared past the house. It started an idea. There at the bottom of the little garden was the railway. The night was dark …

Stimulated by hope, Alcorn's imagination began functioning, and gradually a scheme came into being. He checked it over excitedly and the more he did so, the better pleased he become. Yes, it would work! Let him but carry it out with sufficient care, and he was safe!

The first thing was to give Crisp a motive for leaving the house. There a conversation overheard in the office helped him.

There was some trouble in the Bowling Club. Crisp was on the committee, and Alcorn had heard him say he must go and put his views before Greeves, the chairman.

Greeves lived just across the line a couple of hundred yards away, though it was more than half a mile round by the road. That Crisp should take the short cut would not seem unreasonable.

Alcorn went to the telephone, and, picking up the receiver in his handkerchief, dialled Greeves' number. A girl's voice answered.

"This Leonard Crisp," he said, mimicking Crisp's voice as best he could. "I wanted a word with Mr. Greeves about the Bowling Club. Could he see me if I went round in half an hour?"

"Yes, daddy's doing nothing," came the reply. "He'll be glad to see you."

The first fence taken! Alcorn considered further. It had been wet, and though the rain was now over, Crisp would probably wear a coat. Alcorn found his waterproof and, setting his teeth, managed to put it on the body, Crisp's hat he also found. His shoes would not give trouble; Crisp was wearing an out-of-door pair.

One other item, if he could manage it. Going to Crisp's desk, he found a folder labelled "Bowling Club." This, with its contents, he rolled up and thrust into the pocket of the waterproof.

Now came his worst moment. With immense labour, he managed to hoist the body on to his shoulders. Carrying the hat as well as his own, he glanced round the room to make sure nothing was overlooked. Then, turning off the light, he staggered out to the hall. There, also, he switched off the light, reached the hall door, opened it, passed out, and drew it to behind him.

Already Alcorn was panting and sweating, but he reminded himself that this getting out of the house was his greatest difficulty. The rest of his plan would be easier. It was not completely dark, and while he felt certain he would be unobserved, he could dimly see his way.

He staggered round the house and down the path to the bottom of the garden. There he found that to reach the fence he must cross a widish flower bed. However, that would not matter. A set of footprints had to show in any case, and his feet were about the size of Crisp's — nearly enough, at all events, to pass for them in that sandy loam where only blurred traces would remain.

Reaching the wire boundary paling, he hung the body across it, then stood gasping. When he had regained his breath, he climbed over.

On the grass of the railway ground he had no fear of leaving prints, so was able to make the effort necessary to pull the body after him.

The railway was on level ground, and in a few seconds he was lowering the remains on to the track. He placed the head on the rail and the hat close by.

As a resident he knew the trains. There would be none for 20 minutes. He had had this mind when he told Greeves' daughter to expect her visitor in half an hour. The times would work in.

Feeling satisfied that he had been unobserved. Alcorn now hurried along the railway to where, just outside the estate, there was a farm crossing. He climbed the gate into a lane and hastened on to his accustomed pub.

There, in an unobtrusive way, he managed to call attention to the time. With relief he noted that it was still ten minutes before the train was due.

He stayed in the bar till closing time, then went home. He had now only to stick to his story that he completed his business with Crisp, left the house and strolled to the pub, and all would be well. He could not be suspected. Though his scheme had been improvised, it was watertight.

But when he reached his home his heart sank. The police were there already, and they began with the dreaded warning that he need not answer their questions and that what he said might be given in evidence.

"We found from a private ledger of Crisp's that you were pay- ing him a pound a week. What was that for?"

Alcorn, taken aback, muttered that it was for help in his work.

He was not fully qualified to hold his job.

They appeared to accept this. Then they asked him to let them inspect his shoes.

Panic had now gripped Alcorn, but he agreed without hesitation. "They're a bit dirty," he explained, "but I was down my garden this evening and it was muddy after the rain."

"I can see traces of garden loam on them," they returned. Then the sergeant stared into Alcorn's eyes and added grimly: "Pity it didn't occur to you that Crisp's were clean."

Alcorn stared, then his jaw dropped.

Murder by Deputy

George Mant paused as his housekeeper called to him. "If you're going to the village, Mr. George, I'd be obliged if you'd post my letter. It should be just in time for the London mail."

"Right, Mrs. Cowan."

Taking the letter, George strode sombrely out. He had a letter for London himself, a letter which it had been agony to write, but which was his last slender hope of staving off ruin.

A long run of gambling on the Stock Exchange had ended in complete disaster, and the letter was a plea for an extension of time to the moneylender to whom he had had recourse.

If only, he thought for the thousandth time, his uncle, Adrian Cobb, would die! He was old and past his usefulness, and would be better out of the way. The bulk of his fortune would go to his son, but George and his brother Charles were to get five thousand apiece. Five thousand to George would be the difference between life and death! And Charles, he knew, was in much the same case.

From this to the thought of murder had been but a step. But George had not stopped at thinking. He had decided to kill his uncle if and when he could find a method. He had jokingly suggested joint action to Charles, but Charles's reception of the jest had appalled him. Indeed, George now realised that if he acted alone Charles would suspect him and probably give him away.

The brothers lived alone with their elderly housekeeper a mile from the tiny Cornish port of Tregowan. George was a writer of popular fiction. Charles had been a solicitor, but owing to heart trouble had had to retire on his private means, a mere pittance.

Their uncle, Adrian Cobb, had a big house some halfway to the village. He also lived alone, a man and his wife looking after him. He was interested in conchology, and had a valuable collection of local shells.

On the previous day, George had picked up on the shore an unusual-looking shell, and he thought it would be politic to take it to his uncle and so show an interest in his hobby.

On fine days, the old man sat in a summerhouse overlooking the sea, surrounded by his books.

Now, with the letters, George went direct to the summerhouse. Cobb was there alone.

"Morning, uncle. How're things today?"

The shell interested the old man, and they chatted for a few moments. Then, remembering he had to catch the London mail, George left.

In a couple of minutes he regained the path, which ran along the shore through straggling shrubs at the base of the low grass cliffs on which stood Cobb's house. There he got a shock.

Lying on the path was a man, and when he reached him he saw that it was his brother Charles. A glance showed that he was dead. Obviously his heart had at last given up the struggle.

George's first impulse was to run for help. But a second idea soon flashed into his mind and he grew rigid, thinking intently. For some agonised moments he wavered, then his evil genius conquered.

Quickly he glanced round. The path was secluded and no one was in sight. The risk in what he contemplated would be slight.

Picking up the body, he carried it a few steps from the path, hiding it among the shrubs. Then he took off the shoes and put them on his own feet. Charles was the bigger man and the shoes were too large, but George could walk in them.

He now hurried back along the path to where a person would naturally leave it to visit Cobb, and where he had himself left it. Then he followed his own traces to Cobb's summerhouse.

He had a special motive in this for between the path and Cobb's there was an area of clayey ground softened by recent rain, which it was impossible to cross without leaving footprints. His own previous tracks showed clearly, and those he was now making would prove that Charles had been there too.

He took care in one or two places to tread on the previous prints, so as to leave evidence that his own visit had been earlier than Charles's.

On reaching the summerhouse he knocked and entered. "Sorry to bother you again," he exclaimed, "but I've a letter here that I forgot to show you. I'd like your opinion on it."

He took an old letter from his pocket, and as he handed it to Cobb with his left hand, he picked up with his right hand a heavy stone statuette from a side table.

The old man bent forward over the paper and George brought the weight down with all his force on his head. Without a sound Cobb collapsed. George could see that he was dead.

Trembling and sweating, George wiped his fingerprints off the stone, the door handle, and everything else he had touched.

Then, having recovered his letter, he let himself out and hurried back—again across the clayey ground—to where he had left the body. He was satisfied he had not been seen. He quickly rechanged the shoes, lifted the body back on to the path, and arranged it as it had been.

For a moment he paused to check over what he had done. No, he had made no mistakes. The evidence would show that Charles had followed him to Cobb's, murdered the old man, and hu ried back to the path. The unwonted excitement and effort had proved too much for his heart, and it had given way. Charles was desperately hard up, and his legacy would solve his difficulties. It all worked in, and there was no flaw anywhere.

There remained only the reporting of the affair. At first, George thought of hurrying on to the village to post his letters and "finding" the body on his return. Then he saw that he was already late for the mail.

Here was a snag! He would have to explain his delay. If a question arose, his housekeeper would tell the police he had started in ample time.

Once again the sweat broke out on George's forehead. Here was danger! He must act quickly or he would be lost.

Then suddenly he almost laughed with relief. The problem was no problem at all! There was an easy way out. All he had to do was to report his discovery of the body. His shock and efforts to revive Charles would explain his delay and omission to post the letters. In fact, he now saw that there was no other way in which he could act. The body was lying on the path he was known to have taken.

He hurried to the village, and breathlessly told his tale to the doctor and village policeman. They were sympathetic. The doctor speedily reported heart failure, and the remains were conveyed home.

At lunchtime, Cobb's man found his master in the summer house. George hurried over, his emotion natural under the circumstances. Once again everyone was sympathetic.

That evening, an inspector called with the local policeman. Everything George told him was the exact truth, except that he omitted all reference to his second journey to the summerhouse.

They took the story down and seemed satisfied. Then the inspector began to ask questions.

"The footprints appear to show that you and your brother both visited the deceased. No one else did so, for there were no other footprints from the shore, and the land approaches were under observation by Mr. Cobb's man. I'm afraid, sir, this has an unpleasant significance."

"My unhappy brother," George murmured. "His mind ... He wasn't quite responsible, you know."

"Speaking of it as an abstract problem, the facts prove that the murder was committed by whichever of you visited Mr. Cobb last."

"I understood you to say the footprints showed that." "Footprints are not always what they seem." The inspector's voice had grown grim. "Now, sir, according to your statement you left your uncle and walked straight down to the path, where you found your brother lying dead. How then could he have been the one to pay the second visit?"

"Well don't you see..." began George, then stopped.

Appendix A:
Why I Write Detective Stories
By Freeman Wills Crofts

We are going, you and I, to write a detective novel, or so I am informed. Let us see, then, how we would set about it and what we would find ourselves up against.

Necessarily, we must follow a hypothetical method, for if we asked a hundred detective-novelists how they worked, we should probably get a hundred quite different replies. And we are going to write a *detective* story, which we are doubtless agreed deals with detection and in which the problem is supreme: not a thriller, which depends on conflict and thrills, nor yet a crime novel, which is the history of some particular crime, usually from the criminal's point of view.

Before we begin, we must settle one or two points about our detective. Is he to be a gifted amateur, a professional private detective, or a man from the C.I.D.? Is he to be a "character," or an ordinary humdrum citizen? Is he to work alone or to have a Watson? Suppose *you* settle these points? You have? Then let's get down to it.

If we're lucky we shall begin with a really good idea. This may be one of five kinds. Firstly, it may be an idea for the opening of our book: some dramatic situation or happening to excite and hold the reader's interest. The standard way of finding a body in the first chapter, if hackneyed, is hard to beat.

Secondly, our idea may be for the closing or climax of our book. This must also be dramatic. As an example I suggest the well-known situation in which Tom, who thinks Jack is dead and has impersonated him, is unexpectedly confronted with Jack in a police office or court of law.

Our idea, thirdly, may be for a good way of committing a crime, probably a murder. It should be novel and ingenious—but not too ingenious—and if possible concerned with things with which the man in the street is familiar. This is probably the most usual way of starting work on a book. Every detective fan will think of dozens of examples.

A fourth kind of idea on which to build a book is that we shall write about some definite crime, such as smuggling, gun-running, coining, arson, or frauds in high finance.

Lastly, our idea may be simply to place the action in a definite setting, such as a mining setting, or a golf or fishing setting, or to lay our scenes in a certain place: a bus or an office, an opium den or Canterbury Cathedral.

We may of course build our book on some idea which does not fall under one of these heads. For instance, Dr. Austin Freeman's book, *The Red Thumb Mark*, was probably built on the idea that a fingerprint is not necessarily convincing evidence.

This then is the first stage in our work: getting the idea to start on. Our second stage is more difficult: we have to build up the plot on our idea.

We do this in a very simple, but very tedious way: we ask ourselves innumerable questions and think out the answers. One question invariably leads to another, and as we go on our plot gradually takes shape.

Suppose we have decided on a murder by antimony poisoning. We shall ask ourselves questions such as: Where does the murderer get the antimony? How does he administer it? What is his motive?

Suppose in answering this last question we choose greed: that he inherits money from the man he kills. At once new questions suggest themselves. What was the relationship between the two men? Why had the deceased left money to the other? And so on. As we continue propounding and answering these questions, we shall have the happiness of finding a story gradually growing out of nothing. We continue the good work till the whole happening is built up, from the first thought of the crime right down to its completion, together with the subterfuges the criminal adopts to secure his safety. A rough synopsis is then made, together with sketch maps of the important localities, short biographies of the principal characters, and a chronology of the main events.

It should be clearly understood that this synopsis is of the actual facts which are supposed to have happened: it is not a synopsis of the book. We don't get to the book till the third stage, for which, however, we are now ready.

In this third stage we reconsider the whole circumstances from a new viewpoint, the viewpoint of the person or persons through whom we are going to tell the story. What is the first thing that would have become known? Would it have been the finding of the body? If so, begin with that. What would then be done? The police would be sent for. What would they do? They would make certain enquiries, they would look for motives, they would find out who was in the neighbourhood when the crime was committed.

We continue working in this way till we have completed a second synopsis of the case, this time describing the gradual revealing of the details to the detective. As we do so, we find that we have to supply a good deal of fresh material. That means of course a new set of questions to be answered. There is, for instance, the very important problem of how the detective discovers the truth. He should if possible do so through some flaw inherent in the criminal's plans, unperceived till now by the reader.

Appendix B:
Who Killed Cock Robin?
By Freeman Wills Crofts

The Assistant Commissioner's room at Scotland Yard. The A.C. and Chief Inspector French are discussing business.

A.C.: (*Throwing down papers*). Then that finishes that. Now what about that anonymous communication alleging that some- one of the name of Cock Robin had been murdered?

FRENCH: (*Taking a paper from his pocket*). I've gone into that, sir. I've got the document here.

A.C.: You might read it. I've rather forgotten the details.

FRENCH: It's undated, sir, and bears neither signature nor address. It's written with a streamlined pen on scaled paper and the watermark is stuck on with fish glue.

(*Looks up, then reads*).
"Who killed Cock Robin?
I, said the Sparrow;
With my bow and arrow,
I killed Cock Robin."

A.C.: Quite. I remember now. The Robin was buried as stated, but it was thought to be a natural death?

FRENCH: That's right, sir.

A.C.: But in the face of this very definite statement, we thought we should take some action. Very well, what have you done?

FRENCH: *Shaking his head*). I don't think we're going to make much of it, sir, and that's a fact.

A.C.: Why not? You've got a witness, haven't you? Let's see. (*Takes paper and reads.*)

"Who saw him die?
I, said the Fly;
With my little eye.
I saw him die."

There you are. Did you get hold of the Fly?

FRENCH: (*Unhappily*). No, sir. I got a warrant for his arrest on a charge of buzzing after 11.30 at night so as to hold him, but he got away.

(*The A.C. raises his eyebrows.*)

FRENCH: I sent Tanner and two men to bring him in, but just as they got up to him he passed out of the Metropolitan Area.

A.C.: What did you do?

FRENCH: I wrote to the Chief Constable of Surrey asking him to bring him in.

A.C.: And did he?

FRENCH: I don't know, sir. When I took his answer out of the envelope it went up in smoke.

A.C.: (*Thoughtfully*). Looks as if he had missed him. Well, what else?

FRENCH: I found out about the interment, sir. There was a nasty accident at it. The Bull was tolling the bell, as the information says, because he could pull. But unfortunately, he pulled so hard he brought down the whole caboodle, bell, steeple, and everything else. On himself, too. He was killed. There was the hell of a r—, I mean, the owner was considerably annoyed. He was wanted for steaks.

A.C.: The owner?

FRENCH: No, sir, the Bull. Then I saw the Rook. The Rook was acting as Parson. Excuse me sir. (*Takes paper and reads.*)

"Who'll be the Parson?

I, said the Rook; With my little book."

The Rook made a long statement about the funeral. He said they hadn't had the Linnet there at all. The Linnet had offered to carry the link and to fetch it in a minute. But the Lark, who acted as Clerk, wouldn't attend in the dark. So they had to have the funeral in the daytime. The link therefore wasn't required.

A.C.: Then the Linnet's out of it?

FRENCH: The Linnet's out of it, sir.

A.C.: And the Bull's out of it. But the Rook and the Lark are in it. What about the Owl?

FRENCH: The Owl (*he hesitates and glances at the paper*) dug the grave with his spade and trowel. He was in it to the same extent as the Rook and the Lark. They were all there as the statement affirms, and they all tell the same story. They say they were credibly informed, and believed, that the Robin died a natural death. They said they were only doing their jobs, and that they were paid for it and didn't mean any harm. And it'll be very difficult to disprove their statement.

A.C.: (*Testily*). But good heavens, wasn't the crime common property? The Sparrow and the Fly and the Fish at any rate knew what had happened?

FRENCH: (*Gloomily*). There's more in it than that, sir.

A.C.: (*Shrugging*). Oh, all right. Tell it your own way.

FRENCH: I saw the Beetle next, sir. He admits making the shroud with his thread and needle, but he says he didn't know it was a shroud. He was told it was a sail for the Beaver's raft.

A.C.: Nonsense!

FRENCH: Well, I've seen it. And it's certainly more the shape of a sail than a shroud.

A.C.: Hang it all, you'd think you were out to get these people off. Well, what about the Fish? If he admits catching the blood in his little dish, he was clearly an accessory before the fact.

FRENCH: (*Darkly*). If you ask me, sir, the Fish was at the bottom of the whole thing. The Fish is a twister. He caught no blood in his dish, because there was no blood to catch. But in my opinion it was the Fish who forged the document.

A.C.: (*Staring incredulously*). But the murder?

FRENCH: There was no murder, sir.

A.C.: No murder? But, man alive, haven't you got a confession from the Sparrow?

FRENCH: (*Doggedly*). There was no wound on the body, sir, and no arrow anywhere about. And there was no Sparrow there either. It was a Swallow.

A.C.: (*With exasperation*). I will say, French, you've got me properly mixed up. Let's get it straight. There was no confession from the Sparrow?

FRENCH: No, sir; it was the Swallow who made the confession.

A.C.: But heavens above, why did he confess to a murder he hadn't committed?

FRENCH: I thought at first he was afraid Miss Wren was suspected and was trying to screen her—they've been seen about together, and she was heard to say, "I'm for it, Swall." But Dr. Fox says no, that it was just an ordinary case of narcissistic exhibitionism.

A.C.: (*Nodding*). So it might. Did you check all this up from the Swallow?

FRENCH: Unfortunately, sir, he's gone abroad.

A.C.: Is it known where?

FRENCH: Egypt, it's thought.

A.C.: No chance of getting him?

FRENCH: I doubt it, sir. I went to the P. and O. offices because I've seen it stated more than once that this is the most comfortable route for birds. But he hadn't booked on any of their steamers.

A.C.: (*After a moment's thought*). This is really a most extraordinary statement, French. If it's true, what did the Robin die of?

FRENCH: Dr. Fox thinks of a broken heart.

A.C.: (*Half closing one eye*). That little Miss Robin who lives under the fountain?

FRENCH: No, sir, nothing of that kind. Dr. Fox thinks he was shocked at the depravity of his neighbours.

A.C.: What did he know about it?

FRENCH: Well, they were a pretty low lot, combining to get him out of the way, digging his grave and all that. They weren't even straight. Why, the Rook who read the service had never even been ordained. I sent Willis to the bishop and that's what he told him.

A.C.: But the Robin couldn't have known that till after he was dead?

FRENCH: I pointed that out to Dr. Fox, but he said that considered from the point of view of space-time continuum, that didn't matter.

A.C.: (*Thoughtfully*). I don't suppose it does. (*Then angrily.*) But curse that blessed Fish! Making all this trouble for nothing! If I had him I'd salt him. What was his motive?

FRENCH: As I understand it, sir, he was a Goldfish and his dish was what he lived in: it was round the fountain. It appears the Sparrow used to go and sit on the edge of the dish and jeer at him because his gold had gone mouldy. So when this business of the Robin's death took place, and he heard the Swallow admitting his guilt, he wrote the information and put in the Sparrow instead of the Swallow, hoping to get the Sparrow hanged.

A.C: (*Getting up angrily*). A low down twister, as you say! I'll break his dish and that'll fix him!

(*The A.C. makes a throwing movement. There is a loud crash. French lifts his head. He sees a book has fallen.*)

FRENCH: Bless my soul, I must have dozed off!

Appendix C:
Bibliography

This bibliography builds on James Keddie Junior's pioneering listing of Crofts' work, which was compiled with the author's help and published in *The Armchair Detective* in April 1969. The editor of this volume also acknowledges the help of Hilary Whalley of BBC Archives, Anne Skilton of the Manuscripts Department of the University of North Carolina at Chapel Hill and staff at the British Library and the British Newspaper Archive as well as Geoff Bradley, editor of *CADS* magazine, Roger Bickerton, John Cooper, John Curran, Douglas G. Greene, Jeffrey Marks, and Paul R. Moy. Any additional information is welcomed and may be sent to the editor c/o the publisher at info@crippenlandru.com.

Tony Medawar

I —BOOKS

The Cask. Collins, 1920; Seltzer, 1924. A new edition of the book in 1946 included a specially written preface by Crofts, reprinted in *CADS* 60, May 2011. (Non-series crime novel)

The Ponson Case. Collins, 1921; Boni, 1927. (Non-series crime novel)

The Pit-Prop Syndicate. Collins, 1922; Seltzer, 1925. (Non-series crime novel)

The Groote Park Murder. Collins, 1923; Seltzer, 1925. (Non-series crime novel)

Inspector French's Greatest Case. Collins, 1924; Seltzer, 1925. (The first Joseph French novel)

Inspector French and the Cheyne Mystery. Collins, 1926; Boni, 1926, as *The Cheyne Mystery*. Serialised as *Ingots of Gold. Flynn's Weekly*, 7, 14, 21 and 28 August 1926. (The second Joseph French novel)

Inspector French and the Starvel Tragedy. Collins, 1927; Harper, 1927, as *The Starvel Hollow Tragedy*. (The third Joseph French novel)

The Sea Mystery. Collins, 1928; Harper, 1928. (The fourth Joseph French novel)

The Box Office Murders. Collins, 1929; Harper, 1929, as *The Purple Sickle Murders*. (The fifth Joseph French novel)

Sir John Magill's Last Journey. Collins Crime Club, 1930; Harper, 1930. (The sixth Joseph French novel)

Mystery in the Channel. Collins, 1931; Harper, 1931, as *Mystery in the English Channel*. (The seventh Joseph French novel)

The Floating Admiral, Hodder, 1931. (Crofts wrote Chapter IX, "The Visitor in the Night" of this round-robin novel by various members of the Detection Club: Anthony Berkeley, Agatha Christie, G.D.H. and M Cole, Freeman Wills Crofts, Clemence Dane, Edgar Jepson, Milward Kennedy, Ronald Knox, John Rhode, Dorothy L. Sayers, Henry Wade and Canon Victor Whitechurch)

Sudden Death. Crime Club, 1932; Harper, 1932. (The eighth Jo- seph French novel)

Death on the Way. Crime Club, 1932; Harper, 1932, as *Double Death*. (The ninth Joseph French novel)

The Hog's Back Mystery. Hodder & Stoughton, 1933; Dodd, Mead, 1933, as *The Strange Case of Dr Earle*. (The tenth Joseph French novel)

The 12.30 from Croydon. Hodder, 1934; Dodd, 1934, as *Wilful and Premeditated*. (The eleventh Joseph French novel)

Mystery on Southampton Water. Hodder, 1934; Dodd, 1934, as *Crime on the Solent*. (The twelfth Joseph French novel)

Crime at Guildford. Crime Club, 1935; Dodd, 1935, as *The Crime at Nornes*. (The thirteenth Joseph French novel)

The Loss of the Jane Vosper. Crime Club, 1936; Dodd, 1936. (The fourteenth Joseph French novel)

Man Overboard! Crime Club, 1936; Dodd, 1936, as *Cold-Blooded Murder*. Crofts also prepared a revised 75,000 word version of the novel for an American publisher but this did not appear and the whereabouts of the original version are not known. (The fifteenth Joseph French novel)

Found Floating. Hodder, 1937; Dodd, 1937. Serialised in the *Daily Mail*, daily from 15 July to 21 August 1937. The typescript of the novel was given in four instalments to ex-Superintendent William Hambrook of the Flying Squad, part of the Metropolitan Police. His comments on the story to date and emerging suspicions were published during the serialisation on 21 July, 22 July, 7 August, 9 August and 21 August. (The sixteenth Joseph French novel)

The End of Andrew Harrison. Hodder, 1938; Dodd, 1938, as *The Futile Alibi*. (The seventeenth Joseph French novel)

Antidote to Venom. Hodder, 1938; Dodd, 1939. (The eighteenth Joseph French novel)

Double Death: An Exercise in Detection. Gollancz, 1939. Serialised as *Night of Secrets* in the *Sunday Chronicle*, serialised weekly from 23 May to 27 June 1937 with Crofts' contribution published as "Chapter 2: Secret Fear of Murdered Nurse" on 30 May 1937. Crofts wrote Part Two of this round-robin non-series novel in six parts by various mystery writers —Anthony Armstrong, Freeman Wills Crofts, David Hume, F. Tennyson Jesse, Dorothy L. Sayers and Valentine Williams with an a prologue, published in the newspaper anonymously and in the book credited to John Chancellor. The story was originally published as a competition judged by four senior police officers, including Walter Hambrook – see *Found Floating qv* and George Cornish, see "The Parcel" *qv*. Prizes totalled £100 and the top prize was £50, equivalent to $4,000 today.

Fatal Venture. Hodder, 1939; Dodd, 1939, as *Tragedy in the Hollow*. Also published as *The White Rocks Mystery*. (The nineteenth Joseph French novel)

Golden Ashes. Hodder, 1940; Dodd, 1940. (The twentieth Joseph French novel)

James Tarrant, Adventurer. Hodder, 1941; Dodd, 1941, as *Circumstantial Evidence*. (The twenty first Joseph French novel) *The Losing Game*. Hodder, 1941; Dodd, 1941, as *A Losing Game*. (The twenty-second Joseph French novel)

Fear Comes to Chalfont. Hodder, 1942; Dodd, 1942. (The twenty-third Joseph French novel)

The Affair at Little Wokeham. Hodder, 1943; Dodd, 1943 as *Double Tragedy*. (The twenty-fourth Joseph French novel)

Enemy Unseen. Hodder, 1945; Dodd, 1945. (The twenty-fifth Joseph French novel)

Death of a Train. Hodder, 1946; Dodd, 1947. Serialised in the *New York Daily News* weekly from 4 August to 13 October 1946. (The twenty-sixth Joseph French novel)

Murderers Make Mistakes. Hodder, 1947. (A collection of short stories)

Silence for the Murderer. Dodd, 1948; Hodder, 1949. Serialised in the *New York Daily News* daily from 2 August to 25 September 1948. (The twenty-seventh Joseph French novel)

Young Robin Brand, Detective. ULP, 1947; Dodd, 1948. (Juvenile mystery. The only novel featuring Robin Brand. Joseph French appears as the uncle of Cyril French, one of Robin's friends)

The Four Gospels in One Story. Longman Green, 1949. (Described by

Crofts as "*a religious book on the Gospels*")

Dark Journey. Dodd, 1951; Hodder, 1952, as *French Strikes Oil*. (The twenty-eighth Joseph French novel)

Many a Slip. Hodder, 1955. (A collection of short stories)

The Mystery of the Sleeping Car Express. Hodder, 1956. (A collection of short stories)

Anything to Declare? Hodder, 1957. (The twenty-ninth Joseph French novel)

The Scoop. Published in *The Scoop and Behind the Screen*. Gollancz, 1983; Harper and Row, 1984. (Crofts wrote Chapters VI, "Scotland Yard on the Job" *qv*, and XI, "Inspector Smart Gets a Nasty Jar" *qv* of this round-robin non-series novel, originally broadcast as a radio serial, by E.C. Bentley, Anthony Berkeley, Agatha Christie, Crofts, Clemence Dane and Dorothy L. Sayers). For an entertaining account of the genesis and writing of *The Scoop*, and some further information about *The Floating Admiral*, *qv*, see Martin Edwards' superb history of the Detection Club, *The Golden Age of Murder* (2015).

The 9.50 Up Express and Other Stories. Ohio: Crippen & Landru, 2020. (A collection of short stories also including the scripts of a radio play and a stage play)

II —SHORT FICTION

In his foreword to *Many a Slip*, Crofts noted that, owing to the policy of the *London Evening Standard*, all of the stories in that collection were, as published in the newspaper, "*little more than skeleton plots*" and went on to explain that he had "*now tried to give them some small covering of flesh*". In line with this statement by Crofts, the entries for the relevant stories states they were "expanded and collected in *Many a Slip*". However, it seems likely that the exact opposite is true i.e. that the text of each story as it appears in *Many a Slip* is what Crofts originally submitted to the *Standard*, whose editorial team had edited it for publication.

In his proto-bibliography of Crofts' work, James Keddie Junior noted two stories that have not been traced: "A Matter of Temperature" and "Succour Unavailing". However, there are duplications in Keddie's listing, as well as some omissions, and it is at least possible that these apparently lost stories are alternate titles for other stories listed below.

"The Mystery of the Sleeping Car Express". *Premier Magazine*, 28 January 1921. Crofts' original title was "The Sleeping-Car Mystery." Collected in *The Mystery of the Sleeping Car Express*, 1956. (Non-series detective story)

"The Greuze". *Pearson's Magazine*, December 1921. Crofts' original title was 'The Greuze Girl'. Collected in *The Mystery of the Sleeping Car Express*, 1956. (Non-series detective story. Crofts selected this for *My Best Detective Story: A Collection of Stories Chosen by Their Own Authors*. Faber & Faber, 1931.)

"Mr Pemberton's Commission". *Windsor Magazine*, March 1933. The story has also been published under the title "The Case of the Jade Necklace". Collected in *The Mystery of the Sleeping Car Express*, 1956. (Joseph French. Crofts selected this for *My Best Mystery Story: A Collection of Stories Chosen by Their Own Authors*. Faber & Faber, 1939.)

"The Level Crossing". *Cornhill Magazine*, November 1933. Collected in *The Mystery of the Sleeping Car Express*, 1956. (Joseph French)

"Nemesis". *Roundabout* (Guildford Christmas Annual), December 1933. Although a copy of the original printing of this story has yet to be located the editor of this volume has identified "Nemesis" with "The Suitcase", *Evening Standard*, 9 August 1950, which has also been published under the title "The Sunken Suitcase". Expanded and collected as "The Suitcase" in *Many a Slip*, 1955. (Joseph French)

"East Wind". *Cornhill Magazine*, February 1934. Collected in *The Mystery of the Sleeping Car Express*, 1956. (Joseph French)

"The Affair at Saltover Priory". *Windsor Magazine*, February 1934. Collected as "Saltover Priory" in *The Mystery of the Sleeping Car Express*, 1956. (Joseph French)

"The Vertical Line". *Illustrated London News (Christmas Number)*, 20 November 1935. Revised and collected as "The Case of the Telephone Call" in *Murderers Make Mistakes*, 1947. Collected in *The 9.50 Up Express and Other Stories*, 2020. (Joseph French)

"The Parcel". *Daily Mail*, 17, 18, 20 and 21 April 1936. Published in *Six Against Scotland Yard* (Crime Club, 1936; Doubleday Doran, 1936), a collection of short stories by Margery Allingham, Anthony Berkeley, Crofts, Ronald Knox, Dorothy L. Sayers and Russell Thorndike, together with an analysis of each story written by ex-superintendent George Cornish of the Criminal Investigation Department of the Metropolitan Police. Cornish's analysis of the crime outlined in "The Parcel" was published by the *Daily Mail* on 22 and 23 April 1936. Crofts' original title for his story was "The Package". The story has also been published under the title "Murder by Post". Collected, with Cornish's analysis, in *The Mystery of the Sleeping Car Express*, 1956. (Non-series crime story)

"The Landing Ticket". *The Times [Weekly Edition]*, 12 November 1936. Collected in *The Mystery of the Sleeping Car Express*, 1956. (Joseph French)

"The Hunt Ball", *Holly Leaves (Christmas Issue of Illustrated Sporting & Dramatic News)*, 21 November 1937. *Detective Stories of Today* (1940). Revised as "The Hunt Ball Murder", Crofts' original title, Todd 1943. Revised and collected as "The Case of the Hunt Ball" in *Murderers Make Mistakes*, 1947. Collected in *The 9.50 Up Express and Other Stories*, 2020. (Joseph French)

"The Match". *Detection Medley*, 1939. Revised as "Mr. Sefton, Murderer", Polybooks 1944; and revised and collected as "The Case of the Old Gun" in *Murderers Make Mistakes*, 1947. Crofts' original title was 'The Match Trick'. Collected in *The 9.50 Up Express and Other Stories*, 2020. (Joseph French)

"James Alcorn's Oversight". *Sunday Empire News*, 12 August 1945. Collected in *The 9.50 Up Express and Other Stories*, 2020. (Non-series crime story)

"Murder by Deputy". *Sunday Empire News*, 30 September 1945. Collected in *The 9.50 Up Express and Other Stories*, 2020. (Non-series crime story)

"The Case of the Cliff Path". Adapted from the radio play "The Case of the Torn Song" *qv*. The story has also been published under the title "The Cliff Path". Collected in *Murderers Make Mistakes*, 1947. (Joseph French)

"The Case of the Lower Flat". Adapted from the radio play *qv*. The story has also been published under the title "The Lower Flat". Collected in *Murderers Make Mistakes*, 1947. (Joseph French)

"The Case of the Army Truck". Adapted from the radio play *qv*. The story has also been published under the title "The Army Truck". Collected in *Murderers Make Mistakes*, 1947. (Joseph French)

"The Case of the Invalid Colonel". Adapted from the radio play *qv*. The story has also been published under the title "The Invalid Colonel". Collected in *Murderers Make Mistakes*, 1947. (Joseph French)

"The Case of the Hidden Sten-Gun". Adapted from the radio play *qv*. The story has also been published under the title "The Hidden Sten Gun". Collected in *Murderers Make Mistakes*, 1947. (Joseph French)

"The Case of the Avaricious Moneylender". Adapted from the radio play *qv*. The story has also been published under the title "The Avaricious Moneylender". Collected in *Murderers Make Mistakes*, 1947. (Joseph French)

"The Case of the Evening Visitor". The story has also been published under the title "The Evening Visitor". Adapted from the radio play *qv*. Collected in *Murderers Make Mistakes*, 1947. (Joseph French)

"The Case of the Enthusiastic Rabbit Breeder". Adapted from the radio play "The Case of the Man Who Bred Rabbits" *qv*. The story has also been published under the title "Death of a Rabbit Breeder". Collected in *Murderers Make Mistakes*, 1947. (Joseph French)

"The Case of the Retired Wine Merchant". Adapted from the radio play *qv*. The story has also been published under the title "The Retired Wine Merchant". Collected in *Murderers Make Mistakes*, 1947. (Joseph French)

"The Case of the Home Guard Trench". Adapted from the radio play *qv*. Collected in *Murderers Make Mistakes*, 1947. (Joseph French)

"The Case of the Playwright's Manuscript". Adapted from the radio play *qv*. The story has also been published under the title "The Playwright's Manuscript". Collected in *Murderers Make Mistakes*, 1947. (Joseph French)

"The Case of the Limestone Quarry". The story has also been published under the title "Murder at the Limestone Quarry". Adapted from the radio play *qv*. Collected in *Murderers Make Mistakes*, 1947. (Joseph French)

"The Case of the L-Shaped Room". Adapted from the radio play *qv*. The story has also been published under the title "An L-Shaped Room Upset a Killer's Alibi". Collected in *Murderers Make Mistakes*, 1947. (Joseph French)

"The Case of the Stolen Hand Grenade". Adapted from the radio play *qv*. The story has also been published under the title "The Stolen Hand-Grenade". Collected in *Murderers Make Mistakes*, 1947. (Joseph French)

"The Case of the Relief Signalman". Adapted from the radio play *qv*. The story has also been published under the title "The Relief Signalman". Collected in *Murderers Make Mistakes*, 1947. (Joseph French)

"The Case of the Fireside Mountaineer". Adapted from the radio play, "The Case of the Man Who Loved Mountains" *qv*. The story has also been published under the title "The Fireside Mountaineer". Collected in *Murderers Make Mistakes*, 1947. (Joseph French)

"The Case of the Solicitor's Holiday". Adapted from the radio play *qv*. Collected in *Murderers Make Mistakes*, 1947. (Joseph French)

"The Case of the Burning Barn". Adapted from the radio play *qv*. The story has also been published under the title "The Burning Barn". Collected in *Murderers Make Mistakes*, 1947. (Joseph French)

"The Case of the Swinging Boom". The story has also been published under the title "The Swinging Boom". Adapted from the radio play *qv*. Collected in *Murderers Make Mistakes*, 1947. (Joseph French)

"The Case of the Waiting Car". Adapted from the radio play *qv*. The story has also been published under the title "The Waiting Car". Collected in *Murderers Make Mistakes*, 1947. (Joseph French)

"Crime on the Footplate". *Evening Standard*, 28 December 1949. Expanded and collected in *Many a Slip*, 1955. (Joseph French)

"Perilous Journey". *The Christmas Stocking*, Blandford Press 1949. Collected in *The 9.50 Up Express and Other Stories*, 2020. (Robin Brand juvenile mystery)

"Danger in Shroude Valley". *The Golden Book of the Year*, Blandford Press 1950. Collected in *The 9.50 Up Express and Other Stories*, 2020. (Robin Brand juvenile mystery)

"The Two Bottles", *Evening Standard*, 26 January 1950. Expanded and collected as "The New Cement" in *Many a Slip*, 1955. (Joseph French)

"The 8.12 from Waterloo". *Evening Standard*, 23 February 1950. Expanded and collected in *Many a Slip*, 1955. (Joseph French) "The Medicine Bottle". *Evening Standard*, 18 September 1950. Revised, possibly by Frederick Dannay, and reprinted in *Ellery Queen's Mystery Magazine*, May 1951, as "The Oversight", Crofts' original title. The story has also been published under the title "The Lethal Bottle of Medicine". Expanded and collected in *Many a Slip*, 1955. (Joseph French)

"The Ruined Tower". *Evening Standard*, 26 May 1951. Expanded and collected in *Many a Slip*, 1955. (Joseph French)

"The Raincoat". *Evening Standard*, 30 October 1951. Expanded and collected in *The Mystery of the Sleeping Car Express*, 1956. (Non-series crime story. Joseph French is mentioned in passing)

"Ebb Tide". *Evening Standard*, 20 March 1952. Expanded and collected as "The Icy Torrent" in *Many a Slip*, 1955. (Joseph French)

"Fingerprints". *Evening Standard*, 29 March 1952. The story has also been published under the title "Flaw in a Masterpiece". Collected in *The 9.50 Up Express and Other Stories*, 2020. (Joseph French)

"Gull Rock". *Evening Standard*, 15 April 1952. Expanded and collected in *Many a Slip*, 1955. (Joseph French)

"The Footbridge". *Evening Standard*, 23 April 1952. The story has also been published under the title "Death on the Bridge". Expanded and collected in *Many a Slip*, 1955. (Joseph French)

"The Two Calls". *Evening Standard*, 7 June 1952. Crofts' original title was 'The Boomerang', and the story has also been published as "High Cost of Blackmail". Expanded and collected as "Boomerang" in *Many a Slip*, 1955, and reprinted as "Two Birds with One Spanner". (Joseph French)

"The Photographer". *Evening Standard*, 7 July 1952. Expanded and collected as "The Photograph" in *Many a Slip*, 1955. Revised, possibly by Frederick Dannay, and reprinted in *Ellery Queen's Mystery Magazine*, May 1953, as "Unbreakable Alibi". (Non-series detective story. Joseph French is mentioned in passing)

"Tea at Four". *Evening Standard*, 9 September 1952. Expanded and collected in *Many a Slip*, 1955. (Joseph French)

"The Agent's Signature". *Evening Standard*, 29 September 1952. Expanded and collected as "The Sign Manual" in *Many a Slip*, 1955. (Joseph French)

"The Absent Partner". *Evening Standard*, 29 December 1952. Expanded and collected as "The Brothers Bing" in *Many a Slip*, 1955. (Joseph French)

"The Faulty Stroke". *Evening Standard*, 30 December 1952. Collected in *The 9.50 Up Express and Other Stories*, 2020. (Joseph French)

"The Mountain Ledge". *Evening Standard*, 31 December 1952. Expanded and collected in *Many a Slip*, 1955. (Joseph French)

"The Upper Flat". *Evening Standard*, 1 January 1953. Expanded and collected in *Many a Slip*, 1955. (Joseph French)

"The Flowing Tide". *Evening Standard*, 2 January 1953. Expanded and collected in *Many a Slip*, 1955. (Joseph French)

"The Broken Windscreen". *Evening Standard*, 3 January 1953. Expanded and collected in *Many a Slip*, 1955. (Joseph French)

"Teamwork". *Evening Standard*, 31 July 1953. The story has also been published under the title "Fatal Teamwork". Collected as "Teamwork Felonious", Crofts' original title, in *The 9.50 Up Express and Other Stories*, 2020. (Joseph French)

"The Unseen Observer". *Evening Standard*, 31 August 1953. Expanded and collected in *Many a Slip*, 1955. (Joseph French)

"The Bottle". *Evening Standard*, 4 September 1953. Expanded and collected as "The Aspirins" in *Many a Slip*, 1955. (Joseph French)

"Dark Waters". *Evening Standard*, 21 September 1953. Collected in *The 9.50 Up Express and Other Stories*, 2020. (Joseph French)

"The Target". *Evening Standard*, 14 October 1953. Collected in *The 9.50 Up Express and Other Stories*, 2020. Crofts' original title was 'Tell-tale Target'. (Joseph French)

"Mushroom Patty". *Evening Standard*, 21 October 1953. The story has also been published under the title "The Usual Tiny Oversight". Expanded and collected as "Mushroom Patties" in *Many a Slip*, 1955. (Joseph French)

III —RADIO PLAYS AND OTHER RADIO BROADCASTS

"Scotland Yard on the Job". BBC National Programme (*The Scoop*, Episode VI), 21 February 1931, when it was read by Crofts. *The Listener*, 25 February 1931. Published in *The Scoop and Behind the Screen qv*.

"Inspector Smart's Nasty Jar". BBC National Programme (*The Scoop*, Episode XI), 28 March 1931, when it was read by Crofts. *The Listener*, 1 April 1931. Published in *The Scoop and Behind the Screen qv*.

"Meet Inspector French". BBC Empire Service (*Meet the Detective*), 19 November 1934, when it was read by Crofts. Published in *Meet the Detective*. George Allen & Unwin, 1935, and in *The 9.50 Up Express and Other Stories*, 2020.

"The 9.50 Up Express". BBC (*Detection Club*, 1st Series, No 8). 19 and 21 September 1942. Collected in *The 9.50 Up Express and Other Stories*, 2020. (Joseph French, played by Ronald Simpson)

"The Case of the Old Gun". BBC Forces Radio (*Chief Inspector*

French's Cases, 1ˢᵗ Series, No. 1), 29 October 1943. Adapted from the short story "The Match". (Joseph French, played by Milton Rosmer)

"The Case of the Stolen Manuscript". BBC General Forces (*A Corner in Crime*, 1ˢᵗ Series, No. 2), 5 November 1943. (Dr Carteret[1])

"The Case of the Torn Song". BBC for the Forces (*Chief Inspector French's Cases*, 1ˢᵗ Series, No. 2), 5 November 1943. (Joseph French, played by Milton Rosmer)

"The Case of the Telephone Call". BBC for the Forces (*Chief Inspector French's Cases*, 1ˢᵗ Series, No. 3), 12 November 1943. Adapted from the short story *The Vertical Line* (Joseph French, played by Milton Rosmer)

"The Case of the Lower Flat". BBC for the Forces (*Chief Inspector French's Cases*, 1ˢᵗ Series, No. 4), 19 November 1943. (Joseph French, played by Milton Rosmer)

"The Case of the Hunt Ball". BBC for the Forces (*Chief Inspector French's Cases*, 1ˢᵗ Series, No. 5), 26 November 1943. Adapted from the short story "The Hunt Ball". (Joseph French, played by Milton Rosmer)

"The Case of the Army Truck". BBC for the Forces (*Chief Inspector French's Cases*, 1ˢᵗ Series, No. 6), 3 December 1943. (Joseph French, played by Milton Rosmer)

"The Case of the L-Shaped Room". BBC General Forces (*Here's Wishing You Well Again: A Corner in Crime*, 2ⁿᵈ Series, No. 1), 13 January 1944. (Dr Carteret)

"The Case of the Man Who Bred Rabbits". BBC General Forces (*Here's Wishing You Well Again: A Corner in Crime*, 2ⁿᵈ Series, No. 4), 24 February 1944. (Dr Carteret)

"The Case of the Hidden Sten Gun". BBC General Forces (*Here's Wishing You Well Again: A Corner in Crime*, 2ⁿᵈ Series, No. 6), 23 March 1944. (Dr Carteret)

"The Case of the Swinging Boom". BBC General Forces (*Here's Wishing You Well Again: A Corner in Crime*, 2ⁿᵈ Series, No. 11), 1 June 1944. (Dr Carteret)

---

[1] Dr Carteret, played by Cecil Trouncer, was a coroner detective for whom cases were written by Margery Allingham, E.C. Bentley, John Dickson Carr, Freeman Wills Crofts, Anthony Gilbert, Bruce Graeme and Gladys Mitchell.

"The Case of the Home Guard Trench". BBC General Forces (*Chief Inspector French's Cases*, 2nd Series, No. 2), 24 August 1944. An Arabic translation was broadcast as "A Terrible Mistake" on the BBC Arabic Service, 23 September 1945. (Joseph French, played by Milton Rosmer)

"The Case of the Solicitor's Holiday". BBC General Forces (*Chief Inspector French's Cases*, 2nd Series, No. 3), 31 August 1944. (Joseph French, played by Milton Rosmer)

"The Case of the Retired Wine Merchant". BBC General Forces (*Chief Inspector French's Cases*, 2nd Series, No. 4), 7 September 1944. (Joseph French, played by Milton Rosmer)

"The Case of the Limestone Quarry". BBC General Forces (*Chief Inspector French's Cases*, 2nd Series, No. 5), 14 September 1944. (Joseph French, played by Milton Rosmer)

"The Case of the Avaricious Moneylender". BBC General Forces (*Chief Inspector French's Cases*, 2nd Series, No. 6), 21 September 1944. (Joseph French, played by Milton Rosmer)

"The Case of the Man Who Loved Mountains". BBC General Forces (*Chief Inspector French's Cases*, 3rd Series, No. 1), 30 April 1945. (Joseph French, played by Milton Rosmer)

"The Case of the Burning Barn". BBC General Forces (*Chief Inspector French's Cases*, 3rd Series, No. 2), 7 May 1945. (Joseph French, played by Milton Rosmer)

"The Case of the Stolen Hand Grenade". BBC General Forces (*Chief Inspector French's Cases*, 3rd Series, No. 3), 14 May 1945. (Joseph French, played by Milton Rosmer)

"The Case of the Relief Signalman". BBC General Forces (*Chief Inspector French's Cases*, 3rd Series, No. 4), 21 May 1945. (Joseph French, played by Milton Rosmer)

"The Case of the Waiting Car". BBC General Forces (*Chief Inspector French's Cases*, 3rd Series, No. 5), 28 May 1945. (Joseph French, played by Milton Rosmer)

"The Case of the Evening Visitor". BBC General Forces (*Chief Inspector French's Cases*, 3rd Series, No. 6), 4 June 1945. (Joseph French, played by Milton Rosmer)

"Detective Quiz". BBC Home Service, 2 August 1945. Crofts was a guest, together with E.C. Bentley, John Dickson Carr, Anthony Gilbert, Milward Kennedy, E.R. Punshon and Dorothy

L. Sayers. Val Gielgud was in the chair.

"Detective Quiz". BBC Home Service. 30 August 1945. Crofts was a guest, together with E.C. Bentley, John Dickson Carr, Sir Norman Kendal, E R Punshon and Dorothy L. Sayers. Val Gielgud was in the chair.

"Detective Quiz". BBC Home Service, 27 September 1945. Crofts was a guest, together with E.C. Bentley, John Dickson Carr, Anthony Gilbert, E.R. Punshon and Dorothy L. Sayers. Val Gielgud was in the chair.

"Mr Pemberton's Commission". BBC Home Service, 2 April 1952. Adapted from the short story *qv*. (Joseph French, played by Roger Delgado)

"The Greuze". BBC Home Service, 27 April 1953. Adapted from the short story *qv*. (Joseph French, played by Norman Mitchell)

"East Wind". BBC Home Service, 18 July 1953. Adapted from the short story *qv*. (Joseph French, played by Frank Tickle)

IV —STAGE PLAYS

Inspector French. Adapted from *Sudden Death*. The Barn Theatre, Shere, Surrey, July 1937 (The Otherwise Club); and St Nicholas' Hall, Guildford (Guildford Repertory Company), October 1937. (Joseph French, played by Leslie Coleman)

Chief Inspector French. First revised version of *Inspector French*. Assembly Hall Theatre, Tunbridge Wells, Kent, November 1944. The production was announced as "prior to London" but there weren't any further performances. (Joseph French, played by Geoffrey Saville)

During the Night. Second revised version of *Inspector French*. In 1949 a licence was sought for the script but the application was withdrawn; it has never been performed. Collected in *The 9.50 Up Express and Other Stories*, 2020. (Joseph French)

V —NON-FICTION

Bann and Lough Neagh Drainage: Report by Mr Freeman Wills Crofts to the Rt Hon H M Pollock DL, MP on His Inquiry into the Objections Lodged against the Draft Scheme. Her Majesty's Stationery Office, 1930.

'The Gorse Hall Mystery'. Published in *Great Unsolved Crimes*. Hutchinson & Co, 1935. *New Zealand Herald* (*Unsolved Crimes*, No. 18), 29 June 1935. First UK newspaper publication details unknown. (Analysis of the murder of Rose Harsent at Peasenhall, Suffolk in England on 31 May 1902)

'A New Zealand Tragedy'. Published in *The Anatomy of Murder*, Bodley Head, 1936. An abridged version was published as a two-part serial in *Empire News*: part 1, "Clue of the Wrong Man's Boots", on 27 December 1936; and part 2, "Grim Secret of the Black Smoke", on 3 January 1937. (Analysis of the murder of Christobel and Samuel Lakey in Ruawaro, near Huntly in New Zealand on or about 15 October 1933)

'The Writing of a Detective Novel'. *The Authors, Playwrights and Composers Handbook for 1935*. Nelson, 1936. Crofts' essay was reprinted in later editions of the Handbook and in *CADS* 54, July 2008. Collected in *The 9.50 Up Express and Other Stories*, 2020.

'Moral Rearmament – What it Means to Me'. *Belfast Telegraph*, 5 December 1938. Reprinted with minor edits under other titles in various UK and Commonwealth newspapers for example *Lancashire Evening Post*, 8 December 1938 and *Guildford City Outlook*, February 1939.

VI —PERSONAL APPEARANCES AND TALKS

'Aeroplanes'. New Row Association, Coleraine, Country Londonderry, Northern Ireland. 15 November 1910.

'Esperanto'. New Row Association, Coleraine, Country Londonderry, Northern Ireland. 5 December 1911.

'On Trial'. Crofts was a member of a "gang" of detective writers on trial accused of "faking the evidence". London School of Economics, London, 31 May 1932. Others appearing before Sir Francis Newbolt KC were E.C. Bentley, Anthony Berkeley, Margaret Cole and Captain Alan Thomas. On hearing a guilty verdict, Captain Thomas "took poison" and Margaret Cole "swooned" in the dock.

'How to Write a Detective Novel'. Fellowship of Literature, Ballymena, County Antrim, Northern Ireland 4 April 1933.

'[Title Unknown]'. Foyles Literary Luncheon, Grosvenor House, Park Lane, London. 18 July 1935. The Marchioness Townsend was in the chair and other speakers were the Reverend John Ferguson, David Hume, John Rhode and 'Torquemada' (E. Powys Mathers). Guests included Aleister Crowley, Sir Percy Laurie, Assistant Commissioner of the Metropolitan Police and, as "Guest of Honour", a wax effigy of the notorious criminal Charlie Peace. The occasion was to promote Collins Crime Club.

'[Title Unknown]'. Foyles Literary Luncheon, Grosvenor House, Park Lane, London. 23 July 1936. Dennis Wheatley was in the chair and other speakers were ex-Superintendent George Cornish of Scotland Yard, Dorothy L. Sayers and Russell Thorndike. The occasion was to promote the publication of *Six against the Yard* (1936), which included Crofts' short story "The Parcel" *qv*.

'[Title Unknown]'. National Book Council Exhibition. Victoria Rooms, Bristol. 29 September 1936.

'[Title Unknown]'. National Book Council Exhibition. Brown, Muff & Co Ltd, Bradford, 2 October 1936.

'[Title Unknown]'. Foyles Literary Luncheon, Grosvenor House, Park Lane, London. 23 July 1937. Other speakers were Alderman W.J. Locke, the actress Margaret Rawlings, George West, Bishop of Rangoon, and Brigadier C.R.P. Winser. The occasion was to promote the Oxford Group.

'Writing a Detective Novel'. Guildford Rotary Club, Guildford, July 1941

'Detective Stories'. Guildford Institute Annual Meeting, Guildford, 24 April 1945

VII —ADAPTATIONS OF CROFTS' WORK BY OTHER WRITERS

Radio

"The Level Crossing". Adapted by Harry W. Junkin from the short story *qv*. NBC Radio City Playhouse, 8 August 1949.

"Sir John Magill's Journey". Adaptor unknown, adapted from the novel, *qv*. BBC Northern Ireland Service. 8 episodes, 8, 15, 22, 29 November, 6, 13, 20 and 28 (*sic*) December 1950. (Joseph French, played by an unknown actor)

"The Yang Chi Jade". Adapted by Michael Campbell from the short story "Mr Pemberton's Commission" *qv*. BBC Radio 4, 1 December 1984; rebroadcast 3 December 1984. (Joseph French, played by William Eedle)

"Inspector French and the Starvel Tragedy". Adapted by Alan Downer from the novel *qv*. BBC Radio 4 (*Crime at Christmas*) 29 December 1987; rebroadcast 22 August 1988. (Joeph French, played by Edward de Souza)

Television

Bahnübergang. Adapted by Rainer Erle from the short story "The Level Crossing" *qv*. 1969. Directed by Rainer Erler. With Hans Beerhenke.

VIII —PARODIES

Agatha Christie. "The Unbreakable Alibi". *Holly Leaves* (Christmas edition of the *Illustrated Sporting and Dramatic News*), December 1928. The story formed Chapter 19 of Christie's novel *Partners in Crime*. Dodd Mead and Company (New York), 1929; William Collins and Sons (London), 1929.

(In his essential study of the writer's work and technique, *Agatha Christie's Complete Secret Notebooks* (2016) John Curran describes how Christie contemplated at least two plots involving members of the Detection Club. One, dating from 1931, was for a novel provisionally titled *The 13 at Dinner* in which she and various other crime writers, including Crofts, would attend a meeting of a 'detective story club' at which murder would be committed)

Freeman Wills Crofts. "Who Killed Cock Robin?" *St Martin's Review,* May 1938. Collected in *The 9.50 Up Express and Other Stories,* 2020.

The 9.50 Up Express

The 9.50 Up Express and Other Mysteries is printed on 60 pound paper, and is designed by Jeffrey Marks using InDesign. The type is Adobe Caslon, a group of serif typefaces designed by William Caslon or created in the same style. The printing is by Southern Ohio Printers and the binding by Cincinnati Bindery for the hard cover and the trade paperback version. The book was published in December 2020 by Crippen & Landru Publishers, Inc., Cincinnati, OH.